WENDY JAMES

THE
MISTAKE

But his wife looked back from behind him,
and she became a pillar of salt.
GENESIS 19:26

It's not the tragedies that kill us,
it's the messes.
DOROTHY PARKER

She wakes from that same nightmare of darkness, of heat, of airlessness. In the dream she is stricken, choking and gasping for air; feels her lungs about to burst, her body ablaze. It is hell, but even dreaming she knows that this is only a vision of hell, that the real nightmare is out in the waking world, waiting for her ...

PART ONE

If, before all this happened, before her—before *their*—unravelling, she had been asked how her life was, she'd have said that life was good. Not perfect, of course—when is it ever? In the way of all families, there had been problems, the commonplace complications of marriage and child-rearing, but nothing insurmountable—nothing they couldn't get past, move beyond. They were happy. Happy enough.

Later, when she looks back on that time—the time before it all began to change—Jodie will see that it was more than good, more than happy enough. It was idyllic.

The day before Hannah left for her school's Sydney excursion had been rather ordinary, really, a day busy with humdrum domestic activity. But it was the beginning of spring and the hint of warmth in the sunshine, flooding through the back windows and then in the air as Jodie hung out the washing, had made the day seem somehow special. Arding winters were long and hard and though she had imagined herself impervious after a lifetime's exposure, Jodie had found this particular winter interminable. The change in season was more than just a calendar note, and the colour and warmth brought a palpable sense of pleasure, of anticipation. Spring—the season of hope, of rebirth, of new beginnings.

For once the four of them were home together for dinner. Hannah had to leave for Sydney at some ungodly hour the following morning so there was no homework, nowhere else she needed to be. She had helped Jodie get dinner ready, chatting about this friend, that plan, offering up the odd bit of gossip about teachers, a friend's parent. She had even given in to Tom's pestering and played on the Wii with him before dinner—and was gracious in her defeat, letting her younger brother slay her in a second game, then a third. Angus had arrived home in time to eat with them, relaxed and expansive—asking Tom about his latest cricket score, regaling him with childhood sporting stories of his own, interrogating Hannah on the plans for the week in Sydney, recounting his own escapades during a high-school excursion, giving a comic impersonation of affronted hotel staff, an appalled teacher. Tom had giggled appreciatively, and even Hannah had appeared mildly amused.

Jodie had joined in the conversation only occasionally, preferring to watch them, relishing the scene. It happened far too rarely of late, she thought—all four of them together like this, just enjoying one another's company, being themselves: easy, unaffected. Angus, still handsome in his forties and grown into himself somehow, comfortable in his role; Hannah, her dark curls falling untidily over her face, her quick tongue, sometimes barbed humour, her little barking laugh, so oddly infectious; and the baby of the family, her darling Tom, trying hard to maintain an air of insouciance but failing, his cheeks pink with pleasure, his sentences tumbling together in his excited rush—his father's undivided attention so rare and precious. Here: the family she'd worked so hard to put together—keep together. There were other things in Jodie's life—friends, community—but her family was her core, her centre. This was all she wanted—and all she had ever wanted. All she would ever need.

Later, she will wonder if it is a real memory, or whether the recollection has acquired the rosy glow of nostalgia, making it somehow softer, sweeter, more significant than it ever really was. She will remember this as their last night, although in truth there were plenty more nights when the four of them ate together, laughed together, nights that appeared carefree—but none after this could ever be, for her, as straightforwardly happy. For Jodie, each subsequent gathering came with the bitter landscape of the past and the uncertainty of the future casting their shadows, tainting every moment of joy with dread, with doubt.

It arrives, as such moments always do, without warning.

Jodie had imagined it already, had rehearsed, if not this particular dissolution, then endless variations. When she and Angus were first married, she had obsessively conjured up scenarios of devastation: the police at her door, hats clutched respectfully, eyes downcast, voices hushed. Later, as a new mother, the nightmare visions had become more urgent—waking slowly from a rare undisturbed night's sleep, she would imagine her babies gone blue and cold in the crib; or pushing a stroller along Arding's busy streets she would be assailed by an image so vivid it would take her breath away—an out-of-control truck, the pram and baby crushed, her own life over.

But the moment, when it finally arrives, does not announce itself quite so dramatically.

She's just come in the back door, struggling with a load of washing, is yelling over her shoulder at Tom, who's still in his PJs and standing zombified in front of the TV, to get changed quickly or they'll be late for swim squad, when the call comes. She almost doesn't make it, the contents of the basket spilling all over the table and onto the floor in her rush, but just before the call clicks over to message bank, she reaches the phone.

'Mrs Garrow?'

'Yes?'

'It's Dr Guilfoyle here.'

Jodie notices immediately that the school principal, who she finds rather intimidating with her rounded vowels and precise enunciation, sounds unusually tentative.

'Mrs Garrow ... I'm afraid there's been an accident.'

Jodie feels her throat constrict. 'Hannah?'

'Now, don't panic, she's alive and well ... She's broken her leg.'

'Oh.' And then the draining away of terror, the relief settling; the ground shifts a little beneath her feet, rearranges itself, a chasm closes over. 'How?'

'Well, it sounds terrible, it *is* terrible. She was hit by a car.' The headmistress is brisk now that the worst is done. 'I don't know all the details, but from what Miss French told me, Hannah and Assia had been outside in the middle of the night, retrieving, they tell us, a dropped mobile phone. And somehow … well, somehow your daughter was hit by a passing vehicle. From the information I've been given, it seems it wasn't necessarily the driver's fault.' Her characteristic dryness of manner has reasserted itself completely.

'Oh, dear. And, what? She's in hospital? Can they reset—'

'Well, they've done a temporary cast, but I'm afraid it's a rather nasty break, and she needs surgery—a plate, or pins they're saying—and, well, no doubt you know more about these things than I do.'

'Well, no, it's not really—'

'So I expect you'll want to head down to Sydney immediately. We can't have a teacher stay with her, you understand. And I'm sure you'll want to be there to make decisions about treatment.' The principal's tone is somehow accusatory.

'I do understand, of course. Thank you, Dr Guilfoyle. I'll head down immediately. Which hospital? Is she at Westmead?'

'Actually she's at a small private hospital further west. I'm not quite sure why—beds, I suppose? In Greystanes. Bell something or other. Oh yes, here it is. Belfield Private. Perhaps you've heard of it? Mrs Garrow? Jodie? Hello?'

But Jodie isn't listening. She has the phone clutched tightly to her chest, as if to calm the sudden rapid beating of her heart. She can sense the rift yawning open again; feel the faint but familiar tremor. Belfield Private. Belfield. Of all the hospitals in Sydney.

She closes her eyes, takes a deep breath. 'Sorry, Dr Guilfoyle. I just dropped the phone. I'll make arrangements and get down there right away. And yes, I know where Belfield is,' she hears herself saying calmly. 'I've been there before.'

OCTOBER, 1986

Jodie chooses the hospital quite carefully. She looks for one that is far enough away from her own suburb that she won't have to worry about chance meetings with friends, neighbours, fellow students; a hospital in a less affluent suburb, where her situation won't be regarded as anything out of the ordinary. She makes sure there is a cheap hotel nearby, and books a small and dingy room for the two weeks prior to the due date. What she never considers, though, is the size of the hospital, and as she waits for her first check-up with a midwife (*A little bit late booking in, aren't you, dear? You're almost seven months. Tsk, tsk*) she is struck by how small the maternity wing is. She can see the infants' nursery from where she sits, and it is virtually empty; only two babies sleep on the other side of the glass. The wards themselves are just beyond the waiting room, along a hallway with four doors on either side—which means, she supposes, that there is a maximum capacity of between sixteen and twenty-four beds.

She had imagined, when she allowed herself to think of it at all, that maternity wings were all vast and impersonal, like the wards in the huge public hospital where she'd done her last prac; that to be a patient was like being a tiny bit of plankton in the belly of a whale, that her presence would make no conceivable impact. She would be anonymous, virtually invisible; the baby could be born then instantly whisked away, taken for good and with no questions asked. But here, in this diminutive, cosy room, all timber and worn vinyl and muted colours, the middle-aged nurse on the desk brisk but kindly, it seems impossible that her desire to relinquish the baby will go unremarked—and without judgement.

Jodie is quick to realise that she has made a mistake, but does nothing about it. She could have walked out then, booked in elsewhere—gone to the large hospitals her GP has suggested, RPA, Women's—but instead, when the nurse beckons her over, hands her a disposable cup and directs her to the nearby bathroom, she acquiesces. This baby is going to be born; surely *where* it's born isn't going to be all that significant.

It takes her a little less than an hour to arrange all that needs arranging. To call Angus, her mother-in-law, Tom's school, to pack an overnight bag for herself, a few pairs of pyjamas for Hannah. She is too busy to really think about the situation too much until she is in the car, and then, even with the radio on, it's difficult *not* to think, impossible to ignore the panic edging through. It's enough that her teenage daughter has been hit by a car in a faraway city, that there's some intimation of fault or bad behaviour—there's sufficient here to induce obsessive wondering and worrying, the mind's inexorable, crazy gallop into a nightmare future. Will there be some sort of lawsuit against Hannah? (Car damage, dangerous behaviour, emotional trauma.) Could the surgery provoke a fatal morphine reaction, or worse—addiction, or even death from anaesthesia? (Hannah's never been under the knife.) Or further on, might not there be social isolation generated by the break itself—or the pain, or the scar? (Oh, it requires no effort to follow this trajectory to its inevitable conclusion: from broken leg to depression, self-harm, drugs, suicide ...)

More than enough here to be anxious about, even without the prospect of revisiting Belfield. Her disquiet about returning there is merely a vague and formless apprehension, one she has no intention of examining. Despite her fevered prophesying, Jodie has no real inkling of what lies ahead. She weaves the car carefully up and around and then down the dazzling green ranges, accelerates along the long coastal highway that leads to the capital; rushes blithely, unsuspecting and utterly unprepared, straight into her own catastrophe.

Jodie experiences a slight shock every time she's reunited with her teenage daughter after any sort of separation. When she thinks of Hannah it's always as a younger incarnation—in Jodie's imagination she's still twelve or so, still slender, her chest flat, her hips narrow. This evening Jodie pauses, confused, in the doorway of the hospital room, before she realises with an odd pang that the rather pudgy adolescent lying slumped and dazed, half asleep, mouth open and tongue protruding slightly, a plump, plaster-encased leg hanging from a frame above the bed—is in fact her daughter. But it's only a momentary lapse, and she pushes herself over the threshold.

'Now, here's someone you've been waiting for, sweetheart,' a nurse announces cheerfully. 'Mum's here.' She pats Jodie on the shoulder as she leaves. 'Kids! Can't leave them alone for five minutes.'

Hannah glares at the woman's retreating form before sinking back into her pillows, turns a pale and miserable face to her mother, but says nothing, waits for Jodie to approach. Jodie greets her daughter with a smile, being careful not to appear too anxious, too intense. 'Hello, my darling.' Jodie hates herself for the slight uncertainty in her voice, but can't disguise it. 'Hello, Mum.' Hannah's voice is as plaintive as her expression, and though Jodie would love to wrap her arms around her daughter, hold her tight, she knows better. She accepts the proffered cheek, the brief hug that's made only slightly more awkward by the IV lines, the cannula in her daughter's hand. Hannah had never been an especially cuddly child, but there's a definite distance now, a prickly withdrawal, and even in Hannah's current vulnerable state Jodie knows that to display too much affection would be seen as an unwarranted invasion, likely to be met with not so subtle resistance. Hannah's no real exception—most of the teenage girls she knows are similarly standoffish with their parents—but there's a pang, nevertheless.

She sits on the edge of the bed. 'How is it, Hannie? Are you in any pain? Have they got you on morphine?' She pushes a wayward curl off her daughter's face, gives a sympathetic smile.

'Oh, you know ... it's not that bad, really—I get to shoot myself up when I need to.' Hannah's smile is wry, she waves the little hand pump. 'I'm just really uncomfortable.' She looks uncomfortable too, her leg hoisted up so brutally, her hospital gown pulled at a rather immodest angle, gaping open at all the wrong places, her pillow slipping down behind her head.

'Okay. Well how about I try and get you more comfy while you tell me what happened?'

Hannah makes a face. 'Oh, God. Do I really have to talk about it right now, Mum? I'm just—I just feel really out of it. And I'm really, really hungry. The food in here is totally disgusting.'

'I'm sure it's not that bad.' She eases one pillow out from behind her daughter, plumps it up. 'Come on, tell me, and then I'll go and get you some rubbish from the kiosk. Dr Guilfoyle seemed to think there was some uncertainty about what happened. I'm just concerned.'

'There's no uncertainty. I was hit by some idiot in a car. I said I don't want to talk right now. I'm tired and I'm starving. Why do you have to go on about it?'

'Oh, Hannah, sweetheart, I'm not trying to upset you, it's only because I care about you ...' Jodie's aware that her protestations are not only feeble, but pointless. It's so hard to know how to handle this newly sensitive Hannah—the most innocuous observation can be construed as an affront, eliciting a defence out all of proportion to the original statement. More often than not, Jodie gets it wrong.

'I'm going to sleep.' Her daughter squeezes her eyes shut, turns her face away.

But Jodie has seen the tears welling, heard the slight quaver in her voice. Her own eyes sting in response. She sighs, reties the gaping gown, tugs the blankets across Hannah's rigid body, pats her shoulder gently. She leans over and kisses her daughter gently on the forehead. Receives a sobbing hug in return.

'Oh, Mum. I'm sorry. I'm really sorry.'

By the time the nurse returns, Jodie has provided Hannah with a stack of magazines, a few pieces of fruit and several blocks of chocolate, all bought for exorbitant prices from the hospital kiosk. The specialist has made his visit, has recommended Hannah stay overnight again—just to monitor the effects of the anaesthetic, watch her pain levels. They can travel home tomorrow.

Jodie sits beside the bed, reading a magazine, while Hannah sleeps, sprawled awkwardly, the blankets bunched around her again. The nurse fusses over Hannah for a moment, then approaches Jodie with a clipboard and pen.

'Now, I think we need to get some details from you, Mrs Garrow. If you could just fill out these forms. It's ridiculous, I know—all this paperwork. When I first started out it was nothing like this ...' She chats away, distractedly clearing the chaos that Hannah has somehow managed to create despite being immobilised and confined to a hospital bed. Jodie fills out the forms, only half listens.

'Oh, I nearly forgot. Our matron—well, we don't actually call them matrons, haven't for years, though it's a pity. I like the old titles: matron, sister—they had some dignity. I liked the hats too. And all the starch,' the nurse adds wistfully. 'But anyway, our nursing unit manager was wondering, when she saw your girl's—what's it called, the webbing, the dactyl something or other, between her toes?'

'Syndactyly.' Jodie doesn't look up, responds automatically.

'Right. That's it. Syndactyly. Well, she said that she'd only ever seen one other person with both feet webbed like that. A newborn, years ago. She thought at first that it might've been Hannah here ...'

'Oh.' Jodie stops writing, looks up. 'That is odd. I haven't ... I haven't heard of it either. I mean, I have heard of it, obviously—it runs in the family. But I've never met anyone else ...' She returns to the form, which has blurred. Her hand shakes.

The nurse rattles on. 'But then the matron, Debbie, had the records pulled—and of course it was the wrong date. Another baby, about eight years before Hannah here was born. But here's a funny thing—the mum's name was the same as yours: Jodie. But it's a common enough name, isn't it? She was from

Sydney—Newtown or around there somewhere.'

Jodie forces herself to respond. 'Well, that is an interesting coincidence, isn't it? Maybe she's some,' she hears herself give a weird, high-pitched laugh, 'some long-lost cousin.'

The nurse flicks through the patient file. 'She's left them here for you to look at. Now, what does it say …'

Jodie moves to her side quickly. 'No, it's okay. I'll have a look.' Her voice is low, she looks pointedly over at her sleeping daughter but the nurse ignores her appeal.

'Oh, yes. Here it is: Jodie Evans. I'm not sure what she was doing having her baby here then—it wasn't exactly her local hospital. But look how young she was—only nineteen—'

'Really, I'd love to look, but—' She looks at Hannah again, who is stirring now, yawning, her eyelids flickering.

The nurse goes on, oblivious to Jodie's silent entreaty. 'A little girl, it says here. Elsa Mary Evans. Her mum was only nineteen, but I always think young is better than the alternative. Awful to start pushing 'em out in your forties. I hope this next generation doesn't leave it all too late. I had my first when I was only twenty-one—didn't make the big fuss these older mums do, and I have to say it's kept me young. Plenty of time to do other things—' Her observations are interrupted when a woman, another nurse, squeaks across the threshold, beaming.

'Jodie. It *is* you. I thought this little miss must be your girl.'

Jodie recognises her immediately. She is oddly unchanged after more than twenty years—the slanted blue eyes still sparkling, the friendly smile that makes her look so cheerful, so approachable. 'Hello, Debbie.' She is surprised by how casual, how calm, her greeting sounds, amazed that she has even managed to speak at all. Her breath is shallow, blood pounding; she feels weak at the knees.

'I'll bet you haven't had a thing to eat since you arrived. I know you mothers. I'm on my tea break—why don't you come and have a cuppa with me while Miss Hannah catches up on her beauty sleep?'

Hannah's breathing is deep and even again, her eyes fully closed. Jodie tucks the sheet around her as best she can, smooths her daughter's hair. 'Okay.' She gives Debbie an airy smile. 'Why not.'

The two women sit in the dreary hospital cafeteria, which is almost empty at this time of day. Debbie has ordered coffee but is too busy regaling Jodie with the history of her career to drink it. Jodie sips on watery tea, nodding, dreading the inevitable destination of the conversation, wishing desperately to be elsewhere.

'So, I got out of middy into surgery, and eventually ended up back at Belfield. Bizarre, isn't it? But it's a very different hospital these days—there's no maternity unit, for one thing. It was such a funny little unit, really. That matron—do you remember her? She died a few years ago. Sheila O'Malley?' She waits for Jodie to give a vague shake of her head before continuing. 'Anyway, she was a real old tyrant. Had complete control of the place. No one in admin dared say anything to her—it was like her own little private kingdom. You'd remember what they could be like, those old matrons. You finished your training didn't you?'

'I worked for a few years—a bit of A and E, paediatrics. But I've been out for a while.' Jodie is guarded, reluctant to share more than is strictly polite.

'I took a break after the kids came along ... but not for long. Anyhow, I'm in charge of the surgical team here now, and that's how I got to see your daughter's feet! They're almost exactly the same as the other baby's, aren't they? And I think I remember you saying you had them too? It's really very unusual, according to the surgeon—having the webbing on both feet.' The woman spoons sugar into her coffee carefully—one spoonful, two, hesitates over the sugar bowl and then adds another, smiling ruefully as she stirs. She continues along the same conversational trajectory, determinedly disregarding Jodie's continued lack of response. 'So anyway, when I saw Hannah's toes I thought of you straight away. Initially I assumed that she must have been that baby.' She looks up at Jodie again, notices her expression, gives a reassuring smile. 'Oh, it's okay. I didn't say anything to Hannah. When I checked the notes I realised that the dates were all wrong, and it couldn't be her. And then she said she was an eldest child, so I didn't like to mention it. But, well, I've never forgotten you, you know. You were my first birth. And I've always wondered how you got on. You were so young, younger than me, but you seemed so level-headed, so cool.'

Debbie pauses, looks down, tapping her spoon slowly on the side of her cup, before laying it down carefully on the table. She takes a deep breath, then looks up, her expression fierce, intent. 'So, that little baby. Elsa Mary ...' It takes all Jodie's willpower to stay seated, to resist the impulse to escape this woman's relentless gaze. 'What happened? She ... she didn't die, did she?'

There's no way that Jodie can continue her silence. To have to come here was one thing, but this—her past rearing its head so unexpectedly and so shockingly—is almost beyond belief. If only she could go and not look back, but she can't. She can see that this woman will demand an answer—that she expects, that she needs to know, regardless of any reluctance on Jodie's part. Debbie is implacable, determined, curious, her intelligence obvious, and Jodie can sense that's there's no way she'll let her escape without some sort of explanation. Jodie closes her eyes for a moment, composing herself, before replying.

'No. Not that. As far as I know she's alive and well.' She can hear a sort of desperate pleading in her own voice.

'As far as you know?' The woman is frowning. 'What do you mean?'

'I ... Well, in the end I didn't keep her. I had her adopted out.' It comes easily, more easily than she'd ever imagined.

'You're kidding.' The woman looks stricken. 'God, I didn't realise things were so difficult. You seemed so, well, certain about everything. I mean, I can remember being slightly worried—you were only young, and obviously all alone—but you seemed, I don't know ... so capable.'

Jodie shrugs, tries to keep her expression neutral.

'That's why you were so determined about not breastfeeding, isn't it? You knew you wouldn't be keeping her? And why you didn't want to hold her unless you had to. I guess you couldn't risk all the … bonding stuff, either?'

Jodie tries to smile, to lighten the conversation, to divert her. 'Well, you'll be happy to know that I tried to breastfeed the—'

But the woman interrupts, 'But what I don't understand is why—well, why you didn't tell us that you didn't want to keep her? I mean the midwives, the hospital authorities, the social workers … surely the hospital was the logical place. To start the process, I mean. Usually it's all arranged before the baby's even born. But sometimes it happens afterwards, and the procedures are still pretty straightforward.'

Jodie makes a split-second decision about what to reveal.

'I really hadn't sorted anything out beforehand,' she says glibly. 'I only ever had one antenatal check-up, and then … It was just too hard here. I couldn't face the … well, the feeling of failure. The maternity wing, the nurses, the other mothers. It was meant to be such a … a happy, joyful event. Everyone was so kind, so helpful, so supportive. I felt that if I admitted that I didn't want to keep my own baby, here, that I would be letting everyone down. So then I had to arrange it all myself—the adoption, I mean—once I left.'

Debbie is all wide-eyed sympathy. 'My God, that's … So, where did you go—how did you go about it? Did you take the baby home to your parents? What about your boyfriend, the father? There was a boyfriend, wasn't there?' She pauses, moves her hand over to Jodie's and squeezes briefly. Jodie had forgotten Debbie's casual warmth and easy familiarity, an offhand demonstrativeness that had been—and still is—so foreign to Jodie herself. 'God. You poor thing. You were so young, and having to do all that on your own. I can't imagine.'

Jodie grimaces. 'It was all so long ago, I can barely remember what happened. It was all sorted out quite quickly—she went to a good family. I try hard not to think about it, really. And now—as you can see—my life's so busy ... and I'm sure she's happy, and that we're all better off. It would have been no sort of a life for either of us.'

Debbie gazes at her, shaking her head. 'God. Really, it's just amazing when you think of it. To come back here, now. To this very hospital, after all these years—and to meet up with me. You couldn't have imagined it, really.'

Jodie tries to look pleased by the coincidence. 'No, you couldn't.' She glances at her watch. 'Oh dear, is that the time? Look, it's been lovely meeting you again, Debbie, but I really—'

'Oh, yes, of course. You've driven all that way today, and then all the worry—you must be exhausted. And I should get back to work.'

The two women gather their belongings—bags, papers, keys—prepare to go. Then just as they're shaking hands, just when Jodie thinks it's all over, there is one last question—too intimate for such surroundings, the slightness of their relationship, but delivered in such a forthright, disinterested manner that it makes it impossible to take offence.

'Have you ever thought about contacting her? About contacting Elsa? She'd be grown up now, wouldn't she? In her twenties. There's a register, you know—she could be on it.'

'A register?'

'Well, the adoption laws have changed since you relinquished her. Parents and children, they can choose now—it's reasonably simple to make contact—'

'No.' Jodie's interjection is instinctive, blunt, surprises them both. 'I wouldn't want to contact her. It was ... another life. I know I might seem hard, but I can't ... I can't go back.'

'Oh.' Debbie pauses, considers her. 'But it doesn't just go one way, Jodie. What if she tries to contact you? It's not unlikely, you know.'

The woman speaks slowly, tentatively. 'I could investigate it for you, if you like. I helped a good friend of mine recently—well, in reverse—she was tracking her mother. But I actually have a contact in the department, who can bypass a lot of the official admin stuff. So, if you want some help, I'd be more than happy—'

'Oh, no,' Jodie says, appalled. 'Really. Thank you, but I'd rather not.' Adds more fiercely than she intends, 'I really don't want to know.'

Debbie's voice is unbearably kind. 'I understand, of course. But if you—'

'No,' Jodie repeats firmly, smiling to lessen the rebuff. 'But thank you. It's a generous offer.' She swallows. 'And if I ever do, I'll contact you first.'

Debbie smiles broadly, obviously pleased by this slight concession.

They part ways. Jodie is desperate now to get to her hotel, have a drink. The conversation has left her drained and shaken, but somehow she thinks she managed to strike the right attitude, find the right tone. Anyway, it's all over; she survived. Debbie will finish her shift and go home. Maybe, while the oddness of their meeting is still fresh, she'll want to share it with someone—her husband, her best friend. But eventually, surely—and sooner rather than later—she'll forget all about it.

Jodie helps Hannah get comfortable in the car. She pushes the front seat right back, reclines it fully and straps her in. It's like being a baby again, and Hannah submits to her mother's ministrations without fuss. Her leg, blissfully numb yesterday, is aching a little today, but she's making an effort to appear in good cheer—the journey ahead of them is long. Hannah's half looking forward to getting home—it's not often she gets to experience the helplessness of childhood any more, and there's a pleasure in relaxing and leaving everything to Mum, being waited on, deferred to, coddled. She remembers the strange pleasure of illness when she was sick in bed as a little girl—not so long ago, really. The back of her mother's hand, cool against her forehead, the smell of the special eucalyptus steam, the offerings of soup, lemonade, milky tea. Her mother would sit and read to her, plump her pillows, straighten her bedclothes, dim the lights. Quite often Hannah would drag the convalescence out for a few days beyond what she needed, out of sheer enjoyment.

But now, in the car, her mother isn't quite as solicitous as she'd hoped. Jodie's face is set, she's subdued, inquiring only vaguely into Hannah's wellbeing as they set off. Hannah is slightly disappointed, but in a way it's a bit of a reprieve—her mother hasn't questioned her too closely yet about the accident, and she's been dreading the inevitable questions. She sets her iPod on shuffle, leans back with her eyes closed, is beginning to get nicely in the zone, when with a giddying lurch she remembers. She opens her eyes and sits up.

'Mum?'

'Hmm? Is there something wrong? Is your leg hurting?' Her mother glances at her briefly and then her attention is back on the road ahead, intent on negotiating the unfamiliar city streets.

'No, my leg's fine. But Mum, what was that nurse talking about yesterday? I was half asleep, but I'm sure I heard her talking about someone having a baby. Someone with the same name as you?'

Hannah notices her mother's quick intake of breath, the slight stiffening of her shoulders, but her reply is casual enough.

'Oh, that was nothing, darling. Nothing important.'

'But she said something about a baby ...'

Her mother's voice is tinged with impatience now. 'It was just someone else with webbed toes like yours. A newborn. Years ago. I don't know all the details. It was nothing.'

'And then you went and had coffee with that other nurse. Who was she? How come you know her?'

'She's just someone I worked with a long time ago.'

'But you—'

'Hannah.' Her mother's voice is firm. 'I have to concentrate on getting us back on the freeway now. Not another word.'

Hannah rolls her eyes. She bumps the volume up a notch and leans back again, her plastered leg sprawling awkwardly in front of her. 'Okay, Mum. Whatever.'

There's something going on, Hannah senses that much. Even at the hospital her mother had asked her only the most basic questions about the accident. Hannah had been sure she'd be interrogated, had rehearsed her story over and over in anticipation, making certain that there was no way she'd slip up, but weirdly, her mother has barely asked her anything. It's entirely out of character—she and her mother are really pretty close, and despite the trouble it would no doubt bring, Hannah finds it hard to resist the impulse to confide, to tell her mother what really happened. It's true that they're not as tight as they once were, that things have changed between her and her parents, that she stopped telling them everything years ago. But her connections with both her parents have only become strained in common and expected ways—she finds her mother, her rules, her nagging, her insistence on Hannah's keeping a tidy room and a clean soul, particularly aggravating, and her father, with his irregular but decisive interventions, almost equally so. In this she is no different to most of her friends. For most of them it is as if those formerly powerful symbols of all things good and possible have suddenly appeared in a completely new perspective. Not only have their parents begun to lose their mystery and magic, but they have lost most of their status as major players—have somehow been transformed into hindrances, difficulties to be overcome, mere subplots in the central drama of their own increasingly complex lives. But still Hannah feels enormously guilty about the fabrication, if not about the deed itself, and she would like to get it all over with now, here in the car, get the explanation—the lie—out in the open.

But now doesn't seem to be the time to push it. Her mum clearly isn't in the mood, has other things on her mind, and Hannah doesn't have the energy anyway—the analgesics aren't as strong as the morphine, and the dull ache is ratcheting up in force moment by moment. She lets herself drift off.

The Sydney excursion had promised to be a fun interruption to the usual tedium, a much needed escape from school and family, and Hannah is disappointed that her visit has been so painfully cut short. She and Assia had had a few more unauthorised adventures planned—there was meant to have been a visit to Bondi this afternoon, under the guise of an overnight visit to Assia's parents. The other girls had been sick with envy, their own afternoon and evening filled to the brim with various cultural delights—a visit to the art gallery, the maritime museum and then some lame musical. But despite her disappointment, and perhaps because of the analgesics, Hannah is feeling pretty lucky. Not just because this morning's X-rays have shown that the break is far less complicated than they'd thought, that she won't need a pin, additional surgery. No one in their right mind would call being hit by the car itself good luck, exactly.

But she has to admit that there is an element of extreme good fortune in the fact that the driver didn't hang around to tell anyone what had really happened. She didn't blame the driver one bit—it was her own (and to a lesser degree, Assia's) fault entirely. Somehow they'd got away with the issue of them being outside at that time of the night by telling Miss French that Assia had dropped her mobile out the window and they'd come out to retrieve it, and that the car (driven by some drug- or alcohol-affected maniac) had veered wildly and knocked her down, then sped off again without stopping.

So things could have been and probably should have been far worse. If Assia had been hurt as well, then two lots of parents would have had to retrieve their wounded daughters—what a scandal! The bishop would have been consulted, no doubt and maybe the board. And the teachers—poor unsuspecting dupes—their heads would have rolled. Just the thought of Assia's parents and the fuss they would have made is enough to make Hannah quake.

Oh, not Assia's magistrate father, he's old and vague and completely wrapped around Assia's little finger. But her mother, Manon, is another matter: a weird little elf-like creature with her wild hair, her black eye-makeup, her trendy wardrobe and her wispy, high-pitched voice. The way she can turn hard and sharp, suddenly go on the attack, pulling spiky legal words out of the air, making incontestable arguments, so easily, so coolly. Hannah witnessed her in professional mode once, battling the vice principal over some aspect of the school's disciplinary code. She'd won easily, her eyes slanted with laughter throughout the confrontation, a slightly malicious smile never leaving her face. And Hannah suspects she always wins. So they needed to keep the truth from Manon at all costs, though a part of Hannah thinks it would almost be worth getting her involved, just to witness her rage. Hannah has seen it directed once or twice at poor Assia, who has inherited neither her mother's sharpness of wit nor her father's easy-going nature, and is therefore utterly defenceless against her.

And there's a fair chance that Assia's mother—unlike Hannah's own darling mum, innocent, unsuspecting—would work out that the accident wasn't merely the consequence of the innocent high jinks of spirited teenage girls (like something from *Girl's Own Annual*, where Penelope and Lucy daringly sneak out of their dorm at night, camouflaged by their dark skivvies and black ski pants in a quest to discover the whereabouts of the mysterious trench-coated fellow they've spotted gazing wistfully at their virginal Sports mistress, hoping to somehow orchestrate a romantic union ...). Manon was certain to sniff out the reality.

Which was this: the two girls had met up with a random guy during their few hours of free time between visits to exceedingly dull tourist attractions. Somehow, during a crazy conversation about the origins of LSD, he'd managed to talk them into buying some E. Both Hannah and Assia were novices, both scared shitless, but still curious to try. They'd convinced two of the other girls that they should pitch in, promising that they'd take the pills together when they got back to Arding—in a safe environment, to limit the dangers—and had arranged to meet the boy at the park across the road from their hotel that evening. During the day he had seemed an unlikely enough source— thin, stooped, bespectacled, acne-scarred—and they'd doubted that he'd turn up. But in the gloom of the unlit park, he'd seemed less nerdy, had been satisfyingly sinister, his thin face shadowed, his glasses obscured beneath the regulation hoodie. They had paid up, received their baggie, and were about to hurry back when the boy offered them a complimentary half pill each. There was no real hurry: back at the hotel Sam and Bella were prepared with excuses for Assia and Hannah's absence, and had a coded text message ready to send if the girls needed to return in a hurry. Assia had hesitated, they should stick to their original plan, she'd said, who knew what might happen?—but the boy had been persuasive, and eventually she'd swallowed her fear along with her half of the E. And as he'd promised, it was good stuff.

Hannah couldn't quite remember what happened next, the exact order of events, all she knew was that somehow she and the boy had ended up playing chicken with the traffic. Assia had sat in the gutter, giving an insane commentary on their dangerous antics, giving scores out of ten. Hannah had enjoyed the bizarre game, wondered at her newly discovered co-ordination, her precision, her almost supernatural ability to jump at the critical moment. But this one time the car had sped up, or she'd just plain misjudged the timing, and she'd been winged. If the driver had been a concerned citizen, properly appalled, eager to help, there really would have been hell to pay. A broken leg seemed like a gift by comparison.

Hannah had not admitted to taking anything when the paramedics had asked during her ambulance ride—no drugs, no alcohol—had looked the picture of outraged innocence. *Drugs? What do you think I am!* Despite numerous lectures from parents and teachers about the importance of telling the truth about drug usage in times of medical crisis, she'd decided to keep that bit of information to herself—and luckily Assia had kept quiet too. The effects were wearing off anyway, and by the time she'd been given a shot of pethidine, had X-rays taken, and a surgeon was found to set the bone, there was no need. They'd gotten away with it. And they still had the baggie—Hannah had managed to pass it to Assia when no one was looking.

It seems that Hannah's lies have been more successful than she'd expected—the details of the accident are clearly not bothering her over-protective mother. There's not even the barest hint of doubt; it's as if the butter in her mouth has miraculously hardened to the consistency of a boiled lolly. Jodie's so uncharacteristically preoccupied that there's obviously something else going on, Hannah's certain of that. Just what it is, though, she has no idea.

3

Jodie sits at the outdoor table with Angus. Away from the little pocket of warmth provided by the patio heater, the evening is cold—the temperature forecast to fall to zero overnight, a frost expected in the morning. Mellowed by a few glasses of red, Angus is in a cheerfully chatty mood. He's made it very clear that he's glad to have them return safely, to see for himself that Hannah's condition is not too serious. He has missed Jodie in theory, if not in practice—she knows he will have been far too busy for her short absence to have had any real impact, but even after so many years of marriage, she's oddly relieved to discover that he still cares, that he wasn't happier alone.

She knows that this particular anxiety is one of her own making. It would be easy to assume that her need for reassurance stems from those occasions when Angus has fallen short (and there have been a few), but Jodie knows that it's not that simple, that her uncertainty goes far deeper. That it has no real connection to Angus's behaviour, his stated (and restated) love for her. Even on a night like tonight—when he has clearly made a huge effort to make a little ceremony of their homecoming: leaving work early, bringing wine and Indian takeaway, producing treats for Hannah and Tom, and a sweetly wilting bunch of chrysanthemums for Jodie; when the evening has been filled with laughter and good cheer—even now Jodie worries that perhaps it isn't real, that he's just pretending, making the best of a decision he has come to regret.

It's just the two of them now—Tom is in bed, asleep, and Hannah is holed up in her room for the evening, on no account to be disturbed (no doubt enjoying the 2-litre bottle of Coke, bag of corn chips, and family-sized block of Cadbury's that her father has so thoughtfully provided, along with the entire third season of *Sex and the City*). Angus is telling Jodie about a case he's working on, is explaining some obscure, incomprehensible point of law in exhaustive—and exhausting—detail, and though she nods in the right places, *hmm, hmms* here and there, knowing the patterns of these conversations so well, in reality Jodie is not even half listening.

She makes a decision, breaks into his monologue. 'Darling. Angus.' She puts her hand on his arm. 'I need to tell you something.'

He pauses mid-sentence, and frowns in surprise. 'Oh, okay. Am I boring you?' He sounds huffy, mildly embarrassed.

Jodie strokes his arm in an attempt to soothe him. 'No, of course not. It's ...' She falters.

'What?' His voice is suddenly anxious. 'It's not Hannah, is it? Her break really is straightforward?'

'No. It's got nothing to do with Hannah, Angus. It's to do with me. It's something I've done.'

He raises one eyebrow, gives his best impression of a patronising smirk, 'Don't tell me you've been driving by Braille again—I've told you before that you should stick to embroidery and ...'

She interrupts before he gets to the end of the well-worn family gag. 'No. It's not the car, Angus. And it's not a joke. I wish it was. It was ... well, there's no easy way to tell you this, I suppose. It ...' Jodie is finding it hard to locate the words. She casts about for a place to start the story, but there's nowhere safe, no easy way in.

'Do you remember when you went to London, not last year—the first time. The year before you went to uni—when you were clerking?'

'Oh, yeah.'

'Well, when you were away—before I came over ... I had this thing.'

'A thing? What sort of thing? What are you talking about?'

She clears her throat, her voice descends to a whisper. 'I slept with someone else—a boy. It was nothing—just one night.'

She can't go any further. Her husband is gazing at her incredulously—as if she's mad—and then, then he's smiling. 'Jesus, Jodes. Is this something you've had on your conscience all these years? Sweetheart, I don't mean to disappoint your desire for, well, whatever it is—penance or forgiveness or closure or whatever—but that was a long, long time ago. We weren't married, and we were very young, and I have to tell you, I wasn't exactly celibate myself.'

She clutches his forearm. 'No, Angus. It's more than that. Much more. Just listen, will you? Please?'

DECEMBER, 1986

She comes in to the hospital far too early in the labour, panicked by the first signs of mild cramping, ignorant and afraid, having no idea of what is ahead and not wanting to face it alone. A middle-aged Irish nurse—the matron, she finds out later—is the midwife on duty, and she accepts without question Jodie's carefully prepared story: her parents are travelling in Far North Queensland; her boyfriend, the father of the child, is absent too.

The woman, short and stocky, with her hair in a tidy grey bob, examines her expertly, cool fingers pressing down here and there on her distended abdomen, her eyes distant, face thoughtful. When a pain arrives she stretches her hands firmly along Jodie's belly and smiles down at her reassuringly.

'Well, that's a nice solid contraction, love,' she says. 'There's no doubt you're in labour.' When the pain subsides, she takes a stethoscope and moves it across Jodie's stomach, then stops, listening intently. 'Well, the bub's fine—its little heartbeat is just perfect,' she says soothingly, as if Jodie has made some sort of anxious inquiry. 'Now, how often are these coming?'

'How often? Well, that's about the tenth one, I think. I had to pull over a couple of times, getting here.'

'The tenth one!' The nurse laughs. 'You haven't been timing them then, love?'

'Well, no. I didn't know … I thought that once the pain started it meant … and then there was a bit of blood, earlier this morning, in my undies.' Jodie is suddenly sharply aware of her ignorance, of how stupid she sounds. How stupid she is.

But the nurse's smile is kind; she isn't laughing at her. 'That's okay. The tenth one since when, darling?'

'In the last couple of hours or so, I think. Perhaps an hour and a half?'

'So, they're coming every twenty minutes or so, then.'

'I think so.' She hazards a question, wanting to know more, regardless of revealing her ignorance. 'Is that good? Does that mean the baby's not far off then?'

The woman holds out her hand and helps Jodie pull herself up into a sitting position, panting, breathless.

'Well, it's your first, so it could be … let me see. Twenty minutes apart means that—all going to plan this baby could come anytime from this afternoon to tomorrow afternoon.'

'Tomorrow afternoon. Oh.' Jodie can't keep the embarrassment, the disappointment from her voice. 'So, what should I do? It might be ages then, mightn't it? Should I … should I go back home?' Her eyes fill, her voice quavers, despairing at the thought of heading back alone to the dank hotel room that has been her home for the past fortnight.

'Well, normally, darling.' The nurse helps her to her feet, absentmindedly smoothing down Jodie's crumpled dress. 'Normally I'd be telling you to go home and come back in when they're say, five minutes apart. But as you're all alone, I'm guessing you don't want to make the trip again?'

'No.' She takes a breath, gives a watery smile.

'Well, then,' the nurse says briskly, 'let's get you booked in, get a room sorted. You can watch some telly, have some lunch. It's been a dull, slow day, and to be honest you'll be giving me something to do.'

Jodie is taken to an unoccupied double room. She lies on the bed and flicks through the magazine that the matron has handed her, fearful, unable to concentrate. Her mind grinds over and over the problem, never coming close to any sort of solution: what on earth is she going to do? Who will she tell, what will she tell them? She is almost relieved when a pain comes—at least then she can stop thinking. In a way, now that the time has arrived, bringing moments that just have to be lived through, survived, she feels freer than she has for the past few months. Now at last something must change. One way or another, something will, something must, be decided. A solution will arrive with the baby. This she believes.

The pains go on all day, never really getting much worse, or even closer together. It's not unlike period pain, but much, much fiercer, and lasts forty seconds or so before subsiding completely. They recur every twenty minutes, like clockwork— or, as Sheila puts it during one of her frequent afternoon visits, 'cramp work'.

'And that's what it is, darling: work. That pain is telling you that your body's working for you in a good way—opening you up, to let that bubby out.'

She is casual in her questions, but Jodie can tell Sheila is curious about her circumstances, concerned. And a little suspicious.

'Are you sure your parents know about this?' she asks during a routine examination. 'That your young man knows?'

Jodie makes no answer, gripped suddenly, alarmingly, by a pain of such ferocity that she is unable to do anything but hold her breath. She squeezes the nurse's hand tightly until it subsides.

'Breathe, darling. Breathe.' The matron smiles gently, pushes the damp hair away from Jodie's face. 'Now, my sweet, now *that's* a labour pain. Might be time to give you an internal now. See how much progress you've made.'

But there is no time for any sort of examination. Jodie yells out and stiffens in response to an unexpected reprise of that insane grip. Sheila holds Jodie's hand through it again, strokes her forehead, her voice soothing.

'Relax,' she says, as Jodie bites through her lip in an effort to stifle a moan, a shout. 'Just relax ...'

Afterwards, when it is safely out in the world (*A girl! What a sweetheart, what a little beauty!*), Jodie feels herself floating, beyond thought and empty, almost absent, as if mind and body have been split—although they tell her she has been successfully stitched back together. She makes no move to hold the baby when it has been cleaned, weighed, pinned into its first nappy, wrapped, instead asking them to take it—to take her—away.

Sheila, who, along with a younger midwife, Debbie, has remained throughout the entire ordeal, is used to all sorts of odd postpartum behaviour. She says nothing, exchanges only the briefest of glances with the other nurse. The two women smile sympathetically, understandingly.

'Sure then,' says Sheila. 'We can give the wee thing a suck on a bottle if she needs it, and let this poor sore girl have a rest.'

The young midwife wheels the baby away in a plexiglass trolley, and Sheila stays behind. She cleans Jodie up a little, wheels her back to the ward, then helps her into the shower, dresses her, tucks her into her bed. She brings her a cup of tea, a plate of toast. Through all of this Jodie hasn't spoken, has barely uttered a sound, except for an odd sob that she's hardly aware of, that could be coming from someone else.

4

Happiness. It's not really something Angus thinks about too much. When he does consider it at all, he assumes happiness exists in some separate dimension, no longer accessible beyond the age of consciousness, an ideal connected to dimming childhood memories of circuses and fairy floss, beach holidays and ice-cream. Or perhaps it's merely a construct, a chimera, not quite the fire-breathing monster of mythology, but a kind of illusory carrot used to coerce forward movement—always dangling tantalisingly just out of reach, never quite within chomping distance, regardless of effort.

But his life is running pretty much the way he expected it to run, and he has nothing to complain about. He works hard; his work is challenging and well remunerated. His family life is settled, comfortable. His children, as far as he can tell, are happy, and this is only right. Happiness is—or should be, though in too many instances it's clearly not—the entitlement of all children. Tom and Hannah are well loved, well behaved, not overindulged, and as appreciative of their many privileges as they should be. Jodie, too, seems genuinely content. She is not a demanding wife by any stretch of the imagination; there has never been any pressure on him (a pressure that he sees in the marriages of so many of his colleagues and friends) to perform, to compete. There's not some endless list of outrageous material demands— no diamond rings, no European cruises. Not, however, that Jodie has anything to complain about in this department; they are, by any standards, very comfortably off and if it should ever come up, a European holiday would not be out of the question.

His marriage is, as marriages of almost twenty years tend to be, a little on the humdrum side—but no more than is expected.

Jodie is still an attractive enough woman, can still provoke the requisite lust at the appropriate moment. Angus had occasionally, during the earlier years of his marriage, let more than his eye wander, although he has never strayed too far or too seriously. But he is past all that now—he knows that what he has is good, is worth keeping.

But beyond this, he doesn't think too much. He hasn't time—and nor, it must be admitted, inclination—to go further, to tot up achievements, successes, against losses, regrets. After all, what would be the point? If he's not precisely happy, he wouldn't regard himself as unhappy either. Angus's life is suffused by a slow and steady feeling of fulfilment, and he counts himself a lucky man, satisfied and content.

Even Jodie's revelation has failed to make a seriously negative impression on his customary feelings of wellbeing, of good fortune. Naturally, what she told him has been unsettling, and he has needed a few days to adjust to the idea, to examine the facts and assess the possible consequences. For a few nights he has found it difficult to sleep and has taken himself off to the guest room and subsequently been short-tempered at work and at home. He has sensed Jodie waiting for him to bring up the subject again, to ask questions, dig further—she made it clear that she'd be willing to tell him anything, everything he wanted to know. But after those days of deliberating and after recovering from his initial hurt—that she'd kept this from him for all these years!—he's found himself curiously unconcerned by what happened in the past—wanting only to assure Jodie of his support, his sympathy, his understanding.

'It's not,' he tells her, 'that I'm trying to trivialise the event itself. It must have been unimaginably traumatic at the time. You were so young, still a kid yourself. But that's all over, isn't it, and unless you want to get in contact with her, with the child—and you know I'd support your decision—I can't see how this changes anything. For us, for you and me. And the kids, too. It might seem strange, Jodes, but really my main concern is for you, now—to make sure this doesn't hurt you in any way. Psychologically, I mean. Having it all brought back. And then there's the impact it must have had on you—having to keep this to yourself all these years ... Maybe you should talk to someone.'

It's late, the two of them are getting ready for bed, and though the children's rooms are at the other end of the house, Angus is whispering. When she doesn't answer right away, he assumes she is upset, offended by his reaction.

'I'm sorry if I seem to be treating it too lightly, but I've thought about it, and really, it doesn't matter. I'm not angry or disappointed or anything ...' He breaks off, not quite sure where he wants to go next. 'Actually, you know, I'm not really sure what you expect, how you want me to react—but you must know that this doesn't change anything, anything about us, about how I feel ...' He hesitates, '... about you, I mean.'

'Oh, Angus. I didn't, I don't expect anything from you.' Jodie is smiling widely, is on the verge of laughing. He's not quite sure whether she's amused or relieved. 'I was just worried that this—what I told you—would make a difference. Spoil everything. And I don't want to contact her, I really don't. I can't imagine I ever will.'

Angus is relieved, tries hard not to show it. 'Well, if you change your mind, I'd understand.'

'I won't. Honestly. But if you want to know more ... If you want the details, the father—'

'Oh, no.' He feels a surge of something—dismay, alarm, dread—at the prospect. 'You've told me enough, Jodes. Really. I honestly don't care about that. In fact, I really don't want to know. Maybe some things are best left?'

The panic begins just a few days later, though he doesn't really think that the two are connected. He is lunching with Arding's mayor, Jim Dixon, at the Red Heifer. Though separated by almost a generation, the two are old family friends—Jim had been at his parents' wedding. But the lunch is more business than pleasure, has been set up to explore the possibility of Angus standing as a mayoral candidate in the next local election. Angus's eventual elevation to the position is a long-established but unspoken understanding amongst various local powerbrokers; his reputation in both the commercial and civic communities is solid, his success more or less guaranteed. Jim is a genial Santa Claus of a fellow, a retired stock and station agent, now keen golfer, who has already enjoyed more than a decade in office. He is holding forth, in that expansive elder statesman way, saying something about Jodie, asking whether Angus is sure that she'll be comfortable in the role—would she welcome it, resent it? He knows from experience that the mayor's spouse (*first lady, haw, haw*) is also expected to commit much time and energy, and he hopes it won't compromise their family life. 'You're lucky to have such a young family, Angus—mine are all grown up and flown the nest. And boy, do I miss 'em—in another twenty years you'll know what I mean. These are your golden years, son, you should enjoy them. Life goes by so quickly.' Angus is listening patiently, waiting for a break in the seemingly endless flow, when out of the blue he feels himself overcome by wave after wave of terror. He thinks, briefly, that it is a heart attack—can feel not a pain in his chest, but distinctly, deafeningly, the rush of blood through his arteries, too hard, too fast, too loud. His breathing is inadequate, laboured. Jim is too busy reminiscing to notice, and Angus is able to cover the moment by professing nausea and escaping to the hotel bathroom.

It is a good ten minutes—time spent sitting on the toilet, his head in his hands, taking slow deep breaths—before he can compose himself sufficiently to unlock the cubicle, face his reflection in the mirror. And then another long while splashing water on his face before he can rejoin his concerned friend in the dining room. His first brief glimpse in the mirror reveals eyes that are flecked with blood, and open far too wide, the irises fully exposed, like the blazing orbs of a headlight-dazzled dog just before the moment of impact.

After this the attacks come frequently. First once a week, then twice, then every second day. They come at odd, unexpected times—always when he is at his most relaxed, often when he's alone, and never in moments of stress or crisis. He tells no one—not his mother, his business partner, his doctor, not Jodie—and somehow no one ever seems to notice. Miraculously, he's able to give in to this unwelcome compulsion to run, to escape, to take the necessary time, waiting for his heart rate to subside, his breathing to return to normal, without drawing any attention to himself. He looks up the symptoms on the internet. They are classic panic attacks that he's experiencing, but he isn't impressed by any of the recommended pharmacological treatments, is sceptical about the less traditional remedies. He has no interest in looking for a cause; for the present he accepts the attacks as an inconsequential but unavoidable impairment (a consequence of ageing, like bunions, arthritis?), as if hoping that this lack of serious engagement will make the symptoms disappear. He works hard to minimise the likelihood and the impact of the attacks, and relegates them to the murky backwaters of his consciousness: he does not know, doesn't want to know, what they mean, what they augur.

5

Jodie was surprised by Angus's response. She had imagined he would have been hurt—not by the infidelity itself, how could he be—but by her failure to confide in him, a betrayal of a far more serious kind. The two days of awkwardness, with Angus a polite but cool stranger, the separate sleeping arrangements—this is what she had expected. But his almost airy dismissal of the events, his determination to leave the past in the past, though a great relief, had been thoroughly unexpected. And though she'd had to stifle an initial urge to laugh, she'd found Angus's awkward avowal of unconditional support and steadfast affection incredibly moving. They had made love that night—more fiercely than they had for years—and had talked, though not about anything in particular, nothing serious, until the early hours of the morning. Angus had eventually drifted into sleep, had turned on his side, away from her, snoring gently, but Jodie lay rigidly awake, trying not to think, not to remember. Wishing there was some way she could un-remember—or even better, some way to undo the whole thing—to make it untrue.

But the past looms larger than the present, larger than Angus likes to imagine, throwing its shadow over everything, like some sort of terrifying temporal eclipse.

The act itself was singularly meaningless; indeed, she has so little memory of it that she would be hard-pressed to remember more than a few disconnected details about the man—the boy—himself. Was his hair brown? Or was it reddish? He was dark, rather than fair, surely? His hair was long, of that she's fairly certain, held back from his face in a ponytail. She thinks he may have been tall and thin—but no, she might be thinking of someone else. He could just as easily have been short, stocky—even slightly pudgy. Oh, God. He had been a boy, that's all she really remembers. Just a boy. She thinks of her daughter's male friends: at sixteen, seventeen, even eighteen, the boys' features are still not quite defined; they seem closer to their toddler selves—their brows smooth, jaws soft, eyes clear—than the men they're on the brink of becoming. And that's what *he* had been: just a boy, a long-haired, denim-clad, beer-drinking boy she'd sat next to in the pub. That he was the father of her child, the father of any child, was simply unimaginable.

She'd gone out that night with her flatmate Sharon. Angus had been in London then for more than two months and in all that time she'd dutifully stayed at home on weekend nights, watching videos, reading, or writing long, forlorn letters that she could never bring herself to post. Sharon, impatient with Jodie's shyness, her excuses, had finally talked her into coming out to the pub.

'Oh, come on, Jodie, you're like a bloody old woman. You're eighteen, aren't you? Not eighty. You need to get out a bit, see some life. I'm sure your Angus won't give a shit. You don't really think he's staying home night after night in London, pining for you, do you? Come out and have some fun.'

And so she'd gone with Sharon to some pub in Newtown, not expecting fun, not expecting anything much, really. It was the Sandringham, she thinks, and there'd been a band, a bit of a crowd, and *he'd* been there—was it Gibbo or Hendo or Sheppo or Stevo? A friend of a friend of a friend of Sharon's, up from Melbourne or over from Adelaide or down from Brizzie. He'd bought her a drink, two, three, six, and they'd danced—it had been some sort of a punk outfit as she recalls, though they were already at the tail end of that particular musical scene. What she does recall is the sense of risk—it wasn't the sort of place Angus would have taken her: the pub was dark and seedy, hazy with cigarette smoke, smelling of dope and dirty carpet, crowded with long-haired students, half of them stoned out of their brains, all of them pissed. And Jodie, despite everything, had found herself enjoying it. The dark, the dirt, the heat, the pounding music, the sense of being out of it, being out of herself. She had found herself embracing, for once, the sensation that nothing more than the here, the now, was of any consequence.

And she'd drunk more, and he'd drunk more, and they'd gone outside to share a surreptitious joint—not quite her first, but still, to Jodie a joint was daring, forbidden, vaguely indecent. As the night wore on she'd lost track of Sharon, and had eventually staggered back to the flat, accompanied by this boy, after closing, in the early hours of the morning. They had clutched one another, giggling and swaying, in order to stay upright, had climbed the stairs and collapsed onto her bed. And so they had fucked—drunkenly, clumsily, not out of any real desire, but almost as a matter of course. Because, in those days (and in these days too, she supposes) that's what you did.

Jodie remembers nothing of the sex, really; the only detail she can summon is her dope-induced wonderment at the way a starburst of small black freckles adorning the boy's scrawny shoulder kept dilating and contracting in her vision as he juddered above her.

And that was the end of it. They'd lain there together for a while, not touching, not talking. He'd lit a cigarette (you did that, too, in those long-ago days), ashed on the floor, and then, muttering something about having a train to catch, had pulled on his Levis and his T-shirt and left. He'd gone without so much as a goodbye or a thank you, let alone a telephone number, a name. Jodie had fallen asleep and hadn't woken until late in the afternoon—sick as a dog, vaguely regretful. It was only later that the regret had sharpened into disgust, a mild self-loathing at her weakness, her betrayal of Angus, but she'd resolved that it would never happen again. And it hadn't.

The one thing she does recall quite clearly, all these years later, is that the disgust, even the guilt, though real enough, had dissipated almost immediately. The encounter hadn't really touched her, had left no lasting impression. It was a no-strings-attached sexual experience—unexceptional for a girl of her age, her generation, her culture. There'd been no intent, no preparation, not even a condom in those reckless post-pill, pre-AIDS, abortion-on-demand days of her youth.

So, it was a one-off. Some fun, a notch on her bedpost, perhaps, if she was the type to mark such events, but eminently forgettable. And there was no reason that Angus, that anyone, would ever have to know, was there? No need for confessions, recriminations. There was no need for anyone to get hurt, ever.

DECEMBER, 1986

'Is there someone you want me to phone?' Sheila asks. 'I'd be happy to call for you if you're too exhausted.'

Jodie would like to sleep, but somehow sleep won't come. She still feels suspended, disoriented—even the discomfort in her buttocks, her lower torso, the muscular ache in her thighs that feels as though she's run a marathon, seems distant—as if her body isn't back yet, isn't quite her own.

Sheila seems reluctant to leave her alone, has brought flowers left by some discharged patient, is arranging them fussily. 'There must be someone, sweetie. It's a huge event, a baby. Maybe the biggest in a woman's life. There must be someone you want to tell. What about the father? Your parents? Shouldn't you let them know?'

'I don't want it.' Jodie is amazed to hear her own voice—so certain, so substantial—is surprised that there are still words, and a way to say them.

'Eh?'

'I don't want it.' More confident, louder; this time there's no mistaking what she's saying.

Sheila's eyes widen. She stands still for a moment, considering, then goes back to rearranging the flowers, casually. 'What do you mean you don't want it, sweetheart?' The woman's words are careful, quiet, unstressed. 'I thought you said you had a fellow, that your parents knew all about this?'

'It was a lie. There's no one.' Jodie's voice is flat and expressionless. 'I don't even know who its father is. And I don't want it. I was on the pill—none of this should've happened. If I'd known earlier, I would've had it ... aborted.' It seems slightly obscene to utter that particular word here, in this place created to welcome and nurture new life.

'What about your parents? Won't they support you?'

'No.'

'It's a hard thing, lovey, having a baby when you're so young and all alone, but you know, there are ways, these days. It certainly wouldn't be impossible. There are pensions—not much, I know, but it's possible to live. You'd get help with rent and all the services. I've seen girls younger than you take their little ones home and make a go of it. Often as not, they make wonderful mums.'

'No. I can't have it.' She swallows, steels herself. 'I really need to talk to someone about having it taken away. I want to—to give it up for adoption.'

Jodie glares defensively, trying to conceal her wretchedness, and fearing the woman's objections, her judgement. But her expression hasn't altered.

'Well, it's not a simple decision—not one a girl as young as you should be expected to make so quickly.'

'But who organises these things? I need to find whoever it is that can arrange things.' Now that the words are out, the idea made concrete, Jodie is beginning to feel the air fill her lungs again; her limbs seem as if they might be attached to her body, her body to her mind. 'Isn't there something I can do, something I can sign? I know there are people desperate to adopt out there. You hear all these stories about how hard it is.' She speaks in a rush, as if that will somehow move things along faster.

The woman sits on the edge of her bed. 'Now, Jodie. Hold up a bit. It's not as simple as you think—they won't just let you give the bub away like that.' She takes hold of Jodie's hand, almost absent-mindedly. 'You'll have to have some sort of social worker talk to you, and then she'll refer you on to a psychologist to make sure it's not an impulsive decision, or just a symptom of post-natal depression, for instance—something you'll come to regret. They'll want you to spend some time with the child now—to make sure. Then they'll put the baby into foster care for a while, so you have an opportunity to reconsider. It might be quite a while before it's all finalised. Adoption's not something you can do lightly—there are consequences for both the mother and the child, you know. And it can come back to haunt you down the track. You need to take time and see how you heal, how you think later, when you've recovered. You might feel like there's no way you can deal with it all today, but believe me, so many first time mothers feel just this way straight after they've given birth. You're exhausted, terrified, can't see how you'll cope. What you're experiencing isn't unusual at all.'

Jodie pulls her hand out of the woman's warm clasp, pushes herself up to sitting. 'I'm not depressed, and I'm not terrified—well not in that way.' She speaks slowly now, carefully, wanting the woman to believe that she is thinking clearly, that she means what she says, that it's not spontaneous, a momentary consequence of pain and exhaustion. 'I've had months to think about this, and I don't want it. I really just want someone to take the baby away now. Can't I just sign something and go home and get on with my life? I'm not going to change my mind. Truly.'

Sheila sits quietly, thinking. Jodie can't read her expression. 'Look, you've just been through something huge—even a straightforward birth is an ordeal. You need a good sleep, a proper meal. I'll arrange to have someone come and talk to you then. You haven't even seen your little girl, yet. You really need to—'

'No. Please.' Jodie's voice is sharp with panic. 'Don't you understand? I don't need to see her. I don't want to see her. I don't want to touch her. I want her—*I want her to be gone.* Oh, God.' She turns away, closes her suddenly stinging eyes. 'Isn't there someone who can just make it all go away? This is like some sort of crazy nightmare.' Then, like the child that she is: 'I wish I was dead.'

The woman takes Jodie's hand gently between her own again, rubbing them as if trying to warm her. 'Now, it's not that bad, surely?'

Jodie says nothing, pushes her face into the starchy hospital pillow, tries hard to swallow her sobs.

The woman sits quietly for a moment, then moves closer, strokes Jodie's hair gently, her voice a soothing whisper.

'There is ... there may be something, if you're quite certain you don't want her. There might be some sort of private arrangement that can be made more quickly, without all the fuss.' Her voice drifts, but Jodie, attentive now, waits for the woman to continue. 'The rules for adoption are very ... rigid, and there are sometimes good people out there who can't adopt through the official channels. They might be too old, or not married— just some silly rule that means they're deemed less suitable. But that doesn't mean they wouldn't make perfect parents, given the opportunity.'

Jodie turns to her now. 'Does that mean ... Do you think you can help me?'

'Well.' The woman is stroking her hand with a vague, unfocused tenderness, as if her mind is far away. 'I might just be able to help you, sweetheart. I might be able to find a solution.'

The woman sighs, and lets go of Jodie's hand, patting her on the shoulder. 'Now, you just sit up and wipe your eyes. I'll bring something to eat and then see if you can have yourself a good sleep.' She plumps up the pillows behind Jodie's back. 'I'll get them to keep the baby in the nursery for a while longer—make sure you're not disturbed. And when you wake up, Sheila will have found you a solution. Is it a deal?' She holds out her hand, and Jodie grabs it, clings on. It's a deal.

6

The letter arrives in the week before Christmas. Since the dramas of early spring, life has returned to normal: though she still has a slight limp, Hannah's leg has healed beautifully, and despite the occasional concerned inquiry into her wellbeing from Angus, Jodie has managed to put the whole episode at the hospital to the back of her mind. She assumes that the envelope will only hold another Christmas card to add to the pile, opens the envelope unsuspectingly, doesn't even bother to glance at the back, to check the address. It is only one page, and somehow official looking, though it is handwritten, in small, upright printing, on smooth unlined paper.

Dear Jodie,

I'm writing to let you know that according to a search that was made subsequent to our conversation in September, it appears there is no official record of an adoption being processed for your daughter Elsa Mary. Further inquiries also indicate that her birth was never registered.

As it is clearly my legal duty to report such findings, I have made these discoveries known to the relevant authorities, including the police. However, because our conversation was not strictly official, and what you told me was in confidence, I thought it only right that I should contact you personally with this information.

Yours sincerely,
Debbie West

Jodie crumples the letter up tightly in her hand and shoves it in the pocket of her jeans. She tears open the next envelope in the pile, then the next, briskly adding each bright Christmas card to the display on the kitchen dresser, without pausing to read the inscriptions.

She leaves the paper in her pocket, can feel the ungainly lump through the denim, its slight diminishing whenever she sits down. She extracts it from her pocket later that evening, when both children have disappeared for the night—Tom to Christmas-coloured dreams, Hannah to a movie and then a sleepover. Angus is sitting on the lounge room couch, drinking red wine and channel surfing, and she hands the note to him, crushed and body-warm, without a word, then turns to the window and gazes, unseeing, into the darkness of the garden.

When she's sure he's had time to read the letter through, she speaks, still looking out into the night. 'What I didn't tell you before ... what I didn't tell Debbie, was that the adoption wasn't regular. It was a private arrangement with the matron. Completely illegal, I suppose?' Jodie tells her husband now—this story she's never told anyone—clearly and concisely, never faltering, her words measured, calm.

She waits through an interminable silence, turning back only when she hears him stand. Jodie looks at him, desperate for some sort of reassurance, a clue to what he is thinking, what should be done, but his expression is closed; he doesn't meet her eye. His face is strangely red, and he rubs at his eyes, shuffles his feet; his breath loud and ragged.

'Angus? Are you okay? It's not that bad, surely?' She moves towards him, holding out a hand as if in supplication, but he moves out of her reach. 'Jode, I ... have to—' He rushes past her before he finishes the sentence, exits the room rapidly, almost running, knocking over his half-full glass in his haste.

Jodie follows him up the hall to his study, but the door has locked behind him. She taps, calls out, worried now. 'Angus? Angus, are you all right? Angus. Can you open the door?' There is a long silence, then, his voice comes low and breathy: 'It's okay, Jode. Just remembered something I'd forgotten to do at work. Urgent. Gave me a bit of a shock. I just have to make a couple of calls. I'll be back down in a minute.'

She goes back to the lounge room and mops up the worst of the spill, then waits, certain that he'll return with assurances, answers, some sort of a plan. After what feels like an age, she becomes aware of the dark rumble of Angus's voice coming from the office and she moves back up the hall carefully, trying hard not to make a noise on the timber floor. Even before she can make out the words, she can hear the intonation—Angus's voice has returned to normal, is calm, businesslike, assured. She stands as close to the door as she dares, can just make out his side of the conversation.

'No, no. It must have been illegal—she received some sort of a payment ...

'To be honest, Pete, I haven't really wanted to ask anything else. And if it comes to that, maybe it's better that I know nothing. I don't know which laws we're dealing with here, or what the legal position would be after so many years. But even if the adoption itself can't be prosecuted, I suspect that there'd have to be some sort of investigation. That somebody somewhere's going to want to know why the birth wasn't registered and what happened to that child.

'I don't think so, no. She says she doesn't remember anything about the people who took the baby, only that they were quite old. Evidently the matron arranged it all, told her that everything was kosher.

'Look, do you think you could come over? I know, I know ... I'm really sorry. It's just that I have a bit of a bad feeling about this letter, mate. I haven't even discussed it with Jodie yet, don't want to panic her, but it just occurred to me that we should do something pretty quickly ... go over the possibilities. If there's any likelihood of the police getting involved. Maybe we could make some sort of contingency plan?'

Jodie creeps back into the lounge, grabs the bottle of red wine as she passes through the kitchen. Soon she hears the ensuite shower running and then the low murmur of the television in Angus's office. She wonders about his continued avoidance, thinks about going in and confronting him, asking him why he felt the need to arrange a visit from a solicitor—even if he is their friend—without consulting her, but somehow it's all too hard. Instead, she fills her glass to the brim, waits.

Angus answers the door when Pete arrives, then leads him down the hallway and into the lounge, where Jodie's still sitting, polishing off the last of the bottle of red. Angus answers her questioning glare with an oddly apologetic smile, before backing into the kitchen to get Peter a glass, open another bottle. She gets up to greet him, ready with a quip about the incongruity of him bringing his briefcase when he's so obviously in holiday mode, wearing worn shorts, thongs, sporting the beginnings of a beard, but the joke shrivels on her lips when he evades her outstretched arms and gives her hand a cursory squeeze instead, reluctantly offering a bristly cheek.

'Jodie. How are you? How's Hannah's leg?'

'Well, the plaster's been off for weeks now ...'

But he's not really listening. 'Bloody children,' he says, shaking his head. 'There's always some drama. Sometimes you've got to wonder if it's worth it.'

She is stung by his conspicuous lack of warmth, his awkward formality. 'It's lovely to see you, Peter, at any time of the day.' She smiles to lighten the atmosphere. 'But I'm not quite sure ...?'

'Well. Angus has told me all about ... about your situation, Jodie. Now, I'm not actually a specialist in this sort of thing, though it's a very odd situation and I'm not sure where we would find an expert. Anyway, Angus thought it might be a good idea if we put our heads together and tried to work out a plan of action, work out what sort of, well, what sort of strategies we can put in place to minimise the damage. If it comes to that, which of course it may not.'

He sits down abruptly, and she follows, sits directly opposite him on the long sofa. He pulls a notebook and pen out of his case and places them precisely on the coffee table, as if he's setting up his office desk. He hasn't looked at her properly since he arrived, and now his eyes dart back towards the kitchen. He clears his throat, shifts nervously in his seat.

Angus finally returns, pours them each a glass and sits down beside Jodie. Gives her a reassuring smile, takes her hand.

'So,' Pete says finally. 'Can you show me this letter?'

Angus pulls the letter from his top pocket—folded neatly now, but there's no disguising the evidence of its earlier ill-treatment—and hands it over.

Pete smooths his fingers over the letter's dog-eared edges as he reads. His expression gives nothing away, retains its sober but impassive cast.

'Well,' Angus's voice is edgy with anxiety, 'what do you think? Could it go any further?'

Pete gives him a brief, grim smile, nods his head slowly. 'I'm afraid it could go quite a long way, mate. But before we start panicking and before we think about making any plans, I need you to tell me what you told Angus, Jodie. He's given me a rough outline, but I really need to hear it from you. The whole story.'

Peter sits very still, with his eyes half closed as she tells him, his fingers peaked beneath his chin. He nods now and then, but says little—occasionally double-checking a statement or gently insisting that she keeps the narrative ordered. He wants the bare bones only, he says, is not interested in motivation or explanation—nothing but the facts. Angus paces around the room while Jodie speaks, interjecting at various junctures, worried that she has changed details, or left out some vital element.

When she has finished, Jodie leans back in her chair, exhausted. There's a strange sense of disembodiment connected to retelling the tale, and an unexpected sense of relief, release.

'Well?' She gives Peter a weak smile, and for the first time since his arrival he looks at her properly, his own smile slight, but genuine, and, she imagines, a little apologetic.

'Well.' He sighs and gives his shoulders a little shake, rubs the back of his neck.

'So what do you think, Pete?' Angus sits down heavily beside her again. 'Should we be worried?'

'Oh, yes.' Peter's tone is neutral, but his face is sombre. 'There's quite a lot here to be worried about, I think. In the first instance there's the adoption itself. Look, we can argue that Jodie was young, that she was coerced, but she was over eighteen and it would be hard to argue that she didn't know that what she was doing was wrong. She did it outside the system— knowingly and for money. And then ...' He falters.

'What?' Jodie's voice feels like it's coming from far away.

Peter clears his throat. 'I'm almost certain the authorities will institute a search—they'll have to. Then there's a very strong possibility that they won't be able to locate the child, after all this time, that no one will want to admit to adopting her this way. Why would they, after all? There would have been reasons that this couple didn't go through the ordinary channels. I can't imagine them volunteering the information as they'd be liable to prosecution, too. So then, assuming that the child—the young woman now—can't be found ... well, that will open a Pandora's box.'

'What do you mean? Why wouldn't the police assume what you suggested—that these people just don't want to be found? Why would they take it any further?'

'It's not that simple, Jodie. The investigating police will have to follow certain lines of inquiry. They have no choice. If the search for the child comes up negative, then she becomes, to all intents and purposes, a missing person. Last seen in your company.'

'But I still don't understand what you mean by a Pandora's box. Are you saying that they won't necessarily believe what I tell them if these people don't come forward? But that doesn't make any sense at all. She could be anywhere now. Surely they'll be able to work that out.' Jodie turns to her husband, who is watching her intently. 'Angus?'

Angus takes her hand again, but it's Pete who answers. 'It's not a matter of what they believe, Jodie. A missing person investigation can quickly morph into something else—especially when there's bugger-all evidence to back up your statement. There might be a thousand possibilities that can never be proven—the child could have been taken overseas, she could have been taken by aliens, who knows. And there may only ever be circumstantial evidence to incriminate you—but that can be enough. There are precedents.'

'Incriminate me? Precedents for what?'

This time it's Angus who answers. 'Sweetheart. Pete is just trying to give us the worst case scenario. It's only the remotest possibility, but there's a chance that the police could investigate you, if all else fails, just to make sure that you didn't harm the child.'

'But—'

He interrupts, 'But as I said, it's highly unlikely—so let's not get too hung up on that right now. I'm sure Pete has some genius idea about how we can avoid any unnecessary ... complications.' He turns to his friend. 'So where do we start? What should we do? Should we just wait and see what happens? Wait to see what they—the authorities, the police, whoever—are planning to do?'

Peter thinks a moment, drumming his fingers on his knees. 'This might seem counterintuitive to you both, but I have a feeling that it might be smarter to pre-empt them. Make a huge effort to stay one step ahead.'

'And what would that entail?' Jodie can hear the anxiety leaching from Angus's voice; as his professional self engages, he stops slouching, sits up straight, looking alert. Jodie, though, feels slightly befuddled, knows she has missed some vital point in the proceedings, but is grateful to have it all taken away from her, content to let them take her in hand, take her over. It's almost as if she isn't there, isn't Angus's wife, Peter's friend, but merely a problem to be solved. She relaxes, curling up on the lounge with her wine, contributes little, lets the men's words, their plans, wash over her.

'My instinct is that this will move pretty swiftly. I imagine that your nurse friend must have gone straight to Community Services to check their records, though it's a complete mystery to me why she decided to get involved. Was it something you said? You definitely didn't tell her about the matron?' Jodie avoids Angus's eye when she replies.

'All I said was that I'd arranged the adoption after I left. But she, well, she was very concerned when I told her—she offered to help me find her, to reconnect. I think she said she had some contact in the department, someone who could help me bypass all the red tape. I kept telling her that I wasn't interested, that I didn't want to meet her, but I think she was probably ... trying to help.'

'Oh, God save us all from helpful social-worker types. Anyway, someone at Community Services would have discovered that there was no record of any adoption, and then no registration of the birth, no Medicare notification, and they'll have sent the file to the police. They'd have no option.'

'The police where?' Angus's voice is brisk, businesslike. 'If it's here, maybe I can talk to Don?'

'Actually, I imagine it would be the police nearest to—where is the hospital? Greystanes, maybe? And then on to the detectives at their local command, rather than here. It'll come under their jurisdiction, because that's where the cri—... where it all took place.' He pauses. 'But Don could still be useful. Any contacts you have could be useful. The city detectives will have to liaise with the cops here, if they need to do interviews, I'd imagine. So, if you can get onto Don in, say, the next few days and tell him what Jodie's told us, prepare him—that'll all help. Then when they get in touch he won't be surprised, and you can perhaps, well, you can ask him if he could arrange to have the initial interview here, rather than at the station.'

'Here? Why? What difference will that make? Do we really have to have the police here? Won't ... won't people talk?' Angus's distaste is obvious.

'It just means that she'll have the advantage—you'll be on your own territory. If it's at the station, in an interview room, you'll feel much more intimidated, even if they tell you that it's just a conversation and not an official interview. Here at home you can ask them to sit down, offer refreshments even—and then ask them to leave whenever you're ready.' He gives Angus an inscrutable look. 'But you're going to have to get over worrying about people talking, Angus. It's going to happen.'

'I suppose. But surely we can try and keep it as quiet as ... You know I'm due to stand for mayor this year, and it would be an absolute disaster if—' He breaks off, embarrassed, as if wondering about the relative significance of this particular concern.

'Mate. Angus.' Peter's voice is gentle. 'It's going to be a complete PR catastrophe—there's no avoiding it. You need to prepare yourself.' A slight pause, then he pushes on, 'You might need to pull out of the running if it comes to that. But—and this is what I've been trying to suggest—what if we don't just sit and wait for the blade to fall. Why not make it public ourselves? Make an onslaught on the media before they can make an onslaught on you.'

'What?' Angus sounds shocked. 'What do you mean?'

'This is what I meant about remaining one step ahead. I think we'd be smarter to actually release the story ourselves. Before the police, or the authorities make it public. That way *we* can control the release of the information: say that you've begun a private investigation, that you're actively looking for the child yourselves, perhaps realising after all these years, that something wasn't quite right, that you're concerned for her wellbeing. Maybe you should even offer a reward.'

'A reward?' Angus looks slightly sick.

'Not too much. Fifty grand or so for information leading to the discovery of the whereabouts or positive identification, etcetera.'

'Oh, God.'

There's a long silence. Jodie refills her wine glass, drinks deeply. She is over it all now, would like nothing more than to take herself to bed, to leave them to discuss her future without her. Jodie finds it hard to connect with anything they're saying—the conversation is swirling around her like faint, far-off music.

Then Pete turns to Angus again. 'Look, I know this is difficult to contemplate, but this is as much for Jodie's sake as anything else. We've got an opportunity now to make her appear to be nothing more than a concerned mother, searching for news of a child that she reluctantly relinquished years ago. We have to try and make the story work for Jodie—the court of public opinion is probably more crucial than any court of law, and it can be a very, very tough one. If we leave it to the police to make all the initial statements she'll end up looking a lot worse, believe me. But if we're proactive—if we play the media before they can play us—well, we have a chance. We'll make a public plea—play up Jodie's youth, her vulnerability, her lack of support, the absence of good advice. She can give a press interview or two, maybe even television. We have to make it a sympathetic story: a young mother, despairing, penniless, without a friend in the world—and then make it apparent that she's now genuinely grieving the loss of that child, would like to be reunited ... It'll work. The fact that the matron has died is a mixed blessing—at least she can't refute anything Jodie says.

'I know it sounds cynical and opportunistic. But the alternative ... the alternative is that Jodie'll become a kind of latter-day Lindy Chamberlain. And you know what the press did to her. She'll be tried and convicted and hung in the first five minutes. The public aren't necessarily going to know that the police have begun their investigation—not if we get there first. And if we play our cards right it'll look like the police are helping you with your investigations, rather than the other way around.'

'And what if it backfires? What if the media think that we're covering our arses? What if that nurse speaks to them, tells them how it all came to light? Tells them that Jodie's initial instinct was to lie?'

Peter shrugs. 'It's going to be a shit fight, Angus. There's no getting around it. But at least we can have the *first* word. That's got to count for something.

'The first thing we need to do is to place an advertisement, discreetly, in all the major newspapers. A few regionals. Maybe some of the women's magazines—*New Idea, Woman's Day.* Elsa Mary, is that what you called her? Elsa Mary Evans. It's possible that we're being presumptuous, that the police won't investigate—but I doubt it. However you look at it, there's still a missing person. Even if it goes no further, it's not going to hurt, is it—it'll just be the cost of the ads. And if there *is* any sort of investigation, it's still not going to hurt. It will look, at least, like you're honestly concerned, that you're not interested in covering up, or denying anything.'

'But there's no way of knowing.' This is not an objection from Angus, but a query. 'Say someone does appear? What then? Her identity would have to be proven, wouldn't it? She'd have to undergo DNA tests, I suppose?'

'Yes. And there's the toe-webbing—syndactyly, did you call it? She'd still have it, presumably—or it could have been surgically corrected, I suppose. And you would have had a heel prick test done on the baby, surely. The Guthrie test? It can be used to conclusively establish identity, though obviously we have Jodie for that, anyway.'

Jodie tries to focus. Did the baby have that done? She can clearly remember Hannah and Tom having the test, the way her own heart felt pierced as the tiny new foot was pricked and squeezed, the shocking red blot on the card. But that baby, Elsa Mary—she didn't know, couldn't remember. She had probably left it to Sheila or one of the other midwives. Just one of the essential experiences of motherhood—like the bathing, the feeding, the changing, the nursing—that she had deliberately avoided.

She can't tell whether Angus is excited or appalled. 'So there will be a way—a definitive procedure—to test anyone who comes forward? God, how awful. But I guess that will simplify things, won't it?'

'Well, it's not exactly going to simplify things, Angus—the situation will always be very complicated. But you'd better pray that someone does come forward, that she can be positively identified as being Elsa.' It sounds like a warning; Peter's gaze is fierce, his jaw tight.

'Otherwise?'

'Otherwise ... Who knows?'

Jodie catches Pete giving Angus an odd, imploring look. Angus's eyes widen, then his expression becomes suddenly bland. He yawns, stretches, gets to his feet, gives Jodie a sympathetic grin.

'Jodie, darling—you look half dead.' He holds out his hand and she takes it, noticing how her fingers unfurl, relax in his warm clasp. 'Why don't you go to bed?' He pulls her up gently, propels her with a firm hand in the middle of her back towards the kitchen. 'Pete and I are going to have coffee and sort through a few more details.'

She takes a few unsteady steps, then turns back. 'It's going to be all right, though, isn't it? I'm not going to be ... charged or anything?' It's an effort now to get the words out clearly, to stop them sliding away from her. Angus is back beside her almost immediately. He grips her by the shoulders, his fingers strong, painful. 'It's going to be fine, Jodie. There won't be any charges. I promise.'

In bed Jodie lies awake for what seems like hours, the room spinning in sync with her thoughts. She wonders at her husband's apparent loyalty, his certainty, his faith in her and in the future. Wonders whether it's genuine; whether it can last.

7

The panic had set in as he read the nurse's letter, but had become so severe, so overwhelming, that he had only managed by a supreme act of will, to sit and listen to his wife's account, her revised account, of the adoption. He had escaped as soon as he could, running from the room as if pursued by devils, and the symptoms had taken longer to subside than usual; it had been a full ten minutes—interminable, inescapable—before his heart stopped racing, his breathing returned to normal. Nausea had followed this attack and he'd had to lie down on the office floor, hoping that the churning in his gut would cease without him actually having to throw up. He had tried to think about the contents of the letter, to consider what should be done, could be done, as he lay there, but it had been impossible to focus properly on anything other than his own physical symptoms. When the worst of the churning had ceased, and he could get to his feet without vomiting or worrying about passing out, he had called Peter. But this had been out of an urge to be seen to do something, to show Jodie that he was in control, rather than because he had any particular faith in Pete's expertise.

But it had been a good decision, a perfect decision—he had been pleasantly surprised, even impressed, by his friend's lightning-quick lawyerly reflexes. Despite their long friendship, their parallel careers, he'd never actually seen Peter in action professionally, had assumed that his work persona would be as laconic and dryly humorous as his social persona. He hadn't expected this transformation into a polished but unsmiling— almost dour—legal virtuoso. Even Pete's tendency to plan for the worst—which in other circumstances might have appeared extreme—had seemed merely precautionary, prudent.

After Jodie floats off to bed, clearly smashed, her eyes glazed, face glowing rosily, Angus opens another bottle of wine, persuades a half-reluctant Peter that this is a better idea than coffee, that he can afford to stay longer. It is past midnight, but Angus—as is common after an attack—is wired. He won't be able to sleep for a few hours yet, and although he will regret it in the morning, he knows that a few more glasses of red will help vanquish the inevitable insomnia.

The men take their drinks outside to the front verandah, as far from Jodie and Angus's bedroom as possible. There are cane chairs, a table, but they lean against the verandah rails, sipping their drinks. It is midsummer, but cool and clear; a half moon low in the sky, and a slight breeze makes the swings in the park across the road sway eerily in the bluish light.

Angus speaks first. 'Thanks, man. I appreciate it. I couldn't have … I just couldn't think.' He shrugs, stuck for words.

Pete sighs, shakes his head. 'Fuck, Angus. This is, well, to say it's unexpected is an understatement. It's fucking crazy. When I first got here, I was stunned. I didn't know what to say. Poor Jodes. But she seems amazingly calm, really. Considering.'

'To be honest, I think she's got no idea of how serious it is. All she's worrying about is the illegal adoption business, the trouble she could get into over that. I really don't think it's even occurred to her … What it might mean if this child doesn't turn up. I guess it's a complete long shot, but it really could happen, couldn't it—she could actually end up being charged with …' He can hardly bear to think the word, let alone say it.

'*If* the child doesn't turn up? Mate, it's not that much of a long shot—it's a distinct possibility. Anything could happen— you know that. And I haven't said much about it—but I have a bad feeling that this is going to be a big story. The media will go apeshit with the whole missing baby, hidden life thing. That's why I think it's vital that we try and get public opinion onside from the get go. Trust me: public opinion is going to count for something here.'

'Jesus. Shit. This is nuts.' Angus drinks deeply from his glass, pours more.

'You really didn't have a clue? She never told you anything?' Peter sounds genuinely curious.

'Nothing. I mean she told me about the baby a few weeks back, after she met up with that woman. But she just told me what she told her—that she'd had it adopted out.'

'So she lied to you, too?' Angus hasn't had time to process the fact of her lie, but right now it seems understandable, and inconsequential.

'Well, it wasn't really lying, I suppose, just—'

But Pete isn't interested in his rationalisation, and interrupts: 'It's almost beyond belief—that she would keep something like this to herself all these years. Makes you realise, doesn't it?'

'Eh? Realise what?' Angus slurs the words, hit with a sudden surge of tiredness.

'How fucking mysterious people are. You've known her all this time, you've been as intimate with her as anyone could ever be, and she's never told you ... something so important. So huge. And whatever happened, she's had to live with it. For more than twenty years. Alone.'

'Yeah, well, we know what happened, mate—she told us everything. I mean, I know it was wrong—and bloody stupid— but she was young. Afraid. She had no one to help her. And she didn't hurt anyone.'

'But we only have her side of the story.' Pete gulps his wine, avoiding meeting his friend's eyes.

'What do you mean?' Angus is suddenly wide awake again, his words snappy, defensive.

'We only have Jodie's word for all this, Angus. You do realise that. Whatever happens legally, you're probably never going to be certain. Unless the girl actually emerges.'

'Unless she emerges? Oh, fuck.'

'Exactly. See? You've got no happy alternative. This is really going to complicate your life, mate. Either you'll end up with a stepdaughter that you never wanted or knew about, or you're going to spend the rest of your life wondering where she is.' He pauses, looks down at his glass. 'And wondering whether Jodie knows a whole lot more than she's saying.'

Angus feels a rush of anger welling, then feels it dissipate just as suddenly, extinguished by another wave of fatigue. There's no point, anyway, in challenging Pete's blunt observations. This is how he is, how he's always been, no malice intended. He gives a shiver, rubs his arms. 'Jesus. It must be all of ten degrees. Fucking Arding. Whatever happened to summer?'

'Do you love her?' Peter almost mutters the words, as if he's embarrassed to be asking.

Angus responds in a heartbeat. 'Of course I love her. She's my wife.'

'Then here's my advice to you—lawyer to lawyer. And friend to friend.' His voice was louder now, firmer.

'What?'

'If you do ever start wondering, just leave it, mate. Don't ask. Whatever you do, just don't ask.'

His mother had warned him off Jodie at the outset. Back when Angus and Jodie were first going out, back when it was nothing more than a teenage fling, his mother had, in her usual brutal way, advised him against the connection.

'There's no doubt that she's a pretty girl, Angus, and from all accounts she's bright enough—she'd have to be to get that scholarship. But ...' and here her voice takes on what he always thinks of as her diamond tone—sharp and brilliant, slicing effortlessly through his own convictions, his desires ... 'She's not exactly one of us, is she, dear?'

He could laugh, should laugh, because it is a joke, surely—his mother's insistence on there being a 'them' and an 'us'. Such old-fashioned distinctions in this day and age. The nineteen eighties, he would love to remind his mother, and not the eighteen nineties. But he says nothing, dares not be too open in his defiance.

She has buttered him up with the offer of a beer, a cigarette, if he'd like (*after all, he's a man now, with a man's appetites as well as a man's responsibilities*); he should have been prepared, known what was coming. But instead of walking out in a huff, or better yet, actually defending his girlfriend, he listens, smiling uneasily as she conducts a lengthy and vicious deconstruction of Jodie's character, her potential and—most significantly—her background.

'Have you met the mother, dear? I haven't myself—though I probably wouldn't know her if I fell over her; they live out at Milton, don't they? Not in Arding—but I've spoken to Nancy Butterly about her, and as you know I respect Nancy's opinions on these matters absolutely. She's been working at Grammar for so long—she's an old girl herself, of course—and she was saying that she would never, ever have let the girl in if it had been up to her—on account of the mother. Which says something, don't you think, Angus? Nancy's a very—how shall I put it?—she's a very *egalitarian* sort of person. No one could ever call her a *snob*,' here she waves her hand dismissively, 'although if anyone does have cause to think well of herself it's Nancy Butterly.'

Angus murmurs his assent, wonders how long he will have to sit here, wishes he had taken up the offer of a beer, a whisky, even.

'You might think I'm overreacting—you've only been seeing her for a few months, haven't you? And I do know that these youthful ... entanglements ... aren't likely to be serious. No doubt you'll be hopping in and out of bed with dozens of girls, all sorts of girls, before you find someone suitable.' She gives a tight smile. 'But the thing is, Angus dear, you need to be very careful. A girl like this, from a background like that ...' She takes a breath.

'The thing is, Angus, I believe that this particular girl is likely to be very ambitious. She's pulled herself up this far, from such a very ... difficult background, to a place in a premier girls' school—and yes, that's a remarkable achievement certainly—*but* I have to say that I think your getting involved with such a girl could be very dangerous. I've seen it before—quite a few times over the years, actually. Boys like you, with expectations, responsibilities, position, who get caught by these very clever girls—mushrooms, my old granny would have called them—and it's always, always, *always* an unmitigated disaster.'

His mother frowns at him, expectant, but Angus only shifts uneasily in his chair, gives a nervous smile, says nothing. She sighs. 'Do you remember Bruce Davies, dear? He was an old friend of your father's, boarded at New England when he was a boy; they had a big property out near Moree, Swan Hill. No? Well, he married a local girl, a Moree girl—Susie someone or other. She came from a terrible background—a big Roman Catholic family. The father was a drunk, deserted the family and shacked up with some gin; the mother had to work as a barmaid, or took in laundry, or something equally dreadful, to support them all. But this Susie was exceptionally bright, and quite beautiful to look at, naturally. She went off to teachers' college in Sydney, and then came back to town to teach.

'Anyway, she and Bruce got married, much to the dismay of his parents: there was some friend of the family he'd been keen on for years; they'd expected him to marry her. They were married and almost immediately it all turned to disaster. Bruce did the right thing, gave one of her brothers a job—overseeing the shearing or something like that—and evidently he did something appalling—stole from them, I gather. Terrible business.

'And then the woman herself, Susie, couldn't cope living so far from town; she wanted to keep her job, hadn't realised how isolated they would be, what life on a property was like—the hard physical work, lack of company. Of course when children came along, things got worse. She became an alcoholic, a depressive, and ...' His mother takes a breath, as if steeling herself. 'Well, she ended up killing herself *and* the two children. Drove the ute into their dam one weekend when Bruce was away. Bruce was never the same after that, poor fellow. He went bankrupt eventually, lost the property. He had a stroke a few years ago, not long after your father passed on. He was only fifty-five.'

She pauses a moment in deference to both unseasonably

deceased men. 'I worry about these things, darling. I know you just think I'm terribly old-fashioned, but you have to credit me with some knowledge—some perspective on the way the world works.

'I know we're meant to think that we're all equal these days, that a person from the gutter is just as good—or *can* be just as good—as a prince.' She gives a sad smile. 'But you should never believe it, Angus. I know your Jodie seems like an entirely estimable girl, and I'm sure she'll go on to have a successful life, a career, a decent husband, children.

'But she's not for you, Angus. And if you're—I'm not sure how to put this—if you're conducting an affair with her, you're just not playing on a ... a level field. She'll be expecting something more from you. Girls like that always are. It won't be light, it won't be a fling for her, dear. She's not like Susy Baldwin, or Annabelle Briggs, or the McDonald twins, or any of the other girls you know. She doesn't have security, options of her own. You need to get rid of her, dear, before she hooks her claws in. Before she gets you where she wants you.'

But her cautionary tale seems irrelevant and excessive, her analogy unjust. He can see no drawbacks to continuing his relationship with Jodie, can see no drawbacks in pursuing a relationship with any girl, if it comes to that. Angus is still just a boy, after all, despite what his mother says. He's bright enough, he's not bad looking, he comes from a good family (and in Arding good means old, established, with connections, as well as money), he's a decent bowler, has a powerful backhand, swims for the school. He's not quite school captain material—has never excelled at rugby or public speaking, which are non-negotiable qualities in a leader—but he's a prefect, trusted by teachers, popular enough with his peers. He's a kind boy, responsible, reliable—the type who helps old ladies across the road, chats to parents politely, pitches in to clean up after parties. He helps his older brother with work on their property in the holidays—doesn't even mind shearing—though he's not keen to make a career of farming. Which is lucky, as he won't be—that's his brother's blessing and burden. In the way of second sons, he's been promised to the law already—and the law will suit him down to the ground. He's cautious, unimaginative, methodical. He's easygoing, even tempered. He really never does anything other than what's expected of him, never plays outside the rules, has never caused his mother a moment's grief.

Until Jodie.

Angus had known Jodie—or known of her—for years. She'd been there in the background, at parties, at school dos— known, but not really known, in the way that these things work between boys' and girls' schools. But they'd got together at a bachelors and spinsters, in what he'd thought was a completely spontaneous alcohol-fuelled mutual attraction. Someone (who, Angus can't quite remember, though it may have been one of the McDonald twins) had told him later that Jodie had had the hots for him for yonks, had been working up courage to seek him out, angling for invites to anything he was likely to attend.

He'd taken her to see a film, and they'd ended up together again at some other party—just snogging, nothing serious; they weren't officially an item. But then he had, with no one better in mind, decided to ask her to be his Formal partner. She hadn't said yes immediately, had appeared to consider the question very seriously before giving a strangely grave assent. 'Thank you,' she'd said. 'Thank you, Angus. I'd really like that.' She'd always wanted to go to a New England School formal, she'd confessed. She'd heard that the music was usually fantastic, and the food was always excellent. And this might be her only opportunity. She had smiled slowly, shyly, then, her enthusiasm obviously genuine, if muted. He had expected either the cool, casual consent or over-ebullient enthusiasm typical of most of the girls he knew, so Angus had been surprised, and oddly touched.

It was Jodie's gravity, this quality of restraint that attracted him initially, and that continues (a circumstance that surprises

even Angus) to attract him—almost against his better judgement. Her unselfconscious solemnity made her very different
to most of the Grammar girls: the jolly hockey-sticks and horse-
mad types favoured by his mother—her peers' daughters, the
girls he had known all his life. They were nice enough, fun
with a capital F, bright, cheerful, enthusiastic, endlessly confident, utterly focused, all knowing what they wanted, where
they were going—but all a bit samey to his way of thinking,
interchangeable, with their regulation perms, their regulation
clothes, regulation smiles, their regulation attitudes and aspi-
rations. But Jodie—Jodie was different. She was beautiful to
look at—slender, blonde, her features refined, regular—and
there was no doubt that this had a good deal to do with his initial interest. But there was nothing else that was regular about
her. Not her clothes, nor her manner, her bearing, even her
accent—nothing was quite regulation, nothing was quite as expected. Though she appeared to have plenty of friends, and was
obviously well respected in the school community—like him
she was a prefect—somehow she wasn't entirely in her own mi-
lieu, wasn't quite comfortable. She was watchful, circumspect,
always sparing in her conversation, cautious in her convictions.

He knew that she came from a difficult background, but
when they were together, she wasn't at all interested in talking
about this, about her life. 'So what do you talk about?' one of
his mates had asked him impatiently, obviously put out by Angus deserting him for this girl. 'What the hell do you do with
her all day, Gus, if you're not porking her?'

He couldn't answer. What did they say, what did they do?
They had, the past few weekends, taken a picnic and driven
out to the Wash Pool, a waterhole in one of the nearby national
parks, found a shady spot under a tree, close to the water, and
had spread out a blanket and simply lain there most of the day.
He wasn't porking her, no, but they were close to it and getting
closer (though this was not something he was going to discuss
with his mate). They had spent hours in a state of constant

arousal: touching, sucking, rubbing, moving inexorably towards that moment, yet never quite arriving. They would drink a bottle or two of beer—Angus always drinking the lion's share—eat chips, chocolate, fruit. They would talk abstractedly about this and about that, though he could never recall later what it was they discussed. He talked about his plans, he supposed, and Jodie hers, though he couldn't if pressed have related what hers were: Sydney, he thought. Uni? Nursing, maybe. Or was it teaching? But he enjoyed Jodie's company far more than he would admit to his coarse-minded friend, avid only for titillating details of sexual conquest—her seriousness, her lack of pretension, the odd dignity of her uncertainty, her indefiniteness. But most of all he enjoyed her unquestioning admiration of him, of Angus. An hour or two spent in her presence and Angus felt himself taller, better looking, more intelligent, more in control. Jodie made Angus feel good about himself; she made him feel like a man.

8

Though she's never forgotten her mother-in-law's early attempts to get her out of Angus's life, and her patent disappointment when they actually married (there's not a single wedding photo where Mrs Garrow senior—Helen now that Jodie is 'family'—is smiling), over the years Jodie has managed to get along well enough with her. Both women are united in their approach to Jodie's chief preoccupation: increasing Angus's health, happiness and success, and that of their children. The two women have built up a relationship that, if not exactly friendly, is one of mutual respect, with each recognising in the other certain similarities of character and temperament. Angus's mother respects Jodie's loyalty, her devotion (only what's due) to her son and her grandchildren (whose upbringing she can only fault in small ways—details rather than the bigger picture). Jodie is well aware that in exchange for her efforts in rearing and nurturing this next generation of Garrows, Helen is willing to overlook, even forgive, Jodie's background—which, admittedly, Jodie has done her best to escape. Jodie has ensured that her own family have made no shameful incursions into the respectable world of the Garrows— her mother is kept at arm's length, so there are no painful meetings between the two grandmothers, and her brothers, who don't get out of Milton much, are easy enough to avoid altogether.

Happily, both of the children fit neatly into the Garrow matrix: Tom is really just a miniature version of his father—bright and respectful, easy-going—and is clearly his grandmother's favourite. Hannah is rather a different matter—she is perhaps a little too bright, displays signs of adolescent restlessness, is prone to taking unnecessary risks—revealing a worrying resemblance to Angus's Aunt Ruby, a (reputedly) lesbian potter who lives in the nearby mountains, the Garrows' own blackish sheep. And Helen is critical of her granddaughter's current physical lushness, her plumpness—something she feels Jodie needs to take more seriously. She tries herself with pointed comments about diet and exercise, about the curse of excess fleshiness, all of which Hannah, being the type of girl she is, pretends to ignore.

Her mother-in-law knows, of course, about Angus's past infidelities (is there anyone in town who doesn't?) and though there has been no conversation between the two women about the matter, and confidences would have been awkward, Jodie is aware that Helen respects, even admires her stoicism, her ability to walk with her head held high, to stand by her man. Perhaps Angus's tendency to stray was inherited; Jodie knows from family gossip that her marital experience is almost identical to Helen's own. In any case there is a tacit understanding, perhaps shared by many other women of their particular class and situation, that this is a reasonable price to pay for security and position—and, perhaps, affection.

Angus rings his mother, at Jodie's request, the day after their conversation with Peter. Jodie makes an ineffectual attempt to reorganise the pantry while he makes the call from his study, can hear the quiet murmur of his explanation, a short silence and then the unmistakable sound of the phone disengaging. She gives up on stacking the Tupperware neatly and rushes up the hall and into the office where Angus is sitting at his desk, an odd expression on his face.

'Well? What did she say?' Jodie is slightly shocked by her own intense anxiety, would not have expected she'd be quite so afraid of her mother-in-law's disapproval.

'She was fine.' Angus gives a deep sigh, shakes his head as if to clear it. Jodie notices that his shirt is untucked, the centre button come undone, his pale stomach peeking through. She has to work hard to resist the impulse to move toward him, tidy him up. 'She said that you'd been put in an impossible situation, that she's behind you, behind us, one hundred per cent and that she'll be making her position clear to anyone who cares—or who dares!—to ask.'

'Oh God.' Jodie sits down heavily on the other chair, looks at her husband wonderingly. 'You're kidding, aren't you? I thought she'd be appalled, that she'd—'

'I know.' Angus rubs his eyes, grimaces. 'I did too. She didn't seem at all surprised though, that's the odd thing. But she couldn't know anything about it, could she? You've never told her anything, have you?'

Jodie gives a hard, short laugh, doesn't bother to reply.

'She said she'd call in sometime today or tomorrow to talk to you. To help work out a ... a survival strategy, she called it.'

Despite the notice, Jodie is caught off guard when her mother-in-law arrives late that afternoon. As usual, she tramps up the side of the house to the back entrance, the soft crunching of gravel and the dog's excited yelps signalling her arrival. This is a habit that never fails to irritate her daughter-in-law—the surprise element of Helen's appearance putting her somehow on the defensive, leaving her no time to prepare. Jodie is in the kitchen, simultaneously peeling the potatoes for dinner and helping Tom with his maths homework. Helen stands for a few moments outside the screen door, coolly surveying the scene, before walking in.

'My goodness, Thomas—look at all that homework. They push you children so hard these days. I don't think I ever saw your father do his homework. Then again, I suppose he was boarding at this age.' She plants a kiss on the top of her grandson's head, then turns to Jodie. 'I wonder if Tom could take a little break, watch some TV, play something on the computer, just while I talk to you, dear?'

Tom looks up at his mother eagerly, she nods, and he skips away quickly, before minds change. Jodie hears the slam of his bedroom door, and then more faintly the television, the distant sound of gunfire from his Wii.

Helen sits down in Tom's vacant chair, rifling through his books and papers aimlessly. 'Where's Hannah?'

Jodie shrugs. 'She's out. God knows where. I'm not expecting her home anytime soon.'

'Good. We can talk plainly, then.' Helen motions to the chair beside her. 'Leave dinner for a moment—it can wait.'

'Do you want tea? Whisky?'

'No. Nothing.' Impatient now. 'Just sit down. We need to talk.'

Her life appears to have been reduced to a series of directions to be obeyed, and Jodie follows the command without question, though ordinarily she would baulk at being ordered around by her mother-in-law, would attempt some slight gesture of resistance. She sits down at the table, takes a deep breath, prepares for the onslaught. Despite Angus's assurance of his mother's support, Jodie is wary—she can't quite believe she will be let off without some unpleasantness.

Helen looks at her for a long moment, frowning, and Jodie wills herself to meet her gaze steadily. So closely regarded, Jodie is made suddenly, shockingly aware of her mother-in-law's advancing age, her deteriorating physical condition—her once fine features seem suddenly undefined, her shoulders stooped and frail, her eyes rheumy, dull.

Helen looks away first. 'As I'm sure you know, Angus has told me all about ... everything.' She gestures vaguely, expressing the inexpressible. 'Now, I'm quite sure that between you you've sorted out some very sensible plans to deal with the situation, and you probably feel you don't need my opinion or my advice. But,' she adds dryly, 'I'm going to give you the benefit of my wisdom anyway.'

Jodie forces a gratefully encouraging smile.

'Actually, I'm not going to give you my opinion. It's largely irrelevant, anyway, isn't it? And all I really know is what Angus has told me, which I suspect has been cleaned up somewhat—trying to save me, from being shocked, no doubt.' A slight humorous lift of the eyebrows. 'Though it might surprise him to know I'm pretty unshockable. Anyway, that's neither here nor there—what I do want to give you is my advice on how to handle others—the town, your friends, the children. Angus.'

'Oh, but—'

Helen holds up her hand. It is spotted, wrinkled, but her fingers are still strong and straight, the tips of her long fingernails obviously filed and buffed. Jodie's own hands are work-reddened, her fingers are short, stubby, the nails torn and at this moment slightly grimy from the potatoes.

'Jodie. I know I'm an old woman now, and I'm probably rather out of the social loop—it happens when you get old, you know. Your social, er, garden tends to die off a bit—rather more literally than I'd like, actually.' Again the sudden flash of humour. 'But credit me with some understanding of these matters. You're about to be at the centre of what we in the olden days used to call a scandal.

'I know that to you, the details—what actually happened, whether people believe you—seem terribly important, but in my experience, the particulars of the scandal are largely irrelevant. When this all becomes public, you—and Angus and the children too—are going to find that people you've trusted, even dear friends you've assumed will be loyal, will avoid you. The usual invites will dry up very quickly—though to be honest, dear, you probably won't feel like going out. On the other hand, people you barely know will suddenly want your company, though I've never really understood why. Out of curiosity maybe, or pity ...' She pauses for a moment, considering.

Jodie is curious herself. It's impossible to imagine her mother-in-law ever being an object of pity, or even public curiosity. And it would take a brave person to snub Helen Garrow, particularly the Helen of yore, who was, as she well knows, one of Arding's most formidable and influential social agents. 'Did you—'

'Yes. It's obvious that I've had some firsthand experience, but now isn't the time to go into all that. Ancient history, anyway.

What we really need to talk about is just how you're going to deal with it. Arding will begin to feel very, very small, and the prospect of running away will be very appealing.'

The thought of escape offers immediate relief, and Jodie is surprised it hadn't occurred to her. 'Perhaps we should take a holiday?' she says. 'All of us. We could even go overseas, I suppose. Get right away.'

'Well, of course you could. But it's not really going to solve anything in the long run, is it? This isn't going to go away—whether you're here or elsewhere. Eventually you'll have to come back and … face things. You're not going to be able to leave permanently—Angus has his practice, the children have school, their friends. So we're going to have to work out a way to make it bearable. The way you handle things is going to matter a great deal—not just for your own sake, but for all of you. All of us.'

Us. How it pleases Jodie to be so unequivocally embraced even under these bizarre circumstances. Us.

'So what do you suggest I …' She cringes slightly at the thought of including her mother-in-law in her own sordid drama. 'What should *we* do?'

Her mother-in-law doesn't hesitate. She shrugs off her expansive, almost philosophical mood in an instant, replacing it with a rapid-fire set of instructions that leaves no opportunity for discussion or demurral. Jodie feels as if she is in a war briefing, wonders whether she should be making notes, taking minutes.

Jodie, her mother-in-law instructs her, is to go about her business as if nothing has happened. If anyone asks anything, she's to tell them she's been advised not to discuss the matter. If anyone's rude, Jodie's to ignore them. She's not to get into sentimental discussions over the lost child, her youthful follies or, God forbid, into any sort of argument or conflict over the matter.

If the situation becomes too heated—if public opinion really turns on her—Helen will take the children away to Melbourne, to protect them, at least. There's not much she can do about

Jodie and Angus though; they will just have to ride it out. If the worst comes to the worst and there's some sort of charge—Angus has apprised her of that possibility—well, they'll deal with that when it happens.

'The one consolation,' Helen concludes, 'is that eventually it'll be yesterday's news—not even fit for wrapping fish and chips in, these days.' She leans back in her chair, stretches her legs, lets her head drop backward. Sighs. 'Actually, dear, I've changed my mind. A whisky would be lovely. Make it double. Neat.'

9

When her parents call her in for a serious talk, a few days after Christmas, Hannah's already half prepared to be told something terrible, something earth-shattering.

She's lying on her bed, flicking through *Frankie*, listening to Erykah Badu on her iPod, facebooking, and sending the occasional text, and though she is alarmed by her father's polite request that she come into the lounge room, she's not all that surprised.

Hannah has noticed something going on. Since their return from the hospital in Sydney her mother has continued to behave strangely, her disorienting remoteness during their trip home never quite disappearing. Even though she still seems to participate in all the routine proceedings of family life, somehow Jodie's attention is elsewhere. She might be listening to Hannah's complaints about unfair homework deadlines, or nagging about the state of her room, or whatever, but so often lately it seems to Hannah as though her mother is just going through the motions, without any proper feeling, any real engagement.

And now, over the Christmas break, Jodie has been completely scattered. Christmas is the time when Jodie is generally hyper-vigilant regarding her family's outward appearance: policing their outings, their attire, giving both children constant advice on how to behave around their grandmother and relations, providing a running commentary on their table manners, grammar, accents, on keeping their hair tidy, hands clean, dress sensible and demeanour modest.

Although it had no doubt been going on since forever, Hannah has only really begun to notice her mother's frenzied social anxiety over the last few years—her desperate attempts,

Hannah assumes, to keep up with the Joneses, impress the neighbours, the relatives, even her best friends. She had been invited to stay at Assia's place in Glebe last Christmas (why Assia had chosen to board at Arding of all places was one of life's little mysteries ...), and Hannah had marvelled at the casual way Assia's family muddled through the season's obligations—cancelling dinners, spontaneously heading off to the mountains for the day, or to a café instead of a family barbecue, stuffing the presents willy-nilly into pillowslips instead of wrapping them. It was a whole new experience of Christmas, and of family relations in general, without any traditional observances or painful and senseless formality. Hannah—and, as far as she could tell, everyone else involved—had actually had fun. It had put a very different perspective on her own stuffy, over-catered, convention-ridden experiences. When she'd expressed this to her friend, Assia had just rolled her eyes and said it wasn't a deliberate attempt to create a happy Christmas Day on her parents' part. It had just evolved organically from her mother's hatred of domestic organisation, and her general slackness. Regardless of her friend's scepticism, Hannah reckoned that Manon's way of handling what she liked to call the 'festy' season was far better than Jodie's—and she'd have swapped places with Assia, given the opportunity, in an instant.

But this Christmas had been a little less stressful than usual: her mother seemed to move through the days in a state of vague and vapid cheerfulness—almost as if she were sleepwalking, without any of her usual brittle anxiety. Hannah found herself, for the first time ever, excused from many of the usually compulsory family engagements—she'd even been allowed to leave the Garrow Christmas Eve dinner early and head off to a gathering at a friend's place. Hannah always found this particular family gathering depressingly dull, with no one her own age—her cousins were either Tom's age or adults with partners—and the whole bunch of them were horrendously boring grazier types, with no interest in anything other than cattle and headers, wheat prices and weather forecasts. No Garrow other than Hannah herself, it seemed, had ever read a book, seen a play, taken an interest in music (not counting her leso great-aunt, who sadly was never invited).

On Christmas morning itself the presents had arrived as beautifully wrapped and as satisfying as ever—Hannah received the new iPod she'd coveted, iTunes vouchers, an impressive pile of clothes, as well as a plane fare to Sydney and tickets to the Big Day Out in January; and Tom had scored Lego, some sort of remote-control flying machine, a stack of games for his Wii. Both parents had feigned surprise at one another's gifts, and had expressed genuine pleasure over their children's largesse. But Hannah could sense that her mother's heart wasn't in it.

While Hannah's activities had been radically limited when her leg was in a cast (and there has still never been any serious investigation of the circumstances surrounding her accident—even her father has barely questioned her about that), she has been pretty much left to her own devices since her return. As long as she keeps a low profile, it appears that no one will inquire too seriously into where she's going, what she's doing. And ordinarily this would suit Hannah, of course. But perhaps because it's school holidays, and she has more time on her hands to actually notice what's going on around her, what's going on in the adult world, she has begun to worry that something serious is up. She's tried to find out what it is—has even gone as far as asking her father straight up, a few weeks back, but he gave her a brilliant smile and told her not to fret; there was nothing wrong, nothing to be concerned about. She took him at his word, was reassured for a few days.

But then her father has been behaving strangely, too—has become more considerate than she has ever seen him, like some sitcom dad. Oh, he is just as busy as ever, probably even busier than is usual for this time of year, heading off early to work and then not back till late. But when he's home, he seems really to be there—making a point of seeking out both Hannah and

Tom, expressing a genuine interest in their various activities. And he has put himself out to be helpful around the house, too, Hannah notices: clearing the table occasionally, wiping things down. She has even seen him attempting to put on a load of washing, though he was rather comically defeated in this once he realised he didn't actually know where to put the detergent, or how to turn the machine on.

It seems obvious that both her mother and father are in the grip of something more significant than the customary holiday strains and stresses: there have been whispered conversations, locked-door conferences, unscheduled visits to undisclosed locations. And now both of the parentals are completely vagued out. They're not fighting, it's not that. But they're also not really talking—not to each other, not to anyone.

Now her father stands in her bedroom doorway, eyebrows raised, waiting unsmilingly as she gives him an offhand wave, pretends not to hear. 'Come on, Hannah. Stop playing silly buggers. It's serious. We really need to talk to you both. Now.' She sighs and gives a miserable pout, rolls her eyes.

'What, are you two getting divorced?' She speaks too loudly over the music, trying hard to sound bitchily unimpressed.

'Hannah.'

She sighs and rolls off the bed, limps across the clothes-strewn floor.

'You really have to do something about this, Han.' Her father, who is only occasionally confronted with her room, follows her progress through the clutter with obvious distaste. 'It's completely feral. Can't you ...'

Hannah leans against the doorway with her arms folded, carefully maintaining a blank expression despite her growing alarm, and waits for him to finish, the music still blaring in her ears.

'Though honestly, why I would even bother at this point.' He sighs and gestures for her to walk out the door, but as she's passing, he puts his hand on her shoulder, forces her to turn and look at him, gently prises the iPod jack from its socket.

'Hannah.' His voice is gentle. And frighteningly tentative.

'What?' Her own voice comes out in a squeak, barely audible.

'It's just … This is going to be difficult. Really difficult.'

'Oh God. It's something really awful, isn't it? You *are* getting di—' Another terrifying thought takes hold, explaining it all. 'Oh God, it's Mum. That's why you've both been so weird. She's got something. Cancer …' Her stomach begins to churn.

Her father pulls her to him for a brief hug. 'No, sweetheart. It's not that. It's—' He stops, sighs again, this time more heavily, looks at her gravely. 'Go on into the lounge, darling. And can you please get rid of the iPod? We need you to listen.' He pushes her gently ahead of him. 'And don't worry, Han—nobody's dying.'

Tom is there ahead of her, of course, bouncing about as if he has fleas. Hannah sits as directed on the lounge but moves as far away from her brother as she can. 'Can you just sit still, Tom?' She glares at him. 'It's bad enough having to be here at all.'

Her parents sit side by side on the chairs opposite, both of them looking determinedly cheerful, despite the bizarre formality.

'Well.' Hannah's father clears his throat; he speaks slowly, as if he's not quite certain about what he's saying. 'We've got something to tell you. Some news, and it's not all that good, I'm afraid.'

Tom's eyes widen; his jiggling peters out. 'You're not getting divorced? Mummy?'

Their mother smiles at him gently. 'No, sweetheart. It's not that. It's just something that happened to Mummy a long time ago.' She seems relieved to be able to say something reassuring, but to Hannah the words sound distant, as if they're coming from a long way away. 'And it's really not going to—'

'Jodie,' her father interrupts. 'I thought that we agreed that I'd do the talking.'

Her mother's nervous reply comes immediately. 'Of course, yes. Sorry, Angus.'

Hannah feels irritation flare, unaccountably maddened by her mother's meek obedience, her passivity. Why won't she do the talking? If it's her story, why not tell it herself, her own way? She wonders, half-seriously, whether her mother has sustained some sort of brain damage recently or whether she's been zapped—lobotomised in some tragic psychological experiment. Or perhaps she's started smoking pot. The improbability, the absurdity, of this scenario makes her giggle, but then she feels slightly sick—perhaps this newly distant mother *is* under the influence of some drug.

Her father draws himself up, takes a breath. He gives Tom a steadying glance, looks Hannah in the eye. He tells them.

'Is that it? Really?' Tom says, his relief evident. Then, as it sinks in, adds wryly, 'Another big sister. Awesome.' He punches Hannah's shoulder playfully, shrugging good-naturedly when she gives him an angry shove in return. He turns to his parents, obviously eager to make his escape. 'So, can I go now? I'm almost up to the third level.' He submits to his mother's fierce hug before hurrying back to his room.

But Hannah stays seated. She can't move, can't raise her head. Can barely breathe.

The relief that coursed through her once she was certain that no one was dying, no one was divorcing—those particular fears that still lingered from childhood—has been replaced by a disbelieving rage. Like most children Hannah has only vaguely understood that her mother had really had a life prior to her own advent—and while the details of Jodie's circumstances before her marriage, before Hannah's own birth, have not exactly been shrouded in mystery, they are rarely discussed. Jodie's family— her parents, her brothers—have never had any part in Hannah's own life. They belong to Jodie's past, and from the little she has seen of them, Hannah is glad to leave them there. But this—this announcement, this revelation. It has taken Hannah no time at all to seize upon the ramifications: that her mother might have a criminal past, that her life is about to be made public property. Hannah will be implicated in this; Hannah, along with her mother and father and even little Tom, is about to be publicly shamed.

She can envision her future, has seen it happen enough times to know exactly what awaits her. First there will be the little groups that gather without her; she will have to move through huddles from which she's somehow excluded, that aren't quite welcoming. There'll be false smiles on her former friends' faces, certain invitations she never receives. Her friends' mothers will patronise her, or ask nervously after her mother, and the teachers will look at her differently, regard her as someone to be pitied. Even the people outside school—the university drama group, for instance—will look at her oddly. She'll become a kind of prize, a curiosity. 'Aren't you that girl whose mum ...' It makes her sick just thinking about it.

She has had to work hard to find her place at school—it has taken her years, trying to be both herself and one of them. To fit in. She's far too bright to be ordinary, too plump to be pretty, hopeless on a horse or wielding a hockey stick or any type of ball, and her musical ability is completely underwhelming. But now, for the first time ever, Hannah is happy with the way she is regarded by her peers, satisfied by the place she occupies in the social pyramid. She's got to where she is on her wits—she's the class clown, fun to be around, entertaining. She's not queen of the pile, she'll never be that, but she's well liked and well known. Popular enough. And she's light years away from that painful to remember, desperate to conform, to be approved younger self.

Hannah is smart enough to know that being a Garrow has given her an enormous advantage; that being a Garrow she's considered a social asset by certain others. She knows enough too to realise that as soon as being a Garrow—or being her mother's daughter—carries a different sort of association, her status at school will be non-existent. She will always have Assia, of course: whatever happens, whatever's said, she knows that her friendship with Assia is unconditional, that Assia will never be influenced by anyone else's opinion of her, not even her parents'. But Hannah needs more than just Assia, and she knows that other girls—and, more alarmingly, boys—are not so independently minded.

Hannah realises she should be able to discuss her concerns with her parents sensibly, responsibly, calmly—adult to adult. She's sixteen, after all. But sixteen or not, she can feel her uncontained toddler self—a self she had thought banished years back—re-emerging; a tantrum—all those inarticulable emotions seething and churning—erupting. She feels her eyes prickling with angry tears, sucks her bottom lip in, then bites down on it hard. She can feel her hands turn to fists, her nails sharp against her palms. She pushes harder, waiting for the piercing, the pain, trying hard to contain, or at least rechannel, her fury. But her anger has taken on a life of its own, until somehow it's no longer hers to check.

'This is *so* fucked.' She hisses the words, looking up and beyond her parents. She can sense their paralysed concern, and their inaction puzzles her, and enrages her further—it's almost as if this is exactly what they expected, that they've steeled themselves against it, have already prepared themselves for her fury. 'You have just fucked everything. My entire life. This will be ... Everyone—*everyone* will know! Do you have *any* idea what you've done? Any idea at all?' Her voice comes louder, the rage swelling in her chest like a wave; she can feel it pushing and pounding and expanding inside her, almost breaking through her skin. 'You're so fucking clueless. How could you have done this? I knew there was something going on—back in Sydney, that thing with the nurse.' And then the red-hot question: 'Why the fuck couldn't you just do the normal thing, the usual thing, Mum—you know, what anyone with half a brain would do. Why the *fuck* didn't you just have an abortion?'

'Hannah, I—' Her mother is silenced by a look from her father.

Hannah sees nothing beyond the red that's coursing behind her eyes. She reaches for the antique cut-glass lamp that's standing on a nearby table, feels the terrible inevitability, the necessity of her action, of what she's about to do. Her parents watch her, but remain mutely immobile. It's as if they're waiting for her to act, stunned into acquiescence. Hannah picks up the lamp, the square marble base cold to her touch; feels the solid weight of it heavy, heavy, heavy in her hand, then throws it swiftly and precisely, a metre to the left of her mother's head. The lamp hits the wall base-first with a heavy thud, the crystal shattering, spraying around the room. Her father moves towards her, takes her, sobbing now with distress and fright, in his arms, but her mother just sits there, as Hannah had known she would, impassive, unresisting. Unreachable.

The Australian, Sydney Morning Herald, Daily Telegraph, The Age, Courier-Mail, Adelaide Advertiser, West Australian, The Land, Women's Weekly, New Idea, Woman's Day, Who Weekly, etc. etc. etc.

Substantial reward offered for any information on the past and/or present whereabouts of the child formerly known as ELSA MARY EVANS, born 18th December, 1986, Belfield Hospital. Please contact Peter Silvers at Silvers Wood and Watson, Arding. (02) 6777 2331 or email *p.silvers@sww.com.au*

10

She is in the ensuite bathroom, cleaning her teeth before bed, when Angus tells her—without any preamble—that he'd had a call from Don earlier in the evening. He is busy folding his clothes away in the walk-in wardrobe, has called out the news to her casually, in a by-the-way manner that she knows can't possibly be genuine.

Six weeks have passed since the arrival of Debbie's letter; the notices were sent out a month ago. Don Phillips, the local police inspector and Angus's mate, has counselled them to bide their time, to do nothing precipitate. He had predicted the time lag, almost to the day. 'It'll take some time,' he'd told Angus over a round of golf. 'I'm guessing a month, minimum, to ascertain firstly that your nurse friend isn't leading them up the garden path, though they'll pick up on those ads, the media attention. And then they'll need more time to establish that there's some sort of case worth pursuing. But if there is a missing child—even if that child went missing twenty-odd years ago—there will be an investigation.'

Now, with an instant appreciation of the meaning of this evening's call, Jodie feels her stomach lurch; she retches as she spits out the toothpaste. 'And what did he say?' Her voice is calm, doesn't hint at her agitation.

'It's what we expected, Jodie.' Angus is reclining on the bed, now, his pyjamaed legs stretched out on top of the covers, arms crossed behind his head, still determinedly nonchalant. 'The missing persons unit has begun an investigation. They're sending some detective up to talk to you tomorrow. He said that ordinarily they'd get you down to the station for questioning, but that out of respect to me, and to try and head off the press, they're willing to talk to you here. He'd have preferred to handle the initial questioning himself, but they're sending this young gun detective up and while he's agreed to come here, he won't make any other compromises. They'll be here in the morning.'

She moves towards the bed, sits down beside him, casts about for a suitable response. 'I guess we need to keep it quiet, do we? The police visit, I mean.' He shakes his head—out of bewilderment at her odd response or in an attempt to clear his head, Jodie can't tell.

'Jodes. Jodie. You don't seem to understand the ramifications. This could be huge. At the very least this could destroy your reputation—and by extension my reputation, my career. We could lose everything. If they don't locate this—your child—the question will be open; you'll have it hanging over you forever.'

Suddenly Jodie wants him to say it, to say the word, is sick of the silly game of evasion they've both been playing—the continual ducking and weaving around the truth. 'What question? What question, Angus?'

Angus looks dismayed momentarily—it is impossible to miss the bitterness of her appeal, the underlying anger. But he recovers quickly, takes her hand, waits a long moment before speaking. His voice is low and gentle, as if he really believes she doesn't know the answer: 'The question of whether you killed that baby, Jodie, of whether you murdered your own child.'

Don and the sharply dressed Sydney detective arrive punctually at the specified time. They bring along a local female officer who Jodie has seen now and then around town, always accompanied by a clutch of fractious toddlers. The young woman usually looks tired, harassed, with that slightly stunned look that's habitual to women with very young children. But here, official, in her police uniform, she is a different person: poised, cool, collected, her expression unreadable—and it is Jodie who is floundering, out of her depth.

They have come to the house, the Inspector explains, only because Angus has made a fuss—ordinarily they would have asked Jodie to come to the station. She wonders for a moment why he is explaining this so carefully—she had assumed that as friends this courtesy was only to be expected—and then realises that it is for the benefit of the younger detective, who shrugs and gives a complacent smile.

She asks—good hostess that she is—whether they would like tea, coffee, but the Sydney detective makes it very clear with icy formality that—whatever the normal social procedure of his country colleagues—this is an official visit and no sustenance will be required.

They sit in the lounge room—Angus determinedly guiding the officers to the three-seater, while he and Jodie sit in the single chairs opposite, Jodie on the edge of her seat, her hands arranged in her lap, ankles crossed, like a child awaiting a scolding. An odd numbness engulfs her, descending like the cone of silence in *Get Smart* and extinguishing the sick heat of humiliation and terror that has been burning furiously all through the night. Her panic recedes and everything is muffled; there's a muted buzzing, like white noise, in her head. She feels—as she has so often of late—merely flat, empty, and utterly disconnected. She knows she won't be able to make even the slightest effort to thwart the intentions of those around her, that she must let whatever is about to happen, happen.

She watches with vague curiosity the way that Don—a man who she has known for years, who has visited their home for dinner, whose wife has been on the Grammar fete committee with Jodie, whose son plays on Tom's cricket team—scratches at the side of his nose when he is uncomfortable, as he obviously is now. He clears his throat—rather phlegmily, she observes with faint distaste—and makes an awkward start to the conversation.

'Well, thanks for this, Angus, Jodie. We should get down to business, then. I'll hand you over to DS O'Rooke here. He's going to conduct the, erm ... Ask some preliminary questions. I'm just here as a courtesy.'

Angus raises his eyebrows in a way she is familiar with, and has always found intimidating when directed at her. 'But this is just an informal discussion, isn't it, Don? I don't need to get a lawyer, do I?'

Her husband's voice is cold and hard, and she wonders that the other men don't flinch. But of course, this is a game they're all used to—the power play between legal adversaries means nothing personal to them. Tonight they will go to their respective homes, and forget all about the personas they have assumed, the people they've attacked or defended. Her life will just be a professional problem to be solved, at best. At worst, it will be gossip to be spread about the town.

The Inspector meets Angus's eye coolly. 'Senior Constable Scanlon here will take notes, of course, but no, it's not a formal interview. This has all come from Sydney, Angus. It's out of my hands. But,' he says, turning to the Sydney detective, 'Jodie—Mrs Garrow—doesn't need her lawyer present, does she?'

O'Rooke frowns down at his notes. 'I understand that you are a lawyer, sir?'

'I am, yes. But naturally, I wouldn't be representing my wife, and this sort of business is not my area of expertise. However, if this is a formal interview I can have someone here in five minutes. But my wife won't be saying a word until then.'

O'Rooke looks up from his papers and smiles. His smile is brief, cursory—more like a wolfish baring of fangs.

'That won't be necessary, Mr Garrow. This is only a preliminary questioning. What we're really interested in at this point is finding out where the child—where the young woman, Mrs Garrow's daughter—is now. We can't proceed any further until we've established whether there is indeed any sort of case to answer.'

'What do you mean—a case? I assumed this was just a fact-finding mission. A case would presuppose a crime, and all we've got here is an adoption. And even if the adoption wasn't done strictly according to the law, so much time has passed—surely it's all a bit pointless.' A glare from Angus, bypassing

O'Rooke, directed at Don. Jodie notices the female officer give a slight smirk, which is quickly smothered.

'Well, sir. It's not quite that simple, is it? It's a little more than just an adoption, as I'm sure you're aware. It involved the *sale* of a child, which is a criminal offence. And as I'm sure you're also aware, there's no statute of limitations on criminal cases. But you're correct—that was just a figure of speech; there is no formal case. Not yet.' That brief display of teeth again and this time Jodie can feel a snarl of tension, like a low growl just below her range of hearing, between the two men.

'Perhaps sir, we could, if you'll allow me, just go over the facts.'

'Go ahead.' Angus folds his arms; leans back easily in his chair. 'The facts—that sounds like a sensible place to start.'

'Mrs Garrow,' the detective begins, 'it is our understanding that you gave birth to a baby girl, Elsa Mary, on the 18th of December 1986.'

And it goes on, through her stay at the hospital, and then to the date of her discharge, the lack of any subsequent official registration of the birth, the absence of any record of adoption through the official routes, the legal—he emphasises the word slightly—channels. The lack of proper documentation—no birth entry, no Medicare registration—pertaining to the child Elsa Mary beyond the indisputable fact of her birth—a fact that is clearly verified by the hospital records.

There are no surprises, nothing that she, that they, did not expect. The man relates the facts emotionlessly, asks Jodie frequently whether this or that detail is correct, encourages her to intervene if any fact is untrue or unclear, but doesn't ask her to expand. The DS is as straightforward, as lacking in emotion as Peter had been and Jodie knows that she too sounds calm, composed, her answers unhurried, precise, her demeanour unruffled. On the face of it, they could be talking about someone else completely, could be talking about anybody. Occasionally, Jodie feels a recurrence of her earlier panic, of the giddying fear, but it's only fleeting, like a sudden pang of indigestion, and she is almost immediately able to return to that more comfortable state of detachment.

'Of course,' she answers evenly, when called upon to verify dates, places, names. 'Yes, this is all correct.'

'Mrs Garrow, you can see that it is plainly our duty to investigate this matter further. You must see that we have to ask you,' the detective spreads out his fingers in a strangely theatrical gesture of conciliation, 'what exactly happened next. What you did with the baby. You're the only one who knows, you see.'

She is about to speak, strangely moved by his plea, to reassure him that of course she understands, that anybody would be concerned to find this child, that she will do everything in her power to help the investigation, but Angus speaks first, his voice curt.

'Hold on. You said this would just involve some preliminary questions. You've told us what you know, and Jodie's recollections correspond with all that you've said. Anyway, we've already made this clear—no doubt you've read the papers, seen our notifications. We've already begun looking for this child.'

'Oh, come on. We all know—'

'What we all know, Sergeant O'Rooke, is that my wife is under absolutely no obligation to say anything more.'

'Of course, Mr Garrow. And I'm sure you've told her to say nothing, or you wouldn't be the professional that I'm certain you are. But you do understand, that your wife's status—her guilt or innocence—will be much easier to establish if she assists us voluntarily.'

'Guilt? Innocence?' Angus's anger is undisguised now. 'Innocent of what? I've let you say your piece, check your facts, but it's clear that you're jumping to some fairly spurious conclusions if you're already bringing concepts of innocence and guilt into the discussion.'

'But, sir, we need to establish—'

Angus gets to his feet purposefully. 'Well, gentlemen, as I say, you've said your piece. And now I'd like you to leave.'

The Sydney detective looks vaguely shocked, appeals to Don. Constable Scanlon is looking down at her lap, studiously picking invisible fluff off her regulation skirt.

Don gives his viscous cough. 'Well, Sergeant, I think we may have outstayed our welcome.' He stands, brushes down his trousers. 'Well, thank you both for your time, Angus. Jodie.' He nods. Heads towards the door, followed quickly by the female constable.

The detective stands, his astonishment obvious. 'We'll be back in touch, Mr Garrow. Very soon,' he says stiffly.

'I'm sure you will.' Angus sounds mildly amused. 'But we'll be making a comprehensive statement to the press ourselves later this afternoon. You might want to get back to us after that.'

PRESS RELEASE
Statement of Jodie Garrow

Almost twenty-four years ago, when I was nineteen, I gave birth to a baby girl, whom I named Elsa Mary. On the advice of the matron of the maternity ward at Belfield Hospital, Sheila O'Malley, the child was given in a private adoption, to an older couple that I knew only as 'Simon' and 'Rosemary'. These may not have been their real names, however. I was given $5000 in cash, which was not intended as a payment for the child, but was to help give me time to recover from the birth.

Although I knew that the adoption was not entirely official, I at no point realised that I was engaging in an illegal act, having been advised by Matron O'Malley that everything was above board, and that all the legalities would be handled for me. At my own request, no further details of this couple were ever provided—I was given no surname, phone number or address. I had the impression that they resided somewhere in the Hunter area, but may have been wrong in this.

At the time I was a student, with no support from either my family or the father of the child, none of whom were aware of my condition. I was content that the baby was going to a loving home and that the future being offered to the child by this couple would be vastly superior to any life I could provide.

The baby was handed to the couple on the day of my discharge from hospital. I have had no contact either with the matron who assisted me, the adoptive parents of the child or the child herself since that day.

I have recently come to understand the seriousness of my youthful mistake, and would very much like to re-establish contact with my daughter.

If you have any information regarding Elsa Mary's past or current whereabouts please contact Peter Silvers at Silvers Wood and Watson, Arding. (02) 6777 2331 or email p.silvers@sww.com.au

THE DAILY TELEGRAPH
'Relinquishing mother searches for long-lost baby'

An Arding mother has sent out a nationwide call to help her find the baby that she gave away more than twenty years ago.

Mrs Jodie Garrow of Arding, in the New England region of NSW, was only 19—a nursing student—when alone and a long way from her country home and family, she adopted out her newborn baby, Elsa Mary. The adoption, which was arranged by a member of staff at Sydney's then-public Belfield Hospital, was far from legal, though this was something Jodie—vulnerable and naive—was unaware of at the time.

'The nurse told me she would be going to a good home,' Mrs Garrow told the media, in a short news conference, 'and at the time I was happy to believe her, relieved that the business had been taken out of my hands. I didn't really understand that not going through the proper channels was a mistake. Over the years, like many relinquishing mothers, I have become increasingly eager to establish contact with my daughter.'

Mrs Garrow was not told the adoptive parents' full names but thinks they may have been 'Simon' and 'Rosemary'. Baby Elsa Mary's toes were webbed on both her feet—a rare genetic anomaly shared by her mother and half-sister—and she may have received cosmetic surgery at some point to rectify this.

Mrs Garrow, who is married to Arding solicitor and mayoral nominee Angus Garrow, and who now has two other children, placed advertisements in a number of city and regional newspapers and magazines throughout Australia several weeks ago in an effort to locate her daughter.

If you have any information on the current or previous whereabouts of Elsa Mary, please contact Silvers Wood and Watson, Arding. (02) 6777 2331 or _p.silvers@sww.com.au_

DECEMBER, 1986

Later Jodie will wonder at the speed of it all, the smoothness of the operation—will wonder whether perhaps she was not the first, not the only young mother to have made this very deal with Matron Sheila O'Malley. But at the time haste seemed necessary—how did she have any choice but to gratefully accept the offer, the conditions? She couldn't take this baby home; there was no time for second thoughts, no time for doubt. Expedition was all.

'There are so few adoptions these days,' Sheila tells Jodie; 'young girls—and you, my dear, are the miraculous exception to this—would rather commit murder, kill their unborn babies than carry them to term and give them to all those desperate couples who are not so blessed.' Jodie hears the steel in Sheila's voice, takes a moment to realise that she's talking about abortion and not infanticide.

'And because these babies are so scarce, there are more and more hoops to jump through. So many couples are disqualified while they're waiting to reach the top of the list, betrayed by time, grown too old, the children given to more suitable—younger—couples.

'No one,' Sheila's voice is suddenly full of passion, 'thinks anything of it when a woman gives birth to a child in her mid-forties—it's a natural process and what's to stop them? But for adoption it's different. They're trying to set them up with the "perfect" parents, you see, though how age comes into that, I don't know.

'Anyway,' she goes on, calm again, 'I have some very good friends—I'll call them Ro—Rosemary and um ... Simon. They're good, clean-living, respectable, happily married professional people—the only thing missing in their life is a child. They'd dearly love a little baby—they've been trying for years, but with no luck—poor things. And now they're officially too old to adopt. They'd find one from overseas—a black one or one of those poor little Asian bubbies—but they haven't got the money for all that. And they'd rather a white baby anyway, to be honest. They're not racists,' she adds quickly, though Jodie hasn't made any sort of comment.

Right now Jodie isn't at all curious about this couple and their trials and tribulations, their questionable racial predilections. Her interest in them is far more immediate, far more practical: they want a baby; she has a baby she doesn't want. It all seems beautifully simple—a transaction made in, well, if not heaven, somewhere close by.

'Now, I've told them about you and your lovely little girl, and they're all excited. Over the moon. They wanted to rush over right away and talk to you, see the little bub, but I said they should wait, let me discuss it with you, settle the terms.'

'The terms?'

'Well, as you can imagine, they don't want there to be any … repercussions, later in the piece. Sometimes mums want to give the baby away, but still have visiting rights and so on. They don't want that. It has to be a clean cut, if you know what I mean. And they want to make sure you don't change your mind later.'

'But you know I won't. How many times—'

'Hold on a bit.' Sheila shushes her gently. 'So they're willing,' and her lips suddenly purse as if she's holding in excitement— or perhaps it's disapproval, it's hard to tell which—'they're willing to give you a little bit of cash to smooth things over for you, so to speak. It might make the decision—and all the hardship you've been through already—that much easier.'

'But I thought you said they didn't have any money—and anyway, I don't …' The dubious nature of the offer is suddenly apparent. 'I don't want to *sell* the baby. It wouldn't be right. It's not—it's not moral.'

'Now now, Jodie, don't take it the wrong way; you wouldn't be selling her. It's just to ensure that it's all above board, that you'll be getting something for your trouble, so to speak. And it's not a great deal, they don't have that much money, just a few thousand—just something to tide you over for the next few months, while you get over all this. So you can have some kind of break, and don't have to rush back to working right away. Of course, you don't have to spend the money on yourself—you could donate it to some charity, if you're truly opposed to taking anything. That would be your business. The thing is—they're not just willing to pay, they really *want* to pay, as a sort of thank you.'

'But—'

'First, though,' Sheila goes on, ignoring Jodie's interjection. Her voice is brisk now. 'First you need to give the bubba a name.'

'Oh, but I—'

Sheila interrupts her protest again. 'Now, you don't want

anyone here thinking there's anything odd going on and calling social workers and the like. You will have a visit from the infant health sister at some point, I can't stop that—but we can talk about how to deal with all that later. Now, come on—a name.'

Jodie shrugs, desperate, stricken. 'I can't think of anything.' She has a list of beloved names, names for her fantasy children—but those are not names for this infant, unexpected, unwanted, unknown.

The matron rolls her eyes, impatient. 'It doesn't have to be anything special—it won't be permanent, you know. How about your mother. What's her name?'

'Oh, no, I—'

'Your grandmother?'

'Elsa.' Jodie gives the name—her mother's mother, dead before she was born—without thinking, half in a daze.

The woman nods, satisfied. 'And your other grandmother? For a middle—you need a middle name.'

'Mary.' Her father's mother—long gone too.

'Perfect. That wasn't so hard was it? A good, simple, old-fashioned name: Elsa Mary.'

It's surprising just how easy the whole deception is. Sheila's not there every shift, of course, but she makes it clear to all the other midwives that young Jodie, though finding the transition to motherhood particularly painful, is responding well to her attentions. She is Matron's special protégée, best left to Matron's care. And most of the other midwives are happy enough to do the minimum, to leave her be.

Jodie's main priority during her stay in hospital, Matron insists—as a single mother without support—is to regain her strength. She's to be bothered as little as possible with the baby, who is to be bottle-fed and kept in the nursery as much as possible. The nurses are happy to look after the babies—first time mothers, with their nervous uncertainty, their tendency to weep, their endless lactation difficulties—are seen as slightly troublesome, especially by the older midwives, and as likely to unsettle their own baby as not. So Jodie's desire to see the baby as little as possible isn't regarded as completely outrageous.

And luckily the baby is a placid little thing, sleepy, easily contented, and requires little more than bottle-feeding and changing and the occasional nurse. All of which can be just as effectively done in the nursery. By others.

11

Just as Angus's mother had predicted, their social freezing out, which has all the hallmarks of an old-fashioned shunning, begins slowly, but gains momentum remarkably quickly.

Knowing the viral qualities of small-town gossip, Angus and Jodie forewarn their closest friends one by one before the notices hit the paper. They call them on the phone, or let them know what's coming over coffee, drinks, dinner, in an effort to stem—or at least reduce—the inevitable gossip. Angus tells his good mate David the story, almost casually, over drinks after an afternoon game of tennis and is relieved by Dave's nonchalance, his easy acceptance of the facts as Angus relates them. Angus has already been pleasantly surprised by the supportive attitude of the few people he's told, but still he is hugely grateful for Dave's lack of curiosity.

'Shit, mate.' Dave frowns thoughtfully, gives his bushranger beard a characteristic tug. 'That's got to be a bit of a shock. For all of you.'

He asks after Jodie's wellbeing briefly, and then the conversation changes tack entirely, moving on to a more pertinent discussion of the local rugby team's latest disgrace. This reaction, Angus thinks later, is reminiscent of the way any emotionally charged announcement is handled by most of the blokes he's friends with. With news of an impending birth, a marriage, divorce, death of a parent, there's never much said, never any fuss made—but there's a tacit understanding that the friendship's strong, that nothing has changed, that the mate will be there, unquestioningly, when and if you need him.

But between this conversation and their next meeting—their regular, longstanding monthly dinner with Dave and his wife,

Sue—it appears that something, everything, has changed.

Jodie and Angus are greeted by their friends with all the usual enthusiasm, welcomed into their home with the expected ceremony, or so Angus imagines. Tom and Harry race off to the rumpus room together to play Wii and stuff themselves with chips and fizzy drink; Hannah and Laura head out to a party, rolling their eyes good-naturedly at their parents' customary directives not to drink, drug, or drive. Champagne is poured, beer provided; the two women fuss about in the kitchen, while the men decamp to inspect David's latest motorcycle acquisition.

Angus would count Dave and Sue Forester as being amongst their closest friends—and certainly their best couple friends. Dave, a stock and station agent, a year or two older, is like Angus a grazier's son. They had both been boarders at the New England School before the death of Angus's father and his family's subsequent move to town, and though they hadn't been particular mates in their school days, they'd got to know one another when Dave married Sue, who is almost family to Angus—her mother a friend of his mother. The close proximity of the births of their children, daughters and then sons, had cemented the friendship between the two men. The two women, though cool initially, and with little in common (Sue is an ex-lawyer, now the driving force behind the Arding pony club), have also become good friends over the years.

Angus is comfortable in their house, comfortable in their company. Everything about them feels known, understood, in the way of family. He can almost imagine having just this life, David's life: Susan could so easily have been his wife, and this his home. The house itself—a stately old blue brick in the centre of town—is very different to his and Jodie's contemporary brick veneer on The Hill, but utterly familiar in its run-down grandeur, almost identical to the home he'd grown up in. He is completely at ease with Sue, too. She reminds him of his sisters, some of his Garrow cousins: seemingly devoid of self-doubt, content with herself and her place, reliable and competent, perhaps slightly insensitive to others' feelings—she can be fearfully blunt—but rarely deliberately unkind.

By the time the four of them sit down at the table to eat—the small boys having spirited their dishes back to their gaming den—the adults have all had a fair bit to drink. The meal is delicious as always—Sue is an excellent cook, naturally—and though there is some sporadic conversation, the four of them eat with very little talking. So pleasantly preoccupied is Angus with the quail, it takes a while for him to notice that his wife is upset. Jodie is sitting primly upright, her cheeks red, her eyes wide, and when she speaks her voice has the high and slightly fragile quality that he recognises instantly, one it only acquires when she's feeling out of her depth. He doesn't know for certain, but assumes that there has been some sort of falling out between the two women.

Susan's famous frankness, he knows from experience, can be challenging. She had given him an enormous serve, years back now, when details of his affair with Wanda Robinson had leaked out. She had cornered him at a party and enunciated very clearly her opinion of him (a prick), of Jodie (loyal, blameless), of how he could (and should) redeem himself (go down on his knees and beg forgiveness). 'You can't go on feeling hard done by just because you married your first girlfriend, Angus. You had plenty of opportunities to dump Jodie before you married her—and plenty of encouragement, in case you've forgotten. But you married her, mate, and it's too late to regret that now—you've got kids, and she's been a bloody loyal wife—even if she's not the sort of girl you should have married. Grow up.' At the time he'd defended himself strenuously, but in retrospect he found her plainspoken vehemence more endearing than alarming, and had thought once or twice in a more sentimental mode that she was probably the sort of girl he should have married. Perhaps she would have kept him in line in a way that Jodie, with her uncertainty, with her feeling that the obligation was all on his side, never could. This sort of anger directed at Angus was one thing—he is her equal—but he knows that for his wife it would be different, that seemingly minor slights could be deeply wounding.

He is so busy observing Jodie, trying to catch her eye, reassure her with a glance, a smile of solidarity, he is barely attending to the discussion. So when the conversation suddenly leaves the safe harbour of the general and enters the more dangerous waters of the personal, Angus flounders, unprepared.

'I take it you won't be standing now, Angus? For mayor?' Sue makes the statement quite casually, looking at him levelly across the table. Angus hears a slight gasp from his host, but David glances away quickly, won't meet his eyes.

'What do you mean?'

'Well, I'd assumed that since this—*news*—of Jodie's you'd have decided not to risk losing the election, that you'd pull out, let them put in someone else. Personally, I'm not sure that it was ever going to happen anyway. You know Greg English has been saying he'd like to stand, and he's got all Mardi's family—the Jarvises—behind him, too.'

'Susan. I don't think this ...' David's voice is tight, nervous.

It takes Angus a moment to respond. 'No. That's okay. It's just that—I hadn't really thought about it. This has all been very sudden, as you can imagine. I mean, obviously, I'll get advice—'

'Oh, come on, Angus.' Sue's always very proper enunciation—there's a particular Grammar drawl that Angus would recognise anywhere, one of his public-school mates once described it as a kind of a whinny—has become more pronounced, from drink or hostility, he can't be certain. 'You don't really think that you stand a chance of getting in, with all this happening. The mayor of Arding has to be squeaky clean. In theory if not reality. And this—so-called missing child of Jodie's,' there is a faint jeer in her voice, 'makes you look slightly suspect, don't you think?'

To his astonishment Jodie responds before him. 'I don't see that something that happened to me all those years ago, and that didn't involve Angus, can have any bearing on him whatsoever.

That would be unfair.' Despite his own sense of mortification, Angus is gratified by the conviction of her statement, the dignity of her reply.

'But you're Angus's wife, Jodie. And however absent Angus himself was when your daughter was conceived, your reputation is still going to reflect on him. Short of divorcing you—and I really don't think he'd do that at this juncture—I don't see how he can hope to remove himself from the equation.' Susan takes a few sullen sips of her wine. 'And the way you spoke about that baby just now, Jodie—and the way you told me the whole sordid story—I have to tell you that it gets up my nose.' Her voice is growing louder. 'What sort of woman describes selling off a baby—if that's what you actually did—as something that *happened to them*. That's just appalling. It's not just something that happened to you, you know—it's actually something *you* did to someone else, Jodie. Even if you were only nineteen.'

Angus takes a great slug of beer, a deep breath, glares at Susan across the table. 'Now look, Susan, I don't know where this is coming from, but—' He can hear how ineffectual he sounds, is almost glad to be interrupted.

'Angus, Jodie. I'm really sorry—'

'Oh, come off it, Dave,' Susan interjects. 'Don't be so feeble. We've already had this conversation. You've told us your version of the story, and we've read the statements and articles and, well, it just seems fishy. Why is it that you're only searching now that the police are interested? What's going on? It's been twenty-four years, Jodie. It all seems too little too late, if you ask me. And you might not have asked me, but if we're such good old friends, why shouldn't I say what we think?'

'Susan. That's enough.' David's voice shakes. He pulls at his beard anxiously.

'No, it's okay.' Jodie is startlingly pale, her lips move stiffly. 'Actually, I think you're right, Sue. It is best if people say what they think. At least then we all know where we stand.' As if to illustrate the point, she pushes back her chair and gets to her feet. She looks at Angus across the table. 'I think we should go, darling. You get Tom and I'll meet you both outside. It's a nice night. We can walk home.'

His instinct is to storm out immediately, but he follows his wife's directions, robot-like, collects their belongings, calls Tom. He makes no attempt to soothe David, who fusses about them, almost weeping with shame, assuring and reassuring Angus of his loyalty, his undying friendship, trying hard to explain and excuse Susan's unexpected and violent hostility: 'There was that miscarriage back when we were first married—she took it so hard ...'

Tom skips ahead of them, waiting at each streetlight or running back like an excited puppy, enjoying the novelty of a walk late at night. Now that they've made their escape, Angus feels eviscerated—the episode had been almost frightening in its intensity. Though he can hardly pluck up courage enough to broach it, he's certain that they need to discuss the situation, to debrief, as it were. To consider not just Sue's viciousness, but the entire substance of the conversation. He eventually makes some sort of denunciatory comment about Sue's behaviour, but when Jodie is unresponsive, he attempts to reassure her about his own position. 'You know what she was saying, Jodie, about all this meaning that I've lost my chance at mayor—'

'Well it does, doesn't it?' She is curt.

'Well, maybe. But only for now. When all this blows over ... Who knows?' He gives an airy shrug.

'It's not about to blow over, Angus. We all know that.'

He is bemused by her resistance, the faint belligerence he senses beneath the blunt statement, just as he was surprised by her assuredness during the evening. 'But that's not really what I wanted to talk about. I just wanted to tell you that I don't care about the mayor business. We haven't ever really discussed it, but you know I don't give a shit. It's not important. We'll be okay, you know. It doesn't matter what people like Sue and Dave think. As long as we've got each other, everything'll be okay.

Nothing else matters.' The words sound trite, even to his ears, and he can't help wondering how much of what he's saying is genuine, how much is wishful thinking.

Jodie too must sense his doubts. 'Of course it matters, Angus. Don't be silly. This has changed everything. But I honestly don't give a toss about Sue. She's always a loudmouth when she's pissed. She'll be begging my forgiveness in the morning.'

She increases her speed, catching up with Tom, and the two of them march the rest of the way together, swinging arms and whispering.

Angus has only a brief moment to regret his wife's reluctance to discuss the evening's events, to worry about her very evident doubt, before the panic makes an untimely visitation. He is able, just, to hold himself together for the remainder of the walk home, to check the desperate urge to run, to regulate his breathing. But by the time he reaches the front gate he is almost overcome. He pushes past his astonished wife and son, breathlessly claiming an urgent need to pee. He rushes to the bathroom and locks himself in, then lies prone on the floor, his cheek pressed hard on the cool tiled surface, waiting for it to be over.

12

When Susan doesn't call her the following morning, or even the next, Jodie doesn't know what to think. Though she was hurt (and appalled) by Sue's outburst, she wasn't particularly surprised—Sue is renowned for her propensity to become hostile, to say things she later regrets after a few too many. Jodie's never actually been the object of her aggression before, but she has seen her in action, has been privy to the aftermath a few times. She knows that typically Sue will be eager to restore peace, has anticipated greeting her at the front door the very next morning, bearing flowers, cakes, effusively apologetic, has expected at the very least a conciliatory phone call. But there's nothing.

Despite Angus's assumption that the two women are close, Jodie has never really considered Sue to be a particularly good friend. In fact, regarding herself in the cool and dispassionate way that is lately becoming a habit, it's apparent that though she can boast a vast number of acquaintances, a wide social circle, none of them are truly, exclusively *her* friends. Those she sees most frequently are wives of Angus's colleagues or, like Sue, Garrow family friends. And although she is accepted and included—even in her most paranoid moments she could never say she was ever made to feel unwelcome—Jodie cannot think of one woman she would class as a true intimate.

Giving her news to those she knows best, she had noticed that none had sought further information. She has not had to field any awkward questions, or been invited to confide her thoughts or feelings, or to justify her actions, past or present. The common response from those she's personally informed has been one of mild incredulity, bemusement, and then a furtive, but determined, retreat.

She had noticed immediately on their arrival at the Foresters' a slight but unmistakable change in their manner: the way Sue had avoided looking at Jodie directly, the coolness of her voice, her set expression, David's agitation, his anxious deferring to her, the overwrought laughter, strained conversation. Sue had barely spoken, had declined all Jodie's offers of assistance, which would be eagerly accepted in the ordinary scheme of things. When Hannah and Laura were on their way out the door, Jodie had overheard Susan reassuring Hannah quietly: 'If you need to talk to someone about everything, darling, just give me a call. Any time. You know we think of you as another daughter, so if you ever need to get out ...' Jodie, only a few feet away in the dark hall, had pulled back as if stung, her ears burning.

When the evening descended into utter farce soon after, it had almost been a relief to have what needed to be said, said— to have it all in the open.

In the days following, she notices, as Helen had warned her, an unmistakable dropping off of engagements, both social and otherwise. She can't quite tell, though, whether this withdrawal is external or self-imposed—perhaps it is Jodie herself who is retreating. She has never felt less like meeting up with friends, engaging in chitchat, doing coffee—suddenly all those things that once seemed vitally interesting have become rather pointless. Earlier, when the new school year had begun, she had rung and excused herself from all the various organising committees and volunteer positions she had signed up for in previous years—the trivia night fundraiser for the new school theatre at the New England School, the annual Grammar fete, the school canteen work, sessions in the library covering books. And where once her involvement seemed crucial, her ideas sought, now she sees very clearly that she's not indispensable, that they will all do very well without her. She has stopped playing Thursday morning tennis, too, pleading a pulled hamstring, but when she calls to apologise to her long-term doubles partner, she can hear the quickly disguised relief in Mary's voice, her instant assurance that it'll be no problem to find a replacement, that she has someone in mind. Then the hollowness of Mary's regretful flattery: 'Not that Fiona will really be able to replace you—her backhand is pretty patchy ...' offered up as a consolatory afterthought.

Despite the tapering off of outside occupation, she makes an effort to keep herself busy, trying hard not to think much beyond the here and the now. She spends extra time on the house, doing the jobs she would ordinarily contract out—cleaning windows, touching up wall paint, washing curtains. She devotes extra time to Tom, helping him with the maths homework he loathes, and reading to him at night. They have reached the third book in the Narnia series in as many weeks, though she suspects that he is really too old, and would rather read to himself, that typically of her generous boy, he is only consenting to keep her happy. He hesitates when she asks if he wants to go and see the new Transformers movie with her one evening after soccer practice, looks slightly bewildered. 'Okay,' he says eventually, 'why not?' Then adds, in the most innocent betrayal of his true inclinations, 'I can always go and see it with Harry and James later, can't I? I guess it'll actually be cool to see it twice.'

Most weeknights, Angus, returning home late, eats quickly then retreats to the office; Hannah locks herself in her bedroom, 'studying'. So after putting Tom to bed, Jodie spends the evenings alone, desultorily reading, flicking through the channels, or making shopping lists—itemising ingredients for elaborate meals she'll never make. Occasionally Angus joins her, and the two of them sit together quietly, reading or watching television, but by tacit agreement there is little conversation, no discussion of the madness that is unfurling around them, no consideration of the innumerable what-ifs. Sometimes he leaves the room abruptly, without warning; she will hear the bath running and knows he won't emerge before bedtime.

Following her initial revelation there had been a few weeks of renewed passion, and an atmosphere of tender concern had flourished between the two of them. But after the arrival of the letter, things had changed. He had dismissed her explanation, her attempted apology, saying briskly that it didn't change anything, that he understood her desire to keep the story simple. But nevertheless she had sensed a slight awkwardness, a tension between them. And now the crisis is more tangible, more real—now they're in an odd state of limbo, the police involved, the rumour mill grinding—waiting. They appear to have retreated, both of them, into their own private spaces, have each sought and found solitude with no apparent opposition from the other. There are reasons for it—Angus is busy at work, she knows, and they're both distracted, but there is also a sense of separateness, of disconnection that would alarm her if she let herself think too much into it.

Jodie is expert at not thinking too much into anything—at living in the moment, discarding the unwanted past—after all, she has spent the last twenty years not thinking about so many areas of her life: her childhood, her lonely pregnancy, the labour and everything that followed, and later, Angus's betrayals—the ones she knows about anyway. Even now, when the past is coming at her from all angles, is ever present, she still finds it easy to deflect unpleasant thoughts.

She has taken to going to bed late, waiting until Angus is soundly asleep, so she can concentrate on clearing her mind before sleep, without demands or distractions. She has perfected her own bedtime ritual: a sort of homespun meditation, involving a long gathering of breath, a holding and then releasing, all equally timed, that miraculously maintains her distance from herself, from her thoughts, and ensures that she's asleep within moments of her head touching the pillow. Paradoxically, it is only when she sleeps that Jodie is compelled into awareness, forced into memory, obliged to recall events that would be better forgotten. Asleep, the dreams arrive, uninvited but inescapable, and she is once more locked in that dark, hot, airless place, desperate for relief, for release. Despairing, knowing it can never come.

13

Hannah meets him at a party. Not one of the regular but very exclusive weekend parties attended by the Grammar girls and Newie boys—where parents are still supervising, even if they're not in evidence, and the scene is generally pretty tame—but a much more hardcore party held by a bunch of theatre studies students from the university. She and Assia had auditioned for a student play last summer, a clever adaptation of some Marvel comic, and had both been chosen for small parts in a crowd scene. Hannah had been disappointed at first, certain that she could have handled the main character better than the tall, thin, blonde girl, slightly older, who was given the part. In the end she'd been able to enjoy, with minimal effort or responsibility (and the attendant nerves), the pleasure of ensemble work, which was, she realised, a big part of what she loved about acting—a part she enjoyed almost as much as being able to transform into another person.

The theatre studies group—most of them college kids recently moved out into shared accommodation—were friendly and laidback, and invitations to parties were extended willy-nilly to the younger members of the cast. Getting to the parties had been slightly problematic, but nothing Hannah couldn't handle. It was easy to make these gatherings appear innocent and enterprising—she only had to claim that they were rehearsing, or, when the initial run was over, that they were rehearsing new work, or helping the director with an original script. Her mother had occasionally been suspicious, but her father, always a fan of her moving beyond what he considered the slightly insular Arding private-school scene, enthusiastically encouraged the new social connections.

Though Hannah has absolutely no intention of ever attending what she regards as the only-for-losers local university, she's been surprised to discover that the students—some of them local, a few from Sydney and Brisbane, but most from other country towns and regional cities—are such an easy, fun, non-judgemental bunch. Though there is no way that she really wants to be a part of their boho post-punk hippy scene (with their vintage clothes, their incense, their laconic faux-metro drawls), around them she somehow feels comfortable, at home. She's aware she's not quite right for Grammar, where glamour is in, the most popular girls deliberately, painfully thin, their long hair gleaming and full, their packed-on make-up, their expensive designer clothes. It's all just another aspect of the whole competitive atmosphere—a competition that includes comparative wealth and success of parents, naturally.

Up until the thing with her mother, she had been firmly—and almost comfortably—situated near the top of the tree, socially speaking. But now, just as she'd predicted, she is enduring a slow but steady descent. There is nothing she can put her finger on; it has all been very gradual, very subtle. And it is more than just the bitchiness she'd half expected of her so-called friends. The school itself seems to be in on it—she hasn't been made a prefect, for instance, which has always been more or less guaranteed, and while she can tell herself it has something to do with the Sydney debacle, the fact that Assia and Bella have both received the honour makes her wonder. There is the matter, too, of conspicuously lost invitations to a couple of recent parties (*OMG! You really didn't get my text? We wondered what happened!!! Love u xxxx*) and the suddenly blocked access to certain Facebook pages.

She has made a few attempts to wrangle her way back 'in', but has moved too far from her try-hard past to really want to go back that desperately, and in the end it is easier—and more dignified—to snub those who have never been real friends before they snub her. Of course she has, would always have, Assia.

And now these new friends too—friends whose whole world doesn't revolve around the stagnant pond that is Arding, whose parents, in the main, don't know her parents; kids whose only response when they realise that it's her mum in the papers is an offhand *cool* or *awesome* or *that must suck.*

Here amongst these older kids, kids with no axes to grind, she can relax into being more herself—though she has only the dimmest of ideas about what that—who she—actually is. But she can stop feeling self-conscious, stop holding herself in, stop sneering, stop always being entertaining—get rid of the brittle, bitchy, sharp persona she's developed over the past few years. The drama students are almost an undifferentiated bunch, casually generous, always kind, expecting nothing, seeming to like her for no particular reason, and she can feel herself expanding, enjoying herself genuinely for what seems like the first time since she'd hit the thorny years of adolescence.

There's no denying, too, that she takes a real pleasure in deceiving her parents right now. She's lied to them before, of course, but much less deliberately, much less vengefully. She has no doubt that she'd be in deep shit if they really knew what she was up to— that she was going to real parties, with no responsible adult supervision, everyone drunk or drugged or both, everyone looking to get laid, and with the added excitement of violent gatecrashers, visits from the police. She's in the real world, now—not the protected world they've chosen for her—and the stakes are high.

The boy rocks up to the party late—most of the company, Hannah included, are already completely smashed. The police had left only a few minutes before, responding to noise complaints, and Hannah (understandably cautious—a few parties ago a couple of girls, very obviously underage, had been given an official 'escort' home by some zealous young constables) has just clambered from the wardrobe she and Assia have been hiding in, giggling hysterically.

The boy is leaning against a wall smoking, watching the goings-on around him—it is all disintegrating at a rapid rate, bodies collapsed across the carpet in various stages of consciousness and coupling—with a look of somewhat grim bemusement, maybe even disdain, eyes narrowed, lip curled. He is tall and exotically dark-skinned, with fair dreadlocked hair escaping from a very grimy Rastafarian beanie, and Hannah is immediately intrigued: there is something very authentic about him—something in the way he holds himself, the way he isn't quite a part of the scene; she's sure he isn't just a middle-class boy affecting seediness—his toughness looks real.

She has tried a bit of everything on offer tonight—some E first, a few puffs of a joint, and then a considerable volume of goon—and all her edges have been nicely blurred and blunted. She has no qualms at all about making a beeline for him, ignoring a request from her suddenly queasy friend that they call a taxi and head home.

'Hey,' Hannah offers, leaning into the wall beside him.

'Hey.'

Close up—and she's come far closer than she'd normally dare—he is slightly less exotic. Not Brazilian as she'd hoped, but Aboriginal, maybe, his skin brown, with an odd little sprinkling of darker freckles, his nose a bit too broad, his teeth— bared in his return greeting—crooked and slightly yellow. He's obviously not going to extend the conversation, looks at Hannah consideringly, takes a long drag on his joint. Waits for her to make the next move. Or not.

'So. I haven't seen you around before?' As a pick-up line, it's lame, but it's out before she can think of anything more original.

His reply is terse, flat; his accent broad, with a vaguely Koori inflection.

'Haven't been around before.'

For some reason she isn't in the least put out by his unresponsiveness, his apparent lack of interest.

'Where've you been?'

'Here and there. Mostly there.' Another indrawn breath.

'Sweet.' She holds out her hand for the joint. He hesitates

a moment then bypasses her outstretched fingers—easier to push it between her eager lips.

Five minutes later they are in the bathroom, fucking. She offers her mouth first but he says no, he doesn't want that, pushes her up against the bathroom door. All or nothing.

Assia knocks once, calls out, her voice tentative, slurry. 'Han? Are you in there? You okay? Hannah?'

She smothers his grunts with her hand, manages to gasp out between thrusts that she's okay, that she doesn't give a flying fuck if Assia leaves, that she should go if she wants to, just go. Ignores Assia's urgent reminder that she can't leave on her own—she's staying at Hannah's place.

It's fast, unprotected, noisy—the door banging and banging, the boy moaning loudly, then shouting out—but Hannah's beyond worrying, doesn't care who hears, her hands caught in his tangled hair, breathing in his sweet, slightly woolly, boy smell. She just wants this hard uncommunicative boy; he is all she wants, and all she can see for the moment. This is not her first time, far from it, but it's the first time she's ever felt any real desire, the first time she's really seen the point, the first time it's felt the way she'd imagined it's meant to feel.

After that first night she worries that, for him anyway, it'd been a casual hook-up, nothing more. And ordinarily she'd be happy enough with that—he isn't her type, really, or not the sort of guy most Grammar girls would be seen dead with, not the sort of guy she'd really want to take home to meet her parents. He was a full-on townie, it was clear just from looking at him—his clothes, his dreads, even his crooked teeth were clear evidence of this (no popped-collar polo shirt, no boat shoes, no long shorts, no short back and sides, no sign of ten thousand dollar orthodontics, either). But his dark skin put him in another category altogether.

Ordinarily, she'd have cooled down pretty rapidly herself and dumped him—if not by word, then by omission. It was relatively easy—she'd been on either side of the equation often enough and had perfected her technique. There was the 'walk past and look the other way' scenario, or the 'look through', which was vaguely more humiliating (*hey, I sucked your dick, douchebag—don't pretend you can't remember me!*), or better yet, the 'ignore all texts and Facebook chats'. Then there was the awkward 'let's just be friends' conversation, which she had experienced herself most recently with an old friend from primary school whose regret was so overwhelming that he'd been oblivious to her eagerness (*thank fuck!*) at their next coldly sober meeting.

She has never really been into anything other than the most casual of relationships before, and definitely isn't interested in the old-married-couple scenarios that she's seen some of her friends with long-term boyfriends get sucked into. In the stark sunshine of sobriety the boys she'd been with had transformed back into their pumpkin selves: undersized and pimply, lacking any particular wit or presence. But this guy, Wesley, for some reason she's more intrigued than usual. Even after a few surreptitious meetings—which mostly involve driving out to the dam, parking and fooling around in his car—she still can't work out what it is that she likes about him. He's not particularly quick or clever—in fact he doesn't even speak that much. He's assured enough—but doesn't have the gloss of privilege and entitlement that most of the boys she's grown up with exude. It's a quieter sort of confidence, without the swagger; a confidence built up from experience rather than expectations and connections. It's like his looks. He is good-looking, but he's not an arse about it, and though his body's good—well muscled, hard—it's no big deal, and somehow real, as if developed through solid labour and not as a result of hours of pumping and preening. Right now, when everything else around her is spinning out of control, Wesley is someone to hold on to, someone to hold her down.

Angus is over it quickly enough: over Jodie, over the idea of the two of them, their romance. The way any boy would be. Oh, it was fun, and he was right into her at first, for say, the first six months, when all it involved was occasional visits to her place, a party here and there, a movie, a picnic during the long break between the end of school and the beginning of uni. All done pretty much on the sly, not mentioning their meetings to his mother, avoiding hers.

He is fascinated at first by her freedom. He has never met a girl—or anyone, really—whose family (not quite working-class—almost underclass, he guesses) show so little interest in her whereabouts, her achievements, her doings. Jodie's mother is like some television caricature of a typical Australian barmaid, but without the clichéd big-heartedness: small, sharp, her face coarsely red from too much sun, lines deeply etched around her eyes, her mouth with its cat's-bum smokers' lips, her eyebrows plucked into virtual non-existence, her hair big, her tits even bigger, her accent bursting at the seams. He barely exchanges a word with her, though—once he manages to persuade Jodie that he couldn't care less about the squalor, her idiot brothers—he spends days and even nights in their home. Mrs Evans—*'call me Jeannie, love'*—is always on her way out when he is on his way in. He wonders vaguely if she is a whore; she has the sort of tired prettiness that he associates with ageing tarts, but who would want to sleep with her now? Jeannie's dislike of Jodie is obvious, even on so casual an acquaintance. Their communications are limited to absolute practicalities, but Jodie's mother can make the most innocuous inquiry—*so, you're going to the movies are you*, or, *off on another picnic, eh?*—sound like a sneer, an insult. She is polite enough to Angus during their infrequent meetings, always asks after his mother, who she's had the pleasure of meeting at some 'posh do' she'd waitressed at years before. 'I always remember that Mrs Garrow likes her whisky neat,' she observes somewhat suspiciously, and as she repeats this at their every encounter, Angus is sure that he is meant to infer that his mother is a closet alcoholic.

He has been warned, by Jodie herself and several well-meaning and other less well-meaning friends, that the brothers are not exactly high achievers, or the most respectable members of Milton society. But even so he is unprepared for the reality. The eldest, Jason, at the tender age of twenty-one is already a full-on crim with a record for break and enters, assault, theft—he's done time, and seems bent on doing more. At the moment he is back living at home, accorded full man-of-the-house status. In an attempt to assert his authority, he initially made some threats of violence against Angus, but his mother, aware of Angus's background, his family's reputation, has quickly scotched this. So his visits are tolerated, if not encouraged, by Jason—from time to time Angus is even privileged to receive a grunt of greeting, and once the offer of a beer. 'If you're gonna come around and root me little sister, you oughta have a drink with a bloke,' had been his charming invitation, one that Jodie had declined on his behalf.

The youngest brother, Shane, is a moron; there is no other word for it. He spends his days in front of the TV, smoking, eating chips, drinking Coke and in the afternoons beer, running errands for his bully brother when ordered. He has no occupation, no friends; his appearance is not endearing—with a front tooth missing and others rotting, a face cratered with acne, the beginnings of a small beer belly. He speaks with a stammer, is incoherent and virtually unintelligible. Other than providing physical evidence of God's intransigent lack of fairness when it comes to handing out looks, intelligence, usefulness, there is no reason for his being on the earth, so far as Angus can see. But of all the family—if they could be regarded as forming such a unit—Shane is the only one who appears to treat Jodie with even halfway civility; at least he isn't, or doesn't seem to be, malicious. And Jodie treats him if not with affection then with some attempt at sisterly concern—providing him with a nutritious meal now and then, encouraging him to bathe, washing his clothes occasionally, attempting to curtail the endless drinking.

Thus confronted with her family (and he thanks God that the father—by all accounts a nasty bastard—took off long ago), Angus's admiration for Jodie only increases. How did a girl like her spring from such unaccommodating, possibly toxic soil; and how did she thrive, blossom? Very few people, he thinks, really know what hardships she's faced, what challenges. Her scholarship to Grammar is remarkable, but is perhaps less remarkable than her highly cultivated demeanour. Though he has always been aware that she is, in some intrinsic but indefinable way, very different to most of the girls of his acquaintance, he had never—how could he?—expected this background of extreme disadvantage, of squalor.

So those first months are made exciting by their clandestine nature, the slightly tense and uncertain air of their every meeting, the combination of his mother's disapproval, the scornful indifference of hers. But soon enough, around the time he is getting ready to head off to university, Angus starts to feel cramped, constrained. Begins to look at other girls. To wonder what it might be like to have someone lighter, someone brighter around. There is nothing that he doesn't like about Jodie—it isn't that simple—he hasn't gone off her entirely, not exactly, but he finds himself occasionally wishing for some variety. Fantasising about girls with brown eyes, dark skin, curly hair; about redheads, with downy freckled skin, large breasts. An Italian girl, maybe, or a cool Swede. Even an older woman, married, a mother, going down on him, or a whore, a one-night stand—a series of one-night stands. He begins dreaming about, then wanting, that freedom, though he has no idea how such a smorgasbord of sexual delight could ever be made available to him. He wants to go off to uni free, unshackled; his mates are in his ear bagging him, telling him to *piss her off, man; what did he think he was doing, was he gunna marry her? Why didn't he book himself into a nursing home, like, now?* And he is planning to dump her—without regret and almost without compunction—has a speech worked out, an opportunity arranged. But then, just days before he is due to leave, his mother makes his release impossible.

He has driven down to Milton to pick up Jodie; they are to head out first for a picnic (their code for a fuck) down at the Washpool—a currently half-empty waterhole in the MacDonald National Park. But Jodie isn't home. She's gone for a walk, Shane offers, his expression oddly malicious.

'A walk? But she knew I was coming.'

'Yeah. She probably did, mate. I bet she spends half her life waiting for you to come. Ha. But your old lady turned up about an hour ago—and they had some kind of barney.' Shane gives a burp, turns back to the blaring screen.

'My old lady?' Angus feels his stomach turn suddenly; the blood rushes to his face. 'What do you mean my old lady? Shane? Was my mother here?'

'Yeah, man. Your mum, your *mother*—whatever it is you call her. I call mine an old bag.' He gives a sudden high-pitched chuckle. 'Anyway, this was a fussy lookin' old chook with a pruny face. Drives a big red Mercedes. That's your old lady isn't it? Thought it was one of them seventh day witnesses at first— standing out there with a face on her like the world was about to end—and I was gunna tell her to piss off, but then she asked for Jodes.' He gives a lunatic grin and rubs his gut. 'Jodes went outside with her, and then the next thing, Jodes comes back in here crying and I hear the car drive off. Sounds good, but,' he adds reflectively. 'Them big Mercedes. It's a V8 is it, mate?'

'A what?' Angus is feeling worse and worse; he leans against the wall, suddenly finding it hard to stay upright. He can feel bile rising in his throat, his heart pounding in his ears. He wants desperately to run back outside, get in his car and drive away, fast, but knows that he will have to find Jodie first, find out what has happened. 'So then what? Did Jodie go again? Do you know where? Did she tell you where she was going?' His voice is shrill, quavering. He swallows, closes his eyes briefly, breathes deeply, wills himself to be calm.

'I dunno. She just run out. Maybe she went down the river. There's that old willow with the rope.'

'The willow? Where's this willow?' He can't quite explain to himself the feeling of urgency—he needs to see Jodie, before ... before what? The idiot is unbearably slow. 'Come on, mate. Tell me where it is.' Angus steps towards him, can feel rage welling up along with the fear, thinks he would like to do further damage to the moron's smile.

'Yeah, okay, Angus. I'm just thinking, mate. The best way to explain. You know. No need to get your knickers in a knot. Okay, if you go back towards the highway, then go down Russell Street, and then head straight down to the river from the little park there. You know the one—right on the river. Where that kid got raped last year? Well—the willow's in that park there. It's real big. You can't miss it.'

Angus slams out of the house, runs to the car and drives back down the highway as if his life depends on it. He heads across the park—brown, dreary, the climbing frames rusted, swing chains seatless, the lawn scorched, most of it dust, desolate—and there is Jodie, crouching beneath a giant willow, down on the riverbank. The tree is huge and twisted, but too old now to bear the weight of children; a frayed rope dangles with sinister intent above the dried riverbed. Jodie's eyes are puffy, her face red, but she smiles when she sees him striding purposefully toward her, her expression so expectant, so full of love, of tenderness, of relief.

Angus feels the nausea return; the urge to run becomes even more compulsive. He can sense his future taking shape, feels it harden and then solidify around him. He straightens his shoulders, stands tall. He makes himself smile back widely, reassuringly, keeps walking steadily towards her.

15

It is a Saturday morning, and Jodie has abandoned any pretence at studying, despite an English essay discussing aspects of filial love in *King Lear* being due first thing Monday morning. Instead she has been preparing for a picnic at the Washpool with Angus. This requires considerable effort: a long soak in the bath, legs and underarms shaved smoothly, her body moisturised all over with some musky lotion she'd picked up cheap at the local pharmacy, hair washed and conditioned, then put in curlers while it dries to give her naturally straight hair some body (she couldn't quite bring herself to spend her hard-earned savings on the perms that are currently all the rage at Grammar). She chose her outfit carefully the night before—a short short denim skirt she'd bought only the previous week at the Arding Jean Emporium (size eight, down from a ten; she's done it, finally), and a cute striped cotton top she'd remodelled herself from a man's business shirt bought at Vinnies. She's left the actual dressing and the make-up until the last half hour, wanting to be as fresh as possible, to avoid creases, stains, runs in her mascara.

She can make her preparations in peace. Her mother was out all night and Jodie knows from past experience that she isn't likely to arrive home until late afternoon, just in time to get ready for her next shift. She'll be tired and hung-over, the pouches under her eyes dark, her expression sour, her temper rancid. Jodie is glad she has plans to be elsewhere; even during relatively short visits home—with maybe only time for a shower, a change of clothes, a bottle of beer—her mother is likely to wreak havoc, disrupt any plans Jodie's made, create a scene. Her elder brother too is absent, so she can get ready without his teasing, doesn't have to find something to wedge the bathroom door shut to short-circuit

Jason's barging in and out—the key was lost years ago, and she's had to fill the keyhole with plasticine to stop him peering in at her. There is only Shane, and at least he is predictable, not interested in her movements, happy to loll in front of the television, watching cartoons, the midday movies. He is unlikely to even ask her where she's going or notice who she's going with.

She's just finishing off her left leg, making satisfyingly neat strips in the froth, going carefully over her knee and midway up her thigh, stopping at the precise point where the fuzz of hair seems, almost magically, to disappear, when Shane calls out to her from just outside the room.

'Jode. There's someone here. A lady.' The knob twists back and forth, but he stays outside.

'Well, who is it, Shane? Didn't you ask? Tell her Mum won't be back till late.'

'But she says she wants you, Jodie.'

'Who is it?' She leans over to grab a towel, resigned.

'I think it's his mum. Your boyfriend fella. What's-is-name. Angus. She came in that big car, the Mercedes—the red one you showed me that time.' His voice has lost its customary slowness, is almost snapping with excitement.

'Mrs Garrow?' Jodie's foot slips on the curve of the bath, she clutches at the shower tap to steady herself.

'That's her. That's the one.'

'Tell her ...' Her own voice cracks, fizzes, disappears. She takes a long breath. 'Tell her I'll just be a minute.'

Mrs Garrow stands waiting, smoking a cigarette, outside on the nature strip, facing away from the house. She turns—a small, slender, well-dressed matron, her ash-grey hair tightly permed, clutching a shiny Glo-mesh handbag—as Jodie makes her way down the grassed-over brick path. She knows Angus's mother by sight, has seen her at various school events, and around town, and knows who she is, but they have never met. She is sure that Mrs Garrow has never seen her, wonders how she knew where to find her, what she's expecting. What she wants.

'Well, you took your time, Jodie.' Her voice is cool, the smile cursory.

'Hello, Mrs Garrow.' Jodie doesn't bother smiling. She walks to the gate, but doesn't go all the way through, remains on her side of the fence.

The woman surveys her carefully. Jodie can't remember ever being looked up and down quite so obviously, even by hostile teenage girls.

'Well,' she says slowly. 'You are pretty enough, I suppose. I'd heard you weren't anything special, but you're young—and that counts for a great deal, doesn't it? Your skin's good, your features are regular, your figure's trim enough—everything's still firm.' Jodie suspects her input isn't required at this point, so says nothing, lets the woman continue. 'Now, I'd like to have a bit of a talk with you, dear. I've a ... a proposition—of sorts—to make. We could go to a café if you like—I could buy you a cup of tea, or we could walk, I suppose.'

Jodie half-smiles as the woman looks around doubtfully. There are no designated walking areas, no proper footpaths, in this neighbourhood, just neglected half-dead or overgrown lawns, patches of red earth. The potholed road isn't even guttered.

'I'm sure that anything you have to say to me can be said right here, Mrs Garrow.' Jodie is surprised by the steadiness of her own voice, the clarity, the ease of her response. The woman is obviously taken aback.

'I ... well, that's not what I had in mind.' She frowns, obviously discomfited. 'I'm sure it would be easier ...' She looks hard at Jodie, who is standing solid and immovable on the other side of the fence. She sighs. 'I suppose here,' she gives the overgrown yard, fibro house, neglected street a brief, disdainful look, 'is as good as anywhere else.'

Jodie stays silent, impassive. Waits. The woman clears her throat, but her voice is clear, unwavering.

'I'll be straight with you, Jodie. I think that's always the best way to handle these things. Now, I have nothing, absolutely nothing, against you personally. Indeed your principal, Mrs Doulton, who is a great friend of mine—we have a long history together, both old girls you know, and her mother and mine were dear friends, too—Mrs Doulton has told me that you're a good girl, hard-working, clever, industrious. Well, obviously you are or you wouldn't be there, would you? And that you've achieved a great deal, considering ...' cue another purse-lipped glance at her surroundings, 'considering your background. Anyway, I came here today to ask you something—to ask a favour, if you will.' She pauses, gives a brisk inquiring look, but with no response from Jodie she keeps going, undaunted. 'What I'd like, dear, is for you to stop seeing my son.'

Jodie has been expecting something of the sort, knows that the woman's presence can mean only one thing, but she can feel her stomach turning, her throat tightening, finds it difficult to keep her expression neutral. The woman is watching her carefully, but keeps talking when it is apparent that Jodie isn't going to offer anything.

'Now, I'm not going to go into the reasons for my request, though I should imagine it's quite clear that you and Angus are completely unsuited to one another in numerous ways. And I don't imagine you intend to stop seeing him just because I've asked—although if you had any real regard for Angus's well-being, his future, you wouldn't hesitate. So I thought it might be ... that it might help you to make the right decision, if there were some obvious benefit to you.' She pauses again, as if trying to provoke some sort of response. But Jodie has taken her eyes off the woman, is gazing steadfastly down at her own bare feet, admiring the way her silver toenails shine up out of the surrounding weeds, and says nothing.

'So, dear, I thought that if there was some way I could help you—say, with finances—you might find it in your heart to help me, too.'

Now Jodie does look up. She looks straight at the woman, gives her a twisted smile. 'So, how much?' she says bluntly. 'How much is Angus worth?'

'Well, I don't think you really need look at it quite that way, dear. But I'm willing to give you $5000. Cash, obviously. I hear you're hoping to study, and I imagine you'll need all the help you can get. Five thousand should cover your living expenses for your first year at university if you're not extravagant.'

'But why? We're just going out. We're not engaged. It could all end tomorrow.'

'There are certain ways, ones that I'm sure you're aware of, of keeping a man, of tying young men up, binding them to one.'

Jodie gives a disgusted snort. 'But why would I ... why would I want to do that? I've got my own plans.'

'Yes, well, plans have a strange way of going awry. And there are easier, more effective ways to move ahead—away from this life—than careers, education. And I know my son,' she adds dryly. 'He's very loyal. He finds it hard to hurt people. An admirable trait in many ways. But he could so easily be pressured into doing something he'll come to regret.'

There is a long silence. The two women stand on either side of the fence, the elder smiling slightly, Jodie's clenched fists the only sign of her rage.

'Twenty-five.' Jodie can't quite believe her own words, nor that she sounds so unruffled when her heart is pumping so madly. 'That will pay for my expenses over the whole degree. What point is there in just paying for first year? What am I supposed to do after that?'

The woman looks at her in disbelief, suddenly discomposed. 'Twenty-five? That's ridiculous, girl. Where do you think I'll find twenty-five thousand dollars?'

Jodie shrugs. 'That's not my problem, is it?'

The woman glares, but looks away when Jodie meets her gaze.

'You want twenty-five thousand?'

Jodie smiles, but says nothing.

The woman clasps and unclasps her handbag convulsively. 'How about fifteen?'

'Twenty-five.'

Mrs Garrow gives a long sigh. 'I'll find it, then. Whatever it takes. You're a hard little bitch, aren't you? Extraordinary. But I guess you have good reason. I expect you'll go far.' The smile she gives Jodie appears almost genuine, admiring. 'In different circumstances I might have quite liked you.' She turns, heading back to her car. 'I'll contact you on Monday with the payment arrangements. You can see my solicitor—we'll organise a contract, set up some sort of trust. I'll give you half, we'll open an account—and then you'll have a week to drop him, or dump him, or whatever is the term you children use. You'll see the rest of the money once that's done.'

As the woman goes to open the car door, Jodie leans over the fence, speaking just loudly enough for her to hear.

'Mrs Garrow. I won't do it.'

The woman's panic is unmistakable. 'What do you mean you won't do it? I've just promised to give you what you want.'

Jodie tries hard to suppress her smile.

'You really think you have so much power? You think people can really just be bought off like that?'

'I'll give you thirty, forty.' She swallows. 'Fifty.'

Jodie shakes her head in disbelief.

'Then what do you want?'

'Angus.' Jodie's voice is calm, certain. 'I want Angus, Mrs Garrow. I don't want your money.'

The woman stands as if stricken for a long moment. 'You mean it, don't you? Nancy Butterly was wrong—she thought you would be easy to persuade. But you're far, far smarter than she assumes. Smarter than anyone has guessed.'

'I love him. I'm sorry.'

'Love.' The woman's voice is a hiss, her smile full of contempt. 'There's no such thing. Love is just an excuse for getting what you want.'

What does Jodie want, really? She has told the woman that she wants, simply, Angus—the boy himself. But the attraction is complex, as attraction always is: Jodie also wants, as Mrs Garrow has guessed, a husband. Not just any husband, but one whose status is guaranteed, his antecedents proven, his respectability ironclad, his future assured. Although she's well aware that this desire is somewhat unusual for a girl—a bright girl—of her generation, Jodie doesn't let herself think too deeply about just what this striving for social standing and security through a man says about her, what it means.

What it will mean.

PART TWO

AAP NEWS
'Missing Elsa Mary may be in Tasmania'

A young woman from Hobart will undergo tests to establish whether she is Elsa Mary Evans, the missing daughter of Jodie Garrow. NSW Police have begun a nationwide search in an attempt to ascertain the whereabouts of Elsa Mary, who has not been seen since three days after her birth at Belfield Hospital in December 1986, when she was discharged into the care of her mother. A young woman from Newcastle will also undergo tests ...

DAILY TELEGRAPH
'"Jodie's not my mum"—negative DNA tests shatter adopted woman's hopes'

Two 24-year-old women who share a birthday with Elsa Mary Evans, missing since 1986, have had their identity—and the identity of their parents—put under scrutiny as the nationwide police search for missing Elsa Mary continues.

Jessie Farrell from Hobart and Anna Brown of Newcastle were required by NSW Police to undergo blood and DNA tests, but no biological links to Mrs Garrow have been established.

Miss Brown, a university student who was adopted when she was a newborn, has been searching for her birth mother and says she volunteered for the tests because her birthday is the same as Elsa Mary's.

'It was just a stab in the dark, really. Mum and Dad have always said the adoption was above board, but I thought it was worth checking out anyway, I was pretty disappointed, as I've had no luck making contact the regular way,' she said.

Miss Farrell declined to comment.

AAP NEWS
'Twenty-four-year-old women with webbed toes urged to volunteer for DNA testing'

The search for Elsa Mary, missing daughter of Jodie Garrow, has taken a bizarre twist with police urging any young women born between 1985 and 1987 who have webbing between the toes of both feet (syndactyly) to come forward for DNA testing.

A search for any records of surgery has led nowhere, and a police spokesperson said there is a strong possibility that Elsa Mary's webbing has been left intact.

'According to medical advice, this sort of syndactyly isn't actually physically disabling, and it would really only be corrected for cosmetic reasons,' a spokesperson said yesterday.

THE AUSTRALIAN
'Elsa Mary, where are you?'

Despite a three-month-long nationwide search—conducted through media outlets, as well as many official channels—no evidence has come to light regarding the fate of baby Elsa Mary Evans. Mrs Jodie Garrow, of Arding in Northern NSW, claims to have no knowledge of the child's whereabouts since she allegedly gave her up in an illegally arranged adoption only days after the child's birth.

Despite several false leads, and a $50 000 reward offered by the Garrows, the current or past whereabouts of the child have not been established.

If you have any information on Elsa Mary, or on her alleged adoptive parents, 'Simon' and 'Rosemary', please contact Detective Sergeant Paul Rossi, NSW Mispers, 9765 2323, or toll free 1800 153 153.

AAP NEWS
'Search for Elsa Mary goes global'

NSW Police today confirmed that they would be working with Interpol in an effort to locate the whereabouts of Elsa Mary Evans, missing since her discharge from hospital a few days after her birth in December 1986. Detective Sergeant Paul Rossi, who is heading the investigation, says that 'while we have no particular reason to believe that Elsa Mary was taken overseas, every avenue must be thoroughly investigated.'

DAILY TELEGRAPH
'Jodie Garrow lied: former midwife speaks out'

Debbie West, former midwife at Belfield Hospital, and a central witness in the investigation into the whereabouts of Elsa Mary Evans, says the missing girl's mother, Jodie Garrow, lied to her when questioned recently about her actions following Elsa Mary's birth. Mrs West, who was instrumental in bringing the case to official notice, says that when she inquired into the baby's wellbeing, Mrs Garrow assured her that she had arranged for Elsa Mary's adoption through the 'proper channels'. 'Jodie Garrow is a very good liar,' Mrs West said, 'She's convincing and plausible. When she told me that she'd adopted the baby out I believed her. I only had the records checked in an effort to help her, should she decide to connect with her daughter at some later date. I was as shocked as anyone to find there was no record of adoption, no birth certificate. She's expert at lying—she didn't turn a hair. And what she's saying about Matron O'Malley is a lie too—I had the privilege of working with Sheila O'Malley when I was a young nurse, and she was a midwife who maintained the highest ethical standards. It's a disgrace to have her reputation so publicly damaged.'

NEWS OF THE DAY
Editorial

As the nationwide search for Elsa Mary enters its third month, and with any positive results looking less and less likely, people are justifiably beginning to wonder why the official police investigation into Jodie Garrow is taking so long to get off the ground. Could it be that

Garrow (see inset picture), wife of a prominent Arding solicitor, is being treated very differently to your common, garden-variety suspect? It's another indictment of our so-called fair legal system, where the rich have recourse to the best legal advice before they even need it, and perhaps ensuring they never do. Anyone else so intimately involved in the disappearance of a child—even twenty-four years ago—would be under far greater scrutiny than Garrow, whose statements and media appearances have all been carefully scripted and controlled.

Shame on the NSW police, and shame on Jodie Garrow.

ARDING TIMES
Letter to the editor

I would like to express my disappointment and frustration—sentiments that are shared by many others—at this newspaper's lack of proper coverage of the Jodie Garrow case. Mr Garrow may be one of Arding's most respected citizens, as the paper constantly reminds us, but that should make no difference to the way this news is related. There's still a missing child at the centre of this story, and, most significantly, Mrs Garrow was still the last person to see her alive.

Name withheld,
Arding

16

Jodie knows that if she'd been raped, it would have been an entirely different story.

The whole thing would have been just that little bit easier. There'd have been—what do they call them?—Extenuating Circumstances. Of sorts. So there'd have been some kind of defence. Jodie could have said—or they, others (and there would have been others if this had been the case: women's lobbies, advocates, public figures championing her cause) would have declared Jodie to be a victim, emphasised *her* suffering. She could maintain that she'd had no agency, no choice—at least in the beginning, the conception. It would have been clear that she'd been wronged, that she was more sinned against than sinning.

But that's not the real story, is it? And no matter which way you turn it, looked at from whichever direction, whatever perspective—there's no way that she's the victim here, is there?

No way at all.

A few years back Jodie had been on the front cover of the local paper; her image was practically life-size, beaming cheerily, her hair glossy, eyes sparkling. She had been the spokesperson for some committee or other—wool awards, greening the park, literacy in homes—one of the myriad of community initiatives she'd been involved in over the years, and she'd been flattered by the faint aura of celebrity that surrounded her for the next week or two. *Hey, didn't I see you in the paper? Isn't that you?* She had enjoyed the comments from near strangers, shop staff, the woman behind her in the supermarket queue, as well as her friends—there had been some friendly teasing over her photogenic features, her model potential, the flattering line of cleavage revealed. She had cut out the photograph and article and filed them away with all the other family newspaper cuttings, and promptly forgotten all about it. She had thoroughly enjoyed every one of her allotted fifteen minutes—and it had given her absolutely no inkling into the horrors of public exposure she is currently experiencing.

The local paper has been remarkably discreet—out of some sort of residual loyalty to Angus's family, probably; the proprietor is a New England School old boy, and his father too. The story has been front page news once or twice over the past few months, but the stories have never been accompanied by pictures, and there has been no editorial commentary. But the national newspapers, the tabloids as well as the broadsheets, are another matter. Somehow they've managed to get hold of what must be one of the least flattering photographs of her in existence: anonymously supplied, the picture taken at last year's Grammar Christmas party moments after a minor disagreement with Hannah, and Jodie is frowning, looking sour and rather unfriendly. She has no idea who's supplied the snap or why, but it's devastating to think of so-called friends, or even acquaintances, supplying such material. Then again, she's barely heard from any of her friends since the news hit the street.

Despite her mother-in-law's warning, she had expected a show of support from the women in whose company she has spent the last few decades. She has taken Sue's virulent anger and subsequent distancing with relative equanimity (there has been no apology, no further communication at all, though Angus still sees Dave occasionally), but she would have expected Fiona, Peter's wife, and Karen, a colleague from her nursing days, to be making an effort to keep in touch, ask her out, keep her busy. But even these two—who she counted her best, her most intimate friends—had, after their initial declarations of 'being there' for her, gradually distanced themselves, until they'd virtually disappeared from her life. And there are others, people she has helped out in times of crisis—divorce, infidelity, illness, births, deaths—who she'd expected would appear on her doorstep with casseroles, bottles of wine, with invitations, offering their unconditional support, sympathy, loyalty. But other than one woman, a gym acquaintance who she'd barely counted a friend, who has made a point of ringing to see how she's going, Jodie's been left stranded. Her social encounters now consist of awkward conversations during unavoidable meetings down the street or at school events. She knows she's been summarily judged, condemned and discarded—it seems that even in friend-ship, contrary to popular wisdom, everything's conditional.

She has never been good at friendship, she realises this—even as a child she had always been at the periphery of any group, routinely included but never essential, nobody's partic-ular buddy. The child Jodie had always been slightly different to the other children, mildly aloof—from shyness more than anything else—self-contained. For a short time, in third grade, she'd had a real best friend—Bridie—someone to share every-thing with—every thought, every dream. Jodie remembers her vividly, but Bridie was in her life so briefly, her arrival and de-parture so abrupt and so beset by mystery, that she sometimes wonders whether she'd actually invented Bridie—an imaginary friend for a lonely child.

It's not only Jodie's friends who appear to have abandoned her, but the community itself—the whole sticky web of connec-tions that has always provided support. Now, without the once taken-for-granted buttress of respectability, and the associated assurance of welcome, every excursion outside the house—for shopping, to pick up Tom from school, visits to the solicitor—has become fraught and painful.

She can no longer expect a mildly flirtatious conversation with the local butcher (an old school mate of Angus's) when she buys her meat, for instance, or a chat about the unseasonably warm weather with the local newsagent (a former colleague), or a friendly inquiry about the children's doings from their old baby-sitter (daughter of her old schoolteacher). People tied to her own family in countless ways offer a curt hello, at best, or give her the cold shoulder. And it seems she can't leave the house without some malicious wit calling out to her, can't avoid the refusal to meet her eye, the swiftly down-turned faces of people she would once have smiled at easily in the supermarket. She has even heard the words *fucken murderer* hissed by someone vaguely familiar and has had to lower her flaming cheeks, blink back tears.

Twice she has actually been spat on. The first time it was a high-school girl, sixteen or so, who let out an obscene torrent of abuse after gobbing at her feet. The second time, even more shockingly, it was an elderly woman, well dressed, who stopped in front of her and grabbed at Jodie's hand. She'd assumed that the old woman needed help, that she'd lost her balance, perhaps, and so had allowed herself to be gripped, had tried to steady the frail, birdlike creature. But the woman had pulled her head back slowly, her eyes narrowed. As if in some strange alternate reality Jodie had watched the woman's jaw tense, her throat working as she collected the vile projectile in the back of her mouth, had realised finally what the woman was about to do, had reared back in horror, but it had been too late: the spittle found its target, hitting her in the side of the face. The old woman had hissed something at her, as Jodie pulled free of her clasp, but Jodie hadn't tried to make out the words, had hurried on, trying desperately to remove the shameful gobbet of mucus from her cheek. Utterly humiliated, she had told no one of either instance, had tried hard to forget them herself.

She has no idea how to act in public, whether to hold her head up, to refuse to bend, to look all her accusers firmly and boldly in the eye, or whether she should be timid, apologetic, deferential. To beg her erstwhile friends and acquaintances, if not for mercy, then for their sympathy, their assumption of her innocence, and a resumption of their good will.

Angus merely shrugs and tells her to ignore it when she asks him, genuinely bewildered, how she should respond to her sudden pariah status. But her husband too has continued to retreat in some essential way. There's nothing obvious, nothing she can put her finger on: there is no obvious discord between them. She had expected the tense arguments, the eruptions of anger, that have occurred when things between them have been difficult in the past. She would have preferred this: anger is something she could bear, could understand—could fight.

Jodie now finds that there are days when she speaks to no one other than Tom and Angus and, less and less frequently, Hannah. She goes for long walks with the dog, Ruff—walking for hours some days, from their house on The Hill and out along the dirt roads connecting the small acreages on the outskirts of town. Once, she would have enjoyed the walks, would have had friendly company, Fiona, Karen, sometimes Sue; they would have chatted about this or that, or perhaps walked silently, lost in their own thoughts. But now there's no choice—there's only her own thoughts, or a one-sided conversation with the ever-ebullient Ruff. She imagines herself eventually becoming one of those women— bag ladies, she supposes they're called even in the country—who walk through the streets muttering to themselves, oblivious to everything but their own internal narrative, endlessly reliving the memory of some desperate failure or long-ago success.

There was a girl who'd been at Grammar when she was there—a few years older than Jodie, she had come from an artistic sort of family, was drop-dead gorgeous, smart, popular. She was destined to be something, someone, that was clear: she could act, sing, dance, paint, write. After school she'd moved to the city, and over the years, through this and that avenue, Jodie had heard stories about her life—maybe true, maybe apocryphal: she'd scored a part in a big soapie, sung in some night-club, taken up with a mogul, lived in London or New York, Paris, maybe. She didn't know the full story, perhaps no one did, but the girl—Arabella, her name was—had arrived back in Arding, moved in with her ageing parents, ten or so years ago, a shadow of that former glamorous self. Drugs, they said. Alcohol, love. Her old friends and acquaintances had avoided her; her family just tolerated her. Though she had never known her well, Jodie had been one of the avoiders, not wanting to meet her eye, or be forced to acknowledge her, make conversation. But now when Jodie sees poor Arabella make her aimless circumnavigations about town, it's hard not to empathise.

DAILY TELEGRAPH
'Hospital defends reputation of midwife at centre of Elsa Mary adoption claims'

Belfield Private Hospital last night released a statement defending the reputation of former midwife Sheila O'Malley.

According to claims made by Jodie Garrow, the woman currently under police scrutiny over the disappearance of her infant daughter twenty-four years ago, Matron O'Malley was instrumental in setting up an illegal adoption, in which money is said to have changed hands.

However, Dr Chandler Purvis, CEO of Saratoga Private, who now own Belfield, and a former colleague of the late Matron O'Malley, has publicly repudiated Mrs Garrow's accusations.

'Having passed away a few years back, Mrs O'Malley is unfortunately not able to defend herself. Belfield and Saratoga Private would like to make clear our complete repudiation of Mrs Garrow's allegations,' Mr Purvis said yesterday.

'Matron O'Malley was one of the best midwives this hospital has ever had the privilege to employ, and to suggest that she did anything that was against the law or in any way unethical is a terrible slur against a remarkable woman.'

Investigations into the disappearance of the child, who would now be twenty-four, and a search for her alleged adoptive parents continue.

17

Knowing how painful all social appearances have become for her, Angus has been making a real effort to relieve Jodie, doing some of the shopping, volunteering for much of the running around of children, leaving work briefly to pick up and deliver Tom and Hannah to sporting practice, music lessons, rehearsals, friends' houses. It's an easy way to show his support for his wife both publicly and automatically, and one that requires no real conversation, no emotional effort—all is beyond him at the moment—and he's quite enjoying the extra time spent with the kids. Usually he just drops them off and goes back to the office, retrieving them when they're ready to go, but occasionally he waits. Today, he's surrendered to Tom's appeal that he stay and watch his indoor hockey game at the high-school hall. He settles back on the wooden seat, waves to his tousle-haired, mouth-guarded boy, and prepares to enjoy the noisy battle.

'Angus.' The mother of one of the other team members sits down beside him, gives him a slightly strained smile.

'Mary.' Angus nods. 'How are you?'

'Oh, you know ... busy. How about you?' Her gaze drifts away towards the game, back again, never quite looking at him fully.

'Yeah. We're pretty busy, too.' Drily. He ploughs on, asking the expected. 'And how's Big Jim? Haven't seen him for a while. How'd the soccer season go?'

'Well, he's retired, actually—getting too old. He hurt his leg last winter—tore a ligament ...' He can almost hear her brain whirring as she wonders whether to reciprocate. 'And how's ... how's Jodie?'

'Well, you know. She's okay, I guess. Coping, anyway.'

'Oh. Well, pass on my regards. We're missing her ... tennis, canteen ...' Her voice is edged with anxiety now. She narrows her eyes and stares straight ahead as if following the game intently.

Angus moves the conversation into dangerous territory, deliberately offhand. 'Well, you could pass them on yourself, you know. Our phone number hasn't changed.' He masks the sharp rebuke with a friendly tone, an open expression. 'It would be good if she could get out a bit more, actually, get involved in things again.' He waits for an evasive response, but Mary's side-stepping is more literal than he'd expected—she jumps to her feet, waving manically at someone on the other side of the field.

'Oh, sorry, Angus,' she apologises breathlessly. 'I really have to talk to Christa Underwood about something. Wonderful to see you.' She trips away, her handbag clutched to her chest, her relief at escaping evident.

Angus sighs. He has tried this manoeuvre a number of times, with certain old friends, longstanding acquaintances, and almost every time the response has been the same: shocked embarrassment at Angus's (indecent!) mention of his wife's problem, his implicit plea for sympathy and support. A few of his victims have murmured hasty reassurances, vague promises; others pretended they hadn't heard him, deftly changed the subject, then quickly moved on. Only one woman—the district magistrate's wife, slightly eccentric, renowned for her tart remarks and trenchant opinions—had made an honest rejoinder. It wasn't one he'd enjoyed hearing, but it was honest nonetheless.

'It's right of you to support your wife, Angus,' she had said softly but intently, gripping his forearm with surprising strength. 'But you can't expect everyone to be so loyal—not when we don't know the full story.'

The truth is that Angus doesn't know the full story either. And one part of him—the cool, disinterested lawyer side of him, the aspect that, as the years pass, as his work becomes almost a second skin, has begun to define him—that part of him doesn't want to know the full story, is warning him to proceed with caution. It's complex, almost paradoxical. It's not that he doesn't believe what his wife has told him—he does. It's what she's not saying that worries him. The fact that Jodie's initial impulse had been to omit certain crucial details (come on, she'd *lied!*) really hadn't bothered him at first; he had, just as he'd reassured her, understood. But now, more and more, he finds himself wondering, and the more he wonders, the less he wants to know. And not wanting to know means having to distance himself, and the more he distances himself the less certain he is of Jodie herself—of what she's told him, of who she is.

He sits alone for the rest of the game, distracted, only half watching the boys' clicking progress up and down the wooden boards, though he manages to clap when required, and gives a big cheer when Tom hits a goal. His uncertainty extends beyond Jodie, has transformed his sense of self, his position in Arding, his place in the world. So often, these days, in any public situation, he feels his presence is perceived as almost a provocation to others—as if, given the opportunity, they'd be glad to challenge him, to call him up on his defence of his wife, on his claims to respectability, decency. That they're convinced it's all a pretence—that all these years he's only been acting the role of upright citizen, good father. As if the reality is something else.

People are still friendly enough, respectful—he's still Angus Garrow, after all, and not a person to be casually slighted—but he can sense a certain wariness in some people and occasionally, particularly amongst those who were formerly the most deferential, a barely concealed contempt.

He has, as Susan had predicted, been forced to relinquish his mayoral ambitions, and though outwardly resigned to his sidelining, has observed the local elections with frustration and considerable envy. He has tried hard to contain his bitterness—there have been no recriminations, he has barely even mentioned it to Jodie, but the resentment surfaces at odd moments. His practice has suffered, too—several long-term clients have moved their accounts elsewhere, their excuses so clumsily expressed he'd been embarrassed on their behalf.

His employees—the two PAs, and a young law clerk—have, after their initial unguarded expressions of surprise, nervously avoided mentioning the situation. His partner Gemma, with whom he had a brief and almost perfunctory fling years ago, is even more careful to be circumspect on the rare occasions when Jodie is mentioned.

At home, Angus's panic attacks have become both more intense and unaccountably predictable—occurring now only in the evenings, usually soon after his arrival home, when he should, by rights, be winding down. He has been able to rush off to the study, or the bathroom, claiming work, the need for a long soak, and somehow—so wrapped up in her own worries— it seems that Jodie hasn't noticed anything odd. Though Angus can find no way to explain this change, and though he's grateful that he no longer has to lock himself in his office at work, pleading a migraine, while the panic passes, he fears his virtual absence even at home will eventually create more strain. He is stricken with guilt, knowing that, under their current peculiar circumstances, Jodie will be feeling his absence keenly, that she must feel that he has abandoned her, that he can't bear to be near her. He has thought about confiding in Jodie, telling her what's happening; he would welcome her sympathy, her advice. But Angus can't tell her, won't—he doesn't want to make things any worse, give her more to worry about: however tough he's doing it, there's enough, more than enough, on her plate already.

When the game finishes—the other team winning 3–2— Tom doesn't hang around with his mates for the usual debrief, but wanders over to his father, dribbling the ball despondently. Angus gets up ready to go, ruffles his son's hair.

'Well played, champ. They were a good team—you did well.'

But Tom doesn't reply, keeps hitting and stopping the ball, without lifting his head.

'Tom?' He peers down at his son's half-hidden face, glimpses red eyes, tearstained cheeks. 'What's going on, mate?' But Tom can't answer, is sobbing openly now.

'Oh, shit.' Angus kneels down in front of him. 'What's wrong, Tommy?'

The boy tries to speak but chokes on his words, his lips still clenched around the plastic guard.

'Pull it out, Tommy, will you?' But his son sinks to the floor, as if overcome, his hands covering his face, his chest heaving. Angus half lifts, half drags the boy through the hall and out into the car park, ignoring the concerned faces of other parents, the coach, team members. By the time they get to the car, the worst of his crying has stopped, and he has finally managed to spit out the guard. Tom sits in the back, his face turned away from his father, the occasional painful sob erupting.

Angus waits for a moment before turning on the ignition, his hands gripping the steering wheel. 'What happened in there, Tom? Do you think you can tell me?' He keeps his voice calm.

'Doesn't matter.'

'Please, Tom. It does matter. I need to know. You're not upset about losing?'

'Of course not!' The boy glares at his father, his scorn unmistakable.

'Did someone hurt you—is that it?'

'No.'

'Well then, what? Tommy?'

The boy hesitates, looks away again before speaking. 'They were teasing me—a couple of the boys on the other team.'

'Teasing you? What about?' Angus's heart sinks, knowing what's to come.

'They were talking about you and Mum.' The words are hesitant, his voice half muffled.

'What were they saying? Tom?'

'All sorts of stuff. Sort of whispering it at me when I was down the back. Two boys from St Marks.' The words come in a rush now, as if he's suddenly desperate to be rid of them. 'One of them kept saying that Mum was a murderer. That she killed that baby. That everyone knows it.'

'Oh, Tom.' He is helpless in the face of his son's terror—which is really just a replica of his own.

'And the other one, he was saying you must be in on it too—and that you'd both be going to jail. It's not true is it, Dad? You're not—'

'None of it's true, sweetheart. Your mum did just what she says she did.' He hears his voice: loud, clear, certain. 'And no one—no one—is going to jail.' Angus sounds just the way a father, defender of his family, should—he only wishes he could be sure that he was, in fact, that man.

DAILY TELEGRAPH

Dear editor,

I am writing to you as I am Jodie Garrow's mother and I thought I should tell you a few things about my daughter as people are very interested and there are so many things being said and I thought it would be better to get the story straight.

I live in the small town of Milton, near Arding, which is where Jodie grew up. Since I had my first stroke five years ago I have required full-time care and now live in Restwell Nursing Home. Jodie's older brother Jason and his four children also live here in Milton, so the gossip that is around the place is having a bad effect on more than just Jodie.

I just wish it to be known that my daughter is not quite the do-gooder she makes out to be as she has to all intents and purposes abandoned her natural family. It has been almost eight months since her last visit here, even though Arding is only a ten-minute drive from Milton. She has not been in contact with her brother or his children for over five years, and so far as I know her children have never even met her father, Bob, who now lives somewhere on the north coast.

This is just to give you a picture of the sort of woman Jodie is. She is a social climber who couldn't wait to get away from her background and who has always been ashamed of her parents and her family. We were only ordinary battlers—Jodie's dad was a truck driver and I worked as a barmaid here in Milton, so we were never what you would call a rich or high and mighty family, but we were hard-working and tried our best to give all our kids a decent life. But even as a little girl Jodie was always wishing she came from somewhere else. She was always working hard to be friends with kids who came from real posh families—doctors' and teachers' and university people's children, for instance.

So it didn't come as a surprise to any of her own family, or those who have known her all her life, to find out that she had got rid of that baby all those years ago. She wouldn't have let anything at all come in between herself and Angus Garrow, who she had her sights set on since she was only sixteen or so. I never knew she was pregnant, but I would like it to be known I would have encouraged her to keep the poor little thing, that I would have supported her and there would have been no shame for her in bringing up a little one alone. I would have loved to have been able to be a proper grandma to my daughter's children. It's a great sadness to me that I barely know the two kiddies that she's kept—I suppose we are not good enough for the Garrows!

Anyway, just to set the record straight, it was not our doing or with our approval or in order to not upset us that Jodie did what she did, as we would have been more than happy to welcome her baby and help rear it as best we could despite our own difficult circumstances.

Yours sincerely,

Mrs Jeannette (Jeannie) Evans

18

Jodie reads the letter on the news website on the morning of its publication, though someone thoughtfully pushes the cutting under her door later that day. She spends the rest of that morning cleaning the bathrooms—scrubs every surface, every tile, every millimetre of grout, using the strongest bleach she can lay her hands on, the fumes so strong that it is impossible to tell whether the tears that run in a continual stream, virtually blinding her, and the violent churning of her stomach are chemically or emotionally induced.

Fiona Silvers calls a few days later, her voice uncharacteristically breathy as she leaves a message for Jodie.

'I thought you might like to know,' she says, 'your mum is going to be on telly—on *Today Tonight*. I thought ... I thought you had a *right* to know.' As if she were doing Jodie a favour.

Jodie cannot bear to watch it, but Angus locks himself into the lounge room and listens through headphones. He calls the station immediately and demands a written transcript—a single mention of the word libel and they're more than eager to comply. They email it the following day, and Angus hands it to Jodie on his arrival home. 'It's pretty bad,' he says, his expression full of pity, concern. 'But you shouldn't take it too much to heart, Jodes—she'll have done it for the cash, you know. For the notoriety. And everyone will know that.' She cannot respond, can't even read it in front of him. She snatches the document without making eye contact, walks stiffly into the bedroom, locks the door, sits down on the bed.

'JODIE'S DEVASTATED MUM TELLS ALL'
Interview Transcript

Reporter: Melissa Cartwright
Producer: Samuel Townsend

Melissa Cartwright: Mrs Evans, you wrote a letter to the media last week about your daughter, Jodie Garrow, who's currently under investigation following the revelation that, unbeknownst to her friends and family, she'd given birth to a baby as a young woman—a baby that has since disappeared. I'll just read an extract to the audience.
(Reads excerpts from letter)
Melissa: Well, it was a very honest letter, Mrs Evans, and quite a surprising one. I wonder if you could tell me what prompted you to write such a revealing and heartfelt letter? To make your sentiments so very public?
Mrs Evans: *(clears throat)* Well, dear, a few people around here—those who never really knew us, I'm talking about, because anyone who knows the Evanses will know that we aren't the type of people who'd kick our daughter out if she came home pregnant or with a baby, but there were a few people about who have been making certain, um ... intonations. Saying that poor Jodie couldn't come home, that she couldn't tell her family about it because she'd of been scared. And anyone who knows us knows that there's no truth in that—even though we've had our troubles the same as anyone else, I suppose, there was never any violence or anything like that, but just troubles, like everyone has. But there's no way I'd ever of kicked Jodie out or done anything except what was right by her. When my oldest boy, Jason, was in prison a few years back— it was nothing serious, just a ... a misunderstandment,

and he can be a bit of a lad when he's on the grog—I took on two of his kiddies for a couple of years when his fiancée Laura went off the rails. They're better now, no harm done. And Jason's out and got two more.

Melissa: I can understand you wanting to protect your family's good name, Mrs Evans. But it hasn't occurred to you that in defending your own good name, you may have done some very public harm to your daughter's reputation at this very difficult time?

Mrs Evans: Well, I'm only speaking the truth. We *would* of welcomed Jodes back with open arms. I'd have loved that poor wee baby like she was my own—there was no need for her to do whatever it was she did. It would of been hard—I never had a lot of spare time—or cash—since Jodie's dad left. A deserted mum I was, with three little kiddies, and barely heard from him since. Now I come to think of it, Jodie's a chip off the old block really, he always thought too highly of himself, thought he was too good for us, for Milton.

Melissa: And what is it that you think happened, Mrs Evans? As a mother—and who knows a daughter better than her own mother?—what do you suspect really happened to baby Elsa Mary?

Mrs Evans: What do I think happened? Well, really, dear—I've got no idea, have I? It's a real mystery, isn't it—like they're saying on the telly. I suppose she might of adopted it out, like she says. I mean, there are all sorts of people out there, aren't there? Though, I have to say, I'd have thought Jodes was a bit smarter than to do something like that. Even as a little girl she was quite ... clever ... and not just in a schoolwork type of way. You know what I mean: she always knew which way was up, always good at looking after number one. She wasn't the type of girl you really had to worry about—with boys, getting pregnant and all that. She was a good girl in that way. *(pause)* But I guess we were wrong about that, weren't we? She might of been too good for us, but she wasn't quite as clever as she thought.

Melissa: Perhaps I can rephrase that question slightly. Do you think your daughter would be capable of harming a baby?

Mrs Evans: Oh. I see what you mean. Well, I guess she could of, couldn't she? But she was never a cruel girl. Oh, I guess she had a barney or two with Jason and Shane when they were little. But I don't ever remember her hurting anyone—not physical, anyway.

Melissa: You don't think she'd have been capable of killing the baby, then, and disposing of the body? Perhaps because of her fear of being caught, of putting her relationship with her future husband at great risk? It's not possible that all this, combined with the shock of childbirth, might have driven her to such an act?

Mrs Evans: Well, I ... I don't ... I really don't know, dear. I suppose if she'd had to choose between Angus and the baby ... oh, deary me. Really, I don't think she would. But then, what do I know. She's a bit of a cold fish, Jodie. She's sort of an unfeeling type of woman, if you know what I mean. She's not been a real daughter to me at all, you know, barely has anything to do with me. My sons are wonderful, but at a certain time of life a woman really needs a daughter.

Melissa: Well, thank you for that, Mrs Evans.

Anchor: That was Melissa Cartwright speaking to Mrs Jeannie Evans, mother of Jodie Garrow, from her home in Milton, near the regional city of Arding in Northern NSW.

This time she doesn't cry. Jodie's exhausted her tears, is beyond even anger, stunned, numb. She crumples the printout into a ball, tosses it into a corner of the room. Lies back on the bed with her eyes closed, breathing deeply. She hears Angus's gentle tapping on the door, his apprehensive inquiry—'Jodes. Are you okay? Jodie?'—but ignores it, feigning deafness, sleep. She can't bear the thought of his, of anyone's, sympathy right now, wants to ponder alone the source of this profanity, this betrayal, this clear evidence of her mother's aversion to her.

Jodie's relationship with her mother could never have been described as close—it's quite true that she rarely sees her, though she does her duty: sending birthday presents, cash, paying for any extra nursing that's required. But still she can't understand how their relationship has descended to this. Though she knows that her mother's shameful public critique of her character is vindictive, is more about her mother than her, still it hurts. It's the injustice more than anything: Jodie knows she isn't an overtly warm person—she's self-contained, reserved if not exactly shy—but she's not unfeeling, has never been unfeeling. She has always felt.

Had her mother ever loved her?

She wonders sometimes whether she only imagines that her mother's hostility, and their subsequent estrangement, really stemmed from her childhood, or whether they had only developed this mutual antipathy as she grew into an adolescent. Perhaps before that things had been rather more normal; perhaps Jeannie had been an affectionate, well-meaning, good-enough mother—not entirely besotted by her progeny, but what mother really was (in those long-ago days before a mother's cultivation of self-esteem became more vital to the raising of a healthy child than pasteurised milk)? Or maybe there was some truth to her mother's accusations. Perhaps she wasn't an engaging child—was she prickly, withdrawn, critical? Unlovable?

Her mother's life had been unimaginably difficult. Jodie's father had been in and out of work for years, had been a drunk, occasionally violent. He'd finally left Jeannie with the three of them when Jodie was seven, the two boys eleven and five and by any reckoning a handful. Jason was already hanging around with the type of boys he would always attract—older, tougher, always in trouble—and Shane showing signs of some sort of learning difficulty. He'd be diagnosed with something now, ADD, ADHD, for certain. Looking back, her mother had most likely suffered from some sort of undiagnosed depressive illness for years, but back then she'd done what she'd had to do to make sure they had a roof over their heads, to keep food on the table and shoes on their feet. And that had meant work, hard work: as a barmaid, cleaning, whatever employment was on offer in a small, impoverished place like Milton—which wasn't much, and certainly wasn't conducive to family life.

There wasn't much left of her, Jodie supposes now, to properly nurture her children. Her mother had found her pleasure where she could, obviously regarding her children as an encumbrance rather than consolation. And they—the three kids—well, they'd had a hard time of it too, had virtually reared themselves, had to struggle to survive. There had been a casual arrangement with a neighbour, Aunty Val, who was paid to keep an eye on them—but in reality it was only Shane who needed looking after. Jason's afternoons were spent out on his bike with his mates, causing trouble, while Jodie was old enough and responsible enough to be at home alone. She had spent much of her childhood on her own, mooching about the place, reading books from the school library, watching TV, pretending to be someone else, wishing to be somewhere, anywhere else.

It was as if her mother had given her up as a worthless emotional investment—early on, perhaps even when she was a baby. For as long as she could remember Jodie had existed at a distance from her mother—she'd been on the outer reaches of whatever family unit still existed, and if not unwanted then certainly not understood or approved of. From an early age she'd found her mother vaguely shameful, cringed at her broad Australian twang, her chain-smoking, her stinking like grog even at four in the afternoon; had been painfully aware of the squalor of their housing commission home, her mother's wrong hair, wrong clothes, wrong comments.

Her mother had a more conventional relationship with Jodie's brothers, though; seemed to enjoy their company, in her particular offhand way. This is not to say that they didn't frequently receive the sharp end of her tongue, or the back of her hand, but somehow it didn't mean anything; it was never serious. However unappealing to outsiders, the boys belonged in Jeannie's world—she understood them, approved of them, loved them as much as she could love anybody. Despite the inconvenience of their undeniable problems, unlike Jodie they accepted their home, their mother, their lot in life.

The shimmering oasis in Jodie's lonely desert of a childhood, her one experience of companionship, friendship, is something she still remembers clearly, holds dear, more than thirty years later.

Jodie, eight, has wandered, bored, one afternoon down to the local park to play on the swings. The park has recently been given a makeover during an enthusiastic but short-lived effort to improve Milton's civic infrastructure. Originally just a few swing sets in a dusty clearing, the park now has turf laid in a sweeping area from the river bank to the footpath, saplings have been planted, a small pond and fountain constructed. The area, which fronts a small sandy beach on the river, has become the exclusive hangout of the town's delinquents and bored youths— the perfect place for beer and dope and not-so-surreptitious sex.

But none of this concerns Jodie, who is really only interested in the fact that the revamped park now boasts a swing set with rubber seats, a smoothly spinning pipe-metal roundabout, two slippery-dips, and a house-shaped climbing frame—the whole lot sitting atop a brightly painted cement base with a generous hopscotch grid neatly marked up.

Jodie's mother has been spending most of her afternoons and evenings drinking with a shearer who is in town for an extended bender, and has dumped Shane on her own mother for a period, leaving the older two to look after themselves. Jason, who is twelve, has run wild—joining a bunch of bigger boys every afternoon after school who hoon around town on their bikes and generally cause trouble—while Jodie is more or less left to her own devices, though her mother calls in the late afternoon to check that they are both there, watching television as instructed. He generally cops an earful later, when they're both around simultaneously, for not being there to look after his sister. 'You bloody little shit,' their mother yells, swiping at him as he grins and ducks. 'I'm out there working my arse off trying to support you deadshits. I don't know what for. Jesus! You need to watch her, Jase. Anything could happen,' she adds cryptically, her voice full of some dark knowledge that Jodie can't quite fathom. Even knowing that Jason is never there, her mother makes no arrangements other than a casual directive that Jodie should go over to Aunty Val's if she's worried.

So Jodie, bored and looking for ways to distract herself from the hunger that seems always to gnaw at her, has been venturing alone to the new park, which is only a short walk from home, drawn by the lush grass, the brightly coloured play equipment and the prospect of company.

This particular afternoon there are two unfamiliar children playing, a girl of around her own age, and an older boy, her brother perhaps. The boy, who is smoking a cigarette, is swinging fitfully—dragging his feet in the dirt on every downward swing—and watching the girl climb on the frame. She is worth watching; Jodie stands and shyly watches too. She is obviously some sort of expert, better than anyone Jodie has seen before: she swings neatly from rung to rung, as lightly and easily as a monkey, then spins around on one leg until she is sitting atop the bar at the highest point. She hangs from the rail for a moment, her arms dangling, two neat plaits following suit, then pulls herself up and spins again with dizzying speed. After several more graceful spins, she flies off the bar, her legs bent together, hands clamped about her knees like the young gymnasts Jodie has seen on television. Jodie holds her breath in terror, but the girl lands neatly and securely with two feet together. The girl stands upright, arms before her, eyes closed, breathing slowly, swaying slightly.

Eventually she opens her eyes and turns to the boy, gives him a disdainful look. 'Told you I could do four in a row. You owe me fifty cents. Hand it over.'

The boy doesn't reply, just keeps sweeping through the dirt with his feet. 'Do eight, then I'll pay you.' He flicks the half-smoked cigarette in her direction.

The girl rolls her eyes. Holds out her hand. 'No way, crater face. Pay up now, or I'm telling Aunty Del that you've been smoking—stealing her fags too, I'll bet.'

He mutters as he digs in his pocket, but hands over some change—first a fifty-cent piece, then a few more gleaming coins—before sauntering off.

The girl gazes at the handful of money for a moment, her eyes wide—then turns and beams at Jodie, who is standing en-raptured, still half holding her breath. 'Hi there,' she says breez-ily. 'He's given me a dollar. You can get fifty cobbers for that up at Rafferty's. You want to share?'

Her name is Bridget Sullivan—Bridie—and she tells Jodie that she and her brother Rory are staying with an aunt, her mother's sister, and her husband, a childless couple who own the local newsagency. Her mother has had to go away for a while, she tells Jodie, because of the new man in her life.

She's overseas somewhere, maybe in Italy, or is it Ireland? Anyway, somewhere, but Bridie knows it's definitely not Amer-ica. 'My dad is dead,' she says as they cram as many of the chewy chocolate caramels into their mouths as they can. 'I did ten once,' Bridie confides, 'but I nearly choked to death. True story.' Or maybe her dad just disappeared. She can't be certain. 'But he was definitely Irish and a Tyke, though me and Rory definitely aren't Cathos 'cause my mum can't stand the nuns, and that's why I'm called Bridie—because my dada named me after his own mother, who was a blessed saint. True story. But it's a stupid name, really, when you think about it because I'm not a bride and definitely not going to be because boys are the most stupidest invention ever—my brother is definitely the stupidest—and when I'm grown up I'm going to change it to Vanessa, which is the most perfect name in the world, because you can do that. Or maybe Cassandra, which is better because then I could be Cass. *Cass.* My mum is up to her third husband, though they aren't actually married, and he's an artist and so is my mum but she's a sculptor not a painter like him though she can't really afford to work very much as materials are so expensive, though once there was this man, a millionaire, who gave her a studio and all the clay she needed. True story.'

Bridie is her first, her only, friend. She is like no other girl that Jodie knows, like no other girl in Milton, and Jodie falls headlong in love, in the way that small girls do—spending every spare minute with her, counting down the hours until they can be together. Bridie's not attending school for the short time that she's there—it's only meant to be a few weeks, though it stretches into a month and then beyond—so they spend every afternoon after school together and then the entire weekend, usually at Jodie's place, hiding in the bedroom with the door locked against her brother, or at the park. Bridie has as much freedom as Jodie, it seems, but with the added bonus of money. Her aunt bribes the kids to keep out of mischief, with silver coins and the occasional note. 'We're actually meant to buy our lunch,' Bridie confesses, 'get fish and chips or a sandwich at the café, but I'd definitely rather get lollies, wouldn't you?'

Bridie's life is a revelation to Jodie. For the first time, Jodie's unasked-for freedom from adults seems filled with excitement and adventure instead of loneliness and anxiety. And for the first time she has a companion—one who can give her pointers on how to survive. On the surface, Bridie's own family situation couldn't be more different to Jodie's. Bridie loves her mother, brags about her constantly, quotes her, models herself on her.

It's an extreme contrast to Jodie's already half-ashamed disregard for her own mother—her intuitive knowledge that her mother isn't someone she can look up to, let alone brag about. Bridie even carries a creased photograph of her mother in her pocket. She is young, much younger than Jodie's mum—and much prettier. She has long glossy hair, and wears the kind of clothes that Jodie has only seen in magazines or on television. She is blonde, her face serene, unlined, unworried. Bridie's mother, constantly professing her love for her, promises the world—and Bridie is always expecting gifts and letters and postcards that never arrive. ('I think she's probably somewhere where there's no postman—maybe Africa, right now. Or in Paris and they can't read the address. That would be it. Definitely.') She boasts about what her mother has done, what she might be doing, who she's doing it with. Bridie's mother has told her, has told both her children, that they should regard freedom as a right and a privilege, though to Jodie's eyes the life they're living here in Milton doesn't seem to be all that much better than her own. Bridie's aunt and uncle are constantly mad at her for some misdemeanour or other; her clothes—unlike those worn by her mother in the photograph—seem to be an assortment of hand-me-downs, or worn items bought at thrift shops. ('Mum says that only people with nothing in their heads worry about what they wear.') And though Jodie envies the fact that her friend doesn't have to attend school during her stay in Milton, she doesn't envy her the long days spent in front of the television, or the ten different schools that she has already attended.

During one of their rambles around the park, they discover a willow with branches that stretch right out over the river, easily climbed, and with a natural platform formed by a series of close-growing branches in the centre of the tree—high up enough to feel exciting without being particularly dangerous. They spend hours perched up there with their bags of sweets and the occasional tin of beans or spaghetti that Bridie's aunt's pantry provides, playing pirates, Robin Hood, princesses and dragons. They venture down to use the equipment only when the park is empty, occasionally encountering Bridie's brother, who checks on them from time to time, a stolen cigarette dangling from his lips and a comic book in his hands.

In Jodie's memory Bridie is constantly talking. About her parents, about the places she's lived ('in the desert')—the houses ('a mansion in the most 'sclusive part of Sydney'), the apartments ('a penthouse—which means it's right at the top')—the schools she's been to ('this posh one was the worst where we had to wear hats—and gloves!'), the pets she's had ('a python, and even a monkey, once!'), her plans to travel the world as soon as she's grown up, the jobs she'd like to do ('a trapeze artist or a fisherman'). There's one particular thing she says, though, that is to stay in Jodie's memory for many years; one thing she would, if asked, say transformed her life.

The two girls are at Bridie's place—the visit illicit, as Bridie has been told on no account is she to have Jodie over without supervision. They have stolen a packet of chocolate biscuits from the pantry and filled tall glasses with milk, and have taken them to the bedroom that Bridie shares with her brother. There's a full-length mirror running along the wall opposite the bed, and the girls lie close together, watching themselves closely as they sip from their glasses, chew the biscuits. They watch the chewing—their teeth churning the contents of their mouths into a gluggy brown mush—very seriously, as if they're conducting some sort of scientific research. When the chewing has been completed to Bridie's satisfaction ('You only chewed sixty times, definitely. I was counting. I got up to a hundred. Keep going!'), she considers her friend in the mirror for a long moment.

The two girls are a study in contrasts: despite her blonde mother ('She's a bottle blonde,' Bridie tells Jodie proudly. 'Peroxide. True story.'), Bridie's hair is mousy brown, her body is slight, but her arms and legs are taut with sinew and muscle, she's broad across the shoulders. Her eyes are dark, heavily fringed, her face freckled and elfin. Jodie is shorter, more solid.

Her hair is white-blonde, but dirty, long and unkempt. Her eyes are a washed-out blue, her face long, pale, serious.

'You know, Jodie,' Bride says, 'if you washed your hair and brushed it, you'd be really pretty.'

'Do you think so?' Jodie has never considered herself either pretty or not pretty. It's something she's never really thought about.

'Definitely. All you really have to do is do your hair properly, maybe put it up? You wouldn't have to wear make-up or anything, I don't think. My mum says you're lucky if you can just be natural, if you don't have to work hard to look good.' Solemnly: 'She says I'll probably have to work a bit, to overcome my im—imperfectness.'

Jodie doesn't really understand what Bridie's saying, but she knows a compliment when she hears one, and is happy to accept.

Bridie conducts an experiment: she pulls the tangled mass of hair off Jodie's face, gathers it up in a makeshift ponytail. 'See?'

And Jodie does see. She looks quite different to her usual self, looks suddenly like one of those girls whose mothers pick them up from school, who have their hands held when they cross roads, whose shoes are shined, uniforms ironed, lunches packed neatly into special boxes. One of those girls whose mothers kiss them goodbye and hello—and possibly at other times in between.

Bridie watches Jodie looking at herself, gives a sympathetic smile.

'You know, Jodie, you can actually be whoever you want to be. That's what my mother always tells me. Definitely. Maybe you don't have anyone to help you, but no one's going to stop you either.' Bridie grimaces at herself in the mirror, bares her teeth, widens her eyes. 'I'm not totally sure yet, but I think maybe I'll be a movie star when I grow up. Or maybe an artist, a sculptor like my mum. Or a musician. Or actually ... maybe I'll be a gymnast!' Bridie executes a strange contorted somersault off the bed, landing with a thud on her behind. When their laughter subsides she stays squatting, her eyes meeting Jodie's in the mirror. 'What do you want to be, Jodie?'

Jodie scratches at the side of her nose, picks a loose bit of peeling skin, thinks for a moment. 'You know what?' She pulls her hair back into the messy bunch again. 'I think I just want to be one of those normal grown-ups. The ones with pink lipstick, and high heels, and—and a station wagon.' She purses her lips, turns her head from side to side. She thinks of her mother. Adds: 'And a husband. I'd like a nice, handsome husband. Handsome and rich. *Definitely.*'

Close to the start of the school holidays, Bridie and her brother leave without any warning. Jodie walks to the newsagent and asks Bridie's uncle shyly whether they're coming back, and could she have their address.

'Don't even know where that woman's taken them,' he says, not quite looking at Jodie. 'She turned up in the dead of night with some new fellow in a flash car. Woke those poor bloody kids up and took them just like that. Wearing their pyjamas, not even a dressing gown, bare feet. They didn't have a clue what was going on, but then they never do. And she was six months gone. Women like that ought to be sterilised, if you ask me. Not fit to raise chickens, let alone kids.'

By twelve Jodie has made the decision to get as far away as possible, and as fast as she can. She insists her mother enrol her not at the local central school in Milton, but at one of the bigger comprehensive high schools in Arding. Her mother makes no real protest; there is no reason why Jodie shouldn't go to Arding, no extra expense involved—school uniforms can be bought second hand, and bus travel is free. Her scornful observation—that of course Miss Big-britches couldn't attend school with the local riffraff, could she?—is ignored by Jodie. What, in the greater scheme of things—this whole distant life she is set on creating—does her mother's opinion matter?

From there it is easy to remake herself. In Arding she has no reputation; no one—neither teachers nor parents nor the other students—knows anything of her mother or her brothers. She joins student committees and councils, volunteers for various organisations, works hard at her studies, plays netball, cricket, establishes a reputation as a competent all-rounder.

Convinced that entry to a private school holds the key to her success, Jodie fills out her own Grammar scholarship application in Year Ten, forges her mother's signature, then sits the exam. She has to work hard to persuade Jeannie to attend the compulsory principal's meeting once the scholarship has been awarded, but this one meeting is enough to cement the school's decision: the principal is impressed by this bright and determined young woman, and despite discreet opposition from several old girls on the board, Jodie is welcomed into the school community. Her mother's indifference is made clear from the outset, her refusal to pay for anything additional noted—and a special bursary is set up to provide Jodie with those necessities—uniforms, books, excursions—that aren't covered by the scholarship.

And Jodie proves to be a good choice—she brings honour to the school, winning academic prizes as well as civic awards. The other girls accept her, on the surface at least, and she is included in all the usual extra-curricular activities—invited to parties, for holidays to this girl's property, another's coastal holiday house—and parents are always welcoming and kind. But Jodie's sense of being different, of being not-quite-good-enough never leaves her, keeps her distant, and she develops a reputation for being reserved, slightly cold, aloof. But the reputation is undeserved: if only they knew, she is anything but cold, wishes desperately to be one of them. She works hard to keep her home life as separate from her school life as possible, and hopes that nobody ever guesses how bereft of all the ordinary middle-class privileges and expectations, how wretched her home life really is.

So what her mother had said was true: she had run as fast and as far away from her home as she could. But it wasn't just the poverty that she had run from, or the social exclusion—it was something more profound. What she had been most determined to circumvent was the paralysing sense of littleness, the lack of drive, ambition, simple resolve that seemed so deeply ingrained in the soul of her own family. And for years she has imagined that she had somehow managed to really escape this, has felt herself expand into the Jodie that she knew she could be—the Jodie of her dreams and imaginings. Jodie Garrow is not the mean, lazy, purposeless harridan that her mother was, that Jodie Evans was destined to be. She is generous, hard-working, busy, hospitable, dependable, respectable, and able, with few lapses, to negotiate the complex social proprieties and protocols of her adopted world.

But now, Jodie feels herself shrinking. Almost as if it's a physical reality, as if she's becoming smaller by the day, her sense of herself is contracting into some hard object. Stone-like, impervious, cold. Lumpen and worthless.

Her mother's daughter.

19

If anyone had asked Hannah to describe her mother before all this happened, what would her response have been? Incomprehension? Uncertainty? Bemusement? Describe her mother? For heaven's sake, there's nothing to describe: she's just her mother. Mum.

But lately she's been forced to do just this. First by the police—sitting in her dad's swanky conference room with some dykey policewoman asking questions in what is so obviously a fake kindly manner; with her father, who has only agreed to her being interviewed very reluctantly, on Pete's advice, interjecting at almost every juncture—*not appropriate, not relevant*. The woman asks about her relationship with her mother—do they get on okay? Her father grimaces, and gestures for her to speak, but Hannah finds that really, she has very little to say. She tells the woman the truth, pretty much—they have had their problems, but they're no bigger (well, until now that is) than any of her friends'. They have all the usual arguments—about cleaning her room, doing her homework, spending money, seeing boys, going to parties. Nothing special. Nothing out of the ordinary.

When the woman asks her whether her mother is ever violent, she laughs, and answers before her father has an opportunity to stop her: tells her no, her mother is never, and never has been, violent. She's never hit her. Not even a smack when she was little. And she's never hit her brother. Or her dad for that matter. Here the policewoman glances nervously at Angus, who sits with his legs stretched out, arms folded, his expression unreadable.

'Mum,' says Hannah in the sweetest, brightest, youngest voice she can come up with, 'is a wonderful person. She's kind and she's generous and she's calm and she keeps the house tidy, cooks excellent meals, helps in the community.' Her mother, Hannah is saying, is in every conceivable way exemplary.

Naturally she does not tell the policewoman what she really thinks about her mother—that in fact she does not know what to think about all the claims that are being made, in the press, and by her own appalling grandmother. That she does not know whether what's being hinted at has any basis in fact, or whether it's just gossip, innuendo of the most scurrilous kind. That she has realised, shockingly, that she doesn't really have any idea who her mother is, that this woman she has known—and loved—forever has turned out to be a stranger. That she finds her mother's deep, unassailable ordinariness, her capacity to go on as if nothing is happening, outrageous and incomprehensible. And that right now—when it's apparent that there's a sword hanging just inches from their heads—she finds her mother's utter paralysis, her seeming inability to change anything, stop anything, say anything in her own defence, utterly terrifying.

There have been moments when she has wanted to admit her fears, to fall on her knees before her mother, to be gathered in, comforted, to be a child again. She has wanted to be able to view her in that old adoring light, to have a sense of her as someone solid, essential, inseparably connected to her and providing a safe conduit to the world beyond. But there is no way back. Her father offers what he can in the way of encouragement, support, but though they're close enough, there's still too much unsaid. And too much that's unsayable.

Both Assia and, in his own limited way, Wes have made tentative efforts to talk to Hannah about what's going on in her family. Hannah appreciates their friendship, needs it right now, but cannot bring herself to confide. She would not know what to confide; in truth she finds it hard to articulate what she is feeling, even to herself. Lately it seems the only place where she feels right, the only place where her real self can emerge, is on the stage. Only then—when she's someone else—can she say what needs to be said, only then can she find the way to say it.

Hannah stands before the drama class. The students have been asked to attempt a physical impression of somebody recognisable, someone the class will be able to identify. She doesn't think much initially: when she performs she finds it's best to just do, to be. She turns her back on the audience, makes some minor alterations to her physical appearance. She does her best to push her thickly layered hair into a tidy bob, smooths out the creases in her tights, pulls her school kilt down on her hips so that the hemline sits demurely above her ankles, tucks in her shirt, straightens her collar, sucks in her stomach, shrugs off her fashionably elegant slouch and squares her shoulders. She pulls herself in psychologically, quite consciously now, reins in every random, flyaway thought, and when she turns back to the class she is barely recognisable; it is as if she has discarded completely her own vivid, bulgy, irrepressible self, replaced it with another: taut, cool, opaque. When she speaks, her customary drawl has been abandoned for a more refined accent, her voice has been ratcheted up a notch; there's a faint quaver (indignation? distress?) as she asks of no one in particular—an invisible antagonist, Hannah herself, perhaps—whether she really considers *that* to be appropriate behaviour for an intelligent girl, from a respectable family. The class's laughter is more subdued than she expected, as if the audience recognises that this particular comedic effort is laced with something more dangerous.

'How *dare* you?' Hannah goes on. 'I don't quite know how to express my ... *disappointment*. You were such a sweet little thing, however did you transform into such a difficult girl?' She takes in an imaginary retort, her eyes wide, then her lips compress, she turns away. 'Oh, where did we go wrong?' she moans, shoulders slumped. A long pause. Then: 'And what ... What will people *think*?'

The scene moves swiftly from comedy to drama. Now Hannah is determined to garner more than just the customary laughter, wants some other response from her audience—recognition of something deeper, more mysterious. Suddenly the rather fatuous matron becomes someone menacing—it's hard to see why, to pinpoint exactly how Hannah manages it, as she doesn't speak, but suddenly the character, the caricature—still recognisably the Mrs Garrow they all know—has assumed a darker mien, has become sinister, her intent unmistakably malign. The Jodie grotesque smiles cruelly, then moves forward—toward the audience, her purpose indefinable, but somehow terrifying.

There's a gasp from the audience, and then some suppressed squealing as Hannah moves toward them—and she breaks right there, in a moment of white-knuckle tension. She gives an ironic bow, waits for a response.

There is a gurgle of appreciation from her peers; even her usually scathing Year Eight nemesis Anna breathes an admiring 'Awesome!'. The teacher, Mrs Dennison, is smiling uneasily.

'My goodness, Hannah. That was a remarkable performance. Well done. Though not one for our drama night, perhaps.'

The girls laugh about it, later at lunch, Hannah summarily restored to the fold—for the moment at least. She can sense there's something wrong with Assia, though, who hangs back a little from the crowd, slightly distant, cool, a tension about her that Hannah immediately recognises. Instead of waiting until they're alone, as she usually would, Hannah asks her straight up what's wrong—a gauntlet thrown down in front of all the other girls.

'How could you do that?' Assia says, obviously glad to be given the opportunity to speak her mind.

'Do what?' Hannah affects a nonchalance she doesn't quite feel.

'Do that to your mother. In front of all those people. It was awful. I could never be so cruel. So disloyal.'

Hannah snorts. 'I didn't do anything to her, Assia. And well, no, you wouldn't, would you? Your mother's so cool. My mother's so not. And then my mother has this whole, er, *baby-killing* thing happening.' She says the word loudly, grins defiantly at her friend.

Assia grabs her hand, drags her away from the other girls, whose eyes have widened with delight at the prospect of a scene. 'God, Hannah. How could you say *that*? She's your mother, Han. And she's explained what happened with the baby. You should be sticking up for her. And even if you are angry with her or whatever, you shouldn't be making it into a joke in front of everyone.'

'You're not serious, are you? You have no idea what it's like.' Hannah kicks at a rock, hard, with her new shoe. It leaves a nasty scratch on the leather. She kicks again. Viciously. 'She's been an utter bitch lately. You know that. Then there's all this shit about that fucking baby. And she doesn't do anything, doesn't say anything, doesn't even try to defend herself. What's everyone meant to think? She's so fucking *stupid*.'

'Oh, come on, Hannah. Just because she doesn't let you do whatever you want! Because she expects you to help out occasionally, nags at you to clean up your room? That's all it is, isn't it? She's not that bad.'

Hannah prickles up. 'She *is* that bad, actually. What would you know?' She can feel the words harden, but forces them out like bits of gravel—sharp, biting, hot. 'Your mum's a normal person, not some dumbo Stepford wife who has a major breakdown if the towels in the linen closet don't line up perfectly. If I try and talk to my mother about anything that's important she asks me whether I've done my homework, or put away my clothes. There's nothing,' she screws a finger into her ear, gives a daffy grin, trying to lighten the mood, 'absolutely nothing, up there—except air, maybe.'

Her attempt to be funny doesn't work. Assia's face is red, she's biting at her bottom lip as if to stop from crying. 'Your mum's just normal, Hannah. They're supposed to give you shit about that sort of stuff. They're not supposed to tell you about the great head job they were given by some celebrity or the acid they dropped in the eighties. I know you think my mother's fantastic—she seems so great on the surface, and sometimes she is. But she can turn—in an instant. She's said stuff to me that you couldn't imagine a mother saying. You know she named me after some famous fucking suicide, right? Some poet who killed herself and her kid. How crap is that? Your mother is kind. And she really loves you. And I think what you did in Drama was really, really wrong.' And before Hannah can say anything, Assia is striding away across the grassy playground, lost in the noisy lunchtime crowd.

AAP NEWS
'Search for missing baby fails: case referred to coroner'

After a police investigation has failed to find any trace of either missing Sydney girl Elsa Mary or of the couple who allegedly adopted her, the matter has been referred to the coroner.

Elsa Mary, who will be twenty-four if she is still alive, has not been seen since she was discharged into the care of her mother, Jodie Evans, now Garrow, three days after her birth on December 22nd 1986.

Despite extensive searches, nationally and overseas, NSW Police have not been able to determine whether Elsa Mary is still alive. The coroner, Conrad Westerby, QC, will consider whether an inquest is necessary.

Police ask anyone with information about the circumstances of Elsa Mary's disappearance, or anyone who knows her current or past whereabouts, to contact Crime Stoppers on 1800 333 000.

The photo comes out of the woodwork only a few days after the case is handed on to the coroner. Angus phones Jodie from the office with the news. It's almost eight and he's working late, as usual. He launches straight in, doesn't bother greeting her.

'I've just had a call from someone. They've unearthed a photograph—it'll be in the papers tomorrow.' His voice sounds as it always does lately: steely, held in, as if he scarcely dares to give voice to his thoughts.

'A photograph? And? What's the problem?' The media have released a new photograph every other day, it seems to her. In the newspapers, on television, in every women's magazine that graces the checkout of the local supermarket—she could never have imagined she'd been so profligate with her image. School photos taken at Milton Central, at Arding High, receiving an award at Grammar, photographs of her in her twenties, at uni, nursing, in her thirties, with Hannah as a newborn, wearing a bikini just after Tom (her postpartum stomach stretched and soggy, her thighs maternally dimpled—what had possessed her?). Jodie could weep—every one of these older photographs was evidence of her own complacent acceptance of happiness, of contentment. How could she have not known what was approaching? Her former insouciance seems almost obscene, offensive. Recent photos seem more real—snapped without warning or permission, her face drawn, grim, in one her arm thrown up in an attempt to shield herself from the intrusive gaze of the camera. What more can they show of her? Surely there's nothing left?

But there is something else, it seems: the image of a moment she'd forgotten.

'It's a snap of you and the baby, Jodie.'

'The baby?' she begins stupidly. 'But they've already published those awful pictures after Tom—'

'Of her. Of Elsa Mary.' She can almost hear his teeth clench on her name. 'It was taken in the hospital. Someone who was there when you were and took a photo. They've obviously sold it to the papers.'

'Oh, God.'

'It's not good, Jodes.'

'What do you mean, not good?' Suddenly, she gives a hard laugh. 'How can it be worse than it already is?'

'It's the expression on your face.' Now she can hear the sympathy in his voice, evidence of his residual tenderness. 'You look ... I don't know what to say, Jodie. You don't look like yourself. Everyone knows it's not the best time to take pictures of a new mother—it was probably just hours after you'd had the baby, for Christ's sake; you would have been exhausted, overwhelmed. I can remember what it was like when you had Hannah. But you're looking down at the baby, in this shot—and your expression ... it's ... you're ...'

'What? What on earth am I doing?'

'Well, it's not a loving expression. It's probably just the camera angle—you know what it's like—but you're scowling. You look angry. And the media are running with this, they've pulled out all the stops this time. They've homed right in on your face, you know, blown it up. And they're saying—'

'Oh God, Angus.' She can hear the panic in his voice now, the fear. 'What are they saying?'

'They're saying it's the face of a murderer.'

DECEMBER, 1986

The maternity ward boasts a recently refurbished sitting room for new mothers. It's a friendly space, decorated in bright primary colours, with a tea- and toast-making station, a huge pile of women's magazines (along with the ubiquitous baby-care and breast-feeding guides), a number of comfortable vinyl-clad lounge chairs, and a big wall-mounted television. Most of the new mothers shuffle in a couple of times a day—usually when their babies are asleep—to have a cuppa, a chat with fellow-sufferers, some to have a surreptitious cigarette on the balcony or to spend some time with their other small children, away from the babies.

It's not a place that Jodie frequents—other than to hurriedly prepare a cup of coffee or tea, or, starving again, to take a handful of the cheap biscuits they've provided. But the new young midwife, Debbie, taking advantage of Sheila's morning absence, insists that Jodie join in for a special talk on baby care that she's giving—early, before visiting hours. Following Sheila's advice that she make as few waves as possible where Debbie is concerned, Jodie reluctantly makes her way down and seats herself in one of the slippery, armless chairs. She had hoped to get out of it, to be excused; the baby had been wheeled down from the nursery by an overworked midwife, needed changing and feeding before she could reasonably be sent back, but Debbie had called into her room on her way down the corridor, had pooh-poohed her objections, insisted that she attend.

'Bring the bottle and feed her there,' she'd said. 'It doesn't matter—this is a maternity ward, you know. It'll give you an opportunity to have a gasbag with some of the other mothers.' And then she'd taken the matter out of Jodie's hands, finishing the nappy change herself and wheeling the crib along the corridor, so that Jodie had no choice but to follow along in the woman's determinedly cheery wake, clutching the half-warmed bottle, still in her pyjamas, her hair unbrushed, silently cursing.

She sits through the talk, barely listening, but relaxed, the baby taking the bottle easily for once, without any tussling or fidgeting, and then falling contentedly straight back into sleep on her lap. Debbie rattles off her piece, then answers the women's anxious questions. Though the talk itself covered topics as diverse as supplementary feeding and the developmental benefits of reading aloud to your newborn, most of the women's questions are to do with ways of persuading their babies to sleep: techniques for wrapping, the efficacy of burping, of rocking to sleep, all of them vaguely desperate already to find a way back into this once taken-for-granted state of unconsciousness.

When the questions peter out and the talk officially winds up, most of the women, their infants momentarily content, stay seated, chatting about this or that—comparing births, babies, breasts, rooms. They are friendly enough, though distracted, and obviously exhausted, with a hollow, unreflecting look in their eyes. It's a look Jodie has noticed during her pracs in the eyes of people who have undergone major trauma—death rather than birth—and a look she supposes she has herself. Jodie would prefer to get back to her room, to be alone, but the prospect of disturbing the sleeping baby is worse than the unwanted contact.

One of the mothers, only a little older than Jodie, peers down at the sleeping baby. 'What a cutie. So tiny. A girl?' The woman's voice is gravelly, her accent broad.

'Uh-huh.'

'Mine's a monster—nine pound six. He nearly tore me to shreds on the way out, the little bugger.'

'Oh.' She has no intention of swapping birth stories, would rather not speak at all, but the woman persists.

'It lasted almost eighteen hours. I couldn't believe that it went on for so long—if someone had offered to shoot me in the head I'd have said do it! And then—he got stuck right at the end—literally! I've got stitches from arsehole to breakfast time ...'

Jodie can't repress a bark of laughter.

'So, how was yours?'

'Oh, you know ... Horrible.' It's not something she wants to recall, let alone discuss.

'Amazes me that the human race keeps going—that anyone ever does this twice! Still, it's all worth it in the end, isn't it?' The woman smiles tenderly down at Jodie's baby lying so content-edly on her lap. Half unwillingly, Jodie follows her gaze.

She's spared making any reply—there's a dazzling flash from a camera, and Jodie looks up, startled and annoyed.

Debbie laughs, her bright eyes mischievous, a little instant camera swinging from her wrist. 'I'm just taking a few happy snaps. I really want to remember all this—you're my first lot, you know. It was a lovely moment, Jodie; it'll be a wonderful mother and babe shot—you were looking right down at her with such a loving expression. Perfect.' She gives a satisfied smile.

The other woman snorts. 'I've never understood anyone wanting a photo taken just after they've had a baby. I can un-derstand taking a photo of the newborn, but the mother? *Ugh.* My skin's turned to shit, my face is puffy, and I'm still twenty pounds overweight—at least.' She pushes at her belly. 'I'm hoping there's another baby in here somewhere, to tell you the truth.' She gives Jodie the once-over. 'You don't look too bad, though, considering.'

'She looks great, doesn't she?' Debbie has perched on the vacant seat beside Jodie, is absently stroking the baby's cheek. 'If I hadn't seen it for myself, I'd be wondering if this was really her baby, if she'd actually given birth at all.'

When she opens the envelope—a big manilla sleeve that she assumes contains something official—the cutting falls face up onto the table. If she'd had any idea of its contents she would have tossed it away without a second thought, but now the image is there in front of her, stark and unavoidable.

It is indeed an unflattering shot of Jodie—as Angus told her, she is frowning down at the baby, her face puffy, her lips curled strangely in a not-quite sneer, thin and slightly cruel. Just an odd moment, meaningless—she looks unattractive, it's true, and older than her nineteen years—and it's certainly not a Hallmark image of rapturous motherhood. But it's surely not deserving of the 'Face of a Murderess' headline, either. The bold accusation turns her stomach, makes her gasp in sudden terror, though she barely glances at it, has steeled herself against its meaning, willed herself impervious.

The picture of the baby is another matter, though—Jodie can barely take her eyes off the grainy image. For years she has managed to keep all thoughts of the infant from her conscious mind, insisting to herself that this baby meant nothing, changed nothing—that her birth was little more than a minor knot in an otherwise smooth progression to adulthood. There has been little suffering on Jodie's part, other than in those first few weeks after the birth—no remorse, no real sense of loss or wondering why or where or what might have been. As with all the other things she has managed to bury, somehow she has managed to sweep this too into some dark recess, to bury it and just get on with things.

Her unconscious mind, however, is something else altogether. Once or twice in those first years she had woken with the distinct feel of that tiny burden in her arms, or still kicking safely within her body, or with the sharp awareness of a dream in which she's observing a strangely familiar toddler, attended by devoted parents, playing happily on a swing. A few times there'd been a very different sort of dream—one she could not or would not recall—and she had woken overcome by inexpressible, unbearable sadness.

After she'd had Hannah those particular dreams had stopped, but during those first few months of her new, ecstatically welcomed baby's life, Jodie had experienced an odd sense of loss. She had felt obscurely bereft—filled with incomprehensible longing. She had tried to dismiss it, had put it down to missing the physical sensation of being pregnant, which she'd heard was not uncommon. Luckily, this vague malaise had not lingered too long, had been quickly supplanted by the other more positive sensations.

She had been unable to feed Hannah or Tom herself. The irony of it was something else she did not let herself consider too closely—her young breasts had been so full, so clearly able to fulfil their maternal function, and yet were so determinedly withheld from that first hungry little mouth. And then the physical distress of that withholding—the tender, rock-like breasts, the weeks of leaking, of mess. She had been so set on feeding her other babies, desperate to do the right thing, the best thing, but the milk was no longer there for the taking. Regardless of all the pinching and prodding, the cracked and bleeding nipples, the endless rounds of lactation consultants, doctors, midwives—her body would not cooperate.

Gazing down at the tiny indistinct figure of the infant in the photo, all of a sudden she wants to remember this lost child. With this unforeseen proof of her existence, Jodie recognises, for the first time, the full weight of her lost daughter's being, her humanity—this little person, entire and perfect and wholly separate to her. But still she remembers nothing. Whatever vague recall she'd once had of those features has completely dissolved—she'd deliberately not allowed a picture of the baby's features to lodge in her memory, had worked hard to not preserve her image. She can only recall Tom and Hannah: their cherubic features, and solid energetic limbs, their unmistakable resemblance to Angus—dark hair, dark skin, full lips—their unassailable connection to her.

This other baby had been only six pounds, she remembers: small, pale. Her limbs had seemed delicate—frighteningly frail, alien—whereas the other two had been robust, vital—and known, somehow familiar. Hers. She wonders now whether her impression of the fragility of that baby had merely been a reflection of Jodie's own emotional state, a consequence of her not being anchored securely to Jodie's consciousness.

In the newspaper photograph the baby's face is barely visible, swaddled in a rug despite the summer heat; she can just make out her small, bunched-up features—dark creases for eyes, nose, mouth, like a cartoon character. A tuft of hair—impossible to know the colouring. Just a baby, like any other baby: utterly unfamiliar.

She wonders if Debbie remembers more. It seems impossible amongst all those births, over all those years, that she would really retain a distinct memory of just one baby. But she had remembered Jodie herself, so perhaps she would be able to recall the colour of hair, of eyes, the shape of Elsa Mary's limbs, the weight of her head in the palm of a hand. But there is no way Jodie can ask her; no way she can admit to not recalling, to never noticing. At least some things have been recorded— the baby's weight, length, head circumference—but this small, blurred snap is the only record of her image. And however hard she tries, there is nothing it can tell her; nothing it will reveal.

22

Every Tuesday fortnight, Angus takes an early afternoon to play nine holes with Dave. With both men being so busy, it is often their only weekday encounter with sunshine, the outdoors. Their first few meetings after the dinner party disaster are distinctly uncomfortable, the golf played in almost total silence, and they plead subsequent engagements, not staying for the usual round of drinks. But though the evening is never again referred to—and there are no further invitations from either party—the men's relationship gradually resumes its former laidback character. And soon enough they're back to having their customary post-golf drink at the clubhouse—not the most modish watering hole in Arding, but as good a place as any to while away an hour or so, to enjoy the cheap beer, the easy banter of long-established friendship.

This afternoon Angus has enjoyed himself. He likes to think he is a reasonable golfer—coming at the top of the local competitions once or twice before his working and family life became so all-consuming. Today he played well, a return to form that he had thought lost over the past months. The two men discuss the game over the first drink, then move on to work for the second, both complaining about the constant pressure, the lack of time spent doing things they enjoy.

'I guess with everything that's going on with Jodie, you've got even less time.' David hesitates. 'I hope you don't mind me mentioning it, mate, it's just ... well, you being in the field, a lawyer—it must be hard to switch off, to not look at all the angles, see all the possibilities ...' He falters again, and sips his beer nervously.

'Actually, it's not as hard as you might think,' Angus lies. 'All the media stuff's a bit dire, but other than that I guess I'm not really that concerned. We've got Pete handling all the legal business, anyway. It's not my area.'

'And are things okay? With you and Jodie, I mean. It must be taking a toll?'

Angus is surprised by his friend's continued efforts to discuss what's previously been so carefully avoided. Although suspicious that Dave's been primed by his curious wife, this time he responds honestly, if tangentially. 'Well, I'm just so bloody busy at work—we barely see one another.'

'But when you do? Things must have changed. I can't imagine something this big happening to me and Sue without it becoming world war bloody three. It's bad enough as it is—all those bloody female hormones floating around our place.'

Angus gives a commiserating laugh, tries again to deflect the conversation. 'Yeah. Well, I know what you mean—teenage daughters, eh? Somebody should have warned us.'

But Dave's determined. 'But how are you coping with all the stuff that's being said? All that shit with her mother must have hurt.'

'That old bitch.' Angus dismisses his mother-in-law with a gulp of beer. 'Anything she's said publicly has already been said to Jodie's face. And I guess the important people, Jodie's family, her friends,' here he pauses a fraction, 'know who she is, what she's like. They know what sort of a person she is.'

'I can't imagine what it must be like—for you. I mean, all that publicity. I saw that other television interview—the one last week. With Jodie. Jesus.'

'I imagine everyone in Arding saw it.' Wryly. 'But it wasn't that hard. She really just reiterated her statement, answered a few questions. We'd asked them to come, so it was on our terms. They had to be polite.'

'Still. I dunno how you can stand it—the intrusion. And it must make you wonder.'

'Wonder what, Dave?'

But Dave ignores the question, continues, his voice slurring a little. 'And you really seem like you're doing all right. You're saying all the right things, anyway. I gotta say I admire you, mate.'

'What do you mean?' Angus is more curious than irritated, wonders how far his sodden mate will go, where his next conversational lurch will take them.

'I wouldn't want to be in your shoes, Angus. If it was Sue, I think I'd want to cut and run. But I guess we both signed up for better or for worse, eh, and worse is going to arrive sometime. You just don't get to pick and choose when, or how.' He claps his hand on Angus's shoulder, gives it a friendly squeeze. 'And you and Jodie have been together so long.' He lowers his voice, speaks almost conspiratorially. 'And you've already done the dirty on her—which I have to say I admire too, mate. Always wish I'd been brave enough. But you know Sue—she's a bit different to Jodes. She'd have killed me.'

Angus tries to interrupt the flow, but Dave is unstoppable.

'Y'know, Angus, I've been thinking about it, and I reckon you shoulda got out when you had a chance, Angus. You're over the hill now, mate: your hair's grey, your dick's shrivelled, your stomach's soft. You might've been a player once, but no bird'd look at you twice these days. You may as well stick with Jodie.' He gives a hiccough, adds thoughtfully: 'And you know something? If you tell yourself you love her often enough, it feels like the truth eventually.'

Angus knows that his friend's boozy confidences have far more to do with Dave's own marriage than with Angus's relationship with Jodie. Still, he can't help but wonder how much of what Dave has said applies to him, too. He is conscious of time passing, of course, how can he not be? He is keenly alert to the dispiriting advance of middle age, his own inevitable physical decline. And accompanying this, the shrinking of possibility, the excruciating awareness of unused potential. Even now—or is it especially now?—it prompts the unthinkable questions: Would he change things if he could go back in time? And if he could go back, what would he do?

When Jodie reveals his mother's treachery, that day under the willow, Angus falls in love. His shame and fury at Helen's outrageous interference is inextricably bound up in this renewed passion for Jodie, who has surely proved her love for him in the most profound way. In an instant, his plans to make a comprehensive sexual survey are discarded, forgotten: Jodie is the most remarkable girl he knows, could ever hope to know, not only beautiful and clever, she is like a knight from a medieval fable, or a saint, perhaps, never wavering in her loyalty, her devotion. To him.

Crazily, wonderfully, Angus proposes to her then and there—and crazily, wonderfully, Jodie accepts. They keep the engagement secret, from their friends as well as family, knowing that they will encounter only disapproval, disbelief.

Both Angus and Jodie enjoy the forbidden flavour of their romance, revel in its illicitness. Angus does not understand, at eighteen, how secure these ties of obligation really are, and how difficult to break. He does not realise—at eighteen—how very young he is.

His first affair—if it can really be termed an affair at that age— is almost accidental. His mother, panicked by his continued pursuit of Jodie, suggests he take a working gap year, secures him a clerkship in a London legal firm. Though he's well aware of her motives, he decides to take up the offer to see a bit of the world, broaden his prospects. He defers university and bids an emotional farewell to Jodie. 'It's only a year,' he reassures her. 'And in the long run it'll be worth it, for both of us.'

Angus works hard—commits himself to learning (and earning) as much as he can, knowing that he has been given an incredible opportunity, figuring that observing the workings of a real law firm will confirm his own direction and provide him with an understanding that will stand him in good stead in his career. He starts work early, stays late, goes so far above and beyond his duties that he barely leaves himself any time to really experience London, or get to know either of his flatmates: his putative landlord, Martin (a distant cousin, independently wealthy), seems perfectly happy to keep the dull colonial at a distance; the other, Amelia, an Arts undergraduate, is almost an invisible presence, so rarely do the two meet—the only evidence of her domicile the occasional jug of daisies in the kitchen, the damp underwear left hanging on the back of the bathroom door.

It isn't until a near disaster just outside the flat that they are thrown together. Angus is walking home from the Tube just past seven on a Friday evening. He had been invited out for drinks by colleagues, but declined, not for the first time, instead making copies of several cases that are of particular interest, taking them home to read. He rounds the corner, walking briskly across the road directly in front of their flat—a Georgian conversion in not-yet-trendy Notting Hill—when he sees a car careen through the lights, then skid on the damp congested road, and swerve as if in slow motion straight towards him. Angus has to throw himself out of the car's way to avoid being hit—a feat which he manages to pull off with only centimetres and seconds to spare. The car swerves back into the traffic with a screech, but Angus lies on the footpath for a few moments, dazed, while a crowd of helpers gather about him. They are a rather indecisive lot—no one thinks to call an ambulance, rather they check that he is alive and relatively unharmed—one taking his pulse, another putting him into the recovery position, then helping him to sit up when it is evident that he is intact and quite conscious. There are a few minutes of hemming and hawing and then they all drift off to their own important Friday night engagements, leaving Angus still sprawled in the middle of the footpath, grazed and bruised and utterly shocked.

He would have continued to sit there indefinitely had Amelia not chanced upon him as she was leaving the flat.

Angus is unable to give a coherent account of his being there, clutching his briefcase, his legs bent oddly, his pinstripe blazer torn, tie askew, trousers damp and muddied, and Amelia immediately takes charge. Having ascertained that there has been no serious damage, she enlists two amiably pissed and hefty passers-by to help him up and half drag, half carry Angus—who protests weakly that he is in fact fine, can manage himself, thanks anyway—up the stairs to the flat, where they dump him unceremoniously on the lounge. He sits, stunned and blinking, while Amelia brings him whisky, then sets about tending his wounds in a brisk, matter-of-fact way: helping him out of his damaged blazer, rolling up his sleeves and trouser legs to inspect the damage on his forearms, shins and knees, swiping the grazes gently with diluted antiseptic.

After his second glass of whisky Angus begins to feel less dazed, and though the sting and throb of his wounds is suddenly evident, he finds himself oddly comfortable, in what is by any definition a rather peculiar situation—he is lying prone on the settee, with an almost unknown but extremely pretty (in an understated English way) girl fiercely concentrating on tending him in an extraordinarily intimate fashion. While she unbuttons his shirt, unbuckles his pants, wipes and rinses and pats and rubs and bandages with cool gentle fingers, Angus lies silently, the warmth rising from his feet through to the tips of his fingers, feeling the almost forgotten pleasure of an erection.

Amelia barely speaks all through her ministrations, merely murmuring and tutting, apologising softly in the face of his occasional gasp of pain, but when finally he is cleaned and bandaged to her satisfaction, she sits down on the settee with a sigh, giving him a slow grin.

'Well,' she says, her smile made incredibly sexy by the gap between her two front teeth, 'there you go. My Girl Guide first-aid badge came in handy after all. Don't know what Brown Owl would say about the whisky, though. I don't think that was on the list of approved remedies. I could do with one myself now.' But she stays beside him on the lounge, leaning back and folding her arms. 'Now tell me, Angus, what on earth happened to you?'

His voice is rickety, the story coming in weird little spasms—a rush and a pause, mimicking his heartbeat—but for once he isn't worried about sounding stupid, sounding less intelligent than he really is. And Amelia, who has poured herself a whisky and wriggled out of her trench coat, having apparently given up whatever plans she had previously made, relaxes beside him, asking the occasional question, looking appreciatively appalled, satisfyingly concerned. And for the first time, Angus realises, he is talking to an English person without feeling conscious of being Australian—raw, uncultured, boorish. In his bombed-out state he is incapable of minimising his accent, changing his utterances, reconfiguring his body language from its open Australian looseness to mirror his more rigid British counterparts. Angus notices that he is sitting as he would sit at home, letting his knees hang wide, sprawling, shoulders slumping, stomach muscles unclenching—letting that old upper lip go soft, he guesses—and it has something to do with Amelia.

It's not long before their conversation, too, takes twists and turns and dives that he hasn't experienced since he's been away—and very soon they've ordered an Indian meal from the local takeaway, and are sharing their second bottle of wine— the first having been polished off soon after the whisky.

She's easy to be with, Amelia—interested and articulate. She's a country girl, from a village just outside Worcester, and is finding it difficult, she says, to get used to London. She's come up to study history—although she'd initially been accepted into the local regional university, she'd thought it might be fun to come to the city instead. But it's not fun at all. Although the university course is just what she'd wanted, and she's doing well, she's lonely, hasn't really made friends, feels hideously rural, dull—not up to scratch. All the other girls in her classes seem faster, brasher, cleverer—and they're all happily ensconced in their own social worlds, already connected. And whatever hopes she'd had of creating some sort of cosy alternative home life have been dashed—with both Martin and Angus out most of the time and neither of them much inclined toward social-ising anyway. She has a few friends who've made their way to London for work, study, but their occasional meetings (she'd been heading to one this evening, but was more than pleased to have an excuse to call it off) have grown more and more strained as their lives, and points of commonality, drift further and fur-ther apart. She is, she tells him with a resigned shrug, seriously thinking of calling it quits, heading back home, starting again at the local university. Maybe London life just isn't for her. And she misses her parents, her siblings (four of them) and their small dairy farm more than she likes to admit—she'd been so desperate to leave—and now, she says with a wry shake of her head, all she wants is to be back there again.

Angus finds himself reciprocating, telling her how he's out of his depth in the practice, how he's working like a madman so that no one will notice that he hasn't a clue what he's doing. He tells her—and it's not something he's even admitted to himself, really—that he's not even sure that he wants to do law, that it's just what's expected of him, there hasn't really been a choice.

And then he's telling her, hesitantly at first, about Jodie, about his mother's proposition, their illicit engagement.

'You're kidding!' Amelia appears satisfyingly shocked by his confession. 'But you're way too young. You can't make that sort of decision at this age. That's crazy. It's too early. You could end up married to someone you don't really—' She hesitates. 'I'm sorry. I'm making a big assumption here. It's only that ... Do you actually love her, Angus? Are you missing her, being here?'

'I don't know.' He answers before he thinks, and is shocked by this unexpected admission of doubt—quickly tries to qual-ify it. 'Well, what I mean is ... I do love Jodie, definitely, yes. I love her. But I'm so busy here—I haven't had a moment to miss anybody really.'

The girl's scepticism is obvious. 'You don't actually sound all that definite, Angus. I'm busy too, but I know I'm missing home. That sounds like rubbish.'

Angus shrugs, and reaches out for the wine bottle, fills his glass, then hers.

'Yeah, you're right. I don't know really. I don't know what I think about anything, right now.' He takes a sip. 'To be honest, what I'd like to do is just stay here, forever.'

'What, stay in England? Working your guts out? Doesn't sound like much fun to me.'

'It's not that—I don't mind the work.' He fumbles to find what it is that he means—it's something he's working out now, as he speaks. 'It's just that here, I don't have to *be* anyone ... No one here expects anything of me. I'm just this kind of ... organism, going through life, soaking things up. Nobody has any expectations of me. There's nothing to prove.'

She sounds puzzled. 'But I'd have thought you'd have a lot to prove. All the stuff you're learning, being in a new place, being Australian.'

'Yeah. There's that. But in a way, that's not about me. I don't have to be ... nothing's personal. I don't have to be that person everyone wants me to be, the person I've been all my life. You know—you're from a small town. I'm good old Angus Garrow, always reliable, always doing the right thing. If I go to work here and I'm an absolute arsehole, it almost doesn't mean anything. *I* don't mean anything.'

'But that's exactly what I hate about being here! I hate being invisible. No one knows me, no one cares what I do. It's like here, I don't exist. Like nothing I do touches anyone.' Amelia sounds miserable all of a sudden, close to tears. Angus moves closer, pats her awkwardly on the knee.

'Hey, it's okay. I've met you now. You're not invisible to me.'

She wipes her eyes angrily. 'Oh, it's stupid, isn't it? I thought it would be *sooo* bloody fantastic. You know, you have all those ideas and dreams about university, about making it in the big city—it's something you've waited for all your life. You're grown up and you don't have to do anything you don't want to do and you can make all your own decisions, go where you want, when you want, with whoever you want. But there's no one I want to see, no one to go anywhere with. I go to uni, I hand in my essays, I go to the library, I see all these people hanging out—they all seem to know one another, have places to go. But me, I feel like I'm pretending. I just want to go back home, and wake up in the morning to the sounds of my little sister and brother racing around the house, my mum yelling at me to get up and get ready for school. Everything I was desperate to get away from. God, I'm sorry.' Suddenly she's attempting a grin. 'You've just been practically knocked over by a car, and here I am, moaning. Just ignore me—it's the wine talking. *Wine-ing.*'

Angus thinks for a moment. 'Hey, listen. Why don't we go out to one of those places you always wanted to go—and there are all the places I really wanted to go to, too, before I actually got here. What about a club—we could listen to some music. Is there a show you want to see?'

'Oh, but I'm completely broke,' she says doubtfully, 'and you've had a bit of a shock, you're not really in any state to go out.'

'I've got tons of cash, so it'll be my pleasure. I've barely spent anything since I've been here.' He gives a regretful smile. 'But you're right—not tonight. I am too sore. And to be honest, I'm probably too pissed.'

She touches his knee gently. 'You should probably have a bath and go to bed. You're going to be really sore tomorrow.'

He can feel his erection return, captures her hand beneath his. 'Actually,' his voice catches in his throat, 'a bath is exactly what I need. But I think,' his voice creaky, almost apologetic, he moves her unresisting hand further up his thigh, 'I think I might need some help with that. Maybe you could ...'

She moves closer, he can hear her breathing, fast and shallow, her other hand slips around his waist, under his shirt, her fingers warm this time across his chest. 'I could,' she says. 'Whatever you need, just say.'

It's an odd affair, not an affair of passion for either of them, or so it seems to Angus, but one of mutual need—two lonely transiting souls needing companionship for a few months: a warm body to share a bed, a warm heart to share the occasional bottle of wine, film, trip to the theatre, dance, visit to an art gallery. The inevitability of the relationship's end—it is limited from the start by Angus's necessary return home—doesn't make the whole thing any more urgent or desperate, rather the opposite; they both seem to take a certain pleasure in the temporary nature of the affair.

In the end, it's all over well before Angus's departure—and just weeks before Jodie's surprise appearance—when Amelia returns home to Dorset after her second-term holiday, taking a job as a residential tutor at a local boarding school, deferring her studies until the following year.

Angus misses Amelia far more than he imagined possible. He hasn't heard from her at all—was informed by a bemused Martin of her decision—and spends several weeks working hard, staying back ever later at the office, giving himself as little spare time as possible, anxious to avoid the nagging sense of loss he feels whenever he's at home alone. He resists for weeks the temptation to call and speak to her on the phone, but finds himself hoping, every day, for some word of or from her—a postcard, a phone message. But there is nothing. It isn't until he overhears Martin, on the phone to some friend, mention that he's met up with Amelia's brother, who's told him that Amelia is on the mend, that he has even the faintest inkling that the affair might have meant more to Amelia than to him, and that she'd sensibly taken herself away to avoid getting in any deeper.

He is stricken—and wonders at his own stupidity: of course, this terrible hollowness that he's been feeling, that he thought was merely boredom, or overwork, is the result of missing her, missing Amelia. He determines to see her again—plans a trip into Dorset, has gone so far as to book a room (always hopeful—a double) in a pub near her school, has prepared in his mind a sort of speech, a conversation. And he has half made up his mind that he should, as Amelia—rather surprisingly, considering her reticence about matters personal—had suggested once or twice, rethink his hasty engagement. He has even attempted a 'Dear John' letter, has begun many times, but can never finish, never overcome his sense of cowardice, along with a nagging uncertainty about the real state of his feelings, the possibility that he might be mistaken, that he shouldn't be making such a decision from so far away. Anyway, it was all for nothing—Jodie arrives without warning, just a few days before his planned departure for Dorset. There is no trip, no resumption of his casual affair with Amelia—no test of whether it was in fact something stronger, something more momentous than a temporary affair.

And there is no 'goodbye' letter written to Jodie, then or ever. She stays with him during his last few weeks in London, and the almost immediate revival of Angus's old feelings for her reassure him that his initial choice has been the right one. He knows that he loves her, without any reservations, knows that she is the girl for him. And despite a few unsubtle hints from Martin, who, Angus thinks, rather fancies Jodie himself, Jodie has not the slightest idea of what has been going on.

They return to Australia as planned, move in together, finish their studies. They keep their engagement secret, and disregarding his mother's disapproval and parrying her continued attempts to keep them apart, they marry immediately after Angus finishes his degree. When he secures a position in Arding, the young couple move back, set up home, slipping easily into the town's familiar rhythms.

Even before the children come along, Angus feels himself grow solid, established, sees the pattern of his life stretching out inexorably before him. But he's not, he's never, discontent, is well aware of his good fortune—he loves his career, his kids, his wife, in this he never wavers. He rarely thinks about Amelia, but occasionally he dreams of those first moments between them—the English girl's unconditional kindness, her gentle touch—and wakes feeling inexplicably bereft, almost homesick. It's a yearning that can't be explained, can't be resisted, one that he has always been able to satisfy, up until Wanda, with a fling, an inconsequential sexual adventure. It's some sort of resistance to a life settled so early; or a reclamation, perhaps, of another love, another life, never lived.

SYDNEY MORNING HERALD
'Stepford perfection hides dark interior'
by Caro McNally

I had coffee with a couple of friends the other day, and inevitably the conversation got around to the topic *du jour*, the bizarre tale of Mrs Jodie Garrow and her long-missing child.

Like most of the nation we'd all seen the interviews and statements, gawked over the photos of the blondely pretty, impossibly preserved forty-three-year-old, watched her carefully choreographed television interview and seen snaps of that happy, happy, happy nuclear family.

We're all around her age. One of my friends worked out that she'd actually attended the same small city college at the same time as Jodie. They didn't know one another, of course: Sophia was in Communications, Jodie in the then brand-new Faculty of Nursing, but maybe they sat together at the bistro, or bumped into one another in the library queue. Who knows? We none of us knew her—and we none of us even knew anyone like her. We've all exclaimed in disbelief at her professed naiveté: how could a bright girl of our generation—and I like to think we Gen-Xers were no less savvy than teenagers now—how on earth could such a girl have got knocked up and not known about it until it was too late? And how could she go through the whole birth drama alone, without reading up a little, finding out something about the legal ramifications of adoption and so forth? It's unimaginable, and—we all agreed—frankly unbelievable.

There's something highly 'sus'—in the parlance of our long-ago youth—about the whole thing. It was easier—much easier—to believe that she'd done away with the child (and we could all imagine that grisly act; it's not all that hard to dispose of a not-quite-three-kilo, 22-inch newborn, after all, not hard to drive to a secluded spot—a dam, a river, a deserted industrial bin—to dump said child) than to believe anyone could have been so naive. We're talking about the late eighties here, not the nineteen-fifties.

Not since the Chamberlain case has the story of a missing child so gripped the Australian imagination. In case you're wondering, yes—I was too young to have really understood all the ins and the outs of the Chamberlain debacle, though I do remember (or is it just the footage from the film, masquerading as a memory?) some rather heated discussions, and the polarisation of opinion between those who wanted to shoot the dingo, and those who would have taken pleasure in shooting poor Lindy.

Not since the Chamberlain case has the nation been so galvanised, so shaken from its usual apathy and indifference. Forget about conversations around the water cooler—I've been accosted by little old ladies at the newsagents, those customarily gentle blue-rinse types on their way to bowls, or to meals-on-wheels or whatever, who practically froth at the mouth when confronted with front page pics of the woman in question.

'Just look at her,' one little old lady spat, completely without encouragement. 'So cool, so calm. Not a hair out of place. Ought to be strung up, women like that. There's women out there'd give their right arm to have a baby. Oh, that poor little mite. You hate to think what she did with it.'

There's the photographs the murderers have supplied for use in the media, no doubt to make Jodie Garrow look as mild, as respectable, as appealing, as just-one-of-us as possible. Oh, but how they've missed their mark. The one taken out the front of her—dare I use the term?—McMansion, the rendered, two-storey job that seems oddly out of place in the dignified university town of Arding. (I lived in Arding myself as a student, and chez Garrow is a far cry from the charmingly dilapidated—and utterly freezing in winter—weatherboard cottage of my student days.) Garrow is pictured standing calmly on the doorstep (the front of her 4WD just nosing its way into the viewfinder, though the sleek black Audi coupe is perfectly clear) with her arms around her teenage daughter—who provides the only jarring note with her scowl—and her young son, who's standing beside her looking positively boy-scoutish in his private-school uniform with his short back and sides, his boater. The lawyer husband (from a wealthy grazing family), handsome, tall, obviously supportive, is standing protectively behind them all.

And then there's Jodie herself—her hair neatly bobbed, glistening, the expensive jeans, the padded vest that's *de rigueur* for all good middle-class mums, the single row of pearls around her neck. She's slim, she's pretty, she's blonde; her teeth are perfectly white and even. She's the kind of woman that I—and a lot of women I know—love to hate. No doubt she's a good enough woman—a paragon of a mother (now that it suits her!), a good citizen, working at the school canteen every week, running the netball team, volunteering at the hospital once a month. But what difference does it make in the end? What difference does any of that make to the child that went missing?

In the photos her expression isn't precisely joyous—I mean she's not grinning, no one could be that silly; but she's not exactly grim, either, is she? You can't see any discomfort, any sense of having transgressed in any way, can you? She looks calm, collected, beautiful, cold. Untouched and untouchable. And that's why we're so suspicious. We get the sense that she remains unmoved by her own situation, that she'll be buffered, protected, by all that material privilege. In a way, she's representative of all that's wrong with modern Western culture, isn't she? She's got everything she needs and wants—I suppose so many of us do—but there's no questioning of her right to all these privileges. We all know what her life is like: her house is dirty, she calls a cleaner. The car engine's playing up; she can buy a new one. Her teeth aren't as good as they used to be. Well, cap 'em. Sebastian or Olivia aren't happy at one school, send 'em to another. A baby you don't want? Easy, just get rid of it.

And whatever happened to that baby all those years ago—whether or not she sold it to 'Simon and Rosemary' on the advice of poor old Matron O'Malley; or did the unmentionable, unthinkable—whatever it was that happened to that child, you can almost be certain that it's never given her a restless night's sleep, never added a single wrinkle to that smooth (botoxed?) brow.

You also have to wonder about the Garrows' very savvy manipulation of the media—what sort of people would have the nous to go to the media themselves (surely it's like inviting a vampire over the threshold)? And to offer a generous reward for information just days before the police initiate their search? These people are too clever by half, methinks. Then there's the language of Garrow's public statement: it's as brief and as uninformative as possible, every word measured. There's no way to read anything significant between those lines, because there's simply nothing there. Even in her single television interview she remains chillingly composed: there is no sense of stress or strain, no hesitation, no erring from the script in any way. Jodie Garrow's husband is a lawyer, and no doubt she's been prepped by the best, but still—you'd think there'd be a slight bursting out of emotion, even a quaver.

And then there's her excuse—that she'd been young and silly—that she'd made a mistake, a series of mistakes. Well, it's lame. Actually it's more than lame—it's a criminal misuse of language. We've all been young and silly, and we've all made mistakes.

But this wasn't just a 'mistake', Jodie. This was a baby.

23

Of all the things that have been said about her, this last should mean nothing. She should be immune by now; she has been deserted by her friends, denounced by her own mother, accused of having the face of a killer—and yet nothing has rocked her as much as this. Something in the woman's writing, her tone, has hit something raw in Jodie, something vital. Once—in some former life—that woman, that writer, Jodie can't even bear to think of her name now, had actually been someone whose writing Jodie had admired, whose opinions she'd respected. She'd once assumed they were on the same side—apparently not.

Part of her—and it's a big part of her—still wants to admire this woman. She imagines writing a letter, explaining herself, providing a little potted bio—stories from her not so straightforward life—trying to win this woman over, to have her see Jodie as she sees herself. Look, she'd like to tell her, these were my parents, my brothers, this is the house—not home—I grew up in, this was my life as a child. It's not what you assume; things were hard, I wasn't loved, I wasn't told that I was special, as you no doubt were, as so many others were. I was never told that the world was my oyster, that I could have what I wanted, if only I worked hard enough, used my brains.

She'd like to show this woman just how limited, how stunted, her expectations had been; that everything she had she'd had to fight hard for, sharpened tooth and bloodied claw, that nothing, not one thing—not her neat blonde hair, not the handsome husband, not the two-car garage in the nice suburban street—had come easily, none of this had come, as it were, naturally. She'd like an apology from the woman, like her to offer an alternative story, more sympathetic, a narrative that included not only her mistake, but some understanding of all that had led to that moment—because even now, or perhaps even more now as she ages, as she sees what a singularly diffi-cult road she'd had to travel, now she has more sympathy for that girl—so determined to succeed, so hopelessly unworldly, so desperately alone.

Another part of her would like to berate the other woman, to make her see what she can't see from her own privileged position. She'd like to make her view things differently; like to make her eat her words. She knows exactly what she looks like, the writer, though she has never met her, never even seen a photograph. She knows her type inside out—wearing all black, her hair sleek and straight, her funky IQ-enhancing spectacles, retro-reddened lips, her Camper-clad feet. She knows this woman's position in the schoolroom of yesteryear—she'd have been a popular girl, bright, cool, well-connected, well-heeled, and Jodie knows too that she'd never have been invited to this girl's birthday party, or asked to play on her team. How dare she sneer at Jodie's ideals, her yearnings; laugh at her old-fashioned string of pearls, her outfit, her dull middle-class respectability.

How she'd love to push Ms Caro McNally up to the glass and force her to look at herself, to admit to her own entrenched thoughts about privilege, to concede that if an establishment does exist, a place where the powerful and influential congre-gate, this writer is not, as she so loudly and frequently pro-claims, on the edge, a coolly observant outsider—but smack bang in the middle. She, not Jodie, is the insider.

Jodie knows—as her mother, and this woman have pointed out—that she's had to abandon one life in order to have the life she's living now. Though she recognises, when she can bear to think of it, the immensity of her youthful decisions and actions, and would change certain things if only it were possible, still she is glad of the life she has led, and would not swap it, offer it up as payment. She has imagined, frequently, the life she might have had with that child: she'd have been a single mother, her socio-economic status always low, regardless of her education, occupation; her life one of hard graft, like her own mother's—but even worse, surely, because unlike her own mother, Jodie had been capable of seeing, and desiring, those other possibilities. She'd seen what was waiting for her so clearly—the small rooms, dingy furnishing, grinding work, the bitter stink of poverty, of desperation, desolation; the regret that would colour every aspect of her diminished expectations. She'd known it was possible to live a life that was very different to the one her parents had provided her with—a life of solidity, security, prosperity. And though she knows, now she's older, that grief, sadness, bitterness, sorrow, lurk beneath the surface of all lives, that in the end, death and decay can't be avoided, there's still no denying the fact that most jagged edges can be smoothed, that money and social status can ease almost every journey, every transaction, from birth to death and all that lies between.

All Jodie wants, all she has ever wanted, is a life without grubbiness, without chaos, a life that follows a clear trajectory of progress, of achievement. Surely, she thinks, it isn't that much to ask.

2 4

It seems utterly surreal to Hannah that with all that's going on right now, somehow nothing much has actually changed. This morning before she's even out of bed, her mother comes in to deposit a pile of neatly ironed clothes on top of her television—which is the only area of clear horizontal space available, other than Hannah herself—and makes the usual request that Hannah do something about her room. Bending to pick up a discarded chocolate wrapper, she asks the gods—because what's the point in asking Hannah, who's lying there with her eyes tightly shut, feigning sleep—how it can be that Hannah has absolutely no respect for her own space, all the new furniture, the curtains, the pretty carpet, the computer, her books, her clothes. She gives a final gusty sigh, suggests her daughter get out of bed if she doesn't want to be late for school, and leaves the room. When she's gone, Hannah opens her eyes, but lies still a few minutes longer, marvelling at her mother's capacity to find the time, the energy, to give a shit about the state of Hannah's bedroom. At a time like this.

How can it be that even in these extreme circumstances—she's under investigation, possibly for murder, for fuck's sake!—how can it be that even in these completely jaw-droppingly bizarre circumstances, this woman who says she's her mother (but who knows, given her mother's crazy past, maybe Hannah belongs to someone else. She can only hope) is still keeping religiously to her pre-revelation routine? She is still jumping up every morning, walking the dog, showering, blow-drying her hair, dressing in her sensible trousers, her shirts and quilted vests, applying her foundation, her mascara, her lipstick, all before seven; then emptying the dishwasher and hanging out two loads of washing before waking Hannah and her brother promptly at 7:25 a.m. There will be a rack of warm toast ready for Hannah when she wanders downstairs; a glass of orange juice will be filled without asking. Her mother will be cheerfully cleaning or cooking or perhaps preparing their lunch boxes ... Not one aspect of her pitiful routine will have altered, not one element of the household upkeep will be slipping out of her mother's iron-willed control.

Hannah wonders, briefly, whether her mother succumbs to despair when she and her brother and father are safely out of the house, when she's alone; tries to imagine her mother curled foetally on the bed, tears sliding down her face, wailing, but dismisses this particular idea almost immediately as not being in character. And it's just possible, Hannah concludes as she slides reluctantly from her tangled, junk-strewn bed, and makes a start on her own rather complex morning routine, that her mother is now a shell, and not a person at all.

Hannah's standing in front of the mirror, naked apart from her undies, her hands under her full breasts, contemplating the effects of a combined pushing up and together, when her mother walks in again, this time bearing a collection of discarded shoes. She picks her way carefully across the room and tosses the shoes noisily into the wardrobe, without comment, never once looking Hannah's way. By the time her mother knocks over a stack of precariously piled books, then steps on a half-eaten piece of pizza that's been left on the floor, Hannah's primed for an altercation. She'd do almost anything to see a ripple in that placid surface, a crack in that armour. To find out if there's actually anything underneath.

Hannah puts her hands on her hips. 'You should knock, Mum,' she bellows. 'How many times do I have to say it. This is *my* room. Can't you read? You're always going on about respect—well, why don't you practise what you preach, try respecting *my* space for a change?'

Her mother picks the mangled pizza from her shoe and lets

it fall onto the carpet, treads around it carefully and heads for the door, then pauses, turns back. 'Hannah,' her voice is cool, unhurried, 'I really wish you'd go a little easier on the eyeliner, sweetheart. Dr Guilfoyle won't tolerate it, you know that. You'll end up on detention. And you do look a little—what's the word you girls use?—a little *skanky*, if you don't mind me mentioning it.' She smiles sweetly in her daughter's direction before heading back down the hallway.

Hannah rushes after her, livid. 'You're a cow!' she screams at the implacably retreating figure of her mother. 'Did you know that? You are Such. A. Fucking. Cow.' She sees Tom hovering, peering nervously around his bedroom door. He backs up as his sister advances on him, red-faced, topless. 'And you, you little, you little *cunt*.' She says the word loudly, deliberately. 'You better watch out. She's already murdered one kid, you know— you could be next.' She gives him a vicious little shove and he lets out a squeal, scurries back into his room.

This time she's done it. Finally, Hannah's gone too far. Her mother marches back up the hall, is there before the girl can retreat to her bedroom. She plants herself directly in front of Hannah, blocking her way, her face devoid of expression, but her eyes are cold. She draws herself up to her full height—and it's something of a surprise to Hannah, who has imagined herself to have outgrown her mother, that she's still some inches taller—then draws back her hand and slaps her, hard, right across the face. It's the first time, the only time, that Hannah has been hit by her mother.

'Don't you ever,' her mother says quietly, evenly, her eyes never leaving Hannah's face, 'use that word. Not in this house. Not in my hearing. Not ever.'

25

Jodie is quietly going mad. On the surface things at home seem to be running smoothly, the same as ever. Jodie is good—is a genius, really—at keeping up appearances. The house is as immaculate as ever, the clothes are washed and ironed and put away as efficiently as always, the evening meals as delicious and nutritious as ever, if slightly less adventurous. She is on time for any pick-ups and drop-offs that Angus can't do—though there is no lingering any more, no chatting with the other mums at the tennis court, the drama club, the swimming pool.

And Jodie looks much the same—she hasn't let herself go in any way, though her visits to the gym have been replaced by early morning walks and the occasional session of aerobics using Tom's Wii. She still has her hair done regularly—locating a hairdresser who works from home, rather than visiting her old gossipy salon. She dresses as she usually does—always neatly, conservatively. If anyone was watching—and they are, she knows that—they would not see that anything had changed. But it has. How could it not?

While he continues to be considerate and painstakingly civil, she is sure, by a flicker, a look, that Angus is angry with her. He presents only his blankest, most distant self to her now—his every word measured, every expression guarded. He smiles, he inquires after her wellbeing, but no more. And there is no physical intimacy between them now. There is no cuddling, no half-unconscious proprietary clasping of arm or shoulder, no casually slung arm around waist. They haven't, for some reason, taken that final step of sleeping separately, though why, Jodie doesn't know. There are two spare rooms, both comfortable, each with an adjoining bathroom. But every night they lie side by side, as far away from one another as they can. Their bed is oversized, so there's enough space for each to turn inwards or outwards without encountering the other—they don't touch during the night, not even an accidental roll into the middle.

She is not sure what it's about, what the source of his anger is; Angus has said nothing, has been nothing but outwardly loyal and supportive. Surely, the idea of her betrayal, so many years ago, isn't eating away at him? Perhaps it's the fact that she lied—but she's explained and he said he understood. Surely, surely he trusts her. He has no reason not to, after all. There's nothing she's said, nothing she's ever done in their long history together that could make him doubt her. She, on the other hand, has plenty of reasons to distrust him. She does not dare bring up the matter of his betrayals, of course, but she can barely restrain herself from exclaiming over the injustice of it. Whatever she has done, whatever he believes she has done, Jodie knows that she has never really betrayed Angus. That she never would.

It's true that they skirt around the reality of the situation constantly, that they only refer to what's going on when they have to, when it can't be avoided, but she has imagined that is because he is sensitive to her feelings, that he knows there are constant reminders anyway—that she does not need any more.

The madness—because what else can she call it?—begins after she rereads that McNally woman's piece online. After her first horrified scan of the article, she'd thrown away the paper, but a week or so later, having decided to conduct a somewhat less hysterical evaluation of what she now only dimly recalls, she googles the story and rereads it, an act which only confirms her initial horror and distress. And the online piece differs in one significant way—it does not terminate at the end of the article itself; instead, the piece has been opened to readers' comments, a seemingly endless stream of ill-informed but strident opinions. Despite her growing sense of disgust, she reads all of it—almost as if hypnotised. She is assaulted by the opinion of 'Bess and Annie of Newcastle' that women like her 'are the worst sort of all rich enough to think they can get away with anything she should be put in prison and the key thrown away'. And then there is 'Florence of Pittwater', who agrees with the writer that Jodie Garrow in fact 'represents the very worst of the McMansion dwelling aspirationals, with their increasingly heavy environmental footprint, their privileged private-school progeny'. Three comments discuss the probability of her having had botox (something about the position of her cheeks, and the set of her lips, in particular her forehead, which apparently isn't quite as creased as it should be). There are numerous sentimental outpourings mourning the loss of the baby: *Beautiful Elsa Mary we are thinking of you allways with jesus now. RIP.* There isn't one comment in defence of Jodie, save a suggestion that 'however clear it seems that the Garrow woman has indeed murdered her child, we should not forget that under our legal system innocence must be presumed until proven otherwise'. But the cruellest comment of all, a comment that makes her gasp aloud, has come from 'Anonymous' of Arding, NSW: 'I have known the Garrow woman for most of my life, and though she acts as if butter wouldn't melt in her mouth, she is from a rubbish family and is rubbish herself. She killed that baby. I know it. We all know it.'

She has been unable to stop returning to the site—watching mesmerised as the comments multiply, until there are more than two hundred, then three, four, five hundred posted from all over the world. The affected indignation, the condemnation, the calls to bring back the death penalty, the comparisons with those other infamous mothers of dead or missing children—all of them hard-faced bitches, all of them guilty, all of them heartless murderers who deserved their punishment, or wrongfully exonerated, protected by some powerful agent.

From there she makes the mistake of following the commenters' own links. A handful have begun 'conversations' on their personal blogs, stating their opinions, linking to the article—and then there are more comments on these blogs, more links to be followed. The snowballing effect is clearly visible: as the story moves from one blog to the next, from one discussion forum to another, from one online news site feature to a personal blog, the conversations, speculations, opinions, rants, sprays, commentary spiral endlessly, insanely. Some feature images of her, some of these are distorted or enhanced. There is one picture that has been given a radical makeover. It looks like a photo taken at a charity ball she attended a few years back—she recognises the dress, the background—but her face has been altered. All her wrinkles and creases have been removed so that her skin appears unnaturally smooth, and pale. Her eye-colour has been brightened to a strange and frightening electric blue; her lips have been thinned, made to look grim and hard; and her teeth, originally bared in an awkward smile, have somehow been lengthened until they are almost fang-like. Her hair has become a stiff brassy helmet, improbably glossy. She looks evil, like a monster from some horror movie—a counterfeit human, struggling to contain a demon.

She eventually discovers a site dedicated solely to Elsa Mary, complete with weird, sentimental, hand-drawn pictures of a baby that resembles no child she has ever seen—with ridiculously large (and tear-filled) blue eyes, round cheeks, a perfect pink rosebud mouth. Somehow it's so impossibly sweet that it's sinister. Below this is an artist's impression of what—based on the bleary photograph taken in the maternity ward (also displayed)—Elsa Mary would look like now, at twenty-four. A pale and blandly pretty woman with nondescript fair hair and some vague resemblance to Jodie herself at that age. There are the official web entries too—she comes across the missing persons site operated by the state and federal police, the Interpol bulletin, their requests for information regarding the whereabouts of the child Elsa Mary, born December 1986, at Belfield Hospital.

There is one site in particular that frightens her: jodiegarrow. com.au. Obviously maintained by someone local, it contains little commentary, just images of Jodie, Angus and the children over the years, scanned from the local paper, she imagines, and others, obviously taken recently—snapped outside their own front gate, at sporting events, while shopping; there's even one of Jodie on one of her early morning walks with Ruff. She bookmarks this site, determines to show it to Angus, have it investigated, even though she knows there is little hope of them locating the blogger in the real world, of having the posts pulled down.

This previously unexplored world of the internet both appals and compels her. She reads everything that is written, every day, googling herself, checking out every Technorati reference, and then rereads, transfixed by her own notoriety. At first she limits herself to one hour, then two—then finds she is rushing through her morning cleaning so she can spend as much time as possible in front of the computer. Soon she is spending practically the entire time the children are at school in the study—breaking only for coffee or to hang out a load of washing. She is almost shocked when she comes upon the rare dissenting view, the voice urging calm, circumspection, an end to the idle speculations, occasionally even defending her. Sometimes she can't resist commenting herself—usually something mild and unremarkable: *You should all leave this woman alone—what do you know?*

She shows nobody—not Angus, not Peter—is ashamed, not only of what is being said, but also that she has succumbed to this sad onanistic obsession. It induces nothing but a headachy disgust—a feeling of excess and indolence. Jodie has not felt quite like this since her teens, when she'd spent entire days in bed reading or watching television, moving only to surreptitiously replenish her supply of chips, chocolate, Coke, biscuits.

It is like being sucked into a looking-glass—one that offers up only the most distorted image of herself—depraved, malign, sinister. In a bizarre way it is almost comforting, as if she has already been judged for any act she might commit, past or future. And maybe what she's reading here is the truth: perhaps these nightmare versions of Jodie are revealing something that she's known all along, something rotten at the heart of her.

The one person who keeps in contact, ringing occasionally to see if she's okay, if she's holding up, is a younger woman, known vaguely from the gym, Amber. Other than attending a few exercise classes together, they really don't have anything much in common. They mix in very different circles—despite being in her mid-thirties, a single mother of three very unkempt-looking children, Amber is still very much a student, and a member of what Jodie still thinks of as Arding's hippy community, though the real hippies are long gone—penniless, but eager, clothes worn, slightly grimy, always smelling vaguely of sandalwood and onions. Jodie finds her irritating, but she appreciates the woman's concern, her persistent offers of support, even friendship.

One morning, Amber calls her early, before she's even got Tom out the door for the school bus (having given up driving him since he told her that he'd prefer it if she dropped him several blocks from their regular set-down area outside the school gates). She mentions that she has seen the report of the inquest possibility, her voice breathy and nervous, her statements lilting upwards in a way that sets Jodie's teeth on edge, then asks, a little tentatively, whether she would like to meet for coffee.

Jodie, suddenly wary, says bluntly: 'Why now?'

'Oh. What do you mean, why now?'

'I'm just not sure why you're ringing me now. If you've seen the newspapers. You must know what that means, what's likely to happen next. It's kind of you to think of me, but I've got a lot to think about and I'm not really up to socialising.'

'Oh, I just thought ... I thought you might enjoy the company?'

The woman sounds even more nervous, and Jodie feels herself bending a little—there are so few people, after all, who would voluntarily spend time with her these days.

'Look—you're quite right, it would be fun. Thanks. But I'd rather not go into town today,' she says, risking some slight vulnerability.

'Oh, no. I understand completely. You could come here?'

Jodie can sense some slight reluctance. 'My place would probably be better, I think. Easier.'

'Oh. That would be wonderful.' Jodie hears the relief. 'What day would suit you?'

'Why not today? I haven't got anything on.'

'Fantastic,' says the woman, her voice full of excitement. 'I'll bring the coffee. How do you like it?'

They sit out on the deck with their café-brewed lattes, the younger woman obviously uncomfortable, twirling her hair around one finger, constantly shifting her position on the cushions, coughing nervously before she speaks. Initially Jodie is resigned, gracious; they talk about this and that, their kids, the local schools, a recent council scandal, the outrageous price of supermarket vegetables. Amber is pleasant enough, and the company should be welcome, but Jodie finds herself irritated by every aspect of the woman—her accent, her youth, her pale plumpness, most of all by the intensity of her endlessly banal conversation. She prattles away about the most trivial things, almost at random, but there's a portentousness in her tone—as if there's something significant she wants to say, but is too afraid to say it.

Eventually Jodie loses patience, interrupts a rambling monologue about non-toxic weed-killer. 'Yes, I've heard that garlic's very effective. But I get the feeling there is something else, Amber? Something you wanted ...?'

Amber's cheeks flare, she gives a slight gasp, suffers a fit of coughing. It takes her a moment to recover, but she rallies, makes a tentative admission. 'Well, it's nothing, really. It's just that I wanted to tell you how awful I think it's been for you. And to tell you that there are a lot of people out there who don't agree with what everyone's saying.' She takes a breath, starts again, though only slightly more cogently. 'You know I'm doing a couple of units of a BA? Well, I chose a women's studies subject this term—Women and the Media? And so anyway, we were talking, you know, about the treatment of you in the press and we thought ... well, that you've really been totally victimised, objectified by the media, and—I mean, it's dreadful!' Her eyes are wide, her voice heated, full of indignation. 'It's wrong, isn't it—we all think so, anyway—the way they've taken to you, when there's not even any actual evidence. And, well, it's because you're a woman isn't it? And it's really similar to—Lindy ... um ... you know—the dingo woman?'

'You mean Lindy Chamberlain?'

'Yeah. It's exactly like that. Don't you think?'

'Well, no, I don't think there's really—'

'Not on the surface, but I mean—there was that writer who had a go at you a few weeks ago in the papers, that McNally woman. That was just so nasty, wasn't it? Really bitchy. The way she went on about your looks, about the fact that you're well off. As if that makes any difference. It's almost as if she *hopes* that you killed—' Amber stops abruptly, looking down at her feet, her cheeks and chest flushing a deep crimson.

Jodie feels some sympathy for her embarrassment; but more importantly, she suddenly feels grateful for her support—however awkwardly expressed, however dubiously come by. And the support of these other, unknown women, thinking about her kindly, sympathetically, championing her. God knows why, but it fills her with a kind of desperate cheer, some vestige of hope.

She breaks into the silence. 'Yes, well, the sisterhood isn't exactly barracking for me, is it? They seem to have forgotten about the presumption of innocence. I think you're right—I think there is something really nasty going on—there seem to be a whole lot of people out there who are really hoping that I *have* done what they think I've done. You should have a look on the web. It's a ... a viper's nest. Anyway, thank you so much for passing that on. It really helps to know that there are people out there who aren't calling for me to be locked up. I appreciate it.'

Amber looks up at her, surprised and pleased. 'Would you like to come to our book club?' She blurts the question out excitedly as if the thought has just occurred to her.

'Your book club?'

'Some friends of mine at uni, actually it's our book club—and one of our tutors, as well; she organises it, really. It's fun. We do a book a month. Something topical.'

'I don't know. I'm not really reading anything much at the moment ...'

'Oh, that won't really matter,' Amber says airily. 'Anyway, our next meeting is Friday, so you won't really have time this month. Why not come and just see if you like the group?'

It doesn't take Jodie long to make a decision—the prospect of being amongst a group of sympathetic women, even if strangers, is suddenly very appealing. 'Why not? It's not like I've got anything better to do right now, is it? And I suppose it could be a way of meeting people. Book clubs are more about connecting than books, anyway.'

She goes to the meeting that Friday evening. She has fed the children, left a plate ready for Angus, who is working and not expected back until late, cleaned the kitchen and left Tom with a strangely compliant Hannah. It's dark already; she doesn't have to worry about being seen by anyone, or having to encounter the nervous sideways glances she seems to receive from people who would have waved or smiled just a few months back. The meeting is being held at a member of the group's home, a political science academic, according to the brief bio on a website that Jodie has consulted, who is currently living on campus.

She arrives a little late, nervous; she has misread directions, taken wrong turns, then found it difficult to make out the house numbers on the ill-lit campus streets. A plump dark-haired woman opens the door, greets her, introduces herself as Jillian Stanford, ushers her into the lounge room, where a dozen or so others sit in a loose circle on an assortment of chairs and cushions. A coffee table in the centre of the room is covered with plates of food: slices, cakes, biscuits and cheeses, and there are several bottles of champagne and white wine, and as yet unfilled wine glasses. All of the women are nursing copies of a hefty paperback book, some open, some firmly closed. The conversation falters when Jodie appears in the doorway, and it seems that all the faces are raised expectantly towards her, most smiling widely, welcomingly. There's a short, but intense burst of clapping as she makes her way across the room into the only space left for her to sit—she squeezes between two middle-aged women, who look alarmingly identical, both dressed in black, both with iron-grey hair cut into slanting short-fringed bobs, both wearing steel-framed glasses, long skirts, and chunky purple lace-up boots—Doc Martens, she thinks, though none of her own acquaintances have worn them for years. Jodie looks around, half expecting to encounter someone she recognises, but other than Amber, who smiles at her encouragingly from amongst the floor cushions, they really are all strangers.

Dr Stanford waits until the applause has died down, then beams around the room, makes a short speech. 'What a wonderful, wonderful welcome. Thank you, ladies. And thank you Jodie for joining us. We're really very excited to have you here tonight. I'm hopeful that there's a great deal that you can add to our discussion.' She smiles at Jodie again, her small dark eyes almost disappearing, then waits for her to respond.

'Thank you. It's lovely to have been invited.' She hesitates. 'But I'm not really sure how I can add to the discussion. I'm afraid I haven't even read the book—in fact, I'm not even sure what it is. Amber only invited me the other day, and we decided it was probably too late, that I could start with next month's ...' She trails off, embarrassed and confused by the encouraging smiles of the other women.

'Oh.' Their host looks a little put out. 'Amber, didn't you explain to Jodie?'

Amber is in the middle of chomping on a biscuit, she swallows then gives a nervous shrug, her habitual cough. 'I, well, I thought I did? But you know how it is sometimes. Maybe I wasn't all that clear?' She takes another bite, chews vigorously.

'Well, I'm sorry, Jodie—you've obviously come here under slightly false ... I mean, of course it would be lovely if you could join our book group on a regular basis,' she gives a perfunctory beam, 'but tonight we wanted *you* here particularly—as a special guest. Occasionally we read a book by a local author and have them in to answer questions and so forth, and every now and then when we're reading something more technical, we get in an expert to enhance our understanding—usually from the university. (I always think we're so lucky to have that resource to exploit, aren't we ladies!) So when we chose our current book we immediately thought of you. We could have asked someone from the law faculty, or communications, I suppose, but we thought that a more personal perspective would be far more illuminating. I think hearing about your current experiences might add a whole other dimension to our understanding. As Jess—who's sitting next to you—has pointed out, some of the parallels are quite disturbing. The viciousness of the media coverage, in particular.' The woman falters, as if sensing the mistake, taking in Jodie's appalled silence.

All at once Jodie knows what they're reading, and understands why they've invited her here; the book sitting closed on Jess's lap comes into proper focus. She gazes down at the suddenly familiar cover, speechless. Jess pushes her copy of the book closer so that Jodie can read the title. There's a woman on the cover, her dark hair cut into an unmistakable pageboy, gazing down lovingly at a bright-eyed, bonneted infant. *Through My Eyes: The Autobiography of Lindy Chamberlain.* Jodie keeps staring down at the book, though the picture blurs; she feels her eyes prick, her throat tighten.

The room is silent; all Jodie can hear is her own harsh and ragged breathing. She can barely raise her eyes, can't focus, has to fumble for her handbag, her keys, and stands, gazing blindly about the room at the women, a couple of whom seem embarrassed now, squirming at her obvious distress.

'I'm very sorry,' her voice is thin, but steady, 'but I'd never have come if I'd known what it was you invited me here for. I'm not ... I can't. I had no idea you wanted me as a type of specimen, that you wanted my story.' She takes one last desperate look around the circle, then stumbles through the crowded, silent room, keeping her eyes down, not daring to breathe or look up until she is out of there. Jodie ignores Dr Stanford, who follows her, apologising profusely, runs through the dark to the sanctuary of her car. She drives away fast, without looking back.

She had thought that this was what she wanted: champions, supporters, people who wouldn't condemn, would try to understand. But somehow these women are almost worse than the internet haters. Despite their good intentions Jodie knows she doesn't really exist for them. She represents a theoretical point, provides an exemplar—whether of good or evil, it doesn't matter; she's nothing more than a centrepiece for their arguments, a prop.

When she arrives home, both children are in bed, and Angus has eaten and gone back to the office. She opens a bottle of red, takes it into the study. Sits down behind the computer and pours a glass, downs it quickly and pours another. Sips as she reads the latest links, clicks feverishly through older stories. She doesn't drink often, not in any significant quantity anyway, but tonight she needs the numbing effects of the alcohol. She can see now how it happens, to the Amy Winehouses, the Heath Ledgers, the Michael Jacksons—can understand why they seek the solace of drugs or alcohol or risky behaviour. Perhaps it makes no difference, really, whether they're feted or maligned, adored or abhorred—either way, they're endlessly exposed, their every action scrutinised, discussed, critiqued. They're like butterflies trapped under glass, microbes under a less than benign microscope. Separate. Isolated. Utterly alone.

The next morning Jodie sleeps in, doesn't wake until after ten, which is the latest she's slept for years. She feels horrible—her tongue thick, her eyes bleary, her head aching dully. The television is blaring, but the house is empty, the front door left unlocked. The kitchen is a mess of unwashed dishes, and Ruff is standing on the table, helping himself to leftover toast and egg. Angus must have taken Tom to cricket, and as for Hannah, Jodie has no idea—she never has any idea lately and has given up asking. She shoos the dog off the table and locks him outside, starts clearing away the chaos. Under one of the breakfast plates she finds a note written in Tom's appalling scrawl: *call Briget Sullan*, she reads, *She wants to talk to you about last nihgt.* There's a number written more carefully, though all the sevens are back to front. Deliberately, she hopes.

Bridget Sullan. The name rings no bells. *About last night*, so the call will have something to do with the meeting she'd run out of so precipitously. She would much rather not discuss last night with anyone. Christ, perhaps Bridget Sullan is a journalist with the local newspaper, who's somehow already heard about this latest humiliation, is angling for the story. The way her life is heading now, she wouldn't be surprised. She screws the paper into a ball, tosses it into the bin, starts methodically stacking the dishwasher. In some dark recess of her mind she's glad to have the distraction, a few solid hours of cleaning that will keep her away from the pull of the internet.

But the woman is persistent, calls again that evening. Jodie has finished cleaning up the dinner dishes, is about to iron the children's uniforms, has plans to bake a slice for next week's recess—though she doesn't know why she bothers; these days even Tom rarely seems to eat any of the healthy baked goods she so conscientiously provides.

Angus has gone back in to work for a few hours—it seems he has work to catch up on almost every evening. He has spent the early afternoon helping Tom with a science project, and then a few hours driving with Hannah, who has just got her learner's permit. Other than some inconsequential utterances over dinner he and Jodie have again barely exchanged two words. She picks up the ringing phone without thinking, without checking the number.

'Oh, Jodie.' It's a woman, her voice low, pleasant. 'I'm so glad you answered. It's me. Bridget O'Sullivan.' Jodie says nothing, and the woman goes on. 'I was there last night, at the book club—it was awful, wasn't it? I was so embarrassed. Not for you, but for those women. But it's so strange, you know—until you walked in I had no idea that you were you. I mean, that *you* were Jodie Garrow. This whole thing, I really had no idea. True story.'

True story ... It might be a woman's voice, but it's a voice she knows, a voice she'll remember forever—a voice she still hears in her dreams occasionally—even though she barely remembers the girl it belonged to in any real sense.

'Bridie? Bridie!' Her own voice a whisper, small and light, as if she's been swept back to the past, to her younger self. 'Oh, my God.' A catch in her throat, a half laugh, half cry, of relief, of sudden, unreasonable hope. 'Bridie. Is that really you?'

It is without doubt the same Bridie. She arrives for morning tea the next day, bearing gifts: dandelion tea (good for stress), milk fresh from the cow, a basket of wizened apples (excellent for pies) and, most bizarrely, a two-dollar bag of mixed lollies (heaps of cobbers)—which are all for them, she insists, and not to be shared with the kids. There is no time for awkwardness: Bridie envelops Jodie in a fierce hug, then draws back to take a good look at her face.

'My God, you wouldn't believe how often I've thought about you!' She looks about inquisitively, adds: 'So, it looks like you got your wish. You got your station wagon. Your rich husband. Your ordinary life!' She grins, her bright eyes almost disappearing in a mass of wrinkles.

'God, you remembered! I can't believe I actually said that. But yes, I suppose I did. Not quite ordinary, though,' she adds drily. 'Not any more.'

Jodie hadn't recognised her old friend at the book group, but now, seated across from her, she's unmistakably Bridie. She's still tiny, only just five foot, and thin, but still sinewy, athletic looking. Her face has thinned out, the features matured, a network of fine lines creasing her eyes and cheeks—but her eyes are still fringed by those huge dark lashes, her smile is still wide and wild.

Jodie gazes at her. 'It's unreal, isn't it? You. Us. Meeting again.'

'It was unreal seeing you first in that weird situation the other night. I'd been invited by my neighbour—d'you know Jenna Robards? She's something at the uni, women's studies, maybe?—but I really had no idea what was going on.'

'*True story.*'

'No, really I had no idea. I thought it was just a run of the mill book club—not a bunch of mad femmos, looking for a cause.' She shrugs apologetically. 'If I'd known ...'

'Oh, don't apologise. I'm quite a celebrity these days. The weird thing is that none of my old friends wants to know me, while all these people I've never had anything to do with are suddenly eager to hear my tale.'

'You know, I've barely followed your story. It's not really my thing, I was only vaguely interested because it was local, you know how it is. But it had never occurred to me that it was *you*. I mean, I looked at the pictures, I suppose, and it's not that you've changed all that much. Well, not close up, not really.' She grins, raises an eyebrow, adds with a laugh: 'True story. Anyway, I've been meaning to find out about you since I got up here—find out if you were still around, or where you'd gone. I knew someone would know. I just hadn't got around to it, and it seemed a bit presumptuous too, I guess. I didn't know if you'd even remember me.'

'And I do. *Definitely.*' They grin at one another again, the lame joke somehow endlessly amusing. 'It's wonderful—it's just amazingly wonderful to see you! I can't quite believe it.' She's strangely unembarrassed by her own gushiness. 'And how did you get here? Obviously you know all about me, or as much as everybody around here knows—but what have you been doing? What's happened in your life?' Even as she asks, the strangeness of the question is clear—it's too big, impossible to answer, and it's too intimate, too—not the way Jodie usually addresses other women, even friends. But Bridie doesn't seem perturbed. She gives a short, hard laugh.

'Well, to answer your first question—and all of them, really—I got here in a very roundabout way. Although that'd be putting it more kindly than the reality. It's been the usual thing. To start with I had a totally fucked-up adolescence—too many drugs, too many bad boys—but what would you expect, with a childhood like mine?'

'Did you ... this probably seems really stupid, but did you end up doing gymnastics? You were so talented, so determined—I always thought I'd see your name in the Olympic team or something.'

'Gymnastics? Oh my God—was that my fantasy then? Oh, how funny. I haven't thought about it for years! Nah. I probably nagged at Mum for a while to go to lessons or whatever, same as I nagged to learn the piano, take up horse-riding. But there was no point. We were never anywhere long enough to do anything, really. Except get into trouble. When I finally took off on my own I was always at the fringes of the arty crowd—the same crowd my mother hung in, I suppose. You know, would-be writers, artists, musicians, actors. I dabbled in everything a bit, but never really had any focus. It was more the scene that I was into than the art—drugs, booze, unrequited love. You know the score.'

It's not a score that Jodie's ever been familiar with, but she nods, smiles. 'But now? You're an artist now?'

'Yeah.' Bridie's long fingers plait and unplait the fringe of a cushion. 'Trying to be, anyway. I'm just trying to grow up, really. I had a baby, a daughter—Iris—when I was in my late twenties. Having her made me rethink everything. I wanted a straighter sort of life. Settled, you know. Not quite what you have—I didn't want a station wagon, although a rich husband might have come in handy.' Her warm smile takes the sting out of her words. 'I was on my own, didn't tell the father. Anyway, I got into art school in Melbourne, Mum gave me a reasonable allowance—she'd gone pretty straight herself, married a doctor eventually. My God, our little sister—she was born just after we met—even went to a bloody private school! Anyway, I went and set up a little place, rented a studio, worked hard. Had a few fantastic successful happy years.'

'And then?' Jodie asks the question gently, though she can intuit what's coming, understands suddenly the look of weariness in her friend's face.

'And then Iris died.'

'Oh, no. *No.* God, Bridie, I'm so sorry.'

'It's okay. Well, no, it's not okay. It won't ever be okay.' She pauses. 'But it was years ago. I'm getting used to it, I suppose.'

'What happened? To Iris.'

'It was—well, I could give you the precise medical diagnosis—but let's just say it was a very fast and fatal form of cancer. She was diagnosed when she was three and a half and didn't make it to her fourth birthday. She'd have been ten now. So it was a while back.'

'Oh, it's ... it's ...' Jodie falters.

'Yeah. It's unimaginable, isn't it? When it first happened I thought that I was living in some sort of nightmare, that eventually I'd have to wake up and everything would be the same. Now it's the opposite,' she says. 'Sometimes I think I just dreamed up her whole little life—and that entire wonderful part of *my* life. Anyway. So I've come up here with my partner, Glenys.' A split-second pause. 'She's an artist, a sculptor. Just like poor

Mum always fancied herself. Funny, eh? We wanted to move away from the city. Glenys has two young kids, and it's a better life. You know—we can grow vegies, bake, live simply. And I always had really good memories of Milton. I think it was the happiest time I ever had as a kid. And it turns out that it's the perfect place for people like us. Houses are cheap and there's a bit of a community, you've probably noticed. Somebody told me it's got the highest concentration of gay couples outside the metro area in Australia. Who'd have thunk it, eh? Good old Milton.'

And then Bridget jumps up from her seat, in an unnervingly abrupt move that is somehow utterly familiar. She stalks around Jodie, her hands behind her back, paces back and forth, all the while looking at her consideringly, coolly. It's a professional gaze—almost as if she's measuring her.

Jodie isn't sure whether she should be amused or alarmed, giggles nervously, squirms. 'What on earth are you doing?'

'I'm just thinking, honey. I'm having one of my amazingly brilliant ideas. I have them every now and then.' She gives a deliberately mad chuckle.

'What?'

'I told you I paint?'

'Yee ... es.'

'Well, I actually paint portraits. I've been entering the Archibald every year for yonks—I've been a finalist a couple of times. And I've been runner-up in the Portia Geach. Third place in the Moran. So, you know, I'm getting there.'

Jodie murmurs something appropriately congratulatory, then admits that apart from the Archibald, she hasn't really got the foggiest idea what they are.

Bridie laughs. 'Well you're not alone there, sweet. Portrait prizes aren't quite the Oscars. The thing is, I haven't lined up anyone for next year's Archibald.'

'Lined anyone up?'

'Well, it's meant to be someone significant in the arts or sciences or politics. But that's just "preferential"—you can usually make a case when someone's famous. Or infamous. And there's been plenty of stuff written about you. Anyway, I'd more or less decided not to bother for next year. But maybe there's still time.'

Bridie's still pacing around her, moving backwards and forwards. She opens a blind, closes it again. Peers at Jodie from this angle and that, regarding her through half-closed eyes.

'So how about it? What do you think?'

Even coming from Bridie the request seems ludicrous. 'You really want to paint me?'

'Why not? You'd be better than my last local subject, anyhow. When we first got here I painted Alma McNeeman—you know that journo who lives out near Bundalong, she won all those environmental prizes? The painting was good—it was excellent, really—but that Alma's a bit of a self-righteous cow.' She pauses suddenly, her eyes wide. 'God, I hope you don't know her.'

'Well, I do. Doesn't everyone? But that's okay. She's not really what you'd call a friend. Her husband works with my husband. And she is a cow—I agree. A big fat cow.'

The two women laugh, as silly and conspiratorial as schoolgirls.

'When I was out there I took photos, and then had her sit for a few hours over a couple of days. She was *un*believable—she never so much as offered me a cup of tea the entire time. It was as if I was some sort of indentured servant. And then when I showed her the portrait, God—she actually sneered, I swear. I was too afraid to ask if she wanted to buy it and I don't have a clue what to do with it. I mean, it didn't win anything, or even get an honourable mention, but I think it's a pretty good portrait. It captured some interesting things about her—she's pretty powerful, passionate. Large, in all sorts of ways—but honestly, who'd buy it? Glenys thought we could turn it into an archery target, or a dartboard, but I can't quite bring myself to destroy it. So I've got it stored out in the garage,' she says, grinning, 'facing the wall. Only place for it.' She takes a breath. 'So what do you reckon, Jodie? Can I do it?'

'Well, I don't know. I'm—'

'Oh, come on, Jodie.'

'How long would it take? What would I have to do?'

'Do? Nothing much, just sit there while I work. I'll take a heap of photos, too—and I'll work off those as well. I'd only need you for a couple of weeks, four max, I reckon.'

'Can I think about it?'

'What if I take the photos now and get started with some sketches?'

'Oh, I don't know.'

'Go on. Say yes. You won't regret it.'

'Oh. You're a bloody pest. Okay, then. Yes.'

'Fantastic. I can get some snaps now, and we can do the sittings later—in a month or so. Maybe things won't be quite as fraught then.'

'Maybe. Or maybe they'll be extra fraught.'

'Don't worry. I'll make you sit. Even if I have to visit you in prison.' Their laughter has a slightly hysterical edge—Jodie's as much from the relief of having a companion, someone to laugh with, as from the dark humour of the comment itself.

'Definitely?'

'Definitely.'

Later, looking back, Hannah has absolutely no idea what possessed her, what made her think that it would be okay to bring Wes home after the party, to drag him up their garden path, both of them swaying and laughing, then through the front door—*Oh, my God, the keyhole keeps moving, Wes, I swear. Bloody hell. You do it*—then attempting to creep noiselessly down the darkened hall, past Tom's bedroom and into her own lair, and with the barest of pushes, down, down, down onto the tangled surface of her bed. Well, maybe she does know what possessed her—vodka, lust—but even so, what was she thinking? The answer is: she wasn't. She wasn't listening either, not once they'd made it safely to her room, not once they had pulled off those items of clothing that needed removing, had embarked on that journey of mutual discovery that Hannah has newly recognised as being one of such great pleasure. She wasn't listening, but there was no way of avoiding her mother's horrified expression when she opened the door and switched on the light. Jodie retreated hastily and Hannah and Wes—immediately sober, separate, listening for the inevitable summons, the humiliating eviction—lay blinking at one another in the light.

'Is it Wes, then? Is it because he's black? Would it be less inappropriate if he was a nice white Newie boy?' The argument has been raging for almost an hour, has gone back and forth without any resolution. There's been plenty of time for Wes to make his escape without any more humiliating encounters, for Tom to wander up the hall and into the lounge room, give one brief look and hurry, terrified, back to bed. Far from being embarrassed, ashamed at being caught out, Hannah is giving a good impression of being the victim: it's her right, her bedroom, Jodie should learn to knock; she's legally of age and there's nothing—*nothing*—that Jodie or Angus can do. Of course she would have had the nerve even if her father hadn't been away: it's not about nerve, anyway—*it's her right.* Hannah has been so relentless in her own defence that her mother has barely been able to make her own position clear, other than to reiterate the inappropriateness of Hannah's behaviour. This question of his being black is a new one, dragged up from some obscure place, and she can see it takes her mother by surprise.

'Oh God, Hannah. I didn't even see him. I really tried not to look. I didn't even notice that he was black—the point is I don't want you bringing boys—any boys—back to my home in the middle of the night.'

Hannah ignores what she's just said, continues her diatribe. 'So, basically you're a snob and a racist. And you've so little reason—look at your family. Granny Evans. Your brothers. *You* may as well be black. You're no better.'

Her mother shakes her head, sighs. 'What is going on in that head of yours, Hannah? This isn't about me. This is about you. It's not that complicated, surely? You know the rules. If you must have sex, and I realise I can't stop you—just do it somewhere else.'

Hannah stares at her mother for a long moment. She can see her in triplicate, three figures shimmying across her field of vision. 'How can you say that it's just about me? Right now everything in my life is about you and what you want. If it was just about me, things would be very different.'

'Oh, Hannah, that's just—'

'And don't talk to me about rules. From where I'm standing it looks like you've broken some very big ones.'

'Hannah,' her mother hisses her name, as if barely in control, 'I want you to go to bed. This is stupid. We'll discuss it in the morning. When you're sober. When you're capable of talking sense.'

'But actually, this is what I think. And I'll still be thinking it in the morning. You know, what's the saying? In vino … vino … something or other.'

'Goodnight, Hannah.' Her mother turns to go but Hannah grabs her sleeve, pulls her back. Subjects her to a long hard stare.

'You know, Mum. You scare me. First you dump your family. Then you dump that baby. How could you do that?'

'What do you mean?' Her mother returns her stare, eyebrows raised, coolly inquiring.

'How could you just sell it? If that's what you actually did? And then not tell anyone? Not until you absolutely had to.'

'You know the story.'

'But it's not the truth is it? Not the whole truth.' Hannah feels sick. Her head is spinning, she wants to lie down. And she wants to stop this stream of bile that appears to be going directly from her heart to her mouth, bypassing her brain. She staggers slightly and her mother goes to steady her, takes her arm, but Hannah pulls away, makes herself stand upright. 'Don't touch me.'

'Hannah—'

'Don't even talk to me. I really don't know who you are any more. I used to know you—but maybe that wasn't real, either. You're not my mother. I don't know where my mother is.'

AAP NEWS
'Missing Elsa Mary to be subject of coronial inquest'

NSW's Chief Coroner Conrad Westerby, QC, announced today that there is to be a coronial inquest into the matter of missing infant Elsa Mary Evans, who has not been seen since her mother's discharge from Belfield Hospital twenty-four years ago. Despite extensive searches throughout Australia and internationally for both Elsa Mary and her alleged adoptive parents 'Rosemary and Simon', no evidence of Elsa Mary's current whereabouts have come to light. What now has to be determined, Mr Westerby said, is the likelihood of Elsa Mary's still being alive, and whether this is a matter for further police investigation and possible criminal prosecution.

The Coroner has asked anyone with any information that could assist police to come forward. 'This is a case I would prefer not to investigate, but if no conclusive evidence of Elsa Mary's current whereabouts is forthcoming I will have no choice but to investigate this as a suspect death,' he said.

Hearings are scheduled to begin at the Glebe Coroner's Court in August.

Angus is shocked by Jodie's reaction to the news of the impending inquest. Up until this moment the face she has shown him has been one of almost eerie calm, forbearance, resignation. Now, suddenly, this morning, all her self-possession has disappeared, and she's hysterical, beside herself. Despite the weeks of knowing that a coronial investigation was more or less inevitable, just a matter of time, it is as if it has only just dawned on her how far this thing could go, what could happen next.

He has come back from work to tell her after Pete rang him with the news, has found her standing at the sink, somehow already well aware, sobbing, washing the breakfast dishes with unnecessary violence. Angus has stationed himself beside her with the tea-towel, simultaneously trying to reassure her, while making a valiant attempt to save the dishes from a sorry end, wresting them from her before she crashes them savagely into the draining basket.

'Just give them to me, Jodie,' he hisses. 'It's all right. I can dry them. Will you just calm down? It's only an inquest. You haven't been charged. You won't be charged.'

She slams a froth-covered cup into the basket, breaking off the handle, insists he ring Peter again, that he ring the police, ring the bloody coroner—tell them that it's crazy, that it's all gone too far.

'Oh, come on,' she half sobs, half laughs. 'You're Angus Garrow, aren't you? Surely there's someone you can talk to, surely you can get someone to fix things!'

'Oh, God, Jodie. You know there's nothing I can do. This is how the law works. We've explained it to you a dozen times. You knew this was going to happen if the girl didn't turn up. But it's nothing. The coroner just has to explore the possibilities.' Suddenly he's weary of the whole show. Would like nothing better than to throw a few cups himself.

'It's nothing?' She turns on him now, her eyes red and wild. 'How can you say it's nothing, Angus? I'm really not stupid, you know. These are public hearings. It's my whole life—it'll be taken apart in that court.'

The anger flares, without any warning. 'But it's not just your life, is it, Jodie? You've done a fair job of stuffing up my plans, too. Remember how I was going to be mayor?' The bitterness in his tone is unmistakable, and he sees her flinch. She bites her lip, takes a deep breath, looks at Angus hard, as if waiting for him to say something else, to back-pedal, apologise. But he says nothing, looks back at her coolly.

Eventually, Jodie shrugs, and turns back to the dishes. She picks up a plate, washes it thoroughly. She bypasses Angus's waiting towel, holds it delicately above the tiled floor, watches the suds drip for a moment, then lets it slip, almost casually, through her fingers. She pulls off her rubber gloves and drops each one on top of the smashed pieces of plate, and stalks from the room without uttering another word.

'Oh. My. God.' Hannah, who has skipped her morning class to finish an assignment, is standing in the kitchen doorway surveying the crazy scene, her eyes wide, mouth open. 'What's going on? What's wrong with Mum?'

Angus explains, rather disjointedly, while he sweeps up the shattered remains of the plate, that Jodie is a bit overwrought at the thought of the inquest. 'You can't blame her, though, Han. It's very confronting. But really, I was just trying to explain to her that it'll all be okay. It's just procedure. In fact, the inquest should clear everything up. There's absolutely nothing for any of us to worry about.'

Hannah merely rolls her eyes, as if sensing the hollowness of his reassurances, the bits he's deliberately left out. 'Yeah right, Dad.'

'It'll be okay, Hannie.' Then desperately: 'Anyway, would you be able to help your mother? Finish these dishes?' He passes Hannah the gloves, a dishcloth. 'I have to get back to work. I need to arrange things—we're going to need a barrister.'

Hannah accepts the proffered tools reluctantly, takes his place beside the sink. 'Why don't you get Assia's mum? Manon's a shit-hot criminal barrister, isn't she? A QC, or whatever they call them. She defended that old bloke—you know, the one who was on *Underbelly*—that gangster guy. If anyone can get Mum off, Manon can.'

He has to explain: 'This isn't about getting Mum off, Hannie. The inquest is just to establish whether the child, the woman, is actually still alive—and then what should happen next. This is just to establish the facts—no one has to get Mum off. She hasn't been charged with anything.'

'But how can they establish anything? I don't get it. What if the woman just doesn't want to appear? What if she doesn't even know? That's possible, isn't it? It just seems stupid.'

'It's not stupid, Hannah. It's the law.' His trite explanation appals him, but this is not the time or place to go into the intricacies of the legal system, or to question his own beliefs.

'But what if ... what if the coroner guy decides that the child is dead—even if there is no body? Mum's the obvious suspect, isn't she? Then she could be charged. Everyone's already saying she killed that baby, anyway.' Hannah's voice is perilously high.

'That's the media, Hannie. That's got nothing to do with the law. Your mum hasn't been charged with anything.' He adds, with far more certainty than he feels, 'And she won't be.' He pulls his daughter to him, hugs her hard. 'Now, you get those dishes done—preferably without breaking any more of them. I'm going to give your Manon a call.'

He has encountered Manon before—she is his daughter's best friend's mother, after all. They've met casually a number of times over the years, at school functions, when she's driven up from Sydney for speech nights, drama performances, special assemblies. They've chatted in that perfunctory way that parents do at those events—polite, but vague, scattered, eyes constantly checking the time, scanning the exits. And he knows how much his daughter admires her: Hannah's reports of visits to Assia's Glebe home are always full of stories about Manon— her wardrobe, her advice, her conversation, her eccentric lifestyle. He knows her, too, by reputation, as does everyone in the legal world. She has defended a number of high-profile criminal cases, has a reputation as a tough bitch—and almost always wins her cases. But their legal practices exist in two very different worlds; they have never crossed paths professionally and had been unlikely to—until now, when he needs her skills for personal, rather than professional, reasons.

When he calls her they chat for a moment about the girls, about school, about a forthcoming examination. Unlike most of his colleagues and friends, she asks unhesitatingly about Jodie—she knows most of the public details of the case, of course, but is surprised when he tells her about the impending inquest. She hasn't read today's papers, didn't know.

'Shit,' she says, and he can hear her sharply indrawn breath. But the surprise lasts less than a second; he can almost hear her brain whirring. 'Okay. So this isn't a social call, is it? You're ringing to see if I'll take the case, if I'll defend your wife.' There's a short pause, no time for him to say anything, and then she replies to his unasked question. 'Yeah, okay. Yeah. I'll do it.' He wonders at her quick-fire decision-making—she's had no time to consult either her diary or her PA.

Even over the phone he can tell that he's made the right decision, calling her: in the same way that Peter understood the strategies they should put in place initially, Manon understands right away all the possibilities of what is now destined to be a criminal case, is certain about what's happening, what could happen, and what needs to happen. She fires questions and orders at him, doesn't wait for him to respond, assumes that he'll do as he's told. Which he will, of course—who wouldn't?

'Well, you've obviously known this was a strong possibility, and I expect you've got your solicitor working on it already. But you were right to ring me,' she says. 'This has the potential to be very, very serious. As serious as it gets. We've got a couple of months, but I think it might be best if I fly up as soon as I can. I have court tomorrow, but I'll be finished by three or so. In the meantime, email anything, everything you have. And I mean everything. And I think you need to take an absolute no-comment approach to the media from now on. Don't speak to anyone about the case. Not your friends, not your colleagues, not even your mother. I'll let you know my flight time, organise a car. I'll come straight to your office. Just you—it would be better, I think. You can fill me in. I don't want to talk to Jodie. Not yet.'

She hangs up abruptly, without saying goodbye, without warning.

Angus is not lost, not yet—but even now, the phone dangling, buzzing sharply in his ear, he's left wondering, left anticipating her arrival with considerable excitement, in a state somewhere between irritation and exhilaration.

Their initial meeting is tense. Manon's flight is delayed, and she doesn't arrive until late, after dark. It's blustery and wet, and in Arding—which is a good ten degrees colder than Sydney at this time of year—it's cold. She has driven a hire car from the airport and found it difficult to locate the office in the dark; the streets are badly lit, numbers impossible to read. When he first notices her, looking up from his work, Manon is standing at the door to his office, scowling over at him—her forehead creased, dark brows beetling across her forehead, her thin lips tight.

'I'm here.' She speaks without any expression, but slumps heavily against his doorway, in a movement that is either ironic, exhausted, or angry—it's impossible to tell.

'Hi.'

They survey one another for a long, curious moment. She's small and dark, good-looking in an inner-city way that he doesn't usually find appealing, finds intimidating; it's a look that shouts feminist, intellectual: dark, spiky hair, pale face, her mouth a narrow red slash, glasses that make her look stern and clever and sexy, all in black. She is wearing layers—some sort of clingy tunic, a vest, shirt, long cardigan, tights, heels—expensively chic, but provocative too, somehow, the shirt's plunging neckline exposing a still-firm cleavage, unlined chest. Her style is eccentric compared with most of Arding's respectable middle-aged women, who keep their hair bobbed, their shirts buttoned, their skirts just below the knee, wear sensible flat shoes.

Angus doesn't like to think about what she might be seeing—what's left of a once curly head of hair is grey, thinning; he imagines he stoops a little, though his shoulders are still broad, and beneath his plain white shirt the muscle has become slightly fleshy. Ordinarily he wouldn't give too much consideration to his appearance, but he's oddly uncomfortable under her gaze, embarrassed by his shortcomings as he hasn't been since he was a teenager, painfully aware of his own dull rural respectability.

He gets to his feet, suddenly conscious of the oddly drawn-out nature of their silence. He takes her luggage, her coat, offers her a seat. 'Do you want tea, coffee? Something to eat ... There's a Thai restaurant down the street that's probably still—'

'Actually,' she says, sinking wearily down onto the seat, 'what I'd really like is a drink—I had a couple of thimblefuls on the flight up, but it wasn't quite enough. And sweet Jesus, I needed it.'

'Was the flight okay? Those little Dash-8s are usually very—'

'It was a fucking nightmare!' She gives an eloquent shudder. 'Why didn't someone warn me it'd have bloody propellers? It was like something out of a World War One movie. I kept waiting for some flapper to start doing the charleston out on the wing.' She takes the glass of wine Angus is offering, gulps down half in one mouthful, holds it out for a refill. Sips again, closes her eyes, takes a deep breath. He watches in helpless fascination. She looks up at him then, and smiles for the first time. Her mouth is small, but the smile is unexpectedly broad, and warm. 'Okay then, Mr Garrow. If you can point me in the direction of the bathroom, I'll freshen up. And then we can get to work.'

Manon sits impassively as he tells her as much as he can. The telling isn't chronological; he starts not with the story of Jodie's pregnancy and the birth, but her more recent visit to the hospital—Hannah's broken leg, the nurse who noticed Hannah's syndactyly, then remembered Jodie, asked about the other child. Jodie's confused admission that the baby had been adopted, her lack of honesty about the details. The nurse's subsequent inquiries. Then he tells her everything that Jodie has told him about the events before and after the birth of the child: the one-night stand, the hidden pregnancy, the birth, what she remembers about the adoption, the matron, the adoptive parents. She takes notes all through, but doesn't interrupt or ask questions.

'Okay. I'll be straight,' she says when he's finished, tapping her pen on her teeth. 'I can't second-guess the coroner, but I have to say I'm worried. Best-case scenario: the coroner decides there's not enough evidence to determine whether the child is alive or dead and makes an open finding. Worst-case scenario: the coroner finds a presumption of death, rules it suspicious— and refers it back to Homicide. So what we need to do is to ensure that open finding. We definitely don't want to go any distance down the other road. But at the moment there are so many gaps in Jodie's story. There's absolutely no evidence that any of what she's told us is the truth. Nobody can corroborate— nobody even knew she was pregnant. So we're going to need something—or someone—*else*.'

Angus listens, entranced by her capacity to speak her mind so clearly, and to need no response, no validation.

'I think Peter has done a pretty good job here so far—you've done the right thing, anticipating the media, the police. Making that initial statement. Controlling the media. That was clever. But it let the media genie out of the bottle a bit prematurely, which could also work against us. For some reason the media is mad on this story already. And Jodie's not liked, is she? People aren't sympathetic—they're suspicious. Unfortunate, but it just happens that way sometimes. If the coroner finds that her child is dead, that the circumstances are questionable, it will get a whole lot worse. And public perceptions will make a big difference if it ever gets to a jury. Remember the Chamberlain case?'

Angus is finding it hard to concentrate on her words. Beneath the abrupt tones of her voice she has a faint accent. Eastern European, he thinks, a hint of Zsa Zsa Gabor, Hungarian or Polish, and not French, despite her name.

'So. So.' She leans back in the big office chair, concentrating. Angus watches her, fascinated—he's never seen someone think so vividly, so physically. He can almost see the ideas coursing through her body, like blood, in her rapid breathing, the rise and fall of her chest. And she doesn't ever stop moving: her legs jiggle, feet tap. Her eyes are half closed, but her eyelids flicker, her lips twitch. Only her hands are still, twined tightly in her lap.

She opens her eyes suddenly—glares straight at him. Into him. 'Okay. There'll be something. I can't think what it is, but I know there'll be something, some gap we can split open. Something buried that we can dig up. Something nobody else has noticed. We'll read through everything. Statements, notes, documents. Tonight. Every bit of it. If there's anything there, we'll find it.'

Angus phones home, tells Jodie that he'll be hours yet, that Manon has only just arrived, that they could be here all night.

'So, what does she think?' He can hear the edge of hysteria in Jodie's voice. 'Does she know what's going to happen next? How we should handle everything? Whether I'm likely to be charged?' She sounds slightly slurred, too—either from drink or anxiety, maybe both.

'Jodie,' Angus replies soothingly. 'You need to calm down. Manon has handled this sort of thing before, far tougher cases than yours. Remember, it's just an inquest. Right now you need to go to bed. We'll go over it with you in the morning. Just go on with your ordinary routine for now. Get up, get dressed, get the kids ready for school. Try not to unsettle them, okay? You've got to take Hannah to the physio in the morning, don't you? Well, you do that, drop her back at school and then give me a call. I'll tell you what you need to do next then. All right?'

'Okay.' He can hear her breathing. 'Angus?'

'What?'

'It *is* going to be okay, isn't it? I'm not going to be arrested, am I? Sent to jail?' Her voice is small, young, vulnerable, and he feels a surge of pity.

'It's going to be fine, darling,' he says, looking at Manon. 'Just go to bed.'

He and Manon work through the night, reading, rereading, taking notes. They work side by side at his desk, so close that he can smell her perfume, overlaid, as the night progresses, by the slightly sour fragrance of her sweat. They both drink steadily—first a bottle of white wine and then several glasses of whisky, but there is no apparent diminution in the clarity of her thoughts or her speech, although by her own admission she has been working since five that morning.

She discards layers of clothing as she works—*I hope you don't mind, Angus?*—first her heels, then her stockings, then an outer layer, a vest. Angus pulls off his tie, loosens his collar, rolls up his sleeves, but though he would like to, he does not undo his belt.

It is past three by the time they have finished. Manon sits slumped for a moment on the chair, then stretches, runs her fingers through her hair, yawning luxuriously. 'So,' she says. 'That's done for now.' Before he can ask, she volunteers the answer. 'No. I haven't found the gap. But I know it's there. I can feel it. I'll talk to Jodie tomorrow—see if she can add anything more.' She shrugs. 'Don't worry. I know there'll be something we're just not seeing.'

Angus leans back in his chair, his eyes closed—he is exhausted, and though he longs for sleep, he dreads going home, fearing the panic that he knows awaits him, regardless of the late hour, his mildly inebriated state. When he opens his eyes Manon is looking at him a little quizzically—as if she has noticed that he is a man and not just an automaton for the first time that evening. 'D'you know what I'd like, Angus? What I really need more than anything?'

He imagines that she wants something more substantial to eat than the bag of crisps, the peanuts that are all he has been able to provide, and racks his brain for a shop that will be open this late, but there's nowhere—even the garages close down for the night in Arding. She gives a small inscrutable smile, then says bluntly: 'What I'd really like is a good fuck, Angus. Here. Now. It'll help me sleep better. Clear my head. You've been so very helpful already.' Now her smile is wide, is full of laughter, mischief. 'I don't suppose you'd oblige?'

There had been more than a few affairs since his marriage, but none of them had been particularly memorable—usually they had begun and ended quickly, with little thought, minimal guilt, utter discretion, and zero recrimination. None of them were passionate by any measurement—they had occurred almost as a matter of course. There had been various predictable scenarios—a few weekend flings while away at conferences with almost anonymous women he'd met in hotel bars; others had lasted longer, been closer to home—one or two clients, as nervous as Angus himself about discovery, one of his PAs, and once—an older colleague. They'd been flattered by his attention—what woman wouldn't have been?—had been available, willing to strike while the iron was, so to speak, blisteringly hot, and then had been equally happy to head off into the sunset when the affair had run its course—as they all inevitably did. These women had never wanted more than he was able to offer—which was clearly a no-strings-attached, short-lived sexual liaison. He had been lucky, he supposed, in only ever attracting women with a similarly detached approach: either married themselves or not looking for a meaningful relationship—not with him, anyway.

Only one had been more complicated. His last affair had occurred not long after Tom was born. Wanda Robinson. She had been a young solicitor he'd employed, newly graduated, who had expected serious commitment and had made it widely known—with letters to Jodie, his mother, a glass of wine flung in his face at some function. After the Wanda Robinson debacle, he had had to make a very public decision about where his allegiances lay, had to grow up, as it were, suddenly realising that he didn't want to lose his family. He had sworn to himself and to Jodie: never again. And though opportunities had continued to come his way—after all, Angus was a good-looking, increasingly powerful man in his small-pond city—he had managed to keep his promise.

Until now.

Manon has asked to spend the day alone with Jodie, going over her story.

'It's important that we do it without anyone else around—just so you don't offer the expected version,' she'd explained. 'I'm certain there must be something you haven't mentioned, or haven't remembered. Maybe something that doesn't seem important. Something we can use.'

Jodie makes them coffee, piles a plate with biscuits, and the two women sit in the sun room, in an attempt to make the whole process as casual, as comfortable as possible—though Jodie can sense that this sharp little woman is anything but casual. Manon claims Angus's favourite leather recliner, slips off her shoes and pulls up her slender legs, a notebook perched on top of her knees, while Jodie sits on the edge of the lounge opposite, strangely awkward even in her own home. She has met Manon a few times over the years, and despite her daughter's enthusiasm, her own affection for Assia, has always felt slightly intimidated by her, sensing the other woman's mild contempt for her stay-at-home status and feeling dowdy, rustic, slow, in her company. Now, forced into this strange professional relationship, she is reassured by the woman's undoubted competence, her understanding of what's ahead, her determination to succeed. She feels certain that if anyone can sort out this mess she's in, it's Manon.

She makes Jodie start right at the beginning—from her meeting with the boy—and go to the end. She fires questions: fast, blunt, one after another without respite or any consideration for feelings, emotions: Who was he? Where did you meet him? How many times did you fuck him? No subject is off limits, no topic too sensitive, no wound too tender. When did you find out you were pregnant? Why did you take so long to realise? And then, with the first hint of genuine feminine interest: How did you hide it—how would, how could, anyone hide a pregnancy? Manon confesses that she herself had become monstrous during her pregnancies—her stomach and all parts of her body swelling to elephantine proportions by the sixth month—there was no way to disguise it. Jodie describes the loose tracksuits, big T-shirts, the gradual all-over weight gain, the small swell of her stomach even at term, her housemate's three-month absence during the university break—the only time when her pregnancy was in any way evident. She had had no good friends at uni, and it was easy to stay in the flat, almost completely secluded for those last few months. She had had some savings, and anyway her student allowance was more than enough to live on.

Manon asks about Belfield: this particular hospital—why did you choose it? Jodie explains her reasoning. The distance from home, the improbability of meeting anyone she knew, the cheap hotel where she stayed the weeks before. Mostly—the hope that she wouldn't be noticed there, that she would be just another teenage pregnancy, that an adoption would be easy to arrange at such a place.

Through all of this, Manon listens intently, her head tilted to one side, like an intelligent bird. She asks question after question, notes everything. But it is Jodie's account of the events in the hospital that engage her most concentrated attention. She sits up straight after Jodie's first rendition, her feet sliding back onto the ground. She stops writing, leans forward, closes her eyes as Jodie recites and then recites again each small detail of her stay there—five times, eight times, ten times, until it is only the syntax of her recitation that varies.

'Tell me again about the midwife, about this Matron O'Malley. What she said to you—about keeping you isolated, keeping the other midwives away.'

'She said something like, "Don't worry, I've done this before—it's easy. Just say that Matron is looking after you, and the other nurses will know to steer clear." I mean, they're not her exact words, obviously, but it was something like that.'

'As if it wasn't all that unusual, like it was something she'd done before, no?' There's a suppressed excitement in her voice, all at once she sounds foreign. European. Her voice as exotic as her looks.

'I suppose so. Yes.'

'That's it then!' Manon stands up and yawns, stretches. 'The matron. She'll be your defence.'

'I don't understand. How can she help? She's dead.'

Manon smiles down at her. 'Then she should count her blessings.'

Angus returns home late in the afternoon—he has taken time off, collected both the children and run them to their various activities, arrives home harried, irritable. He gives Jodie—preparing a rudimentary spaghetti bolognese—a perfunctory kiss, then rushes to the study, where Manon has set up a temporary workspace. When the two of them come back into the kitchen together, talking intently, Jodie can tell—and it's not a guess, but knowledge, deep and inescapable. She can see it in the way that Angus speaks to the other woman, the awkwardness, stiffness, the slightly wary holding back. And he's especially solicitous of Jodie, asking what she needs, what he can do to help. There's no apparent sign from Manon, though: she's brusque, blunt, businesslike—her conversation confined to the case, her thesis, their strategy.

His first affair—or what Jodie has always assumed was his first—had come as a shock, about three years into their marriage. Angus had only been a relatively junior solicitor when the woman, Angela—who was considerably older than them, in her late thirties—had joined the firm as a partner. Hannah was only a few months old, and Jodie had been completely rapt in new motherhood—blissed out and bewildered in equal measure, stumbling through the strange new terrain as if half blind—utterly oblivious to anything much beyond the daily round of feeding, changing, sleeping. She had met Angela, of course, at one or two company dinners, but had barely been aware of her existence, and so had been completely unprepared when Angus had admitted tearfully a few years later that the affair had run almost the entire time the woman had been in Arding—over a year—that Angela's decision to relocate had been made only after their mutual determination to end it. There had been others since—some he'd confessed to, others she'd surmised.

After Wanda, the affair that had blown up hugely, Angus was desperate to keep Jodie, to keep their family intact, had promised that it would never happen again. He told her he loved her, over and over. And she'd believed him, trusted him.

His remorse has always seemed so genuine that Jodie has managed to forgive him these betrayals. Forgetting has been harder—she still feels the memory of each betrayal physically—like a sharp blow to her ribs, powerful enough to make her gasp, to leave her momentarily breathless. Even now, when everything has been so pared back that the reality of their partnership seems little more than custom, still the prospect of Angus leaving, of Angus not loving her, fills her with terror.

Now, she serves the spaghetti to the four of them—Angus, the two children, Manon—then delays sitting down with them at the table, finding saucepans to scrub, benches to wipe, all the while surreptitiously watching from the kitchen. She sees the laughing smile Manon gives Angus after some comment or other, the way their fingers touch, swiftly, almost unnoticeably, when he passes her the salad, the way Angus cannot stop himself from looking at her—gazing at her—even when she is only eating, or talking to the children. And Hannah, too, is enraptured, so keen to engage Manon, talking to her intently, hands flying, her eyes alight, enthusiastic in a way that Jodie hasn't witnessed for months. And Manon's response, easy, unaffected, without all the weight and strain that characterises Jodie's mothering. Only Tom is impervious, intent only on his meal, twirling the spaghetti on his fork, eagerly shovelling it in.

And only Tom has noticed Jodie's absence; he looks up when she joins them, and gives her a curious smile. 'Where have you been?' She smiles back, but doesn't answer, sits down beside him and fills her bowl. But she can't eat. Instead, she listens to her daughter giving a scathing critique of some obscure French actor's recent cinema performance, Manon's ironic rejoinder, her husband's amused chuckling. She pours herself a generous glass of wine, and sips, watching them enjoy themselves, savour one another's company, all determinedly disregarding the reason they're all together. Every now and then a comment is directed her way, or Tom's, but the conversation belongs to Manon and Hannah—with Angus providing the occasional fact, the odd quip. As she clears away the dishes, her own bowl emptied by an unapologetically starving Tom, Jodie idly wonders what she should have done differently. What she can do. Wonders whether she has the energy to do anything at all. Wonders whether it's worth it anyway.

30

Angus is consumed.

He wonders vaguely how much it has to do with Jodie—whether this particular betrayal is deliberate, some type of punishment or an unconscious outlet for his anger. For there's no escaping the fact that ever since the announcement of the inquest—and perhaps even before that—Angus has become incandescently angry, and this anger is driving him almost as much as his ardour. He's not really certain what it is he is angry about. He knows that it's not any sort of reasonable response to her unimaginable plight: the desperate pregnancy, the lonely birth, the panic-filled days that followed—how could any of this fail to produce in him sympathy, even pity, for this woman he has lived with and loved, the mother of his children? Though one part of him must judge her youthful actions as stupid, irresponsible—how could she?—he knows that she's a good woman now, that she was a good woman then, at worst possessed of a strange moral innocence that had everything to do with her childhood, her upbringing. And even when he lets himself go to that place where he shouldn't, when he questions her story, wonders whether she is lying, whether she is in fact a cold-blooded murderer—even this is not enough to inspire anger. Disgust, yes. And perhaps dislike, though there are reserves of sympathy in him that could accommodate even that, he thinks. He is not a hypocrite, is well aware that he has failed miserably to stick to the moral straight and narrow himself.

No, it's the mess, the hideous mess that she has made of all their lives—Hannah's, Tom's, his own, even his mother's—that keeps the flame of his anger burning so self-righteously. He can feel the life they have made together, their family—all the hard work, the sacrifices, so many compromises—beginning to disintegrate, dissolve, can feel the cold wind from the chasm, an intimation of the underlying chaos.

But then, perhaps this has nothing to do with his anger. Perhaps he has no excuse, no way of justifying his actions, his desires.

Though he should be concentrating on work, on the coming inquest, right now all he can think of is Manon—her voice, her body, her smell—even a typed sheet of paper that he knows she has touched is a reminder of his unquenchable desire. He notices, just days into the affair, that the panic attacks have stopped—have disappeared as mysteriously as they came. Manon has cured him. He is no longer the sagging, balding, middle-aged has-been that Dave so eloquently described—breathing into a paper bag at the prospect of this being all there is. It's as if his youthful self has been restored, but larger, stronger, more vital—potential conqueror of women, of worlds.

In his mind (absurd, in middle age, to become the sentimentalist he never was in youth!) he composes odes to her apricot breasts, to the soft, briny petals of her cunt, to her deft, muscular tongue. Manon has become the still centre of his spinning world, just at the moment when he knows he needs the world to be motionless, when he needs to see things clearly, more clearly than ever before.

Even in the depths of his madness, it is clear to Angus that Manon does not feel the same way about him. He is merely the provider of physical release, a vessel for her lust. The irony of this unfamiliar reversal does not escape him, but there's nothing amusing about it. He knows there's an end coming, and soon, that the world will cease spinning, that his landing will be painful. But for now he's fixed in his revolutions, observing the world from a distinct, Manon-coloured perspective. Things may be falling apart—but right now he's not at all inclined to keep them together.

Sydney Morning Herald, Daily Telegraph, The Australian, Courier-Mail, The Age, West Australian, The Land, Adelaide Advertiser, News of the Day, *Who Weekly, Women's Weekly, New Idea, Woman's Day,* etc.

Would anyone with any knowledge of any adoption arranged by Matron Sheila O'Malley of Belfield Hospital between 1972 and 1992 please contact Peter Silvers at Silvers Wood and Watson, Arding. (02) 6777 2331 or email *p.silvers@sww.com.au*

31

With the announcement of the inquest it all seems to have got worse: the carefully phrased questions from friends, sniggers from enemies, pitying glances from teachers all driving Hannah spare. And the situation at home is tense, to put it mildly. Her mother is barely speaking, and her father is completely off the planet, too. Even the usually bright and breezy Tom has grown quiet and moody. Hannah wants nothing more than to escape from it all.

She is in town late one afternoon, has been wandering around with Assia—shopping for supplies for their coming weekend at Cosmic, an annual folk festival down in the Valley. It's not an event that she would ordinarily attend, but Wes and a few of the other drama students are heading down, so she's convinced Assia that they should go, too. She put it to her parents, who, distracted by everything else that is going on, agreed without too much questioning. So the girls buy the essentials for camping out—two-minute noodles, Coke, chocolate bars, some tinned fruit, sunscreen, insect repellent, matches, a torch—then visit a café where they share a big bowl of dense potato wedges. It is late when they leave the café and Assia heads back towards school, looking forward to the prospect of dinner later with Manon—but Hannah is too full, too loaded with shopping, to make the trip up the hill home. Instead, she decides to go to her father's office—he will undoubtedly still be there—and bludge a lift.

She doesn't understand what she is hearing, walking up the stairs to the office, has her mind on other things, and the muffled thumps don't resolve into anything meaningful until she actually walks through his door. Her father's secretary (or his Office Manager, as she prefers to be called) has already left, the lights in the waiting room are switched off, but Hannah can see a dim light shining beneath her father's door, and there is obviously some sort of activity going on within. She knocks, opening the door just as an order to wait is shouted, meeting the wild eyes of her father, tie askew, caught in a position that would have been laughably clichéd were it not her father, and therefore beyond disgusting: her dad, pants around his ankles, a woman lying prone on the desk beneath him, half naked. The woman's face is turned away, but Hannah recognises her immediately—knows that it is Assia's mother, and most definitely not her own.

Hannah turns and runs through the office and down the stairs, ignoring the desperate entreaties of her father. She rushes through the alley beside the mall and then as far as she can in the opposite direction to home, pausing only when she's forced to, breathless, a stitch in her side, in a deserted car park beside the car wash, bent over double and feeling sick. She tries hard to wipe the memory—equal parts humiliation and revulsion—from her mind, along with the tears that are suddenly streaming down her face. She texts Wes, almost without thinking, and he arrives, barely five minutes later, holds her while she tells him what she's seen—hesitantly at first and then in a rush. When she's calm, he leads her to his car and they drive up to the lookout in his rusting Datsun. Wes doesn't ask her any more about it—and she's glad of his reticence, glad to be given space, to not be forced to think about it, sort it out. Right now she's in no mood to be offered advice or consolation. Right now she wants to forget that particular scene—wants to forget her parents, forget Manon. Wesley rolls a joint and they sit together, holding hands, passing the joint back and forth, saying nothing, the Cat Empire calling *Hello* from the radio.

From the lookout there's a clear view of Arding—and even from this perspective there's no denying that Arding is a lovely place, aesthetically pleasing in every way, teeming with important historical buildings, charming cottages, beautiful European trees and sensational gardens. It's neat and well maintained, the streets running tidily in a grid surrounding a central busi-ness and church district. It has two grand cathedrals, but nowa-days they're basically deserted, as is the traditional town centre. These days everyone flocks to the two new shopping malls, ugly concrete behemoths that bookend the town.

It's not a bad place to grow up, or it shouldn't be. But right now, with everything that's going on, Hannah hates Arding. She hates its facile prettiness, its eager citizenry, despises its right-on reputation as a tolerant town, its pretensions to being an edgy, artsy, intellectual outpost—a kind of Balmain of the tablelands—almost as much as she detests the desperate gen-tility and subtle snobbery of her own social group. She hates the way nobody ever seems to leave, even her parents—who have had every opportunity—the way the concerns of one gen-eration spill into the next and then the next. She knows that if they lived elsewhere, somewhere bigger, none of what was happening now would matter so much. The Garrows would be nobodies. Gloriously anonymous. No one would know them, know what was going on. And no one would really care.

Almost Hannah's entire extended family is still here in Ard-ing, or around New England—and she wonders whether this geographical torpor is as genetically inevitable as the webbing between her toes. Her mother's father, who she has never met, is the only one of her immediate family to have left. She wishes for the first time that she knew more about him, that she could meet him, perhaps discover someone who can provide a blue-print for her own escape. Because escape is what she craves, escape from the immediate situation, but more than that—es-cape from a future that seems fixed. Her own ambitions go far beyond the town limits, and far beyond the small and stagnant pond that is her parents' world. Marry one of those popped-col-lar boys in boating shoes? Become one of those women with their bobs and pearls? Hannah would rather die.

They watch the orange and pink of the sunset, the lights of the town twinkling below them as the gloom deepens, and eventually Hannah's mind is calm, and then clear, purpose-ful—she knows exactly what she wants, what she needs to do.

'Let's get out of here.'

'Where to? D'you want to go home? Or back to my place?'

'I mean, really get out of here. Out of town.'

'Now? You mean it?' She can't see his expression in the dark car, just the white of his teeth, his eyes, gleaming.

'Oh yeah. I mean it. Let's go.'

'What about your parents? Won't they freak?'

'I'll just tell them I decided to go to Cosmic two days early. They'll be shitty, but who cares? And by the time they find out that I didn't go, well, it'll be too late, won't it?'

He grins, laughs; she can hear his excitement now. 'Where do you want to go?'

'Let's just go for a long drive.' She doesn't want to reveal her plan too early, wants to take it slowly, bit by bit, in case she changes her mind. 'Let's go to the coast.'

They drive in almost complete silence. Hannah has the seat (uncomfortably vintage, she can feel the springs just beneath the thin vinyl) wound back as far as it can go, and although it's dark outside she has left her sunglasses on. Wes has made no effort to talk, after the first attempts at conversation petered out, just giving her the occasional quick glance. She is surprised and impressed (and glad, for once, not to fear for her life!) by his cautious driving, the way he keeps the car within its limits, con-sidering its age and state of decrepitude. He barely even reach-es the speed limit, takes the corners carefully, makes his gear changes smoothly. She lets her head fall back, relaxed for what seems like the first time in weeks. The breeze from the window rushes over her skin, shadows of the trees flicker over her face, *dark light dark light dark*. She gives in, sleeps.

They are almost at the bottom of the ranges, approaching the point where they have to enter the highway, to decide whether they want to head north or south. Wes makes a suggestion: his eldest sister lives in Coffs Harbour—they could stop there for the night. Take their time deciding where they're heading next. Adds in the laidback way he has, 'and you could give your parents a call, you know—let them know you're okay.'

Hannah ignores his suggestion that she call—she has no desire to alleviate in any way the fear she knows her parents will be experiencing—but agrees that they should stay with his sister. 'And then tomorrow,' she says, unable to keep the excitement from her voice, 'I know where I want to go. I've had this genius idea.'

He gives her a quick sideways glance. 'What idea?' he asks. 'What's going on, Han?'

'My grandfather. Mum's dad—I've never met him, but I know where he lives.'

'Yeah?'

'It's up past Coffs somewhere—he runs this tiny little servo just off the highway. Where you turn off to Moon Bay, Moon-town ... Moon something or other, anyway. Up past Sapphire Beach. We've been past it heaps—every time we go to Queensland. Moonee, that's it. Mum always mentions it as we go by the turn-off—she ducks down in the seat just in case he sees her. It's like this stupid family joke.'

'Han.'

'Yeah?' She's too excited to notice the reservation in his voice.

'You don't think there might be a good reason ...'

'A good reason for what?'

'Why your mum doesn't keep in contact with her dad. I mean maybe he's—'

'Mum says he's a prick. Of course, not in so many words—she barely even mentions him actually. But Mum's such a fucking snob—he probably just drives the wrong car. What a hypocrite. She actually grew up in a housing commission place in Milton, one of her brothers is totally retarded, and the other's a crim. And Granny Evans—well, you'd have to meet her to believe her. She's hilarious—a total crazy bitch.' Hannah is raving now. 'She's in a nursing home—she's not all that old, but she's kind of demented, I think, probably from grog. She's really skinny, wears all this lycra—looks like a stick with make-up. Totally terrifying. Actually,' her voice sharpens, 'you probably saw her—everyone else in town did. She went on *Today Tonight*—totally dissed Mum in front of the whole of Australia. Said she wouldn't be surprised if she'd killed the baby. I had to go to school the next day and hear all these kids talking about my baby-murdering mother and bogan grandmother.'

'Yeah, I heard,' he says gently. 'So what makes you think that this grandfather's going to be any better?'

'I dunno. I just keep hoping that someone in my family's normal. All Dad's family are pretty awful, too—though in a different way. And he's the only one of them who's actually got out of Arding. The only one who managed to escape. It's got to mean something, doesn't it?' She shrugs. 'Anyway, it's just a destination. Somewhere to go. Oh God. How much longer?' She's bored now, and hungry. Wishes they could pull over. She yawns, stretches her hand beyond the gear stick, runs her fingers lightly up the inside of his thigh to his groin.

He starts, catches her hand, frowns unconvincingly. 'Oi. Stop it. You want to get us killed, bitch?' He removes her hand, pats it down firmly on her thigh, clamps his own back around the steering wheel. 'It's serious business, this road. I've got to concentrate if we want to make it in one piece.'

'Oh God.' She yawns again. 'I'll call,' she says after a moment. 'When we get back in range. I suppose I should let them know I'm alive, I guess. But I'm not going to tell them where I'm going. Or when I'll be back.'

She can hear the smile in his voice, the approval. 'Good girl. Just say you're going to stay at my sister's place. You don't want them to think I've kidnapped you or anything.' He touches her face lightly with his finger. 'Why don't you go back to sleep? Won't be much longer. I'll wake you when we're there.'

His sister, Eileen, a single mother of two small children who is studying primary education at the local university campus, welcomes them grandly despite the odd hour of their arrival, and the lack of warning. She looks a lot like Wesley, the same honey skin and golden hair, the same full lips, but her eyes are bright blue, and she is tiny—only just five foot—and perfectly shaped. Hannah is slightly envious of the obvious affection between the siblings—they hug fiercely, kiss, laugh, hug again. There's a barrage of questions and answers, and then family conversation, that she's happy to tune out of.

Eileen has made them up a shared bed on the lounge room floor, a comfy nest of cushions and quilts. Despite their best efforts at keeping their voices down, her two young children have woken up and in no time at all there's an impromptu party taking place. Wes is obviously a favourite with the kids—Robert and Lola—who insist on elephant rides, flip-overs and tickles from their energetic young uncle, who is more than willing to oblige. Hannah, who is not fond of children or small animals, hunches up on the lounge, watching. Eileen sits down beside her with a sigh. 'They'll be crappy all day tomorrow,' she says, 'but they'll kill me if I didn't let 'em see Wes. So, have you guys been going out long? He hasn't told us anything about you.'

Away from her brother, Eileen is a little less friendly, her manner brusque, and Hannah feels slightly intimidated by her frank stare, her blunt questions. 'Not that long. I mean, we're not exactly going out. We're just friends, really.'

'Right. So do you want me to get out another bed then, mate?' Eileen pokes at the makeshift mattress with a toe. 'I can put one of the kids in with me, and you can have their bed, if you'd rather.'

'Oh. No, it's fine. It's just that it's not ... official or anything.' She hesitates again, aware of the lameness of her remark, and looks up to find Eileen grinning widely.

'Hey. Don't worry about it, mate. I'm just stirring. You're just a kid. Having a bit of fun, eh? Been there. Done that.' She sighs again, claps her hands together. 'Okay, you little buggers, you can get back to bed now. We've got a big day tomorrow. C'mon Wes,' she says to her brother, who has pinned down his young nephew and is attempting to tie him up in a sheet. 'You let him go, now. You've wound 'em up nicely—now you can put 'em to bed. Hey kids,' she gives another wicked grin, 'maybe you can get Uncle Wes to read you another chapter of that book.'

The two children noisily endorse this, and Wes groans pitifully, gives Hannah a comically hunted look, lets the children drag him down the short hallway and into the bedroom.

Hannah sits awkwardly on the lounge, looks down at the mess of bedding longingly, wishing she could just curl up and go to sleep, wishing she was back home. She leans back, half watching the images on the muted television, drifts.

The next thing Eileen's shaking her gently, handing Hannah her mobile. 'Wes just told me your parents don't know where you are, that you ran off today without telling them you were going. Now you turn your phone on and make that call, girl,' she says. 'Whatever they've done, it's not that bad. Call before you scare 'em sick. And before they get the cops onto you.'

Hannah grabs her phone. 'I will,' she promises.

The woman glares down at her, all her former friendliness suddenly evaporated. 'You wanna make sure you do. You don't want to cause Wes any trouble, do you?'

Later—it's past two in the morning—Wes is sound asleep, curled around a pillow, snuffling softly. He has resisted all of her efforts to get him aroused, or to touch her. ('No way. Not here,' he'd said, panicked. 'Sis'll hear. And what about the kids?') Hannah takes the phone out onto the verandah. The night air is warmer here than at home, and there's a faint tang of salt in the air, on her lips. She turns on her mobile. It registers more than fifty unanswered calls—most from her parents' mobiles. There are texts too—from her parents, from Assia, even one from Tom. She doesn't stop to read them, clicks through the list of names, pauses over her father's mobile, finds her home number, presses call. She lets it ring a few times, takes a deep breath, hangs up. She can't do it; can't face any of it right now. She turns the mobile off and goes inside. She strips down to her T-shirt and undies, climbs back into bed. She wrestles the pillow away from Wes, manipulates his arms around her. His arms tighten, he gathers her up, kisses her sleepily on the forehead. 'Did you ring 'em?' he murmurs. 'Did you let 'em know you're okay?'

Hannah mutters something positive-sounding and he's satisfied, drifts back to sleep. She shoves the mobile, still clenched in her fist, under the pillow, tries to lose herself in his warm, clean smell, snuggling as close as she can. She closes her eyes; prays for sleep.

Angus's first instinct is to chase Hannah. He jerks away from Manon, pulls his pants up, pushes his feet into his shoes. He would have thundered down the stairs in desperate pursuit, regardless of any interested townsfolk, but for Manon's restraining hand, her hissed command that he stay. He looks down at her, perched on his desk, half dressed, slightly dishevelled, but somehow still in control, and still with that feline half-smile.

'There's no point, Angus. The damage has been done. She's either going to run home to Mama or not—you chasing after her is only going to make matters worse.'

'You don't know Hannah—she's—'

'Oh, but I *do* know Hannah, actually. I know that she admires you. You're her favourite parent—currently, anyway. I know that she's highly unlikely to tell Jodie. If you chase her, you'll be showing a weakness that she probably doesn't need to deal with right now. I know teenage girls: she won't despise you for adultery but she will despise you for begging.'

The sense of what she's saying gradually sinks in. Manon relaxes her grip, and he sinks down on his office chair, his body numb, legs jelly.

'Fuck. Fuck.' He puts his head in his hands. 'I can't believe that just happened. Now. What a fucking nightmare.'

Manon is regarding him with undisguised amusement now.

'Angus, really—it's not that big a deal. She knows you have affairs, surely? It's not like I'm the first, is it?'

'No—I don't know. But this is, well, obviously this is a really bad time.'

'Is there ever a good time?'

'Christ. What am I going to do?'

Manon slides down from the desk, walks over to the office door and locks it. She saunters back towards him, her hips swinging. She kneels down before him, cradles his face between her hands, kisses him on the forehead, eyes, nose, lips.

'I know that I'd feel so much better if you would finish what you've started,' she says. Angus feels his blood move again, the heat return to his limbs. 'And I think perhaps, Angus dear, that you will too.'

When he arrives home, close to midnight, the anxiety returns. But it's manageable anxiety this time, different to the attacks. Anxiety with a reason, a focus. He walks slowly up the front steps, his gut churning as he thinks of the confrontation that's possibly awaiting him. How will he face Hannah? What will he say? Even more frightening to contemplate—what will Hannah say? What has she already said? He is about to turn the key in the lock, his hand shaking slightly, when the door is pulled open from inside.

'Oh, Angus. It's you. I'd hoped it was Hannah. I can't get onto her. You haven't seen her, have you?' Jodie is still dressed, unusual at this late hour.

'No.' He tries not to let his relief show, affects a nonchalance he's not really feeling. 'Have you tried her mobile?'

'That's the thing—she must have it turned off for some reason. It's not like her.'

'Have you tried her friends?'

'I've rung everyone I can think of. Evidently she was with Assia until late this afternoon. Assia thought she said she was heading home, and no one's seen her or heard from her since. It's probably stupid to be so worried, I mean she *is* nearly seventeen. And she's probably just with Wes, too busy doing whatever it is they do.'

'Well, you should remember what they do—surely we're not that old.'

She continues as if he hasn't spoken, ignoring his lame attempt to lighten things. 'But I just can't help it—I am worried.'

She pauses, takes a breath. 'Angus, I don't know if you've ever seen this, and it probably has nothing to do with it—I'm probably overreacting. But there's this site, on the internet. There are so many of them. But this one—it worries me. There are all these photos of us. It must be someone here, someone local. Look ...'

He follows her to the study and watches, suddenly worried himself, as Jodie brings up a site on the computer: jodiegarrow. com.au. The site has no header, no text; is simply a montage of uncaptioned thumbnail photos of Jodie, Angus, Tom and Hannah, individually and together, going about their daily business, oblivious. The snaps are recent—there is one of him, walking out of his office, Manon following close behind, that can only have been taken in the past few days.

Angus pushes past her, reaches for the phone, anxiety morphing seamlessly into fear. 'We need to call the police.'

33

They leave early in the morning, before Eileen or the kids are awake. Wes insists that they tidy up their bed before they go, so they fold their blankets quietly, put the lounge back together, straighten up the room. Hannah would like coffee, but Wes says no, that they can get breakfast on the way, stop in at Maccas, a servo.

They travel silently, Wes absorbed in his driving, his own thoughts, Hannah anxious and weary.

'So. What did they say?' Wes asks eventually.

'Who?'

'Your olds. When you rang 'em last night.'

'Oh, yeah. No one picked up. I just left a message. Said I was all right, that I'd call again today.' The lie is necessary, comes easily.

'Did you tell them where we're going?'

'Nah. Wasn't any point.'

'Right.'

The highway is virtually empty at this time, and they travel quickly, arriving at the Moonee turn-off in less than ten minutes. They're not travelling to the town itself, just to a tiny outpost at the junction of the freeway and the road that heads to the larger town, which is on the coast proper. It's just a small clump of buildings set too close to the freeway to be comfortably habitable. It looks to Hannah as if there's never been a point to living here, the long-abandoned houses are fibro, dilapidated—nothing more than shacks. There are two commercial premises, one a bait shop that looks as if it's open less frequently than it's closed, and an old servo with a single petrol pump—presumably the one that's run by her grandfather. It's not open, either, and like the bait shop it doesn't look like it's been used in a while.

'So is this it?' Wes pulls up out the front. 'Are you sure he lives here? At the servo?'

The front half of a big rigger is parked across the road. It's rusted, looks as if it hasn't driven anywhere in a while, and isn't going anywhere soon.

'I'm sure this is right. He used to drive trucks, I think. Mum said she'd heard that he was living here with his girlfriend. That was a few years ago, but ...' She bites on a fingernail, looking over at the deserted petrol station doubtfully.

They climb out of the car and Wes heads across to the building, rattles on the door. Hannah stays put, watching. He swipes at the glass and peers in through the grimy window.

'Nah, there's no one there—looks like it hasn't been open for a while. There's just a pile of crates and tyres.'

He walks across to the high colorbond fence adjacent to the building, looks over the top. 'Hey, there's an old caravan back here. It's kinda derelict, but maybe someone's there. Look.'

She walks to the fence reluctantly, stands on tiptoes to see over. There's an old aluminium caravan, dinged up and rusting in parts, standing in the middle of a paddock, waist deep in weeds and thistles and surrounded by a sea of bottles, cans, fast-food containers, refuse of every imaginable kind.

'Yuck. Gross. Like a castle with a tip for a moat.' She gives a slightly hysterical laugh.

'Yeah, but what do you think, Han? Do you think he lives there?'

What Hannah thinks is that they should get back in the car, that she should head home, run as far and as fast from this god-forsaken place as she can.

'Yeah, I dunno. I guess it could be.' She shrugs, runs her hands through her hair. 'Let's find out.'

They find a gate—rusted closed, they have to climb over—and walk slowly across the damp grass. Hannah can feel her heart thumping painfully; she moves closer to Wes and takes his hand, holds tight.

They pause when they reach the caravan's door—hesitate before climbing the metal steps. The entry is not inviting. A torn screen door hangs, its hinges broken, and the main door is open. A light flickers in the dim interior, she can hear the sound of a television faintly; it takes her a moment to process what she's hearing, moans and pants, a rhythmic grunting—it sounds like porn. Hannah looks up at Wes, tugs on his hand desperately.

'Oh, God,' she hisses, 'what the fuck are we doing here? I can't. I don't. Let's—'

But it's too late. The caravan's occupant has already heard them. There's a growl from inside, 'Who's that?', a thick, congested wheeze. The television goes silent, there's a loud creak, shuffling footsteps, the caravan seems to dip in the middle, and then he's there at the doorway glaring down at them. 'Yeah? If you're after money yez can piss off.' He's a big man, bald, angry, dressed in shorts and a singlet, his powerful shoulders hunched slightly as if to avoid hitting his head in the diminutive van.

'Um ...' Hannah, panicked, looks at Wes, who is carefully avoiding eye contact. 'Um. Sorry to disturb you, but I'm looking for—' she falters, 'Are you Bob Evans?'

The man says nothing for a moment. He looms above her, huge, bearlike, his expression unreadable.

'What if I am? What's it to you?'

'I'm ... um.' Her voice fails her again. 'I think you're my grandfather.'

The man stares down at her for a long moment, then gives a short laugh. 'Well, you're little Jode's daughter, eh? You could have knocked me down.'

He bustles about, making them coffee, surprisingly efficient despite his bulk, in the tiny kitchen space. Inside, the caravan is almost bare, scrupulously clean. There's none of the mess that's on the outside, nothing extraneous. All the surfaces are clean, if worn. There's no evidence of dirty clothes, no un-washed plates in the sink. Just a bed, covered in a bright pink quilt and matching pillows, a television, a DVD player, a towering stack of DVDs (all wildlife documentaries and not a hint of flesh amongst them, Hannah notes, quickly reinterpreting the sounds she'd heard), a small gas stove and a tiny fridge. She and Wes have squeezed into the wall side of the eating nook at the man's behest: 'It's a bit tight, but I sure as hell won't fit—and there's nowhere else. Unless you want to sit on the bed.'

He sees her looking about, coughs self-consciously. 'Yeah. It's a bit of a dump, innit? It's just temporary, but. They're beginning work on the garage in a week or so, and this seemed to be the cheapest thing to do while we waited. One of me old lady's nephews was living here a year or so back—left it in a bit of a state as you can see. So we've had to have a bit of a cleanout. You probably saw all the shit—pardon the French—out the front. But it's not too bad now, inside, is it? It'll do for a few months, anyway.'

'So, you're—married? I didn't know.' She asks the question shyly.

He puts the coffee down carefully, sits down in front of her, beaming widely. One of his front teeth is missing.

'Why would you? Not like I've kept in contact. I've been married to Olga for almost five years, now. She keeps me on the straight and narrow, that's for sure. She's a Pole,' he adds, as if that explains it. 'Haven't seen Jodes since—well not since she was a kid, actually.' He sounds embarrassed, if not regretful. 'I was a bit of a deadshit, a hopeless father. And husband. They were well rid of me, really.' This is admitted without any particular emotion, it seems to Hannah, as if it's something he's said, or at least thought, for years, until it can be stated baldly, without self-recrimination or judgement. 'Water under the bridge, though, isn't it?' He gives a shrug. 'And I'm sure you've heard as much as you want to hear about the bad old days, anyway.'

'Well. Mum's never really said anything much, to tell you the truth. About you, I mean.' Wes gives her a funny look over the table, and it occurs to her that perhaps she could have been more diplomatic. But she knows it's nothing less than the truth—recognises a similar straightness in her own reply, wonders whether her desire to say her piece, regardless of whether it's right or wrong, and with no thought about pain inflicted, has been inherited from this man.

'Nah.' He runs his fingers over his chin; the dark bristle rasps. 'No, I guess she wouldn't. I didn't really have much to say to her, either. I was young and stupid. And drunk, mostly. The boys are a dead loss—take after me I suppose, though it's not like Jeannie's any better. But your mum done well for herself, didn't she? She survived. Got out. Obviously gotta few brains in her head. She married that Garrow fella, I heard. His mum was a bit of a goer. The old man was an old fucker—oh, sorry, love, it's your granddad, isn't it?' It appears that he knows nothing about her mother's current situation, and she has no desire to enlighten him.

'She done good. But no thanks to me. And you—you look like you're doing okay, too, love. A big healthy-looking girl. You don't look much like your mum, though. Not how I remember her. She was always a scrawny piece.'

'No, I don't. Everyone says that.'

'You do put me in mind of someone, though. Maybe Jean's mum. Old Elsa. She wasn't a bad sort when she was a girl— or so they reckon.' There's a long silence, as if there's nothing more to say.

'Well, I better be getting ready. Olga'll be back shortly, and we've got to get into town to see a man about a dog.' He stands up, collects their cups, looks at the clock. Hannah and Wes stand up. 'I don't like to hurry you, but—well, to tell the truth, Olga doesn't know about any of youse. She knows I was married before, but I never told her about the kids.' He dumps the cups beside the little sink, turns back. 'Now, what did you say you'd called in for exactly, love?' He's still genial, but his interest is clearly waning, and it's plain that he's anxious to be rid of them.

'Oh.' She searches for a plausible answer, but there isn't one.

'I don't know really. We were just passing by—heading up the coast—weren't we?' She grips Wes's hand, and pulls him out of the cramped space over to the doorway.

Her grandfather turns a suddenly stern face to Wes. 'And where do you hail from, young fella?' He has addressed all his comments so far to Hannah, has barely looked at Wes since their initial introduction. 'You an Arding boy?'

'No. I'm from Lismore originally, but I'm at uni up there now.'

'At the university are you? More of your lot doing that these days, aren't they? But doesn't change things, does it? You're still what you are—an education can't change that.'

She can see Wes's jaw tighten, a faint flush appear along his cheeks, but his expression doesn't change, he makes no reply.

Her grandfather looks down at Hannah, friendly again.

'Well it was good to meet you, er, Heather. Now, I'd better get ready—the old girl'll be back soon.'

She turns to follow Wes, who has already begun a brisk tramp back through the sodden grass, when it occurs to her that there is something she wants to ask this man; that he should supply her with some information to justify her visit, ease her disappointment—at the very least make up for his appalling treatment of Wes, this rather ignominious farewell. It's an outrageous question, but it only takes her a moment to pluck up courage and ask.

'Was it something you did to her? Is that what's wrong with her? Did you do something to Mum, when she was a kid—fuck her or something?' The words come out as bald and ugly as their meaning.

'What?' The man looks stunned.

'I mean, that's the usual thing isn't it? All those Catholic priests, those filthy teachers, doctors—it was like some sort of epidemic wasn't it, back in the day? I'll bet that's what happened, that's why she's so screwed.' She's surprised by the harshness of her voice—and her own sudden conviction.

The old man's throat starts working, his soft face crumples, he swipes at his eyes. 'Oh, Jesus,' he says—and she sees that he's laughing at her, not crying, as she had initially assumed. 'The things you kids come out with. You think that—Fuck me dead! Go on, on your bike, love. Your boong mate's waiting.' He gives her a gentle push through the open doorway. She can see Wes, hands on hips, leaning on the gate, looking impatient, darkly angry. 'Look, whatever problems your mum's got, they've got nothing to do with me, mate—I can guarantee you that. We're all masters of our own destiny you know—that's something you'll work out. The mistakes we make—they're all our own.'

'So, was it worth it?' Wes hasn't looked at her since they got back in the car, he's driving too fast, his face rigid, a mask. 'Did it help you clarify things, meeting that redneck fuckwit?'

She puts her hand on his forearm, strokes gently. 'Wes. I'm sorry. He is a fuckwit. But there are plenty of them around.' She doesn't say anything about her own disappointment. There's no point—the visit has revealed none of the things that she was looking for, has provided no clear answers, not about her own future, and not about her mother's past.

'Can you slow down, Wes? Please. Maybe pull over?' She points out a looming petrol stop. 'I need to pee. Badly. And we need petrol.'

While he's paying for the fuel, she goes to the bathroom, takes her phone. She turns it on for the first time that day. Now there are more than a hundred unanswered calls, messages, a long column of unread texts. She takes a deep breath, dials her home number, but can't do it, cuts off before it rings.

She exits the bathroom and sees Wesley striding towards her, clutching a rolled-up newspaper. He grabs her arm, pushes her towards the car, his face grim.

'What's wrong?'

'Fuck you.' The words are spat, savage. 'You said you'd called them. Now, look at this, you stupid, *stupid* little bitch. Oh, fuck. Fuck it.'

Wes opens the passenger-side door and shoves her in, thrusting the newspaper into her hand. He slams the door, before stalking around to the driver's side.

She looks down at the paper—the late-morning edition of the *Coffs Coast Advocate*—and there she is: her last school photo, blown up into monstrous proportions on the front page. Her mouth closed, lips tight, eyebrows raised, her supercilious expression disguising gleaming braces. Underneath, there's a smaller shot of the entire family, Hannah standing slightly removed from what should have been a tight and happy circle.

Wesley climbs into the driver's seat and starts the car. He pulls out onto the highway without speaking as she takes in the accompanying headline:

GARROW'S TEENAGE DAUGHTER MISSING
Police fear for second daughter of mother at centre of missing baby case

A search is underway for 16-year-old Hannah Garrow, who has been missing since late yesterday afternoon. Hannah is the daughter of Jodie Garrow, currently under investigation over the disappearance of her infant daughter, Elsa Mary, who has not been seen since she left Belfield Hospital with her mother three days after her birth more than 24 years ago. The coronial inquest into the fate of Miss Garrow's half-sister is due to begin in one week.

Miss Garrow, who lives with her parents in the town of Arding in Northern NSW, was last seen late yesterday afternoon, in the company of a man described as aged 20–25, of average height and build, dark-skinned, with fair dreadlocked hair. Police say grave fears are held for her safety.

> Anyone who has any information, please contact
> Arding Police on (02) 6770 3434 or Crime Stoppers on
> 1800 333 000

'Oh my God, Wes. This is *so* fucking insane.' She thinks of her mother, at home, already overcome with anxiety, having to wait for news of Hannah, fearing not only for herself, but for her daughter. And perhaps—who knows—with the added pain and indignity of Angus's betrayal. Her mother, who has done nothing but love her, who she knows would give her soul to save Hannah's own. For the first time in years, it seems, Hannah feels remorse—painful, sharp—and shame. *Oh God.* What sort of a person is she, to bring this on her own mother? She thinks of that man, her grandfather, who has made good his escape, who denies any responsibility, every connection. She thinks of Jodie—of what she has made of herself, of who she has tried to be—of what she has tried to make of Hannah. Of what it means to be master of her own destiny; maker of her own mistakes.

She puts her hands over her face for a moment, as if trying to hold it all in, hold it back.

She picks up the phone again, dials the number.

Beside her, Wes says nothing, just drives. Takes her home.

34

Jodie is alone in the house. Her mother-in-law has braved the press contingent that has been parked on their front doorstep since Hannah's disappearance—a flurry of flashlights greets every twitch of the curtain, it seems—to collect Tom and Hannah from school and take them to stay with her own sister in Melbourne. Jodie and Angus are to fly down to Sydney early in the evening and will spend the days before the inquest with Manon, going over Jodie's statement yet again. Manon has assured her that she's unlikely to be called for questioning the first day—that will be spent tracking the evidence of officials and bureaucrats, establishing that there was indeed a birth and then a disappearance. But over the subsequent days the questioning could be intense. Manon has warned her that the coroner's surface amiability is deceptive and that a few hours of his relentless questioning can induce incoherence and confusion in even the most seasoned of court players—so it is essential that Jodie is well prepared, and every possible version of every possible question needs to be considered, every possible response formulated and rehearsed.

She has packed carefully, following Manon's instructions regarding her wardrobe: businessy skirts and shirts in neutral colours, conservative heels. Nothing bright or flashy, nothing frilly, nothing revealing, nothing too obviously expensive, no conspicuous jewellery.

Now there is nothing to do but wait for the time to pass. It seems to her that this is what her life has come to over this past year—endless moments that need to be endured, lived through, with little respite, and no prospect of salvation. She is not nervous, not quite, but moves, as she has done for most of this year, it seems to her, in a state of absolute numbness, of unfeeling. Even her face in the mirror is oddly blank—there are no bags under her eyes, no shadows, no signs of her distress or haunting. She has, as has been frequently pointed out, not a hair out of place. She wonders if this is how prisoners feel when they face a firing squad, or take their last steps towards the gallows.

But salvation comes in the guise of a phone call.

'Jodie? It's happened!' Angus's excitement is apparent even in his greeting.

'What?'

'It's unbelievable. We've had three women contact us, just this morning. In response to the notice. Three! Manon was right! Three other women who say that Sheila O'Malley arranged their adoptions, illegally.'

'So—'

'They've agreed to make statements—and two have agreed to appear if it's required. This changes everything. It's amazing, Jodie. A bloody miracle.'

'Jodie? Jodie?' She can hear Angus's voice, faint, mildly alarmed, but she says nothing, can't think of anything to say.

A miracle. A bloody miracle.

It is everything Jodie has hoped for, everything she has wished for, prayed for, since it all began. It's all over—and yet ... Though there's almost instantaneous relief—she won't have to face the coroner, the court, won't have to encounter the accusing eyes of the public as she recounts her tale, doesn't have to consider the ramifications of the coroner's finding—there's not quite the sense of jubilation she had thought she would feel. Instead, it's as if she is still waiting—though she doesn't know what more can happen, what more there is to come.

It's over. And her life can begin again. It will all return to normal. Surely.

35

When her parents give them the news—in a freaky reprisal of that other dire announcement—the formal gathering of the four of them in the lounge room, the two children seated together on the lounge, though both slightly more subdued—Hannah is amazed at the intensity of her relief. It's not just emotional release, but also physical, as if some crushing weight has been lifted from her, as if she can finally move, breathe, think, without constraint.

'Oh.' She wants to say something significant, something meaningful, but doesn't know what, doesn't know where she should begin. 'It's wonderful news. But what does it mean, exactly?'

'It means we don't have to go to old Aunt Cranky in Melbourne!' Now Tom is bouncing again, but this time Hannah doesn't mind, this time Hannah would like to join in.

'Well, I don't know.' Angus is laughing. 'Actually, I think we should let her have you for a few weeks, straighten you out. What do you reckon, Jodie?'

'Oh, but Dad, she won't let me bring my—' Tom realises he's being teased, grins and resumes his bouncing.

Angus turns to Hannah, his face serious now. 'It means that the inquest will be suspended. We'll have to turn up, but once we present this new evidence, that'll be the end of it. And it means that everything your mother has said is true. It also means that a lot of people owe your mother an apology.' He gives Hannah a meaningful look and stands up.

'Come on, Tom. Let's go and get some champagne. And lemonade for you. We could get some pizza, too. I think this news deserves a party.'

Since her return, though she has been contrite, compliant, has created no further stirs, Hannah has avoided any unnecessary contact with her parents, staying away as much as possible, keeping to her room when she's at home. Her father made one tentative attempt to raise the subject of his infidelity during their weekly driving lesson, but Hannah made it clear, through a series of wince-inducing gear changes and some unnecessarily violent braking, that this wasn't a good time for such a conversation. She knows that eventually she will have to deal with what she has seen, what it says about her father, what it adds to her picture of Manon—but right now she is trying hard to pretend that none of it ever happened. The hardest thing is not being able to discuss it with Assia, to keep her knowledge from seeping out—it's almost impossible not to let the disgust and contempt colour any conversations that include the guilty parties.

Now, left alone with her mother, Hannah is suddenly shy. She wants it to be gone—this distance between the two of them, before it becomes permanent, before it's too late. She wants her mother's forgiveness, but more than that she just wants her mother—her real mother—back.

'Mum?'

'Hannah?' Her mother's smile is tentative, a little sad, but unexpectedly familiar and welcoming. Hannah moves without thinking, kneels, laying her face on her mother's lap.

'Oh, Mum.' She's crying, a year's worth—a lifetime—of tears. 'I'm so sorry. It's been so awful. I'm sorry I've been such a cow. I didn't mean to. I don't even know why. I'm so sorry. I just want everything to be the way it was. Before ...'

'You don't have to apologise, Hannie.' Her mother strokes her hair gently. 'We all wish we could go back. Change things. You haven't done anything, darling. It's all my fault. Everything.'

'It's not, though. None of it's your fault. I'm just a crap daughter.'

'Oh, Hannah. You're not a crap daughter. You're a beautiful, wonderful daughter. A mother couldn't ask for a better daughter.' Her mother gives her shoulder a little shake. 'Now, come on. Go and wash your face. Then let's get the table ready for this party.'

Hannah swallows a sob, looks up at her mother.

'It's really going to be all right, darling.' Her mother's smile is genuine, her old smile, is filled with love and humour.

Hannah sighs, wipes her eyes on the back of her hand, returns the smile. It's going to be okay.

AAP NEWS
'Garrow inquest suspended'

The state coroner, Mr Conrad Westerby, yesterday suspended a coronial inquest into the disappearance of Elsa Mary Evans.

Police confirmed yesterday that three other women have come forward, claiming that they had also been involved in illegal adoptions arranged by the late Sheila O'Malley, former matron of the maternity wing at Belfield Hospital.

The women, whose names have been suppressed, are believed to have given birth between 1972 and 1995. One has since been reunited with her adopted child.

Detective Sergeant Paul Rossi, who has been heading the investigation, said that the new evidence would need to be looked at carefully before any decisions were made to proceed with the matter.

'The search is likely to continue for Elsa Mary, but it will probably be a matter for her family and not the police,' he said.

36

Manon ends it, just as she does everything: lightly, ironically. Effortlessly.

It is only a few hours after the suspension of the inquest, and he has sent Jodie back to their hotel, then returned with Manon to her Broadway office to collect some paperwork. The office is in a nineteenth-century import warehouse that has been restored and remodelled. The walls are solid and obviously soundproof, and Manon's own chambers are situated well away from the receptionist or any of the other partners. Nonetheless she draws the curtains, locks the door, requests her calls be held, before they fuck. They move quickly from the desk, to the floor—complete their coupling upright, Manon shuddering against the cedar dado.

Until now, Angus has always been somewhat appalled by his capacity to switch from one mode to another so instantly—from concerned husband, responsible citizen to reckless philanderer, unprincipled, abandoned, oblivious to everything but his own most base desires. It is so commonplace, so farcical, men like him the subject of countless bad movies, but the cliché is real, the contradictory desires genuine, if inexplicable. Wanting the thrill of sexual conquest; wanting his wife and his family, too. But this time it's different—despite Manon's frank avoidance of commitment, so similar to his own, Angus is not sure that he wants anything—anyone—other than Manon. He doesn't know if he loves her, but he does know that for the first time everything else—Jodie, his family, his work, his life in Arding—has receded. Everything but this.

When they have finished, Manon is immediately all business, briskly tossing Angus his shirt, his tie, his trousers, replacing her own discarded clothing efficiently, without offering any conversation. Dressed, she sits behind her desk, dons her glasses, shuffles through a pile of papers, only looking up when Angus has shrugged himself into his jacket, straightened his tie, and lowered himself into the comfortable leather chair facing her.

She looks up, raises her eyebrows. 'So. It's all over.'

'Yes. A job well done, Manon. Thank you. In fact, I can't thank you enough. We should go out, have a drink, celebrate.' He reaches out to take her hand, but she pulls it away, pushing her seat back a few inches.

'A job well done. Yes. But I'm not sure you've any real cause to celebrate, Angus.' Her voice is uncharacteristically solemn, and for once there's no teasing half-smile.

'What do you mean?'

'You've got some heavy shit to sort out. You and Jodie.'

'But that's not—'

'Not my problem? You're right, it's not. I've got plenty of my own.'

'But I don't understand, I thought—' He doesn't really know what he thought, what he thinks, only what he's feeling—shock, a formless terror.

'What? That we could keep all this going indefinitely? That we were playing for keeps? It was fun, Angus, but it's like any good party: it's always sensible to leave a little before you're really ready to go.' The irrepressible hint of laughter is back. She stands up, holds out her hand, and Angus has no choice but to get to his feet, take her slender fingers in his, shake.

'Good luck to both of you.' Manon pulls her hand free of his grip, which has become convulsive, desperate, gives an unmistakably dismissive grin. 'I'll send you the bill.'

Somehow Angus manages to find a taxi. He gives directions to their hotel, then changes his mind, asks to be taken to a hotel in The Rocks, an old watering place from his student days. Once there, he orders whisky, a double, neat, finds himself a secluded table. But even before he takes a sip from his drink (and he's not planning to stop here) it occurs to him that there's no point in getting drunk: what he's feeling now is a close enough approximation of that state anyway; his head is spinning, stomach churning, he can't quite recall who he is, how he arrived here. And he has no idea what he's going to do, or where he's going to go, next.

37

A family dinner. The first they've had together—all four of them—for months, it seems.

Jodie has made Tom's favourite meal: a rich, cheesy lasagne that she knows will give Angus a bad case of heartburn, though this will not stop him insisting on seconds and even thirds. She has made dessert too—Hannah's favourite, a spicy ginger pudding that had seemed an eccentric choice during childhood. The dinner could be an exact replica of that last dinner, more than a year ago now: Tom excitedly relating the outcome of various repulsive experiments he and Harry have been conducting, Angus teasing him gently, Hannah subdued, but relaxed, helpful—she had even volunteered to set the table, had made an effort to fold the napkins carefully, keep the cutlery straight. After the meal the four of them stay seated for another half hour, just talking. Jodie feels as if she has emerged from a tunnel, as if she is taking things in properly for the first time in a long, long while. As if she is catching up on her own life.

When the children go their separate ways—Tom to watch television, Hannah out with Wes—Angus and Jodie clean up. They work together silently, Angus rinsing plates, passing them to Jodie to be stacked in the dishwasher. She is struck by the ease of their proximity, their efficiency, the years of companionship expressed in all the inconsequential touching—the bumping of hands, grazing of hips—though all their movements are neat and contained in the small space. She is keenly aware of the moment's preciousness, and its transience.

'Jodie.' Angus clears his throat. 'Jodes. We have to talk.'

Jodie's movements cease; there is a plate suspended between them, like some grotesque offering, tragic in its banality.

'I think it's time, don't you?' Sadly, gently. 'We can't keep on going ... like this.'

We have to talk. She has imagined a thousand different versions of this phrase—innocuous enough on the surface, but for Jodie, charged, full of portent—ever since she and Angus were first involved. She knows its significance, would have staved off this moment forever if she could. She has imagined, too, her own response to what's coming next—has seen herself like the Wicked Witch of the West, submerged in the watery terror of the moment, shrinking, shrinking, shrinking into nothingness.

She feels a fierce constriction in her throat, a sharp pang in her chest, the muscles in her legs begin to quake, the welling in her eyes becomes a trickle, she takes a deep breath ... and finds herself still there. There is a rush of blood, of life, of feeling. Jodie hasn't, as she feared, dissolved: her breathing is fast but steady, her heart continues to beat; she is still herself, upright, whole. Even her limbs appear to be functioning—her hand moves instinctively to grasp the proffered plate, to lift it from her husband's hand and stack it neatly in the washer. A smile requires effort, wavering through desperately blinked-back tears, but her response is unfaltering, clear.

'You're right, Angus. We have to talk.'

PART THREE

38

The days she spends sitting for Bridie are Jodie's one real solace. Sometimes it seems that it's only when she's sitting in the warm light of Bridie's kitchen, her physical presence all that's required, that she can breathe.

She has been coming twice a week for the past month, which is far longer than Bridie's original estimate, but she doesn't mind. These days spent with Bridie are the best of her week—they have a lovely quiet rhythm about them, something so far removed from her own life, which is unimaginably transformed.

Angus has taken what they're politely calling a sabbatical, but is really a 'trial separation'. He is working for a London firm, has signed a twelve-month contract, and though she is far busier than she had imagined she would be, the ease with which she has swung into life as a single mother has surprised Jodie herself. Though Helen's assistance has been promised (in the gaps between her golfing engagements, her travelling schedule), Jodie doesn't need much help. The job at the hospital is only three days a week, and with Hannah boarding for this final year of school and only coming home every few weekends, or for the occasional dinner, life is quite simple. She and Tom are less lonely than she'd imagined, doing their own thing during the day, and then reading together at night, or playing the odd game of euchre, Scrabble. She is missing Angus less than she imagined, too—he Skypes nearly every day and, as Tom has pointed out, they probably talk to him more now than they did when he was home. Even on the little screen, blurred, the conversation sometimes lagging and distorted, she can tell that Angus is less stressed. He is enjoying the work, he tells them, and has met up with a few old friends. He is looking forward to seeing Tom and Hannah in the holidays, has trips planned to Paris, Prague, Cambridge. ('There's so much we can see while you're here. Pity to waste the opportunity. Though really,' his face suddenly young, wistful, 'all I really want to see is you.')

Jodie has discovered a different self at work, one she had forgotten ever existed. She is amazed to find that her professional self is still so calmly competent, had expected nerves, anxiety, to be full of uncertainty. But she has taken the work itself in her stride and it has quickly become routine. The thing she has dreaded most, the daily encounters with people who know her, know her story, this too has been less difficult than she had imagined. Jodie Garrow is yesterday's news, after all.

But the nights are hard. The vast bed is cold and uninviting, and though tired she avoids sleep—reading or watching television for as long as she can. The nightmares come more regularly now, and have increased their intensity, leaving her drained and edgy.

She is not unhappy, not precisely. There is a hollowness, though, and a melancholy wondering whether all these years of striving, of working to make something real and strong and unified, have all been for nothing. Her family has been transformed beyond all recognition, but she has to acknowledge that it's not all bad, that perhaps they're all stronger for it—Angus, Hannah, Jodie herself, even Tom.

The two days spent with Bridie are an escape into a parallel world. There's the farmhouse itself—set picturesquely in a green valley, desperately in need of renovating, too rambling to heat properly—such a contrast to her own home. And so welcoming: the two exuberant labradors rushing her at the front door, the friendly disorder that a houseful of small children can create, the cup of tea poured from a pot, the comfortable kitchen chair in the square of sunshine where she sits while Bridie paints. There's the smell of the paint or the linseed oil or whatever it is that she can smell, the soft jazz that Bridie has playing in the background, that doesn't quite block out the soft swish of brush on canvas.

Bridie works silently, for the most part, but occasionally they chat about this and that, conversations that touch lightly on many small, inconsequential matters.

But today has been different. Bridie has been in a strange mood from the moment Jodie arrived. Her face unreadable, her voice low and flat, her movements slightly abrupt, jumpy. A fight with Glenys, Jodie assumes, after Bridie makes some catty remark about even female partners expecting too much—that they are basically no different to men in that regard. But perhaps it's more than that—Bridie has become increasingly agitated over the portrait itself, muttering and sighing to herself, pausing mid-stroke, before starting up again frenetically. She scolds Jodie for moving, curtly ordering her to turn her face back, to stop smiling.

Bridie keeps painting, her lips compressed, her motions becoming jerkier and jerkier. 'Oh, fuck it!' She throws the brush down viciously. 'I just can't get it. It's impossible. It's not there.'

Jodie stands uncertainly. 'I should go, then. Let you—'

'Oh, no. Don't go. I'm sorry!' Bridie picks the brush up, grimaces. 'No, it's just that something's not quite right with the portrait. There's something I can't get to—something I can't see. Why don't we just have morning tea? And if I calm down we can get something done after.'

Bridie boils the kettle, cuts cake, brews the tea, pours two cups. The two women huddle around the fuel stove. Their conversation stays general, light, keeps clear of the morning's irritations, and gradually Bridie relaxes, her voice slows down, her movements return to their usual fluid grace. Eventually there is nothing to say, and the two women sit silently, both enjoying the uncomplicated companionship.

It's Bridie who breaks into the silence, her face serious again. 'Jodie. Can I ask you something? I've been wanting to, but it's awkward—and it's never been the right time. There's so much stuff I feel like I know about you—don't you think that sometimes what you know about someone as a child is all you'll ever need to know in a way? But then there's other stuff I don't know. You might think it's none of my business, and ordinarily it wouldn't be, but this is important—you know, for the painting ...'

She leaves it hanging.

'What do you want to ask?' Jodie imagines that Bridie wants to know more about her marriage, her relationship with Hannah, her mother, perhaps.

'It's the baby. Elsa Mary. I've been thinking about it a lot. Trying to work out what you felt about her. What it must have meant to give up a newborn like that. And I wonder how you feel about it now? Do you wonder who she is, that baby? What she's doing? Do you wish you'd kept her?' She asks her questions quietly, looking down at her hands.

It's a question that no one has ever thought to ask. Jodie fumbles for an appropriate response. 'Well, I don't ... It's not ... I really try not to—'

'But actually that's not really what I want to know,' Bridie interrupts. 'The thing is, I feel like I can't finish this portrait—that there's something not quite true in the Jodie I'm painting. It's hard to explain. It's as if there's a part of you that's missing—and I can't think what it might be. It sounds silly, I guess, but I have to paint what I see—and in a way what I'm seeing is a kind of blankness. And that's kind of hard to portray. I mean, you seem impossibly together, considering what's happened. Most of us would be a complete mess in your situation. I know the sort of mess I was in after Iris died. I'm still in it, in a way. And it worries me, your control. And I honestly don't know how to paint it.'

Now Jodie knows what's coming. She looks at her friend steadily. Prepares herself. 'Well, I suppose you'd better ask your question then, Bridie.'

Bridie meets her eye, her own gaze unwavering, her voice clear and cool.

'She's dead, isn't she, Jodie? Elsa Mary. Your daughter. Dead?'

Jodie has signed statement after statement, stat decs, spoken to so many people—lawyers, police, reporters—has told the story over and over and over until she doesn't have to think before she speaks, doesn't even really have to remember; it rolls off her tongue like an oft-told fairy-tale, its happily-ever-after ending intact. But there's another story, too, one with an alternative finale. An ending Jodie has managed to keep hidden, even from herself, for years. But it's a story that should be recalled, she realises now, a story that needs to be told. A story that needs to be remembered.

It is a relief to finally tell someone—someone who knew her before she became Jodie Garrow, someone who knew Jodie Evans. Bridie, she knows instinctively, will not judge, will understand why it happened. Will understand, too, why she has tried so hard not to remember. Will understand Jodie's desperation to stop that sad ending—her mistake—from consuming her, defining everything she does, all that she is.

DECEMBER, 1986

The couple—Simon and Rosemary—are waiting, as Sheila said they would be, at the designated pick-up venue: the bottom of the hospital steps. It's open to the road there, in plain sight and it's hardly salubrious—there's a half-dead gum, a bench, an overflowing garbage bin. Jodie has already made two trips to her car, the first to get rid of her bags, the second to shove the baby capsule that Debbie has insisted she take (*It's illegal to drive without one! Just bring it back when you can*) into the back seat. So she is carrying nothing but Elsa for this trip. The baby is asleep for once and peaceful, bound tightly by Debbie, who has helpfully reminded Jodie that the blanket must be loosened before Elsa is put in the car.

As Jodie makes her way down the stairs she realises that they are arguing. The man—thin and tall, with a straggly beard—is gesticulating wildly with a cigarette, stabbing it in the air as if to make some point. The woman—considerably older, with coarse grey hair pulled back in a rough bun—looks as if she might be crying. She is shaking her head, her foot grinding into the dirt in an angry sort of dance. They are a grimy-looking pair, unwholesome, somehow. Not sinister, but shabby, their faces tight and pinched, their clothes unkempt, and for the first time it occurs to Jodie that the reasons they have not been able to adopt, through the proper channels, as Sheila so briskly put it, may not actually be due to the inherent unfairness of the 'system' but because of some kind of real unsuitability.

Jodie approaches slowly, clutching the baby. She wonders briefly—a forbidden thought!—at the child's future with this couple; if indeed these really are the people who are to be entrusted with her upbringing. Still, she steels herself—it will be nothing to her, this child's future. She has done her part; she has given her the gift of life. But from now on, whatever happens to her will be out of her hands.

Jodie would like to imagine that it all went to plan. She would like this to be the memory. She wishes—*how* she wishes—that she had walked down those hospital steps, the newborn held close, and proceeded confidently to the waiting parents: a young, happy, middle-class couple standing expectantly beneath the shady branches of a flowering coral tree, the light dappled beneath, the traffic a dim and distant rush. The young woman a Burne-Jones style of woman, say, generously built, her hair long, skin glowing, but with a serene motherly core apparent to even the most casual of observers. And the man—she imagines him in his late thirties, clean-shaven, his jaw square, his expression earnest, perhaps slightly melancholy (the unspoken sorrow of his own sterility, she surmises). They watch her approach—yet it is not her that they're watching so avidly, but the squirming bundle that she holds before her now, like an offering. Their faces transform, moving from some undefined anxiety to radiant joy; they're almost quivering with the anticipation of delight, and she rushes (but careful, careful—she cannot trip, not with her, their, precious cargo) and the transfer is made easily, in one seamless movement from her arms to theirs. The woman takes the child to her chest with a half sigh, half moan, her expression rapturous now, the man radiating his own speechless pleasure. And Jodie's giving is without qualms, without doubt—for these are the people who will love this infant as she should be loved, as all children should be loved: they will nurture her, make her life secure, give her the sort of privileged childhood that Jodie herself has only ever dreamed of.

And she—the newly unburdened Jodie, all her anxiety stripped away; the heaviness of her breasts, her uterus, the ache and sting of her heart and her body, this too miraculously gone—she is as she was: young, without care, pure. A child herself, really, with a boundless future—unsullied by regret or trauma—ahead of her.

Instead, in the other story, the real story, Jodie's steps falter as she comes closer to the couple, whose argument has become louder, more bitter.

'No fucken ... can't expect me ...'

'... be mad. I told ...'

'... didn't want ... hardly ...'

'... need to ... baby ...'

'... fucking stupid ...'

The man, virulently accusatory, the woman supplicant, entreating, but both full of a suppressed violence, an anger that Jodie is only too familiar with: simmering, easily triggered, volcanic, the culmination of endless grievance against the world and its treatment. She waits on the steps, hoping that they will stop, look up, that something will change—that this impossible couple will disappear and then reappear magically altered and she will be able to continue her approach with confidence, that she, they, will be welcomed.

Elsa has woken, perhaps noticing the sudden lack of movement. She is squirming in her blankets, her face crumpled, her limbs making little convulsive jerks against her bonds—she will be crying, needing to be fed any moment.

Jodie cannot hand the baby over to these people. She cannot go back up those stairs and into the hospital: Sheila has said that she must not contact her again, that her part in the transaction is complete. It must be as if they had never met. But this will not do. These people will not do. Luckily, they still haven't noticed her; she can creep in the opposite direction before they see, make her way to the car.

She walks numbly across the tarmac car park, seeing her future lying in ruins. She will take the child back to the flat—there's nowhere else to go—and pray that Sharon hasn't arrived back earlier than expected. She can ring the hospital from there, see if they'll give her Sheila's home number, tell them she asked her to stay in touch.

She unlocks her car—somehow amazed that she is still capable of doing something so ordinary, so everyday—and tries to work out how the capsule is meant to fit. But it's impossible—something vital is missing. She gives up and straps the whimpering baby into the bassinet, careful to loosen the wrappings and tighten the velcro band, then manoeuvres the entire contraption, heavy now, from the back to the front passenger seat. She anchors the capsule as best she can, looping the seatbelt through the handle, plugging it in. It's better than nothing, it will have to do.

She stops the car only once during the long trip home, pulls off the highway into a side street to feed the child, ravenous now and screaming. The baby resists the cool formula initially, spitting it out, but she crams the teat into her mouth, persisting even as the child cries harder. She needs changing: Jodie can see the damp patch creeping up her little singlet, but she leaves it—it's too awkward in the cramped space, and she doesn't want to linger. She is desperate to get back, though there is no real comfort in heading back to the flat. But she feels certain that once she has made some sort of return to her own life, however slight, she will find a way to sort out this mess, a way to resolve things.

She pulls back out onto the highway again, the baby lying contentedly now, her eyes flickering, her little mouth opening in a curiously adult yawn. Jodie doesn't think; just drives, slowly, steadily, always conscious that the baby is not safely strapped in.

It is almost midday when she arrives. She parks outside the flat and sits for a moment in the car, conscious of her aching body, her tiredness. Her heart is pounding too quickly, her limbs are heavy and aching, her head throbs. She is shaking—it feels like the beginnings of a flu, but with an additional dull pain coming from her breasts, which have swollen into two rock-like masses. Her breasts are hot, too—emitting a radiant heat that rises up her throat, into her face. Sheila has told her that she needs to keep regularly expressing the milk, warned that there is a possibility of infection otherwise, that she should see a doctor immediately at any sign of a fever. That she would find some comfort—oddly enough—from cabbage leaves laid over the hot flesh.

The baby is sleeping in the capsule, pink-cheeked, her breaths in and out making a faint whizzing sound. It seems simplest to just leave her there, undisturbed, while Jodie takes her bags inside. She unwinds the window a little way, and pushes the door shut as quietly as she can, locking it behind her.

She collects the mail from the box on her way in, flicking through the pile quickly. There is one letter from Angus, she recognises his handwriting immediately, and the others are bills, mail for Sharon, her university results. The flat is cool and dark and tidy inside—the blinds are down, the windows closed, just as she'd left it. She calls out to make certain, but there's no answer. She flicks on the hall light, makes her way to the kitchen, which is spotless—all the benches clear, the sink empty; only the same few cups she'd left drying on the draining board. She taps on Sharon's door, calling out again, before pushing it open. Sharon's room is in its usual chaotic state—clothes strewn over every surface, papers and books, make-up—just as she'd left it. As Jodie had hoped, expected, the flat is empty—she is alone. She goes to the lounge room window, where there is a clear view of the car. She cannot see the baby, but the street is quiet; surely nothing can happen on such a brightly sunny day.

Jodie is feeling sicker and sicker, has begun shaking uncontrollably. She needs to take something quickly, then needs to work out what she should do next. She goes to her own bedroom. It is tidy, clothes folded, the bed made neatly. She digs around in her bedside drawer, finds some aspirin, munches them down without water, wincing at their bitter lemony flavour, gagging slightly as they coat her tongue, the back of her throat.

She sits on her bed, looks at the mail. She looks longingly at Angus's letter, but tears open her university results first. She has passed all her subjects—a credit in Biology, distinctions in Sociology and Psych, and as she had expected, a high distinction for her pracs. She picks up Angus's letter; it is postmarked November 24th—almost a month ago, a lifetime, ago. It is one of those blue airmail envelopes, the paper thin, the envelope unfolding into the letter itself, so she opens it slowly, careful not to tear the sides.

It is only a short letter, and her stomach gives an anxious twist as she begins reading.

Dear Jodie,

You may have already heard—I broke the news to my mum right away, and know what the town 'grapevine' is like—but I've been offered another couple of months' work here, with double the pay and the prospect of a stint in the Hong Kong and then the Amsterdam office—when I actually do my degree—and I have decided to take them up on it. I know it's disappointing and we will have to cancel our week on the coast, as I won't get home until just before uni starts, but it was an offer I just couldn't refuse, as it means that my employment prospects will be that much better—which will be good for both of us in the long run.

They are working me like crazy here and I'm finally getting the hang of it, I think! I will probably keep flatting with Martin—though our flatmate Amelia has recently gone home, so things are a little more expensive for now. We're advertising so hopefully we'll get someone else soon.

Anyway, had better get this off to you—I know you were hoping we'd be together sooner, but we'll just have to settle for a good long (dirty?) phone call.

Love, always, Angus xxx

She is disappointed, yes, but she doesn't know why the tears should come now, when there has been so much else to cry about. They are not gentle teardrops, but like floodwaters, her eyes streaming, spit and mucus mingling; the sobs are coming from some deep dark place, sobs that come almost like vomit, her body heaving and heaving, convulsively, until she can barely breathe.

When the grief has finished with her she lies spent—her head empty, barely able to see through her eyes—waiting for the choking and hiccoughing to subside. She sits up, looks at herself in the mirror; her face puffy and red, her body slumped and misshapen—thick in the middle, her thighs too fleshy, the absurd munificence of her hard bosom. She sits up straight, tidies her hair, pulls in her stomach. She smooths out the counterpane, thinking. She makes a decision—so easily that she gasps, wondering how it has never occurred to her before. She will use her savings, buy a ticket to London, go to Angus, stay with him for the additional few months. She is not going to lose him; if he will not come to her, she will go to him. Soon there will be nothing to stop her, no encumbrance, nothing to put a check on her whereabouts—she will be a free agent again.

She notices, for the first time, the strength of the sun beaming in through the gaps in her venetians; there is even a bite in the filtered streams of sunlight that transect her arms, her head, her lap. She is still warm from the fever, though the aspirin is starting to take effect, but the day is hot, anyway, and getting hotter.

It is time to pull herself together. She will ring Sheila now and get something arranged as quickly as possible, and if nothing can be done that way, if Sheila's unwilling to help, she'll go to the authorities, do it officially, take the risk that there will be some repercussions down the line. By then she will have cleared everything with Angus—all this will be in the past, it will *be* the past. Forgotten. She goes to the bathroom and washes her face, looks at herself in the mirror, and smiles, really smiles, for what feels like the first time in months.

She stands up straight, squaring her shoulders, ready for the difficult tasks ahead. First she should get the baby out of the car; she'll probably be awake now. It's time she was fed, changed. Time Elsa was brought in out of the heat.

ACKNOWLEDGEMENTS

I'm grateful for the input of those friends who've been so helpful in their reading and for their comments and suggestions: Ann Pender, Jane O'Sullivan, Michael Sharkey, Sophie Masson, Rebecca James, and in particular, Felicity Plunkett, whose eleventh-hour edit really made all the difference. And to my daughter, Abi Shepherd, for her thorough proofreading—who'd have thought that one little book could contain so many instances of the word 'uncharacteristically'...?

My eternal gratitude to Jane O'Sullivan—whose stupendously generous offer of a temporary home in Newcastle, just in the nick of time, made everything so much easier.

A huge thank you (along with a sigh of relief) to my wonderful publisher Belinda Byrne, who managed to see the novel that wasn't quite there, and to the brilliant Jo Rosenberg, whose editorial suggestions made this book so much better in so many ways. Thanks are also due to Arwen Summers, for the final touches, to Al Colpoys for the eye-catching cover, and to the Penguin team who've all been so enthusiastic and welcoming.

Thanks again to my agents, Alexis Hurley and Kim Witherspoon, for their confidence and persistence—and patience!

This novel couldn't have been written without the financial assistance provided by the Australian Postgraduate Award I was fortunate to receive, and I'd like to thank the University of New England for ongoing support.

As ever, heartfelt thanks are due to my family—who make it all worthwhile.